SWALLOWING GRANDMA

Katherine Millar is eighteen, and desperate to be thinner and less swotty, and to have cooler friends. But most of all she wishes that she had two parents instead of one grandma, Poll.

Katherine's father was killed in a car crash when she was a baby. According to Poll, the crash was the fault of Katherine's mother, who disappeared shortly afterwards. Poll is pushing seventy, half-blind and utterly poisonous. Her ambition is for things to stay exactly the same for ever, and for Katherine never to leave their pit village of Bank Top; indeed for her to leave the house only when strictly necessary.

Katherine has other ideas, especially when the handsome and self-assured Callum turns up. Katherine can feel that change is coming; the omens are all around her. In the meantime she cleans up after Poll, revises for exams, and surfs the net trying to find out how to be bulimic. What she doesn't quite realize yet is that life won't always wait for you to catch up with it.

SWALLOWING GRANDMA

Kate Long

WINDSOR
PARAGON

First published 2005
by
Picador
This Large Print edition published 2005
by
BBC Audiobooks Ltd by arrangement with
Pan Macmillan Ltd

ISBN 1 4056 1166 9 (Windsor Hardcover)
ISBN 1 4056 2153 2 (Paragon Softcover)

British Library Cataloguing in Publication Data available

Printed and bound in Great Britain by
Antony Rowe Ltd., Chippenham, Wiltshire

For Mum and Dad

Acknowledgements

For help with research:
Mollie Thompson, Jennifer Leeming,
Judith Magill,
Deborah Kelsall, Jane Smellie, Ruby Parr,
John and Margaret Green, and Graham Dixon of
http:/ /www.btintemet.com/—
troubleatmill/speak.htm.
For editorial and other assistance:
David Rees, Kath Pilsbury,
Peter Straus and the team at RCW,
Simon Long, Ursula Doyle and
my friends at Picador.

Chapter One

Dogman turned up on our doorstep at nine o'clock sharp, wolfhound in tow.

'You'll love me,' he said. 'I've brought you a crevice tool.'

'Let him in!' yelled Poll from the kitchen.

He rustled past in his grubby mac and I pressed my back to the wall in case he brushed against me. The dog sniffed my crotch, then trotted on.

'Here you are,' he said, rooting in one of his plastic bags and pulling out the crevice tool for me to admire. It's true, I had been wanting one for about six months. Ours had disappeared; probably Poll threw it out by accident, we lose a lot of stuff that way.

Poll marched in and snatched it out of Dogman's hand. She felt it carefully all over, then took it over to the standard lamp to peer at it in the light. 'Well, aren't you lucky, Katherine Millar? She's always moaning about dog hairs. Winston sheds all summer and all winter, it's a wonder he in't bald. Say thank you. Where did you get it, Dickie? Car boot?'

Dogman grinned. 'I found it.'

Nicked it, more like.

Poll handed it over to me and I squinted at the maker's mark. 'But it's the wrong brand,' I said. 'This is off a Dyson, we have a Lervia. It won't fit.'

'Get away,' said Dogman. 'Bit of duct tape on the end of your tube, it'll be fine.'

I could have inserted the tool into his mouth, Tom and Jerry style.

1

'Are you seriously expecting me to start mauling with duct tape every time I want to use the thing? Putting it on and taking it off? I'm not going through that performance.' I dropped the tool onto the settee. If Poll wanted to claim it, she could do the hoovering herself.

Poll tutted and Dogman shook his head sorrowfully.

'Young people today,' said Poll, 'they want life gift-wrapped, they do. Tek no notice of her, Dickie. She's on t' crest of a rebellion all t' time. I think it's hormones. At least, I hope that's all it is.' She raised her eyebrows at him.

Piss off, I nearly said.

*   *   *

'One day I'll die,' Poll's always going, 'and then you'll be sorry, my girl.'

No I won't. I'll put the bloody flags out. I'll tie a red-satin bow round Winston's neck, dance stark naked up and down Mesnes Park, and put an ad in the 'Celebrations' column of the *Wigan Observer*.

> *She always had a lot to say*
> *She had a tongue sharp as a knife*
> *But now my grandma's passed away*
> *I'm off to start a whole new life.*
> In remembrance of Pollyanna Millar, evil-minded
> shrew and dog-botherer

That night, after Poll had groped her way along the landing from the bathroom, I wrote in my diary:

2

New Year's Resolutions

1. *Stop eating (lose 10 kg by Valentine's Day)*
2. *Get everyone at school to call me Kat, not Katherine, as sounds cooler*
3. *Try to make friends with Donna French X X X lush lush*
4. *Decide what to do about My Future*

Then I lay down on the bed, under Dad's old posters of Blondie, and tried to block out the bad thoughts that always gather about this time by doing A-level essay plans in my head. Finally I turned out the light and blew Dad a kiss, like I always do. It might be mad, but it helps.

I share my room with two dead people. As well as Dad, in his jar on the windowsill, there's Great-grandma Florence, who was Poll's mother, in the bottom of the wardrobe inside a black and gold tin. I never think about her, to be honest, except when I'm hunting for shoes.

The rest of Poll's family are buried in Bank Top cemetery, a sloping field down which the gravestones are moving imperceptibly, along with the wall that's supposed to keep them in. If you climb up on the war memorial in the middle you get a good view, a clear view anyway, of the dirty brick town of Harrop below, with its derelict paper mill and defunct loco works. Surely this can't be where the occupants of the cemetery are headed? I can't see the attraction myself.

My big dream is to be normal. I need to ditch the socks and frocks and be more like other girls, but it's not easy with a grandma like mine.

'Make-up? What do you want to wear make-up

for? You'll ruin your skin. You'll end up looking like a clown or a prostitute, one or t' other. Smear some Vaseline on your face, that's all you need at your age. I were a married woman before I owned a lipstick.'

We have this bollocks continually.

It's dawning on me, now I'm reaching my eighteenth birthday, that actually a lot of things Poll says are rubbish, e.g. that mending your socks while you're still wearing them brings on terrible bad luck. 'It's sewing sorrow to your heart,' she always moans. 'You'll rue.' She also reckons that washing your hair while you're having a period sends you mad, and that sleeping with a potato prevents cramp.

When I was younger I believed her, so therefore all the other kids assumed I was mad too and wouldn't have anything to do with me. I couldn't catch a ball either, and I wore a hand-knitted school cardigan instead of a bought one from Littlewoods. I pretended I didn't care.

'Not everyone has a mother and a father,' I would recite when they cornered me on the rec. 'Me and my grandma are a family too.'

'Piss off, Fatso,' they'd say. 'You don't even call her grandma. How weird is that?'

'She doesn't like it.'

'She doesn't like you. You're mental. Your mum killed your dad and then ran off. Weirdy-weirdo.' Then they'd run away screaming and screwing their index fingers into their temples. Weirdy-weirdo would skulk by the bins for a bit and then go and stand by the teacher till the bell went.

The trouble with Bank Top is that everyone knows everyone else's history.

4

*   *   *

Poll doesn't want people to feel sorry for her—which is lucky, because in general they don't. She's as blind as she wants to be: some days, you'd hardly know she had a problem; others, she's all but bed-ridden. 'It's like having a black spot pasted on the front of your eyeball,' she says. 'If I look at your head, now, all I can see is an empty space.' She's got peripheral vision, though, so you'd be unwise to try anything sneaky.

The Rehab Officer likes to stay upbeat. 'Here, we prefer the term *partially sighted*,' she says when Poll goes to be assessed for extras e.g. hand-rails, magnifiers, large-button phones. Not that she bothers with most of these aids; after all, it's what I'm there for. I'm just a two-legged guide dog.

When she first began to lose her sight she was given this handy booklet, *Coping With Age-Related Macular Degeneration*. It's full of top tips for someone with a reasonable take on life:

• *Use strong lighting throughout the house, particularly on stairs.*

Poll says, 'If you think I'm getting an electrician in you've another think coming. Pass us that flashlight.' Our sockets are loaded to buggery and we have nine table lamps in the living room alone.

• *Tell others clearly what you need.*

No problems with this one. It's all I get, all day and every day. I shop, cook, clean, wash, iron after a fashion, lay her clothes out for her every night and put her eye drops in. She doesn't need the eye drops, she just likes the idea. She needs the ICaps dietary supplement pills, but she won't take them, of course.

• *Use your cane as a signal that you need help.*
Or a weapon. She may only have limited vision but she can always locate an ankle bone from a good height.

• *Don't dwell on your difficulties. Treat your visual impairment as a challenge to be overcome.*
To be fair, she isn't much into self-pity. Anger, petty-mindedness, pig-headedness; now those she does a treat.

• *Get to know your neighbours; build up a community around you.*
Don't know if Dickie the Dogman counts as community; he certainly hangs round our place enough. Poll thinks he's marvellous because he's always posting tat he's got off the market through our dog-flap; loaves with big holes all through them, unperforated toilet roll, bacon that's about 90% fat. And they have these long gossip sessions in the kitchen while Wolfie lolls about on the flags and tries to chew his own paws off.
'You know that woman up Nettle Fold who did Maggie's daughter's wedding dress?'
'Oh, aye?'
'She's a medium.'
'A medium what?'
'No, she talks to spirits.'
'Oh, right. What, part-time?'
'I suppose so. Maggie said she's snowed under with alterations for people.'

'So can she tell the future?'

'Maggie says she can.'

'It's a pity she didn't let on about the groom knocking off the chief bridesmaid, then, in't it?'

I never used to mind Dickie Dogman, in fact I thought he was quite funny when I first knew him. He came on the scene when I was about five, after he knocked on the door and offered us some sand he'd found. 'Mek a nice sandpit for t' littlun,' he'd said. 'Oh, go on, then,' Poll had said, unexpectedly. The pit was a disaster; it stained my arms orange and was a total cat-magnet. But somehow Dickie stayed on the scene. He knew a lot of jokes, and he could do tricks with matches. Sometimes I'd go with him over the fields while he walked Wolfie, or the other dogs he had then. In the spring he'd help me catch tadpoles which would go in a jar on the kitchen top for about two weeks, then Poll would knock them over, or pour melted fat on them, or swill them with bleach. In the autumn Dogman enjoyed identifying fungus, then smashing it up. 'That's fly agaric, that is. We'll have that bastard for a start.' I have a really clear memory of him sitting on a stile once and a red admiral butterfly landing on his coat sleeve. 'Look at that,' he said, watching it dip its wings and unfurl its tongue briefly. 'The miracle of Nature. Oh, it's fucked off.' But his favourite crop was dirty magazines, which grew all along the hedgerows near the lay-by. For a long time I thought he was just litter-picking.

As I hit puberty, I began to see Dogman for what he was; a dirty old man. I kept catching him staring at my breasts and licking his lips. From the time I was fourteen, I never had a cold without him offering to rub Vicks on my chest. Then, one day last year, something really horrible happened.

I came out of the library to find him sitting on the form outside, talking to someone on his mobile. He had his back to me and he didn't know I was there. Wolfie wagged his tail at me but still Dogman didn't notice. He was engrossed in conversation.

'Well, you know me,' he was saying, 'I like 'em big. Yeah, completely topless, nips and all.' His shoulders shook with laughter. 'She didn't know I were there, it were first thing in t' morning. Yeah, massive. Round the back, through t' kitchen window. Hey, hang on, it's not my fault if she parades round wi' no bra on. I was just standing innocently by the back door, me.'

As he was sniggering down the phone, I remembered Saturday and how I'd run down at half-eight to let Winston out for a wee in the garden. I'd not finished getting dressed, but you don't hang about with Winston because his Westie bladder's old and unreliable. Not ten minutes later, Dogman had appeared at the back door with the glad tidings that Lidl were selling off dirt-cheap TVs, and did we want him to get us one. I thought he seemed agitated at the time, but I put it down to the amazingly low price deal.

So ever since then, I've tried to avoid him, he gives me the krills. But it's not easy; he virtually lives here. He's Poll's number-one best friend.

Dogman's not the only pervert round here, either. I've seen a penis, and I was only about eight. This elderly gent stopped me in the street near Flaxton's Chemist and asked me to help him get his puppy out of a drainpipe. 'I know wheer 'e is. I can hear 'im whimpering. What's your name love?

8

Katherine? Well you've lickle 'ands, Katherine, you'll be able to reach in an' cotch 'im reahnd 'is collar.'

'I'll be late for school,' I'd said. Because I *thought* it sounded suspicious.

But he'd taken my arm and hustled me down the ginnel to the yard behind the shop, a scruffy walled area full of rubbish bags and cardboard boxes, and indeed there was a drainpipe sticking out of a mound of earth in the corner.

I stood there straining my ears for the sound of distressed dog and he told me to get down and put my face right up to the pipe. 'Call his name. Go on.' So there I am, down on my hands and knees, shouting, Beaver, Beaver, all the time peering into the dark anticipating the scrabble of tiny claws. When nothing happened I turned my head to ask what he thought we should do next and blow me, he had his tackle out. It looked exactly like he was yanking a plucked chicken head-first out of his flies. ' 'Ave a shufti at this, Katherine,' he leered. I was out of that yard like a pinball off a spring. I still can't go into a butcher's round Christmas time.

I ran straight back home in tears, and Poll was the nicest she's ever been to me. She made hot chocolate and got the biscuit barrel down and we cleared the whole stack of Dogman's Kit-Kat misshapes between us. I didn't even have to go back to school that day, which was a major coup.

'I keep telling you it's a dangerous world out there,' said Poll through a mouthful of wafer. 'Let's get that packet of Jammy Dodgers open an' all.'

One time we had someone keep ringing up then putting the phone down. You'd go, Who is it? Who is it? And there'd be silence, it was dead eerie.

9

Then a few weeks later the nasty language started; I never heard it myself but Poll told me bits and pieces, stuff to do with underwear mainly. She's not one to bother normally, hard as nails our Poll, but it did shake her up. She used to tense when the phone rang. A few times she said, Don't answer it, so I didn't. But one time she picked up and went white, must have been more than knickers. She put the receiver to my mouth but with her fingers over the earpiece, and told me what to say: I had to shout, 'Leave us alone and get a life!' I enjoyed that. Most excitement I'd had in ages. And the best thing was, the calls stopped.

So Bank Top becomes the world in miniature, except it's even worse Outside with serial killers and exploding skylines and famine and anthrax-in-a-bottle.

'Yes, it's a sad world,' Maggie, Poll's bingo-friend, was saying last week over dinner. 'All our age are dropping like flies. I went to three funerals last month. And May Powell died last week, it was in t' paper.'

'May Powell? May Powell as we were at school with?' Poll looked up from her soup.

'That's the one. Th' undertaker's daughter. She was right snooty at school, do you remember? Not that I'd wish her dead. Does anyone want that last crumpet?'

Poll shoved the plate across the cloth towards her. 'She used say her father put her in one of his coffins if she'd been nowty, and closed the lid on top of her.'

Dogman snorted his tea, as if this was the funniest thing he'd ever heard.

'Eeh, and they'd go complaining to Social

Services these days for summat like that.' Poll shook her head despairingly. 'You're not allowed to punish your child at all without somebody poking their nose in. Then they wonder why the kids are running wild. In them days, a parent had some authority. And really, it didn't do the children any lasting harm, did it?'

'No, said Maggie. 'Of course it didn't.'

'So how did May die?'

'Committed suicide.'

'My life's been full of tragedy too,' Dogman piped up. 'Hang about.' He pulled out a hanky and blew his nose hard to clear out all the tea, deliberately making a trumpet noise.

'Has it, love?'

'Oh, aye.' He wiped his eyes. 'I lost my father really young, in an accident.'

Maggie looked at Poll in surprise. 'What happened, Dickie?'

'It was terrible. You know he used to work at the brewery?'

'I didn't, no.'

'Well, he did. He were in charge of one of t' vats. Anyroad, the big paddle they use for stirring got stuck, so he climbed up to see if he could free it. And he fell in.'

Poll put her hand to her mouth. 'Oh, Dickie. I never knew that.'

Dogman nodded glumly. 'My mother was distraught. She said to t' foreman, "Were it at least a quick death?" And the foreman said, "Well it would have been, but he got out three times to go to t' toilet." '

'Ooh, Dickie,' chuckled Poll. 'You're a caution.'

I tell you, we have some hilarious times in

11

this house.

Life seems to be particularly dangerous for our family around the time of our coming of age. We get the key of the door and the hammer of doom at the same time.

The week after his twenty-first birthday, Poll's father lost his arm up to the elbow in a nasty bleach-works accident. We have the photographic evidence; a mild-looking man with sunken eyes and one flat sleeve stuffed into his pocket. The hand he still has is resting on a little table and there's a roll of paper poking out of his fist. 'His Certificate in Textile Technology,' Poll pronounces as if it were a Nobel Prize.

Then of course there was Roger, my dad, eighteen and smashed to pieces in the car that was his very special birthday present, a scarlet Mini Metro Vanden Plas. We all know whose fault that was. (Well, actually we don't, because although it was mostly my mad evil mother having a fit and grabbing the wheel just as a juggernaut was coming in the opposite direction, there's also the school of thought that if he hadn't been bought the car in the first place—which was Vince's bright idea—then the accident could never have happened.) So cars are deadly too and that's why I can never, ever have driving lessons because I will either kill myself or some other bugger, in fact best to stay off the roads altogether if possible (Poll once saw a schoolboy run over by a Selnec bus).

Poll's Aunty Cissie lost her fiancé in the war a fortnight before she came of age; she and her sister were actually cutting up old sheets to make streamers when they got the telegram. She's in her eighties now and she never had another

12

sweetheart, so that was her life over with.

Poll herself got through her twenty-second year unscathed but only, she reckons, because she had a premonition that she'd drown, a recurring dream from childhood that she was stranded on a bare rock with a towering wave about to engulf her. She went to a clairvoyant in Blackpool who confirmed it, so she's made sure she's always stayed well away from water, and thus has cheated Fate.

And therefore because I'm almost eighteen now, and I've had no helpful dreams about avoiding accidents, I ought to be particularly nervous. I could leave Bank Top if I wanted to, I have somewhere to go. But is it a trick? Maybe Destiny has got something unpleasant lined up for me. Sometimes I lie awake at nights gripped with a fear I can't put a name to.

I don't know which is worse; fear or boredom.

Funnily enough Poll thinks she's going to die this year as well. 'Threescore and ten I am. Living on Borrowed Time.'

Yes, well, I think. Play your cards right. It could be arranged.

*   *   *

There are nights I wake up having dreamed about her and wonder then if maybe in those same hours she dreamed about me too. But the detail is never very positive. I'm always crying. Sometimes I'm covered in blood. Once I had her father's head in a holdall that I couldn't put down.

The need to let her know is a physical pull. It's a constant battle. But I have no substance in her life. I'm useless, as useless as a ghost.

13

Chapter Two

What I really wanted for my eighteenth birthday:

- two parents
- a less stupid-sounding voice
- social aplomb
- the tiny bottom half of Courtney Cox

I don't look for a card from my mother any more, haven't done since I was fourteen, in fact I make a conscious effort *not* to. Which is quite mature of me because Poll still checks for one from my dad and he died in 1984.

There were seven cards, plus a small victory, on the table when I came down in the morning.

On Your 18th from Poll and Winston. Picture of a yacht on the front, a design Hallmark clearly intended for a male, although Poll's sight being what it is I suppose I should be grateful I didn't get *With Deepest Sympathy*. The victory was attached to the back of the card by a hinge of Sellotape: two packets of tan tights, reinforced panty, about forty denier by the look of them. 'Well, now you're eighteen,' sighed Poll.

Getting her to admit my real age is an achievement in itself. In Poll's benighted world, it's the Fifties and I've been eleven for the past seven years. I have a print frock for best that's like a sack with arm-holes cut in it, and the rest of the time it's A-line polyester skirts and bargain knitwear. On my legs I've been wearing navy knee socks, pulling them up and over my knee-joints trying to make them look like they might be tights, holding them in place with a double elastic band. In the summer it's white ankle socks which is worse because I've got the calves of a rugby player, hairs and all. Some nights when I can't sleep I've sat up snipping the wiriest hairs off with my nail clippers but they only grow back, twice as fierce. I even have a hair that grows out of my belly, and two on my right nipple. Deformed. Sometimes I think I'm too revolting to live.

I'd been asking for tights since I started in the sixth form. 'What d'you want them things for?' said Poll the first time I raised the possibility. 'You'll only put your fingernails through them, you'll have them laddered in five minutes. Do you think I'm made of money?' No, I nearly said, I think you're made of horse-fly bites and Parazone.

Have a COOL birthday—Card two was a Winston-type Westie wearing a party hat and sunglasses. Aunty Cissie's a complete sucker for anthropomorphism. You should see the walls of her room at the Home, doggies and kittens done up in all manner of garb. No children, see. Sad but vomit-inducing nevertheless.

Birthday Girl!—Dogman's was a flimsy market-job, cartoon of a blonde with a Barbie waist-span and orange minidress.

On Your Special Day—Maggie had left a card with a plastic gold key stuck to the front. 'She's having one of them cameras up her bum next Tuesday,' Poll reminded me, 'so it was good of her to remember.'

Across the Miles I Send to You Happy Thoughts, Good Wishes too—said Great-Auntie Jean in a fancy embossed affair with a silk tassel down the

15

back. 'We have a beautiful new granddaughter, a little Sagittarian,' I read out to Poll.

'I know. I saw.' Poll gestured at her magnifier propped up against the mantel clock. 'And do you know what they've called it? Fat Louse. They've some daft ideas, these Australians.'

The baby's actually *FAY LOUISE* but I didn't reckon it was worth the argument. Jean never forgets my birthday, even though she escaped to another hemisphere before I was born. Far too good for us, says Poll. But I've seen an old photo of a plump little girl, cardigan, print frock and sandals, sitting on a stone wall feeding chaffinches. 'Inverness 1947' is written on the back. Little Jean has a beaming face, and she doesn't look stuck-up at all.

Happy Birthday and here's hoping for a question on Tragic Heroines!!—Rebecca-my-only-mate-from-school clearly did not want me to forget the Modules next week, as if I would, climbing the walls with fear.

Congratulations on your coming-of-age—Lastly a postcard of the Brontës, from Miss Dragon and Miss Mouse at the library; I was really touched.

Cissie and Poll had included money in their cards, although I knew that would have to go straight in my savings account, blink and you miss it. Dogman had dropped off a brown-paper bag containing a pair of 'gold' heart-shaped earrings, though they were for pierced ears and I'm not allowed those in case I get septicaemia and die. There was a pen set from Maggie, and a book token from the librarians.

But the best present was waiting on the doorstep.

I cleared the torn wrapping paper away and went to get my anorak from the hall.

'If you're goin' out, tek the dog. He's beside hisself,' shouted Poll from the living room where she was standing, skirt up, toasting the backs of her legs purple against the gas fire.

So I zipped up my anorak, clipped Winston's lead onto his collar, opened the door and nearly went sprawling over the black binbag that was on the step.

'Have you got your scarf?' Poll again. 'And you'll need a hat an' all. It cuts right through you, that wind.'

'Good idea,' I said, thinking fast because I'd spotted the envelope stuck to the side: FOR KATHERINE — A SECRET BIRTHDAY SURPRISE. 'I'll get my grey cardi too. Hang on, Winston.'

I grabbed the bag by the ears and shut the door in Winston's snout. Then I galloped up the stairs before Poll could see me and threw the bag on my bed. I ripped open the plastic and gaped.

Clothes. Not old jumble; freshly laundered by the smell of them, one or two items on hangers even. I drew out a tunic top in maroon, with one of those keyhole necks and a silver border to the sleeves. The label was sticking out at the back: XL. Heart beating, I pulled open the wardrobe door so I could see myself in the full-length mirror, and held the silky fabric against me. It looked amazing. I was a different person.

I laid it carefully on the bed, and pulled out a matching pair of wide-legged trousers. They formed the sort of suit you'd probably wear to, I don't know, an awards evening, or a posh dinner or something. Next there was a red velvet basque—

17

God, a basque. I'd seen one like it on a poster for *Moulin Rouge*. It wasn't really underwear, more a party top. (Some party like I'd never been to, obviously.) Then I found a stretchy black tube skirt, very long, very vampish. Lastly there was a sexy purple V-neck sweater, again in my size. I was sweating with excitement by the time the bag was empty, and my fingers left prints on the note as I read it again and turned it over to check the back. No clue. The flap had been stuck down, but when I tore it open, the white envelope was empty.

'Are you goin' or what?' Poll yelled up the stairs. 'Because this dog's all set to soil the carpet. I thought you were only gettin' your cardigan. You could have bloody knitted one by now.'

There was a wheezing scuffling sound as Winston tried to start up the stairs, followed by a choke as Poll dragged him back again.

'*Coming!*' I said and scooped the clothes up into a bundle. I threw them to the back of the wardrobe and closed the door on them; I'd see to them later. Poll was waiting by the newel post.

'So where's your cardigan, then, after all that? Honest to God.'

I muttered at her and did a sharp U-turn.

'You mek some noise, you do,' she grumbled as I thumped back up the stairs.

We were nearly out the door when I had my second shock of the day: Dogman, nose to nose with me. He must have been standing on the step, under the impression the bell had rung.

I tried to get past but he blocked my way, holding his arms out.

'Stand and deliver,' he said.

Fuck *off*, I thought, and barged him to one side.

18

It didn't stop him grinning.

'Your money or your life?' he shouted into the living room.

Poll came out with her hands up. 'My life, I'm saving up.'

Dogman pretended to shoot her, and they fell about laughing. 'I've brought a couple of tins of this bathroom mousse,' I heard him say. 'Big 'uns. They were just sitting there, on t' skip near t' council offices. There's no propellant so they don't squirt, but they're full. I bet you could get the fluid out if you stuck a knife in 'em, though.' He raised his voice. 'And I've summat for Katherine too.'

'Wait up!' said Poll, but I was already at the gate and I didn't stop. 'Dickie's brought you a beautiful calendar. It's all pictures of Stratford, and that Shakespeare. Aren't you going to say thank you?'

I knew without looking it would be last year's. 'Get a move on,' I said to the dog.

We inched up the hill to the main road. In my mind's eye I'd arranged all the new clothes on one of those rotary washing lines, and I was gloating over each outfit as it came round. Not that I'd ever get to wear any of them; if I swanned up the village to Spar wearing a bright red basque, Poll would have some kind of Attack. Ambulance men would find her frothing on the front-room floor and clinging pitifully to my grey cardigan. 'It were them tights as started it,' she'd gasp before she pegged out.

Who on God's earth would leave a present like that for me? I gave Winston a tug and replayed the moment when I'd opened the front door. There it had been, my present, sitting on the mat. Maybe one of the neighbours had seen something. Maybe it was one of the neighbours. That wasn't very likely, though, because Poll's fallen out with both sides and I can tell they think I'm just odd. Whenever any of them do speak to me they do it s-l-o-w-l-y, as if I'm backward. Usually I don't bother answering.

Might have been Maggie. But she'd no money, and it wasn't her style, and she'd already given me the pen set. The timing suggested it was a gift from Dogman, but why not say? If it was him, then the level of literacy was higher than usual. Two years ago he'd sent me a Valentine card. *GESS HOW?* he'd printed inside. I'd binned it immediately.

At the top of the Brow we turned onto the high street, the village proper. 'An example of Ribbon Development,' I remember writing in my Y7 geography project. 'Bank Top grew up around the mining and cotton industries, but today is primarily a dormer village for the surrounding urban areas.' It's just a road that runs along the crest of a long flat-topped hill. Exit one direction and you're on the way to Bolton; exit the other and you're Wigan-bound.

Very historical, is Bank Top. General Julius Agricola used it as a vantage point to spy out Britons skulking in the forest below. Panicked Elizabethans lit a beacon here to warn of the approaching Armada, and Samuel Crompton invented his spinning mule just up the road. But time's moved on and, at the start of the third millennium, Bank Top's past its best. It's all very well the local papers publishing quaint photos of children playing on the cobbles; anything remotely picturesque was cleared away years ago. The rows of stone cottages built for the handloom weavers,

20

the Georgian horse trough, the worn granite mounting-block three hundred years old outside the church, were demolished half a century back and the oldest buildings you get now are Victorian terraces. The rest is post-war bland, with some Sixties eyesores thrown in at random.

Bank Top teenagers moan there's nothing to do here, except try and sneak into pubs. (I could go in a pub if I wanted: I don't.) The activity of choice for the underage seems to be to go down the bottom of the Brow of an evening and set fire to a garage. But it's not a bad place, really, there's worse. It's got the library, and it's where my dad is.

Right outside the cemetery gates there's a bus stop. That always used to strike me as funny, imagine the dead queuing up to go off to Bolton, but today it was a damn nuisance because two of Poll's Over Seventies chums were there having a natter.

'It's shocking, it is, honest, they've had all the lead flashing off his roof while he was away—Oh, hello, love. Birthday girl. I've a card for you.' That was Mrs Batley, thickly wrapped against the cold. She rooted in her bag and pulled out a mauve envelope and, bloody hell, a tube of Smarties. She clearly thinks I'm still about six. 'Here y'are, love. How's your grandma?'

I put my head down and looked through my hair. 'OK, thanks. Thanks.' I shoved the Smarties in my pocket and shifted away.

'Will you ask her, love, if she's had a letter about her heating allowance?' Mrs Threlfall, posher coat, furry hat as opposed to headscarf. 'Because we're all supposed to have had one, all them as is on benefit, and if you've not, you've to phone

21

the council—'

I mumbled and nodded, squeezing through the gates onto the gravel path that leads up to the war memorial and Winston now pulling ahead, God knows what he'd seen or smelt. As I walked away I heard them murmuring together. Poor lass, poor Poll, she's a big girl, it's a shame. I bet that was the gist of it. I didn't care. They were going to die before me.

We crunched past the chapel then I bent down and let Winston off the lead. I found my perch on the memorial steps and watched him totter around for a minute till he disappeared behind a gravestone.

I leaned my head back against the granite and stared up to heaven. The sky was perfect winter blue with white clouds streaming across it. My eyes scanned back and forth for the message.

'Are you there, Dad?' I said out loud.

*   *   *

They were playing 'Land of Make Believe' on the radio at the actual moment he penetrated me.

I'd seen Bucks Fizz win the Eurovision Song Contest, watched the girls whip their skirts off for the finale. Never dreamt they'd be the soundtrack to my undoing. He said it would be OK, he kept saying that all the time, till he stopped talking altogether and started jerking around and biting my neck.

He was clever, string of O-levels already, predicted top grades for his A-levels—which he got, despite everything. But the clincher was he said he knew, he'd studied women's bodies and there was a cycle and it was an impossibility that an egg could be fertilized during that particular window. He had a textbook with a diagram in it; we had it open on the bed as he took his trainers off.

Mum was in hospital dying by inches, I had no one I could ask. Trust me, he said, I'm nearly a doctor.

Chapter Three

My dad left me:

- his posters, LP records and cassette tapes
- a collection of stringy ties
- a pair of nail clippers decorated on the front with an enamel violin
- some medical textbooks
- a stack of science-fiction novels
- a gold ring set with a sovereign

He didn't specifically leave this stuff to me, but Poll's never said I couldn't have it. She threw everything else away after the crash. 'Why did you keep his ties?' I asked her one time she was in a better mood. 'He looked so bonny in a tie,' she said, then locked herself in the bathroom for an hour afterwards. Neither of us can get the ring on, Poll with her super-size knuckles and me with my sausage fingers, so it lives in my jewellery box, on a velvet hummock.

My mother left me: a single 6"x4" photograph. I found it in between the pages of *An Illustrated Biology Course*. It was under Symbiosis, although I don't think that's significant. I've left it there because that way it's safe from Poll. When I first came across it, at thirteen, I looked at it every day.

She's blonde and plump, and *young*; but then she'd only have been my age. Her hair's flicked into two wings at the sides of her face and she's wearing blue eye-shadow, a black T-shirt and a knee-length floral skirt. You can't see her feet because they've been cut off the bottom of the picture, so I don't know what kind of shoes she favoured. She's resting her hands protectively on her big bump of a stomach—me—as she leans against the bonnet of the deadly Metro. I'd say she looks fairly happy. She doesn't look like someone who's about to abandon their baby.

I can't place the house behind her. It's certainly not this one, because the window to her right has little octagonal leaded lights. We used to have two small stained-glass panels at the front, but when it came time for replacing them, Poll made Dogman cart them off to the tip to save on repairs. Although I bet he sold them to a reclamation yard, thinking about it.

Pictures of Dad are easier to come by. Poll's got dozens, charting his progress from babyhood to A-levels. He goes from a cute, cheeky-looking boy to a really handsome man, with dark brown hair swept across his brow, an intense gaze, and evidence of a slight mullet at the collar. He reminds me of the drawings in Auntie Jean's old *Dr Kildare* annuals.

I know Dad's back at the house in his jar, what's left of him. But for some reason I feel closest to him in the cemetery. It's so still, a space to think, and you're up on the highest point of the village so it's closer to the sky.

The year I was finally booted out of primary school for spooking the normal kids, I used to come up here a lot. If I wasn't holed up in the library, this is where I'd be. It was

that summer, just when things were getting desperate, that Dad sent me his kiss. Some people might have said it was two aeroplane trails cutting across each other, but I knew it was a giant white kiss he'd scrawled across the ether.

So I look to the sky for messages; and sometimes they're there, and sometimes not. Usually, if you search hard enough, you'll see something significant in the cloud formations. I'm sure, for instance, that a Westie-faced cumulus told me Winston was going to be OK after his op six years ago. And going further back, when I was waiting to see if I'd got into the grammar, I came up here convinced I'd failed and there was a flat grey ceiling of nimbostratus. Then, as I watched, the sky broke open and a thin shaft of sunlight beamed down over Bolton. I don't know if it was shining precisely on the grammar school, but the next day I got the letter offering me a place. Last spring I was convinced I'd messed up a French module, but a band of cirrocumulus showed me a row of ticks. I got an A.

It was cirrocumulus again today, making a fantastic curving spine right above me, anatomically correct down to the number of vertebrae and the little tail of a coccyx; now that had to be Dad. I took my mile-high backbone to mean How were the resolutions going.

Well, first off, I'd kicked the diet into touch. They're rubbish, diets. I've tried them before. You start off hungry and virtuous, the next stage is light-headed and high, then ravenous and unreasonable with a blinding headache, as if someone has

25

attached a couple of jumbo bulldog clips to your eyebrows. That's where the diet begins to fall apart. Eating is my top pleasure, it even beats reading; also, food's not just food in our house. It's sugar-coated guilt, full-fat reproach, high-sodium defiance.

'What's going on? Why have you left your chips?' Poll said last time I tried to cut down.

'I was full.'

'Full? Full? You normally have twice this number, and a steak pie on top. And afters.'

'I was trying to lose a couple of pounds.'

Poll rolled her sleeves up crossly, then leaned over to pick up the plates. 'I've told you before, you're wasting your time. Your shape's genetic. Off your mother. There's no way you can change what you are. You were just born fat.'

'People aren't born fat. It's what you eat,' I said, without much hope.

She patted her rounded stomach. 'No, it's inescapable. Look at me. Legs like sticks and a great pot belly. It's the Southworth Stomach. Cissie's got it too, all the woman down that line have. You got Castle genes: big all over. You can't fight your heritage. Thank your lucky stars that's *all* she passed on. You might have been certifiable. Now, are you having a vanilla slice?'

Far above me, the spine had melted into long wispy fingers, ghost fingers pointing to the south. I stepped back up onto the memorial. 'Dad? If you're still there—I really could do with some help. About the future. Can you give me a sign?'

I watched my breath mist in front of my face, and waited. A helicopter chopped faintly in the distance. Two metres away from where I stood a

26

wren flittered onto a hawthorn branch, bobbed about, took off again.

Winston chose that moment to reappear with something hideous in his mouth. I bent down to prise the thing from his jaws but he was too quick for me; he threw his head back and bolted whatever it was down, gagging and snorting. Probably he'd be bringing it back up later, on the living-room carpet. 'Come on, mutt; home,' I scolded. 'You always have to ruin the atmosphere, don't you?'

I thought again of the backbone when I got in. The TV was blasting out of the lounge, *House-Strip-Neighbour-Swap-Challenge*. Still in the porch, bending to unhook Winston's collar, I called; 'I've been having a think about things, Poll, and I want you to call me Kat.' I said it quite loudly, partly because there was this bouncy theme tune to contend with, and partly because I wanted her to understand right from the word go that I was serious about it.

Poll's frowning face appeared round the door. 'You want me to call you a cat?'

'No,' said Dogman's voice from behind her. 'Don't be daft. She wants you to call her a cab.'

Winston walked stiffly off and I hung his lead up. The urge to impale myself on one of the coat hooks was tremendous. Instead I wrenched my mac off and pulled it down over the hook so hard that the collar ripped. Poll didn't see this, luckily.

'Come in here and tell us a proper tale,' she said.

'Can you turn the TV down?'

'I'll put it on mute,' said Dogman.

I wish I could put you on mute, I thought.

'So what do you need a cab for?' asked Poll,

27

bristling at the thought of any extravagance.

I sat down heavily on the settee. 'I don't. I *don't*. Want a cab. I just had an idea.'

'We're not having any more pets, if that's what you're after. It wouldn't be fair on Winston. And I'm not keen on cats, they bring in dead things.'

'Aye, that's right, they do.' Dogman shook his bristly head. 'Or sometimes things that are still alive. My mother had an infestation of mice once after her Bruno brought in a pregnant one and it got away under t' cooker. I said to her, I thought cats were supposed to get rid of vermin, not attract it . . . ' His voice trailed away as, on screen, a busty woman in a T-shirt bent forwards over a workbench.

'Not cats, not cabs. Just listen, will you? All it was, I wanted to change my name slightly.'

'What for?' Poll shifted her weight onto one foot and started fiddling with the leg of her panty girdle. 'What's wrong wi' t' one you've got?'

'Nothing.'

'So? What's there to change?'

'It'd be easier.'

'How?'

'Well, Kat, it's shorter than Katherine.'

They were both staring at me.

Poll said slowly, as if she was humouring a mad person, 'You want us to call you "Kat"?'

I nodded.

'And shall we get you a collar wi' a bell on it, an' a little dish for your milk?' She started chuckling, and Dogman joined in. Laughter all the way. 'Kat? By, you come out wi' some stuff, you really do. Kat. I mean. Whale, more like. Elephant. Tell you what, we'll call you Ellie, if you like.'

I got up to go and pushed past them both, treading on Poll's slipper as heavily as I could.

'Ooh, bloody hell, watch where you're going,' she gasped.

'Pussy,' I distinctly heard Dogman mutter before I could get to the stairs.

*   *   *

That midnight found me basqued up and buzzing. On the other side of my bedroom wall, Poll slept the untroubled sleep of one who has no conscience. We'd had another row after tea because it was nearly a month since I'd gone to see Auntie Cissie, and because I wanted to read a book instead of listen to how ill the butcher's daughter's neighbour had been after eating squid on holiday. Before she'd gone up I'd mentioned casually about some new outfits, maybe, with the birthday money. She paused at the bottom of the stairs and checked me up and down while I was standing under the hall light.

'You are a bit scruffy at the minute, it's true.' She peered forwards, frowning. 'Your jumper's hanging funny; that's you pulling at the cuffs. Still, you've had your wear out of it.' She nodded. 'I'll have word with Dickie. He says there's some Marks and Spencer's seconds coming on Munawar Noor's stall next week. Munawar told him he could have first pick.'

'What like?'

'I don't know. Knitwear, I should think. That's what he mainly sells, in't it?' She turned away and started to pull herself up the steps. Behind her back, I stuck my tongue out as if I was being sick.

29

'He'd some nice embroidered cardies last time, do you remember? But they'd none in your size. I'll ask Dickie to watch out for them coming again.'

'Could I not have something a bit more, a bit more, young? Like, I don't know—' as if the idea had just that second occurred—'a trouser suit?'

'Trouser suit?' She paused in her tracks and half-turned, clutching the banister with a freckled hand. 'What would you want a *trouser suit* for? You look like the side of a house as it is. Backside like yours, you're best off in skirts. Trouser suit? You'll be wanting jeans next. And a sight you'd look in those an' all. There's more to life than fitting in with the crowd.'

I should bloody well hope so, I thought. 'Palazzo pants are quite flattering if you're curvy.'

'Palazzo pants? Are they them long trousers where you walk on the hems and get them all dirty? You're not having any of them, they'll be in holes in no time, I haven't the money to—'

'No, listen, they're sort of loose—'

'Oh, I know, them ones like they wear in the army with about fifty little pockets in all your nooks and crannies—'

'No, they're wide-legged trousers—'

'Yes, well they'd have to be wide-legged for you to fit in 'em—'

Bitch! Bitch! I wanted to scream at her, but the air had gone out of my lungs like it does in a nightmare and left me with a helium whimper.

'You *never* treat me—Oh, forget it,' I squeaked, and flounced off to the kitchen.

'You've got to be realistic, I'm only saying,' Poll called after me. 'You can't get away with such as these slim 'uns. You don't want to make a fool of yourself. Have you forgotten that time you walked around in a strappy top? And you weren't as big then as you are now. You cried your eyes out, after. I could have told you.'

Pause.

Die, you old witch. Do it now. Lose your footing and crack your skull against the skirting board. Lie there pleading for help. In agony.

Creak creak up the stairs.

I stood in the moonlight, burning. It helps, times like this, to press my fingers into my scalp, very hard. One day I might push too hard and my fingers'll go *splot* into my brain.

Far-off flush of the toilet. Hiss of the pipes. I conjured Dad up for an out-loud moan; had him sitting at the kitchen table, looking sympathetic.

'It wasn't a proper top, that was why the other kids laughed.' He nodded at me encouragingly, like he does in these interviews. 'It was a thermal vest that Poll made me wear under my jumper, even though it was July. She said, "You'll be outside a lot, seeing the animals. Stop complaining. We never had any school trips when I was your age." '

I imagined Dad smiling. He'd have known what she was like.

'On the coach no one would sit next to me, so I got a book out and pretended to read while the other girls swapped bits of packed lunch. Julie Berry kept kneeling up on her seat to chat to Clare Greenhalgh behind, and Mrs Kirtlan kept turning round and shouting at her to sit down and put her belt on. Everyone was drawing love-hearts on the windows, then shrieking and rubbing the initials out. Part of me really, really wanted to join in but I just lifted my book up higher, like I was too gripped by the story to bother with anyone.'

'I've done it myself,' Dad said silently.

'And it struck me then, how do people know what to wear? Because when I looked round, all the girls seemed to be in on some great clothing conspiracy which meant friendship bracelets, and tiny twin plaits framing your face, and turned-up jeans were de rigueur. And yet if I'd dared to appear that morning wearing any one of those items, it would have gone out of fashion *the night before.*'

'It's a lot easier being male,' said Dad.

'All the girls had these little vest-tops on as well, even Sally Ralphs who was the other fatty in the class and should, by rights, have been a target too. She's got a boyfriend now, I saw them in the bus shelter before Christmas.'

'You'll get a boyfriend.'

'Don't want one. They're too much trouble. Anyway, halfway round the zoo, when I was nearly dead from heat-exhaustion, I thought it might be an idea to strip off the jumper and tie it round my waist. I thought I could get away with it.'

'You were more developed than the other girls, even at ten. They were probably jealous.'

'No, I think they just thought I was a blob in bad underwear. They were whooping so loud Mrs Kirtlan had to blow her whistle.'

'I'd have sorted them out.' I imagined my dad making a fist on the tabletop and scowling.

Above the kitchen, Poll's bedroom door clunked shut, vanishing Dad. I opened the cupboard over the sink, drew out a box of Frosties and ate a dozen handfuls while the moonlight streamed in, bright parallelograms on the specked lino. I was thinking about Sally Ralphs' big arms.

Once the house was quiet and the sugar had kicked in, I tiptoed upstairs and listened at Poll's door. Then I crept into my room, put a chair under the handle like they do in films, and pulled the rustly binbag from the back of the wardrobe.

It was amazing to get all the clothes out again and look them over in detail, like Christmas to the power of ten. The sweater and skirt were obviously brand new because they still had their tags in and I had to snip them out with my violin nail clippers. The basque I think had been worn before, because it had a tiny black bow at the front that was coming loose. I just clipped it off and the neckline was as good as new.

Then I set to trying all the outfits on, one after another. The clothes themselves looked fantastic. My stupid face stuck on the top spoilt the effect a bit.

I combed my long hair over my face, like Esther in *Bleak House* does the first time she looks in the mirror after her terrible disfigurement. Peeping through the strands, I thought maybe I didn't look too bad. Yes I was big, but I went in and out, I had a waist, and the flesh was pretty firm. Poll's arms are thin, but the muscle's all slack and hangs and swings under her biceps in a truly repulsive way. I gather there are men who find big girls attractive (Dogman, apparently).

I felt drunk on possibility. Perhaps I had an admirer. A secret lover had spotted my potential from afar, and left me these clothes as a token. I wondered what shoes you wore with an outfit like this. Not the brown sandals I had on now, that was for sure. A mum would know such things, but I didn't have one handy.

I so wanted Dad. Handsome, clever, sitting on the bed; I could nearly see him. Chatting about my plans, my escape; giving crucial advice. I wanted the life that went with these clothes.

Why couldn't I have a normal, alive father instead of a bloody dead one?

*   *   *

I put the stained sheets in a binbag and dumped that in next door's garden. Mum might have noticed, but I knew Dad wouldn't. Blood for blood, as it turned out.

Chapter Four

'I was up all night,' sighed Maggie, clicking sweeteners into her tea.

Poll shook her head and tutted. 'Me an' all. Couldn't get off. Two o'clock, three o'clock. I kept thinking, What are the Gothic elements in Charlotte Brontë's *Jane Eyre*? And to what extent do they help shape the narrative structure?'

'It's the ending that bothers me,' said Maggie.

'Oh, me too. Have another biscuit, go on.' She nodded at the flowered plate.

'Ta, I will thanks. No, it's the religious parallel with the story of Saul, and the whole redemption angle I'm uncomfortable with. To me, the plot's too didactic, too bound up in biblical teaching; the emotional force of the novel becomes, ultimately, diluted. A Romantic writer like Brontë should never have confined her artistic scope within the narrow boundaries of Victorian Protestantism. The two elements are, by definition, diametrically opposed.'

'Dickie thinks the same.' Poll screwed up her face. 'He reckons it's like serving custard with bacon.'

Actually, this never happens.

*　　　*　　　*

When Maggie and Poll do get together they talk about illness or the good old days or crime rates. They like to sit with the local paper divided up between them, picking out the shock horror reports about elderly ladies getting beaten senseless for tuppence. If I'm in the room with them, I'm either part of society's decadence or, if Poll's in a good mood, a shining exception. Youth as it should be when it's been properly brought up. 'She's a whizz at *Countdown*,' Poll will often remark. 'Even the conundrum at th' end, no problem.' I keep quiet. It doesn't do to be too clever round here.

Sometimes we play Scrabble with a giant board, but even that's problematical. If I win, it's, 'Well, no wonder, you're studying English. I never had a proper education, me.' If I lose; 'Eeh, and you with all your brains, fancy.' Meanwhile, Dogman cheats for England. FUNT, he puts down. YESKER. NONING. When I challenge this shite, he claims they're dialect words and Poll tells me to stop picking on him.

If only life were an exam.

In real life, for instance, I can never think of anything to say, plus I hate the sound of my own draggy voice. Somebody says, 'Hiya, cocker, how's

35

tricks?' and I panic, even if it's someone I know; especially if it's someone I know. I died a thousand deaths last month when Mrs Threlfall asked if I was courting yet.

I spend a lot of time smirking dumbly at the floor. But on paper I'm as articulate as anyone. (*In a sense, Mrs Threlfall, your question, though innocently meant, is redundant, for you should know that I have decided to shun the twenty-first-century mating rituals in which the majority of my peers are engaged. In today's Britain, women can lead happily independent lives, unencumbered by the erroneous expectations of a patriarchal society. So put that in your Ty-Phoo and sup it.*)

They're underrated as a pastime, exams. There's something about the adrenaline rush, the legitimate isolation, the whole regulated nature of the exam experience that makes me feel the school hall is my natural element. I don't enjoy exams like, say, I enjoy a box of Maltesers, but I am fantastic at them whereas I seem to be crap at everything else. Ten A-stars, me; you'd never guess it if you didn't know. Some days I wear them round my brow like a crown, but mostly they form a constellation called the Sad Act.

When I walked out of that last English module, I felt elated. I'd been pulling *Sons and Lovers* to bits, brilliantly, because of course I am an expert on Destructive, Stifling Relationships, and Frustration generally.

Halfway through a wasp landed on the paper. It crawled onto the first question I'd answered, sat for a moment waving its feelers, wandered onto the second question, then took off to bother Lissa Hargreaves in front of me. She had a fit, of course, because it wasn't her wasp. It was my wasp and it had come to tell me that I was going to Oxford. Eventually Mrs Wills came over and shooed it away with a copy of Rules for Candidates.

I finished with five minutes to spare, had a quick read through, tingling; then, as Mrs Wills was cruising the aisles with treasury tags, I took all my hair-grips out and checked all the tops on my highlighters. I was high as a kite. When she said to us all, You may go now, I pulled my cardigan on, grabbed my little plastic bag and half-ran for the door. Rebecca caught me up and we fell into step, comparing notes. Really though I was thinking of the bacon bap I would shortly be ordering in the canteen.

'I was *so* not prepared for that Lawrence question. I've made a total mess of the ending, I ran out of time. I just hadn't revised enough,' she gabbled.

We both knew this wasn't true. It was something you said, schoolgirl etiquette. 'Me neither,' I said.

We made our way down the stone steps and past the gallery of school photographs, all those glossy Head Girls and Prefects, and on the bottom row a decade of guide dogs bought with silver foil.

'Don't you wish you could have your essays back for another hour, sort them all out?' Rebecca glanced back at the office with a convincing expression of longing. Maybe she had cocked up. 'Which Hardy question did you do?'

Now we were walking through the undercroft, nearly at the canteen. The wind blew Rebecca's short straight hair up off her high forehead. Her plainness annoys me at odd moments, and I know it's unreasonable, people in glass houses and all that. At least she wears better clothes than me. And if she's got no bust to speak of, it seems a small price to pay for not having a vast backside.

'The one on landscape.' I grimaced. 'Aren't we all just flies crawling across the giant tablecloth of fate?'

'Plus, we'd gone over it in class. Yeah, I think I did OK on that question.' She held the door open with a slender arm, then a frown creased her brow. 'God, I don't know, though. I might go and see Mrs Clements about it after dinner, get her to talk me through it. Do you want to come?'

'What's the point?' I ducked past her into the canteen; the smell was wonderful. 'It's finished now. Try and forget it.' I nudged her into the back of the dinner queue and we leant against the wall while Year Sevens dithered at the front. 'Listen, while I remember, I want to ask you something. I've been thinking of changing my name.'

'Your name?' Rebecca looked at me as though I was mad. 'To what?'

'Kat. I want you to call me Kat from now on.'
'Why?'
'Well, I like it. I think it's more *me*.'
'Kat?'
'Yeah.' I soldiered on. 'Haven't you ever wanted to change your name? Becky, Bekka, Bex, Beckham? You know, for fun?'

Rebecca shook her head. 'Actually, I hate it when people shorten my name.' You would, I thought. 'But if you really want me to call you Kat, I'll try not to forget.' There was just that hint of disapproval in her voice. Kat? *Kat?* What next? Tattoos and class-A drugs? The line shuffled forward and she started to get her money out.

Suddenly I slapped my sides with a sensation of panic. 'Bloody hell.'

'What's up?'

'Oh, *hell*, I've gone and left my purse in the exam room.' I knew exactly where it was. I'd got up and walked out with it draped over the back of my chair. It's another pre-exam ritual I have, the removal of the purse. Besides, it digs in when I lean over.

'Do you mean your belt thingy?' Rebecca began to rummage through her bag. 'I might have enough change, well, if you just wanted a snack. I could lend you—'

'No, it's all right. I'll have to go and get it, I can't leave it there for somebody to nick.'

This would, in fact, have been unlikely. For a start there was hardly more than a couple of quid in there, and more importantly, the belt itself was gruesome. Maggie's niece had made it for me back in Year 9, when the official school purse belt—a freaky item worn only by the socially inept—became too small even on its longest setting. We had a row about it. Poll said it was safest to carry your money on your person. I said what about pockets, but she pointed out that I was always poking my fingers through mine till they were all in holes. So Maggie had this mega-belt run up for me in navy, a school colour, and I've been wearing it ever since. Glamorous it is not, but it is handy, though I'd rather have pulled my own tongue out than admit this to Poll.

I panted back along the undercroft and up the wide stairs to the hall. I plunged in through the swing doors and stopped dead. The details of the scene flashed up and burned themselves on my brain forever.

At the far end of the hall the gigantic red and gold organ pipes rising in asymmetrical slopes to the hammer-beam ceiling. In front of them, the wooden stage with its lonely lectern, and formal seating at each side for visitors. Then, below and stretching towards me, ranks of wicker-bottomed chairs that squeaked on the parquet when you sat down.

All of it I knew, I'd seen before in a thousand years' worth of assemblies and speech days: but never with this detail in the window.

Unbelievable, at first. Two girls framed in the tall stone-arched window on my immediate right, where the chairs gave way to the rows of candidates' desks. Donna French, *Donna French* and Nicky Hunter, in slim profile, touching. They were standing face to face, belly to belly, in what looked like an embrace; laughing in a stifled, secret way.

They jumped in shock at my entrance and again at the bang of the door behind me, but, weirdly, they remained clinging together.

'Oh!' cried Donna, her face a mixture of dismay and hilarity.

Nicky let out a shriek and turned her head away towards the windowpane. Donna put her arms behind her back and dropped her eyes to the floor. I saw them arch their backs simultaneously, their willowy bodies curve apart like an Art Nouveau design, but I still didn't understand. Then there was a small thud and my purse belt, which had been around the two of them, hit the wooden floor.

Released, the two girls moved apart, Nicky giggling with embarrassment. She still had her face turned from me but I could clearly see her reflection in the glass. Her eyes were wide with horror and she was grinning stupidly.

I just stood there like a lump. Donna moved first, bent down and picked up the belt. Nicky took this as her cue to slide out and make a run for it.

'Sorry,' mumbled Donna, holding the belt out to me. She was trying not to snigger though at least she'd had the grace to blush. 'I was going to hand it—'

We both heard Nicky's far-off snort of laughter, and Donna's self-control dissolved. She flung the belt on the table nearest and stalked out. As the door bumped shut behind her, the belt slithered off the varnished surface, buckle end first, and fell in a coil. It lay there like a dead snake, with me hating it.

*   *   *

He'd first spoken to me half a year before, under the horsechestnut trees. A day like summer, although it wasn't. We were the new Upper Sixth; lords of the playing fields, monarchs of the benches. 'Come and see this,' he shouted as I walked past, nose in a book. When I looked up he was perched on the back of the Wasserman Memorial Seat, huge shoes planted on the slats. Even as I swooned I thought, someone'll sit there, in all that mud he's wiped across it.

I approached warily, in case he hadn't meant me at all.

'What are you reading?' He took the book out of my grip and scanned the cover. '*Mansfield Park*? Looks a bit old.' He shaded his eyes and smiled, though it wasn't a straight smile, if you know what I mean. I

41

thought he was making fun. 'You can read too much, you know. Books aren't life. You have to live. Catch.'

I managed to grab a corner as it flopped down, drew it back up, then hugged the novel against my chest. I wanted to defend it or, failing that, I wanted it to defend me. 'It's good,' I said lamely. I didn't dare mention the heroine was called Fanny. Behind his back a conker thudded to the ground but he never even flinched.

'No,' he said, 'this is good. Here.'

He held out his hand and showed me a conker-case, green mottled with brown. I could see where the little dark spikes had dug into his palm.

'Here.'

I took it off him gingerly, held it in my fingertips. Some joke, probably, this was. In half an hour he'd be back in the common room, laughing with his mates about me.

'Open it. Go on.'

'Why?'

He sighed and took it back. 'I'll do it, then.' He squeezed the sides and a dark crack appeared in the green. Then the crack opened like a mouth and a segment of the casing fell away and tumbled into the grass. With his long fingers he eased the other two pieces apart and let them rock slightly on the cushion of his left hand. The conker lay in the centre like a precious bead. 'There.'

I leaned forward to inspect the pattern, beautiful fingerprint whirls, and the shy nude underbelly of pale skin peeping out on one side. It was so glossy it looked almost liquid; a bubble of molten wood. When I poked it, its back was waxy, glossy, like something alive. I drew back. There was another thud inches from my right foot.

'Do you know what's special about that?'

He placed the bits of shell down on the bench by his feet and began to roll the conker between his hands.

'It'll grow into a mighty tree one day?' I clung hard on to my book. I was going to fail this test, whatever it turned out to be.

'No. Can you not see?'

I shook my head, wishing I was back in the library doing an essay.

'It's brand new. Never been seen before. You and I were the first people ever to lay eyes on that conker.' He tossed it high into the air and caught it neatly between two palms. 'So it's special, in't it?'

'Yeah, I suppose so.'

'Feel that.' He passed me one of the spiky casings and I took it more confidently. 'Not the outside, that bit's a bastard. The white stuff inside.'

I had to lay *Mansfield Park* on the arm of the bench to follow his instruction. Then I cradled the piece of shell and stroked the lining. 'It's really soft. It's like, like silk; no, suede.' He had made me marvel.

He nodded. 'Fantastic, in't it?'

I stretched out my arm to give it back but he clapped his hand quickly up under mine and the shell went sailing into the lower branches and disappeared. My heart nearly stopped with shock.

He laughed at my expression and I laughed with him.

'Tell me something,' I said. 'How come you're sitting under this tree with conkers falling all around you all the time, and you've never been hit?'

He pretended to inspect his head, rubbing his fingers across his scalp, then grinned. 'No, no it's true, no injuries to speak of. It's me, I'm magic. I'm charmed.'

I thought, It's me that's charmed.

Chapter Five

The day had begun badly.

Dogman had appeared after breakfast, looking terrible. 'Wolfie's dead,' he'd announced, and collapsed onto the settee. I'd had to go and make him a cup of tea for the shock, although it turned out Wolfie had joined the dog-angels yesterday evening. 'He rolled over and gazed at me wi' his big eyes, as if he were saying, I've had enough.' Poll sat on the chair opposite with her hand to her cheek. 'He'd been on his last legs a while. But I knew this were summat different. And the vet said his kidneys had failed, that was why his breath smelt, and it would be a kindness to put him to sleep.'

Poll was in tears. 'Nobody loves you the way a dog does,' she sniffed.

'Aye, that's true,' Dogman sighed.

I left the scene before they drowned in grief; before I lost my temper and told Dogman it was just as well they didn't put humans down for having bad breath. I should have felt sorry for him, dogless Dogman, but I didn't.

I was too hungry. The sky above me was filled with clumps of mashed potato and clotted cream. By the time I got to Cissie's I was feeling faint; I could have dug up and eaten the daffodil bulbs by the front gate. Only the thought of the purse belt got me past the vending machine in the entrance.

'So they put in a catheter and drew out *two pints*

44

of black . . . Yes?' They know me at reception, but this was a new woman, pie-crust collar, big pearl earrings.

'Cissie Southworth.'

'Sign in the book, if you would.' She slid the page at me through the glass hatch. I caught the biro-on-a-string as it swung past my stomach and scrawled my name, then checked as usual for any other visitors Cissie might have had since I last came. Just her ex-hairdresser, Edith—she must be in her sixties herself—and the vicar. Well, who else is there left?

Apart from the tragic fiancé lost in the war there's her sister, my great-grandma Florence, whose ashes live in my wardrobe: died of a stroke over twenty years ago. Poll's one-armed dad, who would have been Cissie's brother-in-law, came down with fatal peritonitis about the same time as the Coronation, so he's out of the picture too. Of her three nieces, Mary died in childhood, Jean's alive and well but in Australia, and Poll has to be dragged here because they always fall out whenever they meet up. I sometimes look in the visitor's book for Vince's name, but I don't really expect to see it.

I don't mind visiting Cissie. She's at least someone I can talk to without bursting into flames of embarrassment. I can sound off to her about Poll and get a sympathetic hearing. Also, she—ha ha, this is really mad—believes I have a life. If I could ask anyone (not dead) about leaving Poll, it would be Cissie.

She was sitting in the TV lounge watching *Watercolour Challenge* with a shrunken, oddly shaped woman. 'He's made a right dog's breakfast

45

of that, now han't he?' Cissie was saying. 'You can't tell which way up it's meant to be.' Then she spotted me and her face lit up.

'Ooh,' she said, grasping my hand, 'our Katherine, what a treat. You're looking bonny, love. Come next door.'

I hoisted her to her feet and she cast a smug smile at the woman left behind with just Hannah Gordon for company. 'It's a shame,' she whispered to me. 'She's nobody.' I wondered whether Cissie meant she has nobody or she *is* nobody. Maybe they're one and the same.

We walked slowly along the corridor to her room and picked our way through her soft-toy collection. 'I've a few more since you were here last,' she said cheerfully. 'Edith brings them me, oh, and I won that pink 'un in a raffle for Heart Disease.'

'Don't the staff bother? I mean, it's all very nice—' I scooped a brace of dog-creatures off the armchair and looked round for somewhere to lose them. 'I'll just lie them down here,' I said, shooing them under the bed with my foot. 'Having so much stuff must make it difficult to clean round. Do they not mind?'

'I suppose so; they're very good wi' me. But we're not allowed pets, and you get to my age, you need summat to stroke.' She gave the dog a pat, as if it was alive, and I watched as a hank of white fur detached itself and floated to the floor. 'This is new. I'm going to call him Dulux.' It lay splayed across her thigh like road-kill.

Ally from the kitchens put her head round the door. 'D'you want a drink, you two? I'm just coming round with the trolley now.' Ally gave me the creeps. I used to think she was about fifty, but

46

one day she was talking about the time she left school and I realized she was only ten years older than me. It's true her skin was unlined and her permed hair was brown, not grey. But she was enormous. Biceps like giant hams, hips that barely made it through the door frame. The sort of fat that makes strangers stop and stare in the street; morbid obesity. I should have felt some kind of solidarity with her, fatties united, but I just found her repulsive. That's the way you're heading, a voice in my head warned whenever any of Ally's flesh was on display.

'My Cuddly Carer,' said Cissie. 'We'll have two teas and a Penguin each. Forget your figures, eh?'

Ally winked roguishly. 'Coming right up.'

Everybody loved Ally.

'No sugar in mine,' I shouted after her massive back.

Ally handed out rations, beaming, and lumbered out of the room. Cissie checked over each shoulder, careless talk costs lives, and lowered her voice. 'So how's your secret boyfriend?'

A tricky one, this. 'Give us your biscuit here, I'll do it.' I tore open the plastic and my stomach rumbled as I caught the scent of chocolate. (Imagine that, went my head, imagine that in your mouth right now.) I handed it back.

'We've had a row,' I said decisively.

'Aw, love. What a shame. What happened?'

'He was too possessive. I needed my independence.' I thought of Donna silhouetted in the tall window and felt a stab of physical pain in my chest. 'And he didn't respect me enough. He wasn't as nice as I thought he was.'

Cissie tutted and looked sad. 'I tek it Poll still

47

doesn't know? Very wise.' She bit her biscuit and chewed thoughtfully. 'A fall-out, eh. And can you not make it up?'

'No. I need my own space for a while. I've got my exams . . . '

'Aye, well, you've got to concentrate on your exams, that's true. Are you not having your Penguin?'

'I had a huge breakfast.' (Weeny tub of diet yoghurt. Took me about thirty seconds to eat.) 'I'll save it for later, smashing. Cissie, I was wondering, is Poll really poor? I don't mean starving or anything; obviously she gets by day to day. I mean, has she any savings that you know about? Or antiques to sell, that sort of thing? Long-term nest eggs?'

Cissie wiped the chocolate off her mouth with a tissue. 'It's not really any of my business, love. I don't think she has, she's never mentioned anything.' She screwed up the tissue in her fingers. 'You know I've nowt to leave. I've already given her that mantel clock of Florence's, not that I had much choice in the matter. I've a tiny bit in the Abbey National, that's all, and that's coming to you, with my mother's rings—'

'Oh,' I said, embarrassed, 'I wasn't thinking of that. Anyway, you're not going anywhere for a good while, are you?'

'I should hope not.' She laughed, but what she said next was drowned out.

'He*llo*, playmates.' It was shiny-head Mr Poole, ex-Bank Top butcher. 'And how are we today? Excuse me while I park here a mo.' He steadied his Zimmer frame against the door jamb. 'Mind my bike! I'm en route for reception, but I needed a breather. So I thought, why not drop in on the lovely Mrs S?'

Cissie was all smiles. 'It's that man again.'

'Testing, testing.' Mr Poole tapped his hearing aid. 'Can y' hear me, Mother?'

'Can I do you now, sir?'

'I don't meynd if I do.'

They're worse than kids when they get going.

'An' how's your Poll?' Mr Poole said to me when he'd got his breath back. 'Still a rum 'un?'

I saw Cissie nodding out of the corner of my eye.

'Pollyanna Millar, terror of the playground sixty year ago. Our John's still got t' scar wheer she kicked him to mek him join th' Ovaltineys. After a gold badge, she reckoned. She all but crippled 'im for months.'

'She got one in t' finish,' said Cissie. 'Wore it to school every day, I remember Florence pinning it on. But there were a lot of blood spilt ovver it. She went round all t' littleuns, mekkin' 'em sign up. An' a lot o' t' juniors were frittened of her an' all.'

'He's the scar on his shin *till this day*.'

I looked from one to the other. 'Yeah, but, sixty years ago. You wouldn't still have a scar, not after all that time.'

'You would if you'd been clouted wi' a clog.' Mr Poole wagged a knobbly finger at me. 'Vicious things. They'd a' iron band all round t' sole. She cut our John's shin reight oppen. She were a nowty wench, your grandmother, when she were younger.' He glanced at Cissie. 'I'm not speykin' out o' turn, am I?'

Cissie shook her head. 'You're not, no. She deafened an American serviceman with a liquorice stick. Perforated his eardrum.' I started to giggle.

49

'It's not funny. Poor lad. They were our allies.'

'That wasn't Poll's fault, though, was it? She's always told me it was because he was interfering with her. She was only a schoolgirl. He said some rude words and she took fright; that's the version she told me.'

'Did he 'eck as like. That's what she told everyone so's not to get into bother. Does she hit you?'

'Nah.' I laughed at the idea. 'Not since I was tiny. I'm twice her size these days. I'd just dodge, if she ever did.'

'She's an evil tongue on her, though, there's more than one way to skin a cat. You forget,' Cissie concluded, 'I've known her longer than you, and I've seen you in tears often enough. She can be really sharp when she wants.'

I felt my cheeks flush and put my face down till it passed.

Mr Poole nodded. 'Mustard. She nearly took Eric Benson's finger off wi' a home-med firework, do you remember? Collecting cartridge cases and filling 'em' wi' gunpowder she'd filched out of t' quarry. She thought she were a boy, that was half the trouble.' Then, after an awkward pause, he went on, 'Still, we all do things as we're not proud of when we're young.'

'Oh aye, that's true,' said Cissie.

'Anyways, I'd best be off. People to see, pills to tek.' He patted his chest. 'Leave you two ladies to your gossip.'

'TTFN,' said Cissie, blowing a kiss. Dulux slid away and dropped on the floor but she didn't notice.

The rubber tips on Mr Poole's Zimmer made a

squeaky noise that got fainter and fainter as we listened. Cissie seemed subdued.

'I suppose we're all a bit nowty, once in a while. I remember throwing all our Florence's make-up out of an upstairs window. I were angry with her because her husband was still alive. Velouty de Dixor all ovver t' flags. It meks no sense, I can see that now. You do some daft tricks when you're young.'

I couldn't think what to say, so I bent down and retrieved the sheepdog for her.

'Here you go. He was making a bid for freedom.'

'Eeh, y'are a love. So, tell me again about this boyfriend. Donny, in't it? Tell me again what happened. Are you *sure* as you can't patch things up?'

I came away feeling strung out. I'm not a natural liar, despite all the practice I get fending off Poll's incessant probing. I only invented the boyfriend for Cissie. I thought it would cheer her up, give us something to talk about. I didn't invent him for myself. I'm not that sad. Maybe I could kill him off, a drugs overdose or a drunken stroll up the railway line after closing time. Mind you, then she'd be scouring the *Bolton Evening News* every night and there'd be a whole new load of questions to answer.

As I walked up to the entrance I caught sight of Mr Poole sitting half-hidden in a winged chair behind a weeping fig. He had a tea towel over his lap and his hand beneath it was jerking up and down, up and down. Christ, I thought. Even in here it's full of pervs.

I veered slightly so that I would pass near him, and hissed, 'You're disgusting,' at the top of his head. He looked up, surprised. His face seemed

51

odd and naked. As I glared at him the cloth fell away across his knee and I could see that he was holding a pair of glasses in his lap. His flies, I noted, were completely closed.

'Just a sec,' he said, sliding his glasses onto his nose.

'That's better. Couldn't see a blessed thing before.' He peered up at me. 'Now, what's tha sayin'?'

'It needs dusting. This place.'

He tipped his head to one side. 'Does it? I corn't tell.'

'That's probably why your glasses were so dirty.'

'Aye,' he said.

'So what's happened,' the woman at reception was saying down the phone, 'is she's fallen on top of her umbrella and the spoke's gone in her eye.'

I fled the place, cramming the Penguin down my throat as I went.

$$* \qquad * \qquad *$$

Dad let me have Radio One on as we drove in that last morning. Goody goody two-shoes. I was busy making deals in my head. All the songs had messages in them, but none of them mentioned death, so I thought we'd be all right.

My dad spent ages with the doctor while I read a magazine article about the glory of Venice. Then a nurse came. She took me into a side room and said, 'You know your mum was very sick. She's been really brave but she was a very poorly woman. Sometimes you can't fight illness. Sometimes the body's just too badly damaged.'

I looked at her.

'Your mum died during the night. She wasn't in any

pain.'

I said, 'Well, she bloody should have been. I am.' And all the time, this song kept going round and round my head, getting so loud I couldn't think. It was as if my brain was broken. 'Where's Dad?' I managed to ask. 'I need to see him.'

'Give him a few minutes, love,' said the nurse. 'I'll take you to your mum.'

'What's the point?' I shouted.

'I'll leave you for a minute, then,' she said.

I stood totally still for a few seconds, then I lay down on the lino floor and started punching my stomach as hard as I could. I never even saw the doctor come in.

Chapter Six

For all his evil nature, Vince sorted out a lot of household jobs before he left. He re-papered the chimney breast around the new gas fire, he laid lino over the chipped tiles in the porch, and he took out the hedge and replaced it with a larch-lap fence so it'd be less bother to maintain. He even creosoted it afterwards. He was quite thoughtful, as cheating love-rats go.

But that was nearly two decades ago, and although the flowery wallpaper and the lino were still good, the fence was now collapsing in the middle and several of the laps had dropped off. Dogman had been drafted in to help replace a couple of critical panels.

'You don't want to go paying garden-centre prices for stakes,' he'd told Poll. 'They charge silly

53

money. I can get 'em for you. I've a mate.'

So on this sunny morning, Poll was in the garden holding a sharpened pole upright while Dickie hammered it into the soil with a mallet, and I stayed out of the way. They were singing advertising jingles to each other and laughing in a stupid way. I could have snatched that mallet and seen them both off with one good swipe. I was trying to watch a programme that would change my life.

So the next time you visit your grocer
Tell him no other sausage will do
And to all his replies tell him, 'No, sir,
It's Donnelly's sausage for you.'

I strained to hear over Dickie's yodelling.

'I was a mess,' the young woman with maroon hair was saying. 'I really was. A total wreck. My skin was, like, yellow, and I had these great bags under my eyes. And my teeth were a state, all the enamel coming off, the dentist used to go mad so I stopped going. But the worst was the sore throats, I always had a sore throat. I always felt like sh—, like a wreck.'

'And you were "hung up on control", you said before.' The presenter pointed the microphone back at her face.

'Well, it was like, I can't control that side of things, you know, the eating, so I wanted to control everything else. Smacking the kids for tipping their toys out because I couldn't, you know, cope with the clutter. Do you get me?'

'I'll come back to you, Elaine,' said the presenter, leaping lightly up an aisle to kneel at the side of a middle-aged woman in a red suit. 'What was it you wanted to say—?

'Jo.'

'Jo. Have you a question for Elaine?'

Jo leaned in close towards the microphone. 'Same thing with me. Five, six times a day. I got through a load of toothbrushes. And air freshener. Our upstairs stank like a harem.' She gave a short laugh, and the audience joined in supportively.

'And your husband never knew?'

'Never.'

'He didn't have his suspicions, when you disappeared off to the toilet after every meal, and came down reeking of freshmint and perfume?' Close-up of presenter looking surprised.

'No. You see, you get very, erm, cunning; you do these tricks, scams. You might say, "I'm going to have a nice hot bath"—and do it while the taps are running to cover the noise. Or have the radio on. And when you've been doing it for a few months, you get so you can, you can be really quick. And you can hide your empty packets and till receipts, stick them at the bottom of the bin or whatever; I used to burn ours on the fire.'

There was a muffled shout from across the studio; the presenter sprang to his feet and jogged back to Elaine. 'Yeah, plus, there's a lot of husbands and boyfriends who don't *want* to know. Even if they suspect. It's easy to block out what you can't face.' Much nodding. 'I mean, how do you come out and say it? To your, to the person you so-called love and trust? How do you say, "Oh, darling, are you making—deliberately making—yourself sick all the time?" I mean, it's just disgusting, isn't it, to say that?'

The camera lingered on Elaine's expression while someone said something else in the background. The presenter put his hand on her shoulder for a moment.

Then the shot changed to a dowdy woman, fiftyish, sitting in the front row. Some doctor or other, written a book. Get off, you fat cow, I snapped at the screen. She droned on about levels of electrolytes and long-term damage to the oesophagus while I cursed myself for not having switched on sooner. Poll wandered in and asked if I wanted a hot-cross bun because she was doing one for Dickie. I said yes just to get her out of the room.

I'd actually put weight on. Would you believe it. Six days of starving, really going for it, then it was as though something snapped inside me and I ate and ate. You can't diet when you're the one in charge of cooking and shopping. How can I sit down to a bowl of soup and a couple of slices of Nimble when Poll's across the table tucking into toad in the hole? It's no contest. Poll was delighted when I started eating again. 'I thought as you were sickening for summat,' she said, ladling out the custard. 'You've been miserable as sin. Do you want to finish it off?' I did, I had. Then I went up to my room and tried the basque on and it barely did up.

For a minute or two I was so angry I could have scraped my cheeks raw with my fingernails or banged my head against the wall until I saw stars. In the end I went downstairs, opened the kitchen drawer and got out the big scissors. Then I went back up and cut my grey cardigan to tiny pieces. Poll would be furious when she found out, but she could stuff herself. My thumb was burning by the time I'd finished and I had a red welt coming

56

where the scissor handle had rubbed. That was good.

Stupid to get upset in one sense because I'd never, ever wear the basque; but still. It had looked nice before. Like I could have had another life.

The credits were rolling as Poll came in with the hot-cross buns, a whole plate of them. 'There you go. I might have put too much butter on 'em, I don't know.'

She'd cut her hand too with the bread knife, I saw, so there was also blood on some of the buns. I snatched a clean one and focused my attention back on the TV.

'If you've been affected by the issues raised in this programme, then you can ring our helpline, or visit our Web site at www.talkinghelps.co.uk.' Even though you couldn't see him, the presenter's voice was full of concern. I could imagine lonely women all over the country rushing to the phone to ask him how to sort out their lives. Then the credits finished and his tone changed to something more upbeat. 'Have you experienced a holiday romance? Did you meet your other half on exotic shores? Or did your sloe-eyed lover turn out to be nothing but a foreign cheat? If you're interested in appearing on a future show about long-distance love-affairs, why not contact us . . . '

'Bloody beltin', these,' Dogman mumbled. I tried not to look but I could see the mashed-up bun and butter in his mouth.

'Bloody being the operative word.'

'I sometimes reckon you've swallowed a dictionary,' he quipped, spitting bun on me as he passed.

'In that case you must have swallowed *Spot the*

57

Dog,' I snapped. 'You've the vocabulary of a four-year-old.'

He grinned and showed more gluey bun.

'Watch your mouth, you,' said Poll. 'Dickie's never had your advantages. His dad used t' beat him if he saw him reading so much as a comic. He never had a bedroom of his own, neither, used t' have to sleep on t' landing, didn't you?' Dogman nodded tragically. 'So. Think on. And shift up. He's come to watch the racing.'

Time to move.

'I'm off to the library, then. I'm not taking Winston either, he can go in the back. I've revision to do.'

Poll didn't think much of libraries. 'Waste of a good building,' was her verdict. Apparently when she was young, the school library was a seven-foot cupboard that opened right out, and it served the whole village too. 'It was plenty big enough for a place like this,' she told me many times; usually as I was putting my coat on, books ready by the door. 'I don't know what you want to keep trailing all the way up there for. It's good telly tonight.'

Since its days as a cupboard, Bank Top Library's come a long way. The front elevation is modern smoked glass and breezeblock while inside it's cosy with its orange carpets and blue beanbag chairs, a fish tank, posters, funky mobiles. Best of all, in the far corner, there are three computer screens, because Bank Top Library is at last hooked up to the Internet.

'Let me know if it cuts you off,' said Miss Dragon, peering at the home page suspiciously. 'It's been misbehaving. I'm going to have to ring up. See how you go on, and come and get me if it

58

disconnects itself.'

I watched her stride off. I almost love Miss Dragon, Miss Stockley to her face. She's a stone-faced woman, traditional, solid. Everything about her says, I'm not here to be liked, I'm here to run a good library. Large-print Western, drugged-up political rant, historical passion; Miss Dragon knows instantly where to locate it. She stands behind the front desk and frowns as punters rifle through the books with their grubby fingers. She wears her grey hair bobbed, and always a print blouse under a long knitted waistcoat. You'd think she was a right old misery, but you'd be wrong.

The time blind Poll knocked *Pride and Prejudice* into a full washing-up bowl, she was lovely with me. 'It's the sort of thing I do myself,' she said when I explained I'd had it propped open behind the taps because I couldn't bear to put it down. She said it was nice to come across a youngster who appreciated the classics, and had I read any Dickens? I told her I'd once started *David Copperfield* and given up, and she led me to the D shelf and found me *Bleak House* instead. She said, 'I shall ask you what you thought of this next time you come in.' I was back in three days.

'Well?' she asked. 'Didn't you enjoy it?'

'No,' I said, 'it made me cry.'

'Do you wish you hadn't read it?'

I thought about it. 'No.'

She seemed pleased.

One month after that conversation, I was expelled from Bank Top Primary in disgrace and it was Miss Dragon who helped pick up the pieces. She even offered to come to my first parents' evening at the grammar school, when she heard

Poll wasn't going. I sometimes look at Miss Dragon and I think, she wouldn't have given up a baby and swanned off into the blue.

Nowadays she lets me have first pick of any books they're selling off, and asks my opinion on the ones they order in new. My opinion; fancy. And when I mentioned to her about calling me Kat, she didn't laugh.

'Kath?' She put a hand behind her ear.

'No. Kat. With a K.'

'Kategorically?'

'Katastrophically.'

'I hope not. I'll katalogue it in my brain, though it may take a while for my mouth to make the switch.'

I knew Miss Dragon wouldn't disturb my research, and if anyone else asked, it was a school project. I typed in the Talking Helps address and waited for the page to load. Scrolled up and down, found the right link, and clicked.

Here we go, I thought.

Bulimics (people who make themselves sick after eating) often have LOW SELF ESTEEM. They may have experienced A MAJOR STRESSFUL EVENT in their lives. They may have difficulty dealing with NEGATIVE EMOTIONS such as ANGER or LONELINESS. Some people who suffer from bulimia say they feel an overwhelming NEED TO BE IN CONTROL of their lives by strictly monitoring what they eat. Almost all say they are under SOCIAL PRESSURE to be thin from TV, magazines, peers etc.

The site had clearly been put together by a panel of doom-merchants.

<u>Physical Dangers associated with self-induced vomiting:</u> dizziness, weakness, confusion, temperature sensitivity, low blood pressure, high blood pressure, low platelet count, hyperactivity, chronic fatigue syndrome, brittle nails, hair loss, swollen legs, muscle wasting, cramps, bloating, constipation, diarrhoea, incontinence, coeliac disease, osteoporosis, arthritis, degeneration of the jaw hinge, loss of periods, infertility, tooth erosion, easily bruising skin, hypoglycaemia, hyperglycaemia, diabetes, anaemia, respiratory infections, hairiness, temporary paralysis, peptic ulcers, tearing of the oesophagus, gastric rupture, gastrointestinal bleeding, cancer of the oesophagus, cancer of the larynx, seizures, kidney failure, liver failure, brain damage, blindness, stroke, arrhythmia, heart failure, death.

Well, OK, but the main thing was you'd be losing weight.

I clicked onto the next page, but it was all about **breaking out of the cycle** and **loving and valuing yourself**, absolutely nothing about what to stick down your throat. So I called up a search engine and started looking for Eating Disorders. What I wanted was a sort of user's manual.

I caught a movement out of the corner of my vision. Miss Mouse, Miss Ollerton, was wandering

61

over, clutching a stack of books and looking sad. She always looks sad. She's very nervous too, never looks you in the eye. I couldn't imagine her doing any other job than this, living anywhere other than in this castle of words. I leaned over the screen casually, blocking out what was loading; occasionally it's useful being so wide. Miss Mouse drifted past in her long droopy clothes, gave me a half-smile, and disappeared into the Hobbies and Crafts section. I could hear the gentle thump thump through the back of the shelves as she slid each volume into its correct place. Her skin and hair are so pale I think she sleeps inside a book cupboard.

When I sat back, the computer was displaying a blue sky bisected by a rainbow, and a sparkly waterfall in the bottom left-hand corner. Welcome to *Cherry's Home Page*, it twinkled. It didn't look like a site about making yourself sick.

Cherry-not-her-real-name was twenty, and at college in Wisconsin. Her hobbies were collecting buttons, horse-riding, and bulimia. She'd been bulimic since she was seventeen, and it was a *load of bull* that it made you ill. Her friends thought she looked great, and in any case it was her life and her body and if that's how she wanted to run the show, who had the right to tell her otherwise?

There were links to *My Button Collection* and *Some Great Pics of Horses*, and *Cherry's Guest Book*. In spite of myself, I had to check out the button page. Possibly what we had here was somebody even sadder than myself. I mean, buttons? Poll's got about five hundred of them in a tin under the stairs, mainly boring old shirt ones of Vince's.

Turned out she meant badges, which wasn't

quite so nerdy. *I have over 2,000 buttons! I have catalogued them as follows: Animals, Brand-Names, Drugs, Humor, Miscellaneous, Music, Places, Political, Portraits, Religious, Vintage.*

I skipped to the Guest Book.

Congrats, Cherry, on your great site. You tell it like it is. I use a toothbrush! was the first entry I read, from The Kookie Monster. Cherry had replied: *Yeah, I tried that one time, but it scratched my throat.*

You weren't using the bristle end were you?!!! The Kookie Monster had typed.

Doh! Was Cherry's response. *Trust me to get it wrong! Ha-ha, only joking, stay Cool!* There was an emoticon of a laughing face next to some kisses.

In the next thread, Genius-Girl was tickling her tonsils with a ruler because she didn't like to smell vomit on her hands afterwards. *Kind of appropriate as I'm a math grad.*

Anni86 was still living at home with her parents, but she'd come up with a brilliant excuse for hogging the bathroom. *I say I'm using a face-pack and don't like to be disturbed for twenty minutes. Then I turn up the radio real loud. I always make sure I dab a little of the face pack round the sink or on the taps before I come out, and sometimes I leave a smear round my hair-line or jaw.*

That is so smart.—Cherry

I'll try that one myself.—Forestsprite

Has anyone here used a proprietary emetic?—Deepsouth

Too risky. You have no control over where you puke. People start asking questions.—Genius-Girl.

Wanna swap some buttons? Mail me with your wants list.—Maddyfan.

I unrolled the messages slowly, taking in the good bits. It was true what they said about the Internet, how it opened whole new worlds.

Thanks a bunch, girls, I could have added. *It's been a real eye-opener.*—Barm-cake.

I closed the site and heaved myself out of the swivel seat. With luck, racing from Chepstow would still be on for another hour.

*   *   *

Sometimes think I lost my virginity under a horse-chestnut tree, by moonlight. That there was moss under my head, and the leaves rustled as we moved together. Shadows played across his closed eyelids; I couldn't stop looking at his beautiful sad face. 'Your hair's the colour of conkers,' he whispered. The rain began to patter on the leaves as he entered me, but I didn't feel it on my skin till afterwards. He whirled the stars around the sky the way a child waves a sparkler. There was no pain. 'I shan't go to university,' he said. 'I couldn't bear to leave you now.'

Chapter Seven

I reckon Poll's got an eating disorder, of sorts. That larder's stocked for a siege, terrorist attack, deadly virus outbreak, asteroid collision, economic collapse, etc. Cissie says it's to do with the war and being forced to make three square meals a day out of potato peelings and thin air. She tells tales of having to make tea-substitute (grate a pile of carrot onto a baking tray and dry it out on a low heat) and jam-substitute (mix in a pint of appropriate-coloured jelly and re-pot) or almond substitute (crack open a prune stone and dig out the kernel). She's cooked with blackcurrant leaves, onion skins, dandelions and nettles; she knows a recipe for fatless pastry, can bottle fruit without sugar, and scramble one egg to feed two people (add half an ounce of cornflour in with your butter).

'What's for tea?' the infant Poll used to ask her mother.

'Three jumps at t' cupboard an' a bite at t' knob,' Florence would reply, flicking through her Ministry of Food leaflets. Desperate times all round.

It's from these lean years, Cissie says, that Poll's developed her skewed relationship with food. So we have *two* bread bins, one for bread, and the other for sticky no-brand cakes with lurid icing and foreign writing on the packet. She buys these off Chorley market, or they get brought along in tribute by the Dogman, and they don't last two minutes. 'It's a shame to let 'em go stale,' she'll say, licking hundreds and thousands off her fingertips. For breakfasts we have tram-scotcher toast—slices two inches thick—and condensed milk sandwiches for suppers. In between it's compulsive chain-snacking. The only reason Poll's not built like a sumo is she's Queen Fidget.

My trouble is, I spend too much time sitting on my bum and reading.

My trouble is, having Poll around.

*   *   *

'It's in your best interests,' I remember them saying. They said it when they took my clothes off, and when

65

they put me in a dim room and when they tried to show me the screen. I wouldn't look.

'There's no damage,' I heard the doctor say to the nurse.

There is. There is! I wanted to shout. There's damage in my head. How can that thing be alive when Mum's not?

But I didn't say a word, just bit the side of my hand hard.

In the end they switched the scanner off because I just kept my eyes tight shut and my head turned away. In the darkness I saw:

Him, holding a spray of lilac to my face. Close your eyes, he told me.

I did.

Open your mouth, he whispered.

I parted my lips and he placed something cool and moist and flat against my tongue.

Now eat it.

I chewed, carefully.

Keep smelling the lilac as you eat, he said.

I opened my eyes and saw him holding the apple and the penknife apart, then bringing them together and smoothly cutting another thin slice of white flesh. He passed it to me on the blade.

Do it again, he said.

Why? I asked.

Because I want you to, he said. I want you to experience life.

When they turned the lights back on, there was a crescent of purple teeth marks across the edge of my palm. I put my hand quickly behind my back, but the doctor saw. 'Have you any questions at this stage?' he asked me, picking up his notes. The nurse behind him had a face that would have soured milk.

'Yes,' I said. 'How did I get to where I am now?'

'I don't understand what you mean,' he said.

'I mean, this shouldn't be happening. I want to go backwards. Rewind. Six months ago, I was happy. Now I'm stuck in here and you're telling me a pack of lies. You can't keep me here, you know.'

I thought they'd give me my clothes then, but they didn't. They brought Dad through instead.

'They're wrong, Dad,' I cried. 'There's no baby. There can't be, I've not even had sex yet. Honest. They're making it up.'

But his eyes had gone like glass and he shook his head at me. It was about that time they were wheeling my mother down to the basement.

*   *   *

It hadn't been too hard to conceal my new hobby from Poll, although Maggie caught me once just after a session in the bathroom and gave me a few searching looks. I stayed to ear-wig on the stairs.

'What's up with your Katherine?' I heard her ask.

'What do you mean?'

'She looks as though she's been skrikin'.' Poll probably shrugged because she didn't reply. 'Has Dickie said summat daft?'

I nipped back down and wandered in all innocent, blowing my nose noisily into one of Vince's large hankies. 'I tell you what,' I said, 'my hayfever's been terrible since old Rowlands planted all that rape at the bottom of the Brow.'

'Ah,' said Maggie. She was sitting by the gas fire drinking her tea from a sugar basin. She's not one to complain, isn't Maggie. 'Now, I've summat for you, if you'll howd on a minute. Fetch my shopping bag from t' kitchen, will you?'

I brought it in, trying not to snag my tights on the vicious raffia decoration.

'Here. Try this on for size. I spotted it in Scope and I thought, I know who that'll do for.'

She handed me a plain brown leather purse with a length of thong wrapped round and round it.

'What is it?' Poll squinted and reached for her magnifier. I unwound the long strap and passed it over to her. 'Hmm. Very nice.' She mauled it between her fingers, undid the top and sniffed inside. 'Leather. What do you say?'

'Thank you.'

'Well, I still think it's awful, them rough boys taking your purse belt and throwing it out of the bus window. You did report them, didn't you?'

I nodded. 'There wasn't any money in it.'

'That's not the point. You'd think you'd be safe on a bus in the daytime. It's getting so you can't go out. Bolton's becoming a war zone. Over here, love.' She motioned me to bow my head so she could slip the purse on. 'You wear it round your neck. And I've a picture, see. It was in a magazine at th' hairdresser's.' She unzipped the purse and drew out an A4 page folded into squares. It showed a hippyish model with half a dozen scarves on, plus this purse dangling below her neck, and all sorts of jewellery hanging against her red hair. She looked gorgeous. Maybe it was a magic purse that would make me look like that. 'You can be really with-it, wearing this. And it's plenty big enough to fit your bus pass, your keys, all sorts. Kitchen sink, if you want.'

'Thanks,' I said.

'You suit your hair back, though, we can see your bonny face. She's a pretty girl, in't she, Poll? Hiding behind all that hair. How d'you expect the lads to see your bonny smile if you brush your hair all down like that?'

'I'm not interested in boys,' I said, pulling out the elastic on purpose and shaking my head like the girl in the Pantene advert.

Poll tutted. 'Tek no notice, Maggie. She's a lost cause. I've given up botherin', me. Now. Are you stoppin' for your dinner, cause I've a prayta pie and some pickled cabbage as wants eatin' up.'

'Hmm.' Maggie patted her belly. 'I s'll be awreet wi' t' pie but I might have to pass on the cabbage.'

I buzzed off back up to my room, purse swinging. Boys? Yeah. Right.

*   *   *

I've lost my wife and my daughter on the same day,' I heard him say as he walked out of the room.

*   *   *

Nothing ever turns out exactly like you imagine it. That's what allows you to play Cheat-Fate, where, for instance, you *imagine* unwrapping your exam results and getting a line of U grades then, because you've imagined it, it can't happen. I play this game all the time, but sometimes I can't stop myself fantasizing about good things, which is stupid because simply predicting them will prevent them from happening.

What I'd role-played for months was that I'd get put in a General Studies group with Donna French

69

and that, being forced into close proximity to me, she'd suddenly realize that I was OK really and just needed bringing out of myself. Then she'd invite me on a few one-to-one shopping trips or meetings in coffee bars, and she'd quickly come to like me so much she'd decide to have me as her best mate. Rebecca would leave the school, or get herself a new friend, basically find some way of disappearing, as would all the rest of Donna's gang.

Under Donna's influence I'd become slimmer and smarter, because she'd find me the right clothes to wear and teach me make-up, and also tell me what music to listen to (at the moment I mainly play Dad's old 80s cassette tapes, hiss hiss, wurp wurp. All Rebecca ever listens to is classical).

Then, one day, Donna would invite me back to her lovely house, and it would look like a page of *Hello!* magazine. And, in the privacy of her super-cool bedroom, something would occur. A kiss, maybe. An embrace, endearments. Possibly some hair-stroking.

But now it was too late because we would be leaving school in half a term, and I hated her anyway because of the Belt Incident. I'd had Donna killed several times since; once on a ski trip, some kind of collision with a rock; once by a jealous ex-boyfriend who'd waited till she came out of a pub and then run her over in his sports car; and once a good old-fashioned tumble down the stairs in her high heels. The same for Nicky Hunter, too, only perhaps with just the sustaining of major injuries because I hadn't been in love with her.

Yet there we were on this Wednesday morning, Donna and me sitting at opposite ends of the common room during a midday free, and she was still alive and I was still fat. She was at the far end, half-hidden by the drinks machine, plugged into her Discman, and apparently engrossed in highlighting pages of notes. I was in a corner, covering my face with a book. There were only half a dozen other people around and I thought, if it ends up just me and her left on our own, I shall get up and walk out.

The door swung open and there was Mrs Law. You don't mess with Mrs Law; she's Psychology *and* Acting Deputy Head *and* Careers. If she decides she doesn't like you, that's your UCAS form down the pan. The Lower Sixth call her Judge Dredd, and she knows, and likes it.

'I'm looking for volunteers,' she announced.

Everyone shuffled but no one made any positive movement.

Mrs Law did her lighthouse-flash gaze round the room. 'Jenny? Lissa? What about you?' They got to their feet, frowning suspiciously at each other. 'And you, Sita? Come along; Alex as well. Just a quick job, helping out your fellow students in the sports hall. Won't take five minutes of your valuable time. Jasmine and Zoe, surely you're not hiding behind that curtain? That's it, out you come, a break will do you good.'

I saw Donna glance round and register alarm at the emptying common room. She unplugged her headphones swiftly. 'I'll come too, Mrs Law.'

Mrs Law smiled in a surprised way as Donna half-ran across to join her. Then she turned to go and, at the last moment, spotted me. 'And Katherine.' *I thought you liked me*, I wanted to say. But she only fixed me with her death-ray eyes and

71

held open the door. I laid the book down and got up as slowly as I could, hoping she might walk on ahead and I could peel off and take sanctuary in the toilets till the coast was clear. No such luck. She ushered us all out, then brought up the rear like a collie.

'God, if we have to do circuit training or something, I'm going to tell her to get stuffed,' muttered Lissa.

'She can't *make* us do PE.' Alex swivelled her bracelet as she walked. 'I mean, we're out of this place in six weeks, forever. What can she do to us, really? Give us lines? I'd like to see her try.'

'She could stop us sitting our exams,' said Jenny.

'What, for saying no to this lark, whatever it is? I *don't* think so.'

Jenny shrugged.

We did as we were told.

When we got to the sports hall we saw there were four sets of equipment waiting for us. In each corner there was a short row of chairs, a stack of clipboards, a crash mat, a pile of newspapers, a roll of parcel tape, a ruler and a small polythene bag containing strips of black plastic. It looked as if we might be going to play some sort of hideous party game. A little group of Lower Sixth came forward to greet us.

'This is my psychology class,' said Mrs Law. 'They need you to help them with an experiment.' I saw Alex roll her eyes and slump against the wall bars, arms folded. Mrs Law mustn't have seen because she carried straight on. 'Emily, do you want to explain?'

A stocky girl stepped forward. 'Hiya, thanks. Thanks for helping out.' There were no answering

72

smiles. 'Yeah, well, what it is, is we want to set you a competitive task. We're going to observe the different strategies people use to deal with it, the task, and evaluate which one is the most successful.'

Bollocks, I thought. Psychologists *never* tell you what they're observing.

'So we need you to get into pairs.'

No one moved.

'Chop chop,' said Mrs Law.

Alex sighed and slouched forward, pulling Sita by the hand. 'Sooner we get this started, sooner we can get back. To our A LEVEL REVISION,' she finished, glancing back over her shoulder at Mrs Law. Jasmine nodded at Zoe and I thought, oh fuck, I can see where this is headed.

'Jenny, do you want to go with me?' I asked, in an utterly crap, pathetic way. But Jenny and Lissa were already turning to go, together, which left –

Donna's head was well down. 'I feel sick, Mrs Law,' she mumbled. 'Need to go and get some Paracetamol.'

'Paracetamol won't help with nausea,' said Mrs Law briskly. 'What you need is to take your mind off it. Get cracking now; you're holding the others up and I don't believe they'll thank you for that.'

Donna and I trudged across the slippery gym to where our knot of Lower Sixths were seated, holding on to their clipboards. Donna flopped down onto the crash mat and lay full length on her front, as if she was sunbathing, while I stood above her, chewing my nail and feeling like hell.

'Right,' said Emily. 'I need you all to watch this carefully.'

She peeled a page of newspaper off the pile

nearest and began to roll it up diagonally so it formed a long, thin tube. A Lower Sixth assistant handed her a bit of parcel tape and she stuck the final corner down so the tube couldn't unravel itself. Then she took the ruler, held it against the middle, and bent the tube down at both ends. 'You need to make each central strut exactly thirty centimetres long,' she explained. 'Do you see? Mand, can I have those ones I did earlier?'

Assistant Mand scrabbled under the wall bars and pulled out a bundle of other tubes, all with their ends bent over.

'Now, what you're going to do is use these struts to build three regular solids. A tetrahedron, a cube, and a dodecahedron.' Mand started rooting in some binbags that she'd hauled out from behind the benches.

'Come again?' said Alex. 'I quit maths after Year Eleven, you know.'

Emily wasn't fazed. 'Like this.' She held out her arms and Mand handed her two finished shapes, well-jointed with parcel tape and plastic ties. They were pretty rigid considering they'd been made from paper. 'Can you all see? A tetrahedron, like this, is a *four*-faced solid, and a cube, here, has *six* faces, and a dodecahedron, that's what Mand's holding, has got *twelve*.' Silence. 'OK? Great. And because this is a competition, we don't want you to talk to any of the other couples, or ask us anything either. We're here to observe. Ignore us. We're invisible.'

'Is there a prize?' Alex again, just this side of insolent.

'Yes,' said Mrs Law. 'A beautiful box of Belgian chocolates for the winning couple.'

'Oh my God, really?'

'No. Emily?'

Emily shouted, '3-2-1-*go*,' as if it was a proper race. The competitors exchanged disgusted glances, but started anyway.

Two minutes in and it looked as if Donna and I were going to be winning a category all of our own; the only team to complete the task without actually speaking. We sat at opposite edges of the crash mat with our backs to each other, while the clipboard girls scribbled away. I started rolling up tubes and taping them, because I'd worked out we only needed six to make up the tetrahedron and it seemed sensible to start with the easiest. Then, when I got to the fifth, Donna said, '*Shit*,' under her breath. 'Shit shit shit.'

I moved aside my curtain of hair and peeped out. Donna's shoulders were jerking oddly but I couldn't see what she was doing.

'All right?'

'Shit,' she said, without looking at me.

I turned back to my rolling.

'Katherine?' she said in a tight voice. 'How do you get these bloody things off?'

When I looked again she'd turned round and was holding her arm away from her body, and it was all stripy red round her cuff with scratching. A black cable tie bit into the skin just below the bone of her wrist and you could see the purple flush as the blood built up.

'I can't get it *off*,' she hissed. '*Fucking* thing. The more I try, the tighter I make it. It's agony. How do you undo it?'

'I'll ask those girls.' I glanced over. Still writing.

'No, don't! I feel such a div.'

'Well, you can't undo them once they're on, they've these little notches, can you see—'

'My hand's about to drop off—'

'Hang about.' I felt around in my purse and drew out my nail clippers between two fingers. 'You might be able to use these to shear through the plastic.'

She took them off me and I saw her hands were trembling. She squeezed them experimentally near the flesh but she couldn't get the angle. 'Oh! Shit.' The clippers flirted onto the crash mat, then bounced onto my shoe. I scooped them up and handed them back. She had another go and this time nicked herself properly. 'Ow, fuck, look at that. Hey,' she said with an effort, 'can you do it?'

Putting my skin on hers, even though it was only fingertips on a wrist, made me want to die. I concentrated totally on the cable tie, and she might even have closed her eyes. Any moment now, I thought, Mrs Law's going to glide over and ask us what we're playing at. I wondered what the observation team were putting in their notes: *Subjects went into what at first appeared to be a consultation huddle but within minutes had developed into lesbian-style groping. They made very little progress with their polyhedra.*

The tie pinged off and Donna yelped with relief. 'Christ. Thanks,' she said, rubbing the dark line where the notches had dug right in. 'God, I'm so stupid. What a bloody bloody stupid thing to do. I'm always doing stupid things. Mum calls me Little Miss Dizzy. I just dive in, I never stop to think—'

'Have you got any struts made yet?' I asked quickly.

'Too busy mutilating myself. Sorry. What can I

76

be doing?'

'Well, I'm nearly ready to make the pyramid. I might need you to hold some pieces in place while I tape the others together.'

We got into a kind of rhythm: peel, roll, stick, bend-bend, and I sneaked glances at her while we worked. Her hair was so sleek; different shades of blonde fell across each other, then back into place when she moved her head. Her thighs were so slender that even when she sat on her haunches, they hardly spread at all. There were light freckles on her heart-shaped face. I watched her till it hurt.

Donna had started talking like a radio DJ, rattling off questions and laughing a lot. 'That's such a neat pair of clippers, where d'you get them? I've never seen ones with a violin on the front. Cute. Hey, look at Lissa's group, they're making hexagons. Should we be making hexagons? Don't you need hexagons for the dodecawhatsit? No? Shall I tell them? Won't it be funny when they realize they've done it wrong. Hey, you could use those tie things if you were a criminal, bind your hostages up, they'd never escape. Shall I tear off some pieces of tape for speed? Oh, ow, *ow*. My God, look at that, I've taken all the hairs off my forearm. I bet you could use this stuff instead of waxing, bloody painful though. Mind you, so's waxing. Can you believe there's women who pull their own hair out, for kicks? I mean, on their heads, so they go bald? Mental.'

We got two shapes completed before the bell went for dinner, so technically we beat everyone, although none of the Lower Sixth said that. They didn't even tell us what they'd been observing.

As we filed out of the gym, Donna was saying,

'We won, didn't we? Didn't we win?'

'You are so sad, Donna French,' said Alex, but in that way which means it's only a friendly thing to say and not bullying.

'Sad yourself, loser. Look, I've made myself a victory wreath.' She was stringing cable ties together into a large-looped chain. 'Smart, eh? Might wear it tonight, essential clubwear.'

'Looks a bit spiky to me,' said Lissa. 'You'd have somebody's eye out if they came up for a snog.'

I was hanging at the back of the group when Donna turned to me. 'You are so fucking clever, though. You deserve this.' She draped the plastic chain over my hair. 'Honest,' she turned back to the others. 'You should have seen her. Dead organized, worked out how many struts we needed for each shape before we started, had a proper strategy, no, stop laughing, to finish each shape before we started the next because that was quicker—'

I was half-smiling in case it was a piss-take, to show I was in on the joke.

'No, seriously,' Donna went on. 'If you're ever in desperate need of a paper polyhedron and time is of the essence, Katherine's your girl.' She raised her palm to me.

I gawped for a second, then it clicked what she wanted and I slapped her hand. 'Yo,' she said.

'Actually, it's Kat,' I said. 'My name. Kat. I've changed it.'

'Miaow,' said Alex.

Nicky appeared round the corner and Donna let out a squeak of joy. 'Nicks, Nicks, wait up.' She broke into a run. Nicky held her arms open for Big Hugs.

'See you then, Kat,' Donna shouted over her shoulder.

*   *   *

I don't know how long I was there. Time's different in hospitals. I don't even know if it was another part of the same building, or a different place altogether. There was still that giveaway smell of cleaning fluid and canteen. There was still nowhere to be private, people asking you questions constantly and putting needles in your arm. I didn't take much notice. I kept my eyes closed a lot of the time because it was better in my head.

The night before we did it, he took me to a playground and sat me on a swing. He swung himself like a maniac.

'You could launch yourself off into the sky, it'd be easy. Lose yourself in all them stars,' he shouted as he swished past me. 'Go higher. See if you can go right over the top bar. I bet you could if you got enough momentum up.' His hair flowed round his face, then back, blown tight away from his hairline. I slowed down to watch, saw the chain links shift, heard the creak of the giant bolts.

Then, without warning, he jumped right off in mid-swing, legs flailing. He landed hard and staggered, but didn't fall. 'Hit the ground running, that's what they say. That's the secret,' he called across the darkness.

He strolled over and stood close in front of me, gripping the chains near my hips. 'There's no need to be scared. I'll show you something.' He drew the swing seat towards him and held it for a moment, then let me fall away. 'Come on.'

I remember scuffing my shoes hard into the grass

to stop myself, and the whole metal frame shuddering around me. He took my hand and led me over to the roundabout.

'We're at the centre of the universe, you and me,' he said.

I laughed.

'No, we are. I can prove it. Hop on.'

The roundabout was a solid cylinder shape with bright tube handles intersecting the top into cake-slices. We each sat in a slice and he pushed hard on the ground with his foot to start us moving.

'Lie back. Go on.'

I rested my neck on a cold handle.

'No, don't close your eyes. Look up.'

Orion whizzed round, Ursa Major wheeled from one edge of my vision to the other.

'I told you. The stars revolve around you. You're the centre of everything. We are. Us.'

A nurse came in. 'You've got visitors,' she said brightly. 'Shall we have these curtains open, let a bit of sunshine in?'

I wriggled myself up in bed, heart beating in case one of them was Roger, or Dad. I knew it wouldn't be Dad, though, really. 'You'd have broken your mother's heart with all this,' he said, the last time I saw him. 'You were everything to her. Whatever made you do it?'

'Love,' I told him.

'You don't know the meaning of the word,' he said, and started crying.

'I do!' I shouted. 'Roger loves me. He wants this baby.'

'Does he heck. He wants shut of you.'

'He says he'll look after me.'

'He's too busy looking after himself. Drunk on his

80

own charm. Well, you go your own way from now on, it's nowt to do with me. You've made your choice as far as I can see.'

'Are you decent now?' asked the nurse. 'Come here and let me put a comb through your hair. Have you any cologne?'

The door opened and an elderly woman in a black and purple shell suit walked in, followed by a grey-haired man in a patterned sweater and baggy pants. I turned to the nurse in confusion.

'Who are they?' Because I didn't like the look of them at all. Especially her.

'I'm your rescuer, that's who I am. I'm family. My name's Pollyanna Millar, and this is Vince. We've come to tek you home.'

Chapter Eight

The invitation was in my pigeonhole on the last day of term.

Skool's Out
Summer's Here
and Donna's 18!!!
Come and get slaughtered before the results!!!
The time: 7th August, 9pm –1am
The place: Steem
Dress: Bad Girl!!!

I checked Rebecca's pigeonhole to see if she had one too, but it was empty, spotless. Everyone was clearing out. Lockers were being moved, ancient pieces of food and forgotten books being

81

unearthed, while Mrs Law barked instructions across the common room and handed out binbags.

'We want *no trace* of you by twelve o'clock,' she yelled above the noise of the radio. 'Anything left at the end of the day will be *thrown out*.'

I stuffed the invite in my purse. Obviously I wouldn't be going, but it was nice to have got one. The last party invitation I'd had was completely bogus. It had come a week after my birthday and had looked like a proper card from a real person. *PULSE invites you to rave the nite away with your mates*, the gold ticket said. 'It's a con. They get your name off th' electoral roll,' said Poll, destroying my last vestige of hope. 'It's a computer as sends 'em out.'

'Oh, that,' sniffed Rebecca when I showed her Donna's card. 'I heard them twittering on about it yesterday. Her dad's paying for the whole lot, you know. Club hire, drinks, everything.'

'Are you going?' I asked, madly.

'No, of course not.' Her eyes bulged at the idea. 'Anyway, I didn't get an invite.'

A little thrill of mean pleasure went through me.

'She probably thought you wouldn't like it.'

'Which I wouldn't.'

'Hey, you could come as my guest, though. It might be a laugh.' I tried to keep my voice light, as if I might be joking.

'You're not really going, are you?' She stopped ramming folders into carrier bags for a moment and goggled at me.

I considered for a second or two, and this is what went through my head:

1. Aerial shot of Ibiza-type rave crowd, lots of

82

happy faces and bare shoulders.
2. Me, squeezed into the middle of it, flushed and petrified, in my basque.
3. Outside the front of my primary school, me standing crying in front of a felt-tip poster announcing COME AND GROOVE AT OUR DICO.
4. Donna and Nicky, joined at the hip.

'I've got a recital that evening, anyway. You're welcome to come to that if you've nothing else on.'

'I'll have to check,' I said, which was polite speak for Even if Poll allowed me out after dark, I'd rather watch Maggie knit dishcloths.

*   *   *

'I've been invited to a party,' I told Cissie, for something to say.

We were tucking into crumpets and jam and I'd crammed down four, on the grounds that they'd be making a reappearance later.

'Ooh, how lovely. Whose is it?'

'A girl at school. I don't know her so well, she's inviting all sorts. Loads of people. She's in Badminton Club and Choir and Dram Soc, one of those types with a hundred close friends.'

'And will it be at her house?' Cissie's always keen to hear reports on how other people keep their homes.

I shook my head. 'It's going to be at Steem.'

Cissie looked blank.

'That big building opposite W. H. Smiths. The one that got set on fire.'

'Used to be Ethel Austin? I'm with you.' Cissie

was disappointed. 'Funny place for a party. I tek it they've put a roof on now. You'll need to watch your purse, there's thieves everywhere.'

'I'm not going.'

'Why ever not?'

I let a huge lump of jam drop off the spoon and kept my eyes on it while I answered.

'It wouldn't be fair to leave Poll on her own at night. She's not been well.'

'First I've heard of it. What's up wi' her?'

I took a bite of crumpet while I thought of something. Do you ever wish you'd not started a conversation?

'She's had pains.'

'Where?'

'In her legs.'

'Pains in her legs?'

'Her feet, really. She's having trouble with her ankles swelling. And she gets bad headaches from straining to see.'

Cissie narrowed her eyes. 'She's had those a while. She teks her tablets and they soon shift. Are you sure she's not trying it on? I mean, we all get swollen ankles at our age. Look at that.' She pulled her pleated skirt over her knee and twitched a slipper at me. 'I used t' have beautiful ankles, me.'

'You still do, love,' shouted Ally from the door. 'Put 'em away or you'll cause a stampede.' She waddled in, chuckling. 'She's a minx, your aunty. We have to watch her, you know.'

'Great-great-aunt,' I muttered, seeing the sleeves strain across Ally's upper arms as she stacked crockery. I stuffed the rest of the crumpet in quickly to clear the last plate. Then I sat for a minute with my jaw working like a cow because you

84

have to chew stuff well, otherwise it's hell to coax back up.

Cissie was admiring Ally's new ring.

'It's a belter, in't it?' said Ally. 'Alan give it me last time I was in Leeds.' She lowered her lashes and put her head to one side as if she was posing for a photograph: the Thoughtful Bride.

Cissie gasped dramatically. 'He's never asked you to marry him?'

'Yeah. It was brilliant. I din't have a clue. I was in t' kitchen and he shouts, "Oh, just fetch my tool bag in here, will you?" So I carried it into t' living room an' he says, "Open it up for me." ' Ally was growing pinker. 'So I said, "Do it yourself"— 'cause, to be honest with you, I have trouble bending right down—and he said, "No, go on, I've a surprise for you." So I did, and there it was.'

'How lovely,' said Cissie warmly. 'Is it a diamond?'

'Yeah. And that's white gold, not silver. He said he wanted summat a bit different.' She stretched her hand out and tilted the ring experimentally. 'We've not set a date yet, he's waiting for his mother's hip replacement.'

'And how long have you been seeing him now?'

'Only three months, I know, mad in't it? But we'd been emailing since before Christmas.' Ally winked at me. 'I got him off th' Internet, Webhearts it's called. It's dead easy, and there's photos. You should give it a go, Katherine. There's someone for everyone. You should get yourself logged on.'

You should try sticking your fingers down your throat, I thought.

'I'm not interested in boys,' I said.

85

'She's exams,' said Cissie. She reached over and patted Ally's hand. 'Eeh, I am pleased for you, love. When is it his divorce comes through?'

I went home in a terrible temper. The sky was just clouds, and it started to rain as I got off the bus. I don't know why I was so furious. What had Sad Ally's life got to do with me?

'Poll? Poll?' I shouted from the porch. Silence. She must be round at Dogman's. I stomped upstairs into the bathroom and locked the door. Then I threw myself on my knees, whacking the toilet seat up so it clapped against the cistern, and jabbed my fingers at the back of my mouth. A surge of relief came up along with the crumpet; anger and tension poured down the pan. I retched till my stomach hurt, then laid the side of my head on the edge of the bowl.

'Get Dickie in to sit wi' Poll if she's mekkin' a fuss about being left. They can watch the telly, he does a great running commentary,' Cissie had said. I told her I'd think about it, which I would, endlessly; only I knew I'd reach the same conclusion every time. I was more likely to win the Bogle Stroll than walk into a nightclub on my own.

Another home improvement was under way when I came back downstairs. Poll had returned with Dogman and they were carrying a biggish cardboard box between them.

'Careful now,' said Dogman. 'You don't want to chip them.'

'It's not heavy but it's awkward. There.' Poll slid her end of the box onto the table, then spotted me. 'Come and look. Dickie's been busy.'

I edged over as Poll undid the flaps and drew out a two-foot garden gnome.

'Jesus,' I said.

'I know, aren't they smashing? Look at this one, he's sitting down. And this one's got a hedgehog on his shoe.'

'A squirrel. The mould didn't tek so well there. If I can do some more, I'm going to flog them at car boots,' said Dogman, stroking one of the gnome's heads as though it were a newborn.

I picked one up gingerly. 'Why has it got pock marks all over it? It looks like it's got a disease.'

Poll tutted. 'You're allus finding fault, you are.'

'Air bubbles. I'm working on that one. I maybe should have med the mixture with more water. If you put the paint on thick enough, it fills up a lot of the dents.'

I stood my gnome back up on the table, and saw that my palms had gone red. 'God, have you seen this? The paint's coming off. The paint's dissolving, Dickie. What the hell did you use?'

Dogman looked upset. 'They were out of a kit.'

'Slap some varnish on, they'll come up a treat,' said Poll. 'And don't wipe it off on the sofa, Katherine; I saw that. Go and get a dishcloth.'

Poll was arranging the gnomes in a tableau when I came back from scrubbing my hands under the kitchen tap. 'Don't they look smart? That one favours Patrick Moore.'

'Dickie,' I said, 'what did you make them out of? Because they're very light.'

'Plaster of Paris.'

'So what'll happen when it rains?'

'I did wonder about that.'

'Fantastic. What next, birdbaths carved out of soap? Chocolate sundials?'

'Tek no notice of her, Dickie.' Poll stood back to

87

admire the overall effect. 'They're great. I shall put them in our back, near the fence. I bet next door'll want one when they see them.'

'It might be an idea to wait till I get them varnished,' said Dickie, frowning.

'Nonsense. They'll be fine.'

I could tell she was livid with me. Those gnomes were being planted or she'd die in the attempt.

I prayed for rain, and when it hadn't come by 9 p.m., I filled a watering can and went off to imitate a monsoon. Poll finally found me in the dark, dousing the gnomes.

'Look at that,' I pointed gleefully at their melting heads. 'They've lost some weight, haven't they?'

'You know your trouble?' she said. 'You can't bear anybody else to succeed at something. It always has to be you on top. You're seriously disturbed, you are.'

*   *   *

She installed me in the front bedroom in the middle of a lot of dark pre-war furniture. I never want to see another lozenge motif as long as I live. Roger's books were everywhere and I was growing fatter by the day.

'There'll be more space when he goes off to Sheffield. He'll be tekkin' all his clothes and papers with him,' said the Poll-woman. 'I suggest you stay here and rest up for now. There's nowt to go out for, and it's piddling down anyway. Get yourself settled.'

'I've got to go to school,' I said. 'I think I've got exams. Have I got exams?'

'Put your feet up, I'll bring you some Ovaltine. Roger gets through a tin a week.'

'I need my books. I've got to revise.'

'Look,' said Poll, 'you've missed 'em. Th' exams are finished. You weren't fit to do 'em. It's no good crying, that chapter's over. Do you tek sugar, or not?'

When Roger came back from town he'd bought me a bunch of pinks.

'That's bad luck, that is,' said Poll.

Roger laughed in her face. 'How are pinks bad luck? You're soft, Mum.'

'Pink's for a girl,' she said darkly. I swear she looked more pregnant than me.

Vince sat at the dinner table and studied the coaching inn on his place mat. He had thin cheeks and comb-over hair, Brylcreemed down.

'Is your dad a mute?' I asked Roger that night, after Poll and Vince had gone up.

'No. He's just lost the will to live,' said Roger.

'You won't leave me here, with them, will you?' I said.

'We've got to think in the long term now,' he said, which was ironic really as he only had another seven months to live.

Chapter Nine

'I'm going to get a summer job,' I announced to Poll across the bed we were making.

'Ooh, hark at her,' said Poll, even though there was nobody else in the house.

'Well, I need some money, and you've none to spare, so I don't see any alternative.'

I snatched the sheet out of her hands viciously and pulled her off balance. She toppled forwards onto the mattress, swearing.

'Oops, sorry,' I chirped. 'I thought you had hold of it. Are you all right?'

'No thanks to you.' She struggled to her feet again and glared. 'If I didn't know better, I'd say you did that on purpose. I don't know what's got into you recently; you used to be so meek and mild. Bad blood coming out. What sort of a job had you in mind?'

'Whatever I can get, after the exams have finished. Secretary, maybe.'

'You can't type.'

'Shop assistant.'

'You'd never manage. All them strangers, you'd have a fit. You've to look people in the eye when you serve 'em.'

I took in a good breath and let it out again, slowly. 'There's girls at school have got jobs selling tickets in a booth. You just sit there, take the money and hand over the ticket. It's a piece of cake. You'd be able to sit there with a book, read all day if you wanted to.' I thought I could cope with that.

'What sort of tickets?'

'Charity. Registered, all legit. You don't get much for it but it's cash in hand, the girls say.'

Poll pulled a face. 'Oh aye, and think how vulnerable you'd be. In a booth on your own; you'd be a sitting duck for all kinds of funny characters. You attract that sort, you know you do. You'd have hooked yourself a stalker before you could say *Prime Suspect.*'

One of these days, one of these days Poll'll say to me, Oh, that's a good idea, I agree. Then I'll faint dead away. In fact I'll be in a coma for weeks and they'll have to play tapes of Carol Ann Duffy's poetry to bring me round.

I stood up straight while I rammed a pillow down into a clean pillowcase. 'I'm going to have to do *something*, at *some* point. In three weeks the exams'll be over. Then what am I going to do with my life?'

Poll opened her mouth to speak and I waited. 'You've years yet—' she began, but suddenly there was a terrible squeak of pain down by her feet. 'Oh, hell fire,' she gasped, 'I've trod on Winston.'

I crawled across the mattress and hoiked him up. He weighs nothing these days.

'Did I tread on your paw? Eeh, poor love, are y' awreet?' Poll stroked his yellowing head tenderly while I lifted one paw for inspection after another. There didn't seem to be any damage. 'He were in among t' dirty sheets. He mustn't have seen me. Poor thing.' She put her hand under his chin and lifted his muzzle. 'Oh, see his little face, his eyes are all glazed.'

He didn't look particularly bothered to me but I left her to her fussing. I straightened the pillows, finished tucking the sheets in both sides, and pulled the duvet and bedspread up on my own while Poll sat in the Lloyd Loom chair nursing the dog on her lap. They'd have made a good study for one of those collector's plates, *The Faithful Pal: see the fine detail of the matted sheepskin slipper, admire the workmanship needed to capture the tiny bobbles on the inside-out cardigan*. After a while she raised her head and said, 'He's gettin' owd.'

'Right,' I said. We were both thinking about Winston dying, and I didn't want to. 'I'll make some dinner, shall I? Will that gala pie be all right

91

still, or does it want binning?'

She left Winston on the bed and came down after me. While I was cutting slices of pie with the huge sharp knife she came into the kitchen and slapped her hand down on the worktop next to me.

'Here,' she said ungraciously. 'If it's that big a deal. Of course, we may not be able to heat the house this winter.'

Like bollocks we won't, I thought, unrolling the five-pound notes. Thirty quid! 'Thanks,' I muttered. It was probably my child benefit anyway.

'I say, I don't know what you want it for. You've everything here. Young 'uns today, they expect everything on a plate. My best blouse when I was little was med out of a pair of bloomers my mother never wore. Pink silk. And very smart it was too. I never had a dress as a girl that didn't have a flaw somewhere in t'material.'

One quick thrust with the knife and we'd have had an instant end to all these stories of wartime hardship. I could wipe the blade on the Bailey's tea towel and carry on cutting pie. No jury in the land would convict me.

*   *   *

By September, I felt like a whale.

'Ger away. You've a long way to go yet,' said Poll, Job's Comforter in tracksuit bottoms. 'It gets so's you can barely move. And if you go overdue, like I did wi' Roger, well. I can't tell you. It's terrible, that last six week.'

Late that night Roger took me outside to get cool. We perched on the low front wall, me facing the house opposite and him side-on with his back against the gatepost. You could barely see the stars. I was looking for Orion.

'Hey,' I said, I thought he'd be pleased with this, 'I've just noticed something. If I look straight at that tiny star to the left of Orion's belt, I can't see it. It disappears. But if I turn my head and squint at it out of the corner of my eye, it comes back again. It's magic. Is it magic? A magic star?'

He was using a pair of nail scissors to unpick a badge from the knee of his jeans. 'No,' he said flatly. 'It's to do with the receptors in your eyes.' The badge was coming away, thread by thread. 'The ones at the corner of your eye are better at distinguishing variations in light, the ones in the middle work best at picking up colour. So if you want to see something faint but monochrome, you look sideways at it.'

'That's fascinating,' I said.

'It's only science,' he said. The badge peeled off completely and he threw it over his shoulder into Poll's rose bushes. 'I'm going Tuesday. You do know, don't you?'

I nodded.

'Are you coming with us?'

For a second I thought he was asking me to go and live with him in Sheffield. Hope leapt up inside me like a spurt of blood.

'Vince is driving over to help me unpack. You can come up in the Metro with me, and go back with him in the Manta.' He said 'the Metro' like it was the most sacred phrase in the English language. Vince had taken him to see it on his birthday, at the start of August, put the deposit down, and they'd picked it up from the garage on Results day.

'I don't know if I want to or not,' I whimpered, the tears starting.

'For God's sake, don't lay this guilt on me now,' he shouted, throwing up his hands in a way I'd seen Poll do.

With a tremendous effort of will, I stopped crying. 'I'm all right. I'm fine. Shall I take out those loose threads for you?' There was the ghost of a rectangle fringed with orange cotton across his kneecap.

He shrugged. I leaned across and began to pinch out the threads one by one.

'Don't get in a state, though,' he said when he saw I'd got myself under control. I tried to smile. 'Because we need to look after this baby.'

Notice he didn't say anything about looking after me.

After Vince and I came back, that Tuesday, I fled upstairs to Roger's room to have a good weep. But the door was locked, and I could hear Poll sobbing her little shrew heart out behind it.

*   *   *

So I took the money sharpish, and went off to Bolton to spend it on normal-girl clothes. Half at the back of my mind, and slimmer than a shadow on a cloudy day, was the idea that maybe, if I found the right outfit, I would go to Donna's do.

I wasn't allowed to go into town by myself till I was sixteen. Poll thought it was too risky and I wasn't bothered enough to argue. If I wanted something from the shops, e.g. chocolate or books, I could walk up the hill into the village, or down into Harrop, which is the smallest town in the universe probably. Serious catch-a-bus shopping I associated with crashing boredom; trailing after Poll while she held packets, boxes, labels up to the

94

light and demanded to know what was in the small print. Selecting the right coins for her out of her tatty old purse. Flashing looks of apology at the staff she was rude to.

'Can't you see I'm partially blind?'

'Yes, madam, but you still can't bring back soap if you've used it.'

'It's not on, this, it in't. I'm nearly seventy, you know.'

But once I'd got my GCSEs it mysteriously became safe to get on the 214 alone, as long as I didn't sit next to any men. This sudden change might have had something to do with the fact that Poll urgently needed me to go and see about a new gas cooker, but she was laid up with flu at the time and Dogman had gone to Barmouth for a week. 'Stop mithering,' she'd croaked through the big white hanky. 'I've written it all down for you.' Huge biro capitals dancing between the lines on my jotter. 'What can possibly go wrong?' And even though that afternoon there'd been a bomb scare and all round Boots was cordoned off, and then I'd got stuck in a crowd of Bolton Wanderers supporters singing swear-songs, I came home in one piece.

You can't get much new for thirty quid, but there's good pickings to be had in charity shops. I found another ankle-length stretchy skirt, black with grey flowers on it, and a long black blouse with white collar and cuffs. 'That suits you,' the woman behind the counter said unexpectedly when I stepped out of the cubicle to get a better view in the mirror. I went scarlet and dragged the curtain back across. Beneath the hem of the skirt my brown school shoes stuck out. It's hard work, reinventing yourself.

Next I went to Debenhams to see what they had in their footwear department, just on the off-chance they were giving away the ultimate pair of solve-your-wardrobe shoes for twenty-one pounds.

I wandered past the make-up and perfume counters, and noticed how many cosmetics are named after things you eat. Grape, candy, toffee, vanilla, I counted off. Cherry, fudge, cinnamon. Clever marketing, that; your teenage girl's so busy trying to avoid real food she'll run a mile from a proper toffee, but she's still greedy for the idea of one. I've seen these girls, thin as whippets, inhaling choc-mint lipgloss like it was cocaine.

Even the mascara was called Liquorice. I picked one up and read the blurb along the side. *2000 CALORIES*, it said. That was never right. How could a mascara have two thousand calories in it? That made it as fattening as an entire Black Forest gateau. Presuming you ate it. Surely to God you didn't eat it?

'Can I help you?' said the assistant.

I had a quick look. Smooth oval face, neat arched brows, mouth in, I'd say, Frosted Ginger. Not much older than me.

'Oh. I'm sorry. I was only . . . I don't wear . . . '

'It's pretty daunting, in't it, all these colours, knowing what suits you. We see some women come in here, well, I shouldn't say really, but some of 'em look like clowns. You'd think they'd used wax crayon instead of make-up, honest. The old ones are the worst.' She giggled and leaned towards me. 'I'll not last two minutes here, will I? It's only my first week. I bet I'm not here by Sat'day.'

I couldn't think how to reply. I smiled back for

politeness, but began to edge away.

'Tell you what.' She stepped out from behind the counter. 'Shall I give you a mini-makeover? We're really quiet. I could show you which colour spectrum suited you. You're an Olive Tones, so you'd look fantastic in some of these eyeshadows over here, and we could even you out with this base, take out some of the redness in your cheeks, I know this stuff looks funny being green but I swear it really works, and you've lovely strong brows, we could bring those out with a dark pencil, give them more definition and balance your features . . . '

I shook my head. 'No thanks. I don't wear make-up. My grandma says it's bad for your skin.'

'OK.' Her face fell ever so slightly. 'Do you want a free sample of foundation, though? You could try it at home, it's dermatologically tested, it's actually good for your skin 'cause it contains sunscreen, filters out harmful UVA and UVB rays, and then if you like it, you can come back some time and I can show you how to blend it with some of the cream blusher, which'd really bring your cheekbones out.'

I reached out for the sachet, thinking it might be worth a go with when I got home, just to see, and then I spotted her hand. It was odd somehow; very small and boiled red beneath the smart white cuff of her overall. I didn't stare but it looked, in that split-second flash, as if at least two of the fingers were missing. Her other hand, fluttering over the display counter, was beautiful, with long white-tipped nails. A burn? A birth thing? Her eyes met mine but there wasn't a flicker of anything, only eagerness.

'Go on. You know you want to.' She grinned. 'And if I make you look like Liz Hurley, tell my

97

supervisor, will you?'

'All right,' I said.

'Come round, then, sit in the chair.'

I did as I was told, although my heart was thumping with shyness. 'Bet you won't find any cheekbones.'

'Bet I will,' she said.

After she'd finished and swivelled me round to see in the mirror, she smoothed my hair away from my brow.

'I'm not a hairdresser,' she said, 'but I reckon if you used some straighteners on this, and had a wispy fringe cut in, it'd really, really suit you. The way your hair is now, no one can see your face.'

My strange reflection made me giggle with nerves. The assistant laughed too, only in a non-hysterical way.

'I look like somebody else. It's like, like turning from black and white to colour.' I couldn't take my eyes off myself. I knew I wasn't beautiful, but I was, kind of, tidied up. Drawn-in. More *there*.

She was busy pulling out drawers and tipping up miniature cartons.

'I've found you some extra samples.' She handed me a smart little paper bag with string handles. 'There's more or less everything here that's on your face, not the same lipstick but close, and we've no mini-eyeshadows at the moment, but your blusher crème's there, I already put you in a foundation didn't I, oh and we've a vial of scent going begging, I'll stick that in an' all.'

In my head I heard Poll say, She only did it 'cause she likes a challenge. I drowned her out by asking to buy a full-size mascara, then nearly had a fit when it was fourteen pounds. *Fourteen pounds*. I paid up, though.

'It's a lot, in't it? But you get what you pay for, it's really good quality, dun't flake or anything, you buy these cheap ones and they're halfway down your cheeks by the time you've got to t' bus stop.'

She shut the till and gave me a huge smile. 'Go an' knock 'em dead. And don't forget about the straighteners.'

What do you think you look like? said Poll's voice as I walked out into the fresh air where everyone could see me. I wanted to touch my tacky lips, but I knew if I started mauling I'd ruin the effect.

On the way back to the bus station I spotted a pair of black ankle books with low spiked heels in a charity shop window. SHOE EVENT said a banner above. I went in, checked the soles and, call me Cinders, they were my size. Four pounds I paid for them, and I don't think they'd been worn.

No perverts sat near me on the bus. I got a window seat so I could check out my reflection when we went past anything dark. There'd never be a day as good as this again.

As we got to my stop, I wondered whether to wipe some of the slap off in case Dogman made a song and dance about it and alerted Poll. Poll might even spot it all on her own if I was standing near a window. I knew the sort of thing she'd say. She'd go, Do you want to attract sexual deviants? Or; Is that what you spent my heating money on? Or; At the end of the day, you're still like the side of a house, there's no make-up'll hide that.

I could feel my insides winding themselves up as I stepped down from the bus and my body stiffened as I walked away, imagining her face. Just as I was

99

getting into a big mental argument with her, I became aware of someone staring.

He was my height, my age, about. Thick dark hair, slightly wavy; white shirt with a granddad collar, and a black waistcoat over the top, like a gypsy. You'd call him handsome, although his neck was on the thick side. He was leaning against the wall of the Feathers, smoking; drugs, I shouldn't be surprised.

I put my head down and walked past him.

'Hey,' he called after me. 'Hey, wait!'

I quickened my pace, exactly like they say not to on *Crimewatch*, and made to cross the road.

'Wait,' he shouted again. 'Katherine.'

I stopped in my tracks.

'Katherine Millar. Wait for me. I only want a word.'

It was daylight and we were near a busy road junction. If he dragged me into the bushes and slit my throat before perpetrating a dreadful sexual assault, there'd be loads of witnesses. I turned round and glowered.

'Hi,' he said, flicking his tab-end into the hedge and hooking his thumbs into his belt loops. 'Do you mind if I walk you home?'

'You what?'

'I want to talk to you.'

'What about?' I gripped my keys in my fist so that the Yale was poking out through my fingers. This is a very effective weapon if you jab it in the eyes, and you can't be prosecuted the way you can if you carry Mace around with you.

He took a step towards me. 'I can't tell you in one sentence. Let me walk with you, a little way. Up to the timber merchant's.' I couldn't place his accent but it wasn't local.

'How do you know which way I'm going?'

'Oh,' he said calmly. 'I know where you live.'

*   *   *

I'll always associate Phil Collins with extreme pain. Every DJ who came on played 'You Can't Hurry Love', it was number one. I'd rather have had silence, but Poll said the radio would take my mind off the contractions.

'When is it time to go to the hospital?' I kept asking. Phil went ching-ching-ching, ching-ching-a-ching.

'You've ages to go yet, I was hours with Roger. They get nowty at th' hospital if you turn up too early. Walk about a bit. Keep active.'

It didn't matter whether I sat, lay or stood.

'When's Roger coming?'

'We've left a message. It's an hour and a half from Sheffield. He'll come as soon as he can. He's a good lad. I only hope he teks care, there's some maniacs on t' motorway.'

He rang at teatime. That's it, I thought, time for action. When Poll put the phone down and turned round, I was waving her china
beggar-girl high in the air. 'I'll smash this on the hearth NOW if you don't run me to hospital,' I shouted.

She rushed outside to where Vince was building an impromptu rockery. He'd started at lunchtime. A lot of it was broken bricks, I could see. Poll made a screwing motion with her finger against her temple, then saw me looking through the window and pretended she was scratching her head. I still had the beggar-girl in my hand. Vince came in at once and I

101

handed him the car keys.

When we got to hospital they examined me straight away. 'You're well on,' said the midwife. 'Goodness, I should say this baby's more or less ready to be born. You left it till the last minute, didn't you? Try not to push till we get you to the delivery suite.' I was wheeled off at top speed, Phil-in-my-head sang, 'No, you'll just have to wait.' The best bit was leaving Poll standing, furious, in the corridor.

The best bit was when the pain was over and I could flop back and close my eyes.

The best bit was when they handed me the baby, wrapped in a white blanket.

The best bit was when Roger opened the door, even though he was followed immediately by Poll and Vince.

'God,' he said. 'I've thrashed that car to death. I swear the engine nearly jumped out of the bonnet. They posted a note up in the hall foyer, but I was in the library and I didn't see it till I got back in. I wish somebody would invent a phone you could carry about.'

'It's a girl,' said Poll bleakly behind him. Then she went out again, pulling Vince by his sweater sleeve.

'Still,' said Roger, 'it's pretty cool. Hey, I'm a dad.' He had a quick peer into the blanket, but the baby was just lying there with its eyes half shut. Its skin was red and flaky, like bad sunburn.

He sat down on the edge of the bed. I really wanted him to kiss me. 'You look grim,' he said. 'Did you have a rough time? Why didn't you let my mother in?'

I thought having the baby would make him forget about Sheffield. I thought once it was born, he'd stay with us.

102

I've never been too good at predicting the future.

Chapter Ten

If you're a fatherless lesbian, chances are you don't know a huge amount about penises. This was all the information I'd garnered so far:

- they could be extremely dangerous
- they looked quite like a plucked chicken
- they featured on Greek vases a lot, pointing forwards like little signposts
- they worked on a hydraulic principle
- there were several components to the wobbly mass down there, although I still wasn't totally sure how many. Obviously I've seen giant willies spray-painted on bus shelters, and side-on most of them look like sports whistles. In these diagrams, the geography of testicles and phallus seemed fairly straightforward. But on the occasions I'd been flashed at, the confusion of slack pink danglies was less clear. When I was seven and innocent, I thought men had one thing in their trousers, and one thing only. Then, what happened to me behind the chemist's when I was eight showed me there were in fact two attachments hanging down between a man's legs. Straight after, an unreliable boy at school tells me there are supposed to be three. Three? He used the phrase Meat and Two Veg. So then I thought, maybe I'd misheard and it was tentacles, and not testicles, and it was possible there was a

whole clutch of wobbly bits, bunched together like a squid. Later, at secondary school, the diagrams in our biology textbook clarified the Two Veg part of the story, sort of. But even at eighteen, I wasn't clear whether the balls were arranged in separate little sacs, or one squashy cushion.
– Unless he's been the victim of a terrible accident, every man has one.

I remember the day that particular truth dawned on me; about a week after the non-existent-dog chase. The idea sent me into shock and I could barely cross the doorstep for weeks in case I bumped into a man we knew, e.g. Mr Porter at the newsagent's, Mr Rowland the vicar, the paperboy. Worst of all, that year at school I had a male class teacher called Mr Walker. So when he was settling on the carpet at storytime, I could see his penis flopping about with my X-ray imagination. And when he stood up to write the date on the board, I saw it again, swinging gently against the leg of his pants. I made it worse for myself by checking the back page of the Ladybird book *Your Body* every damn night and I think I'd have gone mad if it hadn't been for the summer holidays, and the promise of dry old Mrs Kirtlan next term.

It all came back to me, that time of horror, as I started to run away from the gypsy boy towards the brow. He wasn't going to rape me, I got that, but he kept shouting out for me to stop and talk, and that he knew me. He damn well didn't. I'd have remembered someone like him. It was a scam, maybe for money, maybe just to make mock. I was too wise and also too out of breath to reply. How the fuck though did he know my name and my address? Part of me wanted to turn round and see how close he was, but I was too focused on making it up the hill.

At last, when my lungs were ready to rupture and I was seeing blood-pressure stars, I let myself pause and look behind. He was still there but a long way away now. He hadn't made any attempt to pursue me at all, just stood there staring. As I watched, he raised his arm and waved. I turned and puffed on. But even as I gained the hall and slammed the front door, I thought, he still knows where to find me, any time he wants.

*   *   *

He read poetry when the pain got bad, and held my hand as she was being born.

'I wouldn't have missed this for anything,' he said as we cradled the baby together. 'Look at her. Our love meets in her tiny heartbeat.'

When I started crying for my mum, he wiped my tears away and said, 'We have to suffer loss so that new love can come into the world. It's the circle of Life.'

He always knew what to say.

*   *   *

He appeared again three weeks later, in the library. I was in the research corner, supposedly leafing through Job Opportunities in the *Bolton Evening News*, but really making a list of my all-time top-ten Emily Dickinson poems. I'd got 'I Felt a Funeral in my Brain' down at number one and I was debating which was better, 'Heaven Is What I Cannot Reach' or 'I Heard a Fly Buzz when I Died'. Then, out of all the voices, internal and external, my brain picked out someone saying 'Millar'. I jerked my head up and there he was, by the front desk.

He was standing chatting to Miss Dragon, and what was weird about it was her body language. Normally she's very stiff and brisk, and she likes to hug a bundle of books to her bosom like a breastplate. But even though gipsy boy was casual in the extreme, with his longish hair and pierced lobes, his combats and his leather wrist bands, she was leaning towards him as though she'd known him for years. And she was smiling. At one point she touched her fringe, like I've seen the girls at school do when they're talking to someone they fancy.

I tuned in more and heard her say, 'It's an unusual spelling,' and 'I had an aunt who lived in Nantwich. A beautiful church, I remember, with a square or a green in front of it.'

'We're not big church-goers,' he said. 'Mum's a pagan, if she's anything. But it is pretty nice, yeah. I like churches, they've got power. Specially the Gothic ones.'

As I watched, his eyes met mine and I started in my seat. I could have crawled under the desk, but too late, Miss Dragon was turning my way and nodding her head, then coming out from behind the desk in a purposeful way. He stood back for her politely and she noticed, and gave a tiny twitch of her lips.

'Kath-Kat,' she said, as she came up close. 'I have a young man here who'd like to meet you.'

We could all have been at a cocktail party.

106

'Hello,' he said, standing at a careful distance. 'My name's Callum. Callum Turner.' Big grin, eyebrows well up. I noticed he'd got a necklace or something peeping out of his collar.

'Callum's been doing some research into his family tree,' said Miss Dragon, looking down at me kindly. 'He's been travelling round the country searching out distant relatives.'

'Well, I'm going to. This is my, you know, first stop.'

I turned to Miss Dragon, excluding him. 'I don't know anyone called Turner, Poll's never mentioned any Turners.'

Miss Dragon inclined her head, inviting him to speak.

He said; 'I might be your cousin. I think, and obviously I could be wrong, but I think my mum was your mum's sister.'

I had a hot flush while his words sunk in. I must have gone a funny colour because Miss Dragon said, 'Come in the back office. You'll be private there for half an hour or so.' I didn't move. 'Come on. It's not an offer open to everyone.' She went behind me and took the back of the chair in her hands. I got to my feet.

'My mother isn't here,' I said, swallowing. 'We don't know where she is. She ran off eighteen years ago. When I was a baby—Oh Christ, do *you* know where she's living?'

'No,' said Callum. 'God. Sorry about that. Bummer.' Miss Dragon glanced from me to him, and ushered us towards the Private door.

When we were nearly there, Miss Dragon put her hand on my arm and drew me away. 'Excuse us for a moment,' she told Callum. Then she lowered her voice. 'If you don't want to speak with him, Kat, say. I thought you'd be excited to meet someone who knew some more about your family, but I didn't realize he was going to come out with something of that magnitude. I had absolutely no idea. I may have acted precipitately. So please don't feel you have to talk to him.'

'No, I do.'

'It might be, well, disturbing if you don't hear good news. You don't know what he's going to tell you. Or he might not tell you anything.'

'I know.'

Miss Dragon nodded. 'Would you like me to stay, then?'

'You can't, can you? You need to be on the desk.'

'Miss Ollerton could . . . No, you're right. I do need to be out front. But I'm only just outside if you need me. Yes?'

'Don't tell anyone what he just said, will you? No one *at all*.' I heard the tremor in my own voice.

'Of course I won't. It's not my secret to tell.' She showed us through the door, and scanned round the room quickly. 'Make a coffee if you want one, the kettle's in this corner, and there are some chocolate digestives in the Ryvita tin. Don't touch that bag of bananas, though, they're Miss Ollerton's. Shift those catalogues, that's it. I'll pop back in twenty minutes or so.' Then the door was closed behind her, and we were on our own.

'This is a big privilege,' I heard myself say.

'What, talking to you? I know it is. I'm honoured.'

'No!' I was gabbling. 'I mean being in here. It's Miss Stockley's territory. The whole library belongs to her, well not really, but she thinks it does. So being in here's like the Inner Sanctum.'

'Procul, o procul este, profani,' said Callum.

'You know Latin?'

'My mum taught it me. That's from Virgil. I know some Greek too. Are we having a drink, or what?'

He got up and put the kettle on, while I thought about clashing rocks and whirlpools. If the situation got out of hand, all I had to do was open the door and walk out.

'OK, me. I'm seventeen, and I'm in the sixth form at Crewe College.' He was moving round the room, opening the coffee jar, rattling spoons, teasing open milk cartons. 'I live in Nantwich, which is in Cheshire, with my mum Jude. Our flat's above a book shop where I sometimes do casual work, although mostly I sit and read the stock instead of serving customers. Luckily the owner fancies my mum, although she doesn't fancy him because he's so old. My dad exited the scene when I was still little, and I don't care because my mum's so cool about everything. She doesn't bother much with men, it's me and her, we're pretty close. My best friend's called Sam Haslam, my favourite film of all time is *Reservoir Dogs*, I hate McDonald's and my ambition is to buy a croft in north-west Scotland.' He picked up the kettle to pour and paused. 'That's about everything. My life in fifteen seconds. What you see is what you get; I'm the straightforward type.'

My heart rate was slowing a little. It was a small, safe room we were in. Install a bed and I could have lived here quite happily. You could tell everything was in its right place; the marker pens

109

snug in their plastic wallet, the files on the shelves in alphabetical order with their fronts all flush, even the row of pencils had been arranged in order of height. This was the kind of environment I could imagine working in, one day, maybe, with Miss Dragon to watch over me.

'I'm sorry I ran off, before.'

He gave a short laugh. 'Christ, no, don't apologize, Kat. That was my fault, I did it all wrong, what a dickhead. You must have thought I'd escaped from somewhere. I'm amazed you didn't ring the police. The trouble with me is I just jump in.'

'You were quite scary.'

'What, me? Ha ha, I like it.' He waved a teaspoon triumphantly in the air. 'My mates would piss themselves if they heard you say that. My nickname's Mary at college. My motto is, if there's any trouble, leg it. Anyway, I'm sorry for frightening you. I just really wanted to speak to you about the family. Do you take sugar? Oh, there isn't any. Here you go.'

He placed the mug down in front of me, slid into his seat opposite and then pushed the tin of biscuits into the middle of the table. I shook my head. Even one would have choked me now. Up close I could see the dark bristles on his chin and the hairs on his forearms, the way the necklace chain rolled across his throat when he spoke. What was he seeing when he looked at me? Was he disappointed? He didn't seem it. I tried hard to sit still and not keep shifting in my chair.

'So your mum's a teacher?' I asked, more to break the silence than because I wanted to know.

'You must be kidding. Well, except in the sense

she taught me. I got six GCSEs and I never set foot in secondary school. But I'm at college now just to see if I can bag a couple of A2s at the end of next year. Mum doesn't believe in formal education, she reckons it stifles individuality. School stifled her; she spent all her time rebelling against the system. Then she went off to uni and totally went off the rails.'

'What did she do?'

'Well, she had me, for a start.' He laughed. 'Big surprise for everyone.'

I shivered at the coincidence. 'Is she older than my mother? Why aren't they still in touch?'

'I don't know anything about her, not a thing. Sorry. Mum won't say a word. I managed to get out of her about your mother being involved with a man called Roger Millar, and his mum's name being Pollyanna—there aren't many Pollyannas around. That's how I tracked you down. But I guess they had some kind of major row before that because Mum won't even talk about their childhood together. It's like a closed book. I don't think she's got any idea her sister disappeared, what did you say, eighteen years ago?'

'Will you tell her?'

'I don't know. This family tree is something I'm doing for myself and I don't want to go upsetting Mum unnecessarily. There's something really hectic in the past that she just won't discuss.'

A sepia Philip Pullman looked kindly down at the back of Callum's head. You know, I'm normally dead shy with strangers, I felt like saying. But the situation here was so extraordinary. My heart was beginning to slow, I felt ready to tell him something back.

'Well, we don't talk about Elizabeth in our house 'cause my grandma hates her. Loathes her. Won't have her name mentioned.' How to convey to him the emotions attached to my mother.

'Because she ran away and left you?'

'That, and . . . Poll—my grandma—feels Elizabeth was responsible for my father's death.'

Callum's jaw dropped. 'Shit. That's terrible. Was she?'

'Yes, basically. God, do you really want to hear this?'

'If you want to tell me.'

Through the pane of glass in the door I saw Miss Dragon give me a little wave. I felt a surge of excitement that he was going to listen to every word I said. For once I'd be in control of the narrative.

'Yeah, it's all right. I mean, if you're family, I suppose you should know. It's not like it's a big secret, everyone in this village knows the bare bones. But we don't ever discuss it now at home. Poll told me the once what happened, then whenever I asked again she'd just clam up. My great-aunt Cissie's filled in some of the details.'

I took a deep breath.

'They were in his car, coming back from Sheffield, when they started arguing. I don't know what about; Poll says they were always at it. Elizabeth was very bitter about having to give up university and stay at home with a baby. Because *she* got pregnant while she was still at school, which is weird—and she resented Dad his freedom, so it was probably that they were rowing about.'

Callum was leaning forwards, frowning. 'So what happened? Did they crash?'

112

'Yes. She grabbed the steering wheel and a lorry was coming the other way . . . She admitted it all at the inquest. She didn't try and hide her guilt. Apparently she wasn't injured at all, not one scratch. And luckily I was at home in my cot, with Poll. I was only a few months old.'

'My God,' Callum breathed. 'So your dad was killed outright?'

'I think so. In his new car that he'd got for his eighteenth. Poll's world more or less fell apart, and she took it out on her husband Vince, and on Elizabeth.'

'Why on Vince?'

'Because he'd bought the car, I suppose. I expect she hated everybody. Mostly she hated my mother. I'm not surprised Elizabeth ran off, rather than live in that house of venom, but you'd think she'd have taken me with her, wouldn't you? What sort of sick mind leaves her baby in the care of a woman she detests? Anyway, sorry, she's your aunt, maybe you can see a better side to it.'

Callum was looking dazed. 'I don't know what to think,' he said.

'Then Vince went too, pretty much at the same time, so that left me and Poll, and that's been the household ever since. She made it legal by adopting me when I was about four, although sometimes I think it was just so she could avoid having a Castle around, that was my mother's name; your mother's name, obviously. I wish I could say we were as close as you and your mum, but we're not. I look after my grandma because she's disabled and she needs me, but at the same time she hates relying on me so she's usually in a foul temper. I can't ever call her Grandma to her

113

face 'cause that's too cuddly a name. She's not a cuddly sort.'

'Sounds grim. So where did Vince go? Is he still in touch?'

'God, no. Poll would have him shot if he ever turned up on our doorstep. He didn't just leave, he ran away with a fancy-woman; I heard that part from Cissie. And we've not heard a dicky bird from him since. Alien abduction, emigration, the Foreign Legion; take your pick. He's not coming home again though, that's for sure. Not unless he wants a bullet through his neck.'

'Jeez,' said Callum, swirling his coffee mug round and staring into it. 'Hey, you don't think they're together, do you? Elizabeth and Vince? Love on the run?' He smirked in a way that made me cross.

'No I bloody don't. He was old enough to be her dad, for a start.' I wondered then if I'd told him too much. Just because he knew some Latin didn't necessarily mean he wasn't up to something. 'By the way, how come you're not called Castle, Callum Castle?'

He laughed easily and drained his cup. 'My mum married my dad. David Turner. They may only have been together for a year but she kept the name. Couldn't be bothered to change it, probably. Any more questions?' He put his head on one side, and his earring glinted in a way that made me think of the Ladybird book of *Pirates*. You'd suit a bandanna, I nearly said.

'Yeah. How come you didn't go to your maternal grandparents first if you had questions about your aunt? They'd be the ones with the info, surely?'

He sighed and folded his hands on the table in

114

front of him.

'They'd have been my first port of call. But my gran's got Alzheimer's, doesn't know me from a root vegetable, and my grandad, ahm, passed away eighteen months ago. At Christmas. Not a good time to lose someone. We knew he'd been ill, although my grandma was having trouble taking it in, Alzheimer's makes you totally selfish, you know. Then she wouldn't believe he'd died. Mum was on anti-depressants. It was—'

He broke off.

'Sorry. I wasn't casting doubt. I was interested in the process of finding someone.'

He got to his feet, scooped up the mugs by their handles and placed them on the draining board. 'Sure, of course.'

I stood up automatically to rinse the cups clean and, for a moment, I almost put my hand on his arm. I didn't, because a zillionth of a second later I came to my senses and turned the movement into a stretch towards the tea towel.

'All right?' he asked, turning round suddenly.

Through the glass, Miss Dragon raised her eyebrows at me. I gave her a smile but she carried on watching until old Mr Gardner tapped her on the arm and thrust a newspaper clipping under her nose. She led him away to the photocopier and I heard myself saying, 'I've got a photo of her, of Elizabeth, if you want to see it sometime.'

'Cool. I could get to meet the one and only Pollyanna.'

I was pulling the door open as he spoke, but I turned back to stare at him. 'Haven't you understood what I've been saying? Don't you get it at all? She hated your aunt and she'll hate you on

115

sight. She'll probably attack you with her stick. No way are you seeing her. *No way.*'

He shrugged. 'Whatever. I don't mind. I'd really like to see this picture, though.' He took hold of the door and held it for me, and as he raised his arm I smelt a sharp tang of, not sweat, but maleness. His forearms stretched showed the shape of muscles under the tanned skin. His face was close to mine. 'It would mean,' he said, 'an awful lot.'

*   *   *

Part of the problem was my weight. I thought the weight got expelled along with the baby. I'd never been fat before in my life, but I was now, just when it really mattered. I took his Debbie Harry poster down in the end, I couldn't stand to see her tiny thighs. When he complained, I burst into tears. I said to him, 'This isn't me, you know. This is not my body.' Not my baby either, it felt like.

This is what I felt for that baby: zero, zip, zilch, nothing, nowt. 'That's normal,' said the health visitor, the nasty big liar. You look at the front of all the parenting magazines and what you don't see is photos of bloated mum sulking in the background while the baby cries its lonely lungs out a few feet away. New motherhood was meant to be a naked pastel heaven, smiley smiley hormones, and little gums clamped on your breasts. I thought that was gross and I said so.

When he came home that Easter, I was miserable. It had been just me and the girl-baby, stuck in his bedroom. Poll clattered about downstairs, beating up the furniture it sounded like, and Vince hung around the garden, prodding at the frozen soil. I couldn't go

116

out. At first I'd wanted to, before the baby was born, but Poll kept saying everyone would stare. So I tried, and they did. Village of the Damned. Everyone stopped to gawp but no one spoke to me. I don't know how Roger stuck living here for so long. So then I used to sneak into the fields where you hardly met anyone, and that was better. Poll didn't like it, though. 'Don't go so far. What if that baby comes and you can't get to a phone? Max Jolley across t' road were only in his back yard when he had a heart attack and died.' I took no notice; I'd have gone just to spite her. But then, after the baby was born, I stopped wanting to go out. I don't know why. I stopped wanting to wash and get dressed as well.

I made an effort when Roger came home, though. 'Blimey, you've put some meat on,' he said when he first saw me. In the back of the car, Poll smiled; I caught her in the mirror.

The first few hours he seemed pretty cheerful, but he got twitchy towards the evening. He went up the village for a breath of fresh air and he palmed a stack of ten-pence pieces before he went. When he got back, they were gone, I checked his pockets.

That night he became furious with the baby. 'Haven't you got her into a routine yet?' he snapped. 'She shouldn't be waking all through the night. You're doing it wrong.' He took a blanket out of the wardrobe and stomped off downstairs, and I've never come so close to hurting Katherine as I did during those next few hours. I didn't, though, and I'm proud of that.

I'd looked forward so long to him coming home, and yet it all went wrong. I knew there was something on his mind, it wasn't just dealing with the baby. 'Can't you shut her up?' he kept saying. Whenever Poll had her, Katherine went quiet as a lamb. 'You have to know how to handle them,' she said smugly, 'I've never had a peep out of her.' But a month after the accident, I found out she'd been slipping her sugar lumps to suck on, and teaspoons of brandy. So no bloody wonder.

Even Poll noticed something was up with Roger. 'You've ants in your pants,' she said, patting his hair as she walked round the back of the settee. 'Are you missing your pals in Sheffield? I bet y' are.'

All I could think of was that song, Please please tell me now. Except I didn't want to know, and if he hadn't told me, he might still have been alive.

This is how the last few minutes of his life went:

Roger   I'm glad you're coming back with me for the weekend. It'll give us a chance to catch up.

Me   Yeah, on sleep.

Roger   Yeah. And I can show you where I hang out. I know you've seen my room but you've not been to the Students' Union yet. I thought we might go up to the Mandela bar this evening.

Me   Let's not stay too late, though, I'm really tired.

Roger   Aw, don't be a drag. How old are you, about forty? Anyway, I want you to meet a friend.

Me   Who?

Roger   She's called Judith.

Me   Oh.

Roger   Yeah, she's really nice. You'll have loads in common. I think you'll be soul-sisters.

Me   You just jumped a red light there, you know.

Roger   Did I? Oh well, we're still here to tell the tale. Yeah, she's really, really great, you'll really

	like her. And she loves babies. You'll have loads to talk about.
Me	I didn't want to talk about babies this weekend.
Roger	No, well, there's other things you've got in common, I'm sure. Are you all right?
Me	Just resting my eyes.
Roger	Right. Right. It's a funny thing, though, modern culture. You know, the way we have rules for everything. You know, like, say, marriage and relationships.
Me	Mm.
Roger	Yeah. I was reading a book on it before I came back. Fascinating stuff. There's love, this timeless, er, thing, and then every hundred years or so, a new set of conventions attached to it by the so-called moral guardians of society. I mean, the Ancient Greeks were much more fluid about love. They didn't have this rule, this arbitrary rule about how if you love one person then you can't love another. They said that the more you loved, the more love there was to go around. That trying to use up love was like trying to empty the sea with a cup. And that trying to put a fence round your love was like tying a rope around a beam of moonlight. Couldn't be done. Because love, particularly sexual love, you know, passion, is an elemental force. You can no more govern it than you can command the tides. It's too powerful.
Me	Mm.
Roger	And, if you think about it, no one who has more than one child is ever seen as

119

betraying their firstborn by making it share its parents' love with someone else. Society accepts the sharing of love in that context, no problem. Which is right. Love isn't finite. Love feeds on love. Love begets love.

Me   Mm?

Roger   So, this twentieth-century fashion for monogamy is really unnatural, and actually spiritually stifling. It's really unhealthy. For instance, if you said you loved someone else, another man, I wouldn't be fussed. I wouldn't. Because that wouldn't necessarily mean you loved me any less. It might mean you loved me more, because your life had been, what, enriched, and you'd grown emotionally. You see, the more you love someone, the more you want to give them their freedom. That's the mark of a really strong relationship. And there aren't many people who'd be . . . advanced enough to accept that. That's why I'm glad I've got someone like you.

Me   You what?

Roger   Because I know you'll accept the situation with Judith for the reasons I've just outlined.

Me   The situation with Judith?

Roger   You can help each other. Judith's a lot like you, she's a clever girl. She's reading classics, you should hear her talk. Really interesting. You'll like her. And what I'll do is, I'll set you up in Sheffield together, find a little terrace. 'Cause I know things are tough with my mum; well you can move out and come and be near to me. That's what you wanted, isn't it? And there's no need to worry, Judith

120

	knows all about you and Katherine. She's very interested in your situation, supportive—
Me	Are you having an affair with her?
Roger	That's a very bourgeois term. I didn't think you'd be so judgemental, I've always admired you for your independent thinking—
Me	Shit. Is she pregnant? Is she? She is, isn't she, I can tell by your face. Answer me. Oh for Christ's sake, look at me, at least bloody look at me when you're pulling my world down around my ears. Stop driving, pull over now and LOOK AT ME! LOOK AT ME!

It's true, I did want to kill him at that precise moment but I'd never have had the wherewithal to do it on my own. It was his bad luck about the lorry on the other carriageway.

Chapter Eleven

We met again in the library, with Miss Dragon as unofficial chaperone. I wasn't ready to have him in the house, I couldn't be doing with the subterfuge just yet.

'Is it not a bother to keep coming all the way up from Nantwich?' I asked as we settled ourselves into the study corner.

He pulled off his backpack and shoved it under the table. 'Soon as I pass my test I'm getting a Micra, Mum's promised she'll go halves with me. In the meantime she runs me into Crewe and there's a train goes straight through, although I seem to be the only one that ever gets off at Bank Top. I think it carries on to Blackpool. One day I might stay on it. I've never been, have you?'

'Not since I was about ten. My dad used to go a lot, to see the waxworks. Apparently there was a fantastic display of diseases there.'

'How do you mean?'

'Wax models of an arm covered in the measles rash, a foot with gangrene, various degrees of burns on flesh. You were supposed to be over eighteen to view them, but he used to march in long before that and no one ever challenged him.' Poll had told me she thought this display had been responsible for making Roger want to go into medicine. 'He used to pore over them cases,' she said. 'All the other children wanted to see the famous murderers, but not my Roger.' There were some terrible venereal diseases on display too. It was from Poll I learned that syphilis can eat away your nose and make you mad. She didn't tell me there was a cure. Sex was dangerous, all heartache and humiliation, she said; and a waste of time for women. Think on.

'Tell me about him, Kat.'

'Who, my dad?'

'Yeah. He sounds really interesting.'

'I've hardly said anything about him.'

'But his story's so tragic. Really sad. And I'm interested in the whole family.' He smiled at me the way Errol Flynn smiles at Olivia de Havilland in *Captain Blood*. I'd never seen such eyelashes on a man.

Across the room a grandma-type sat engrossed in *Peepo* while her toddler pulled out the contents of her handbag, one by one, and stuffed what

122

would fit behind the nearest bookcase. Miss Mouse was returning videos to the carousel stand by the door, and glancing at the wall clock every ten seconds.

'I thought you wanted to see this photo?' I said, pulling it out of my carrier bag. I'd stuck it between the pages of my Emily Dickinson.

'Yeah, I do, I do. Pass it over.'

I slid it across the polished table and he caught it with his fingertips and twirled it round so it was the right way up. The effect on him was extraordinary.

First he stared, sort of shook his head, then stared again. Next he flipped the photo over to look at the back, but there's nothing there at all, it's completely blank. He turned it over once more and I could see his gaze sweeping up and down it, from one side to the other. He leant right over it, peering, and when he raised his head, his cheeks were flushed.

'Haven't you seen a picture of your aunty before?' I asked, surprised by the level of emotion he seemed to be feeling.

He was silent for a moment, then said, 'This is your mum?'

'Yeah,' I said. 'It was in the pages of my dad's textbook. That's why it survived; Poll threw everything else out after my mother left. She must've missed this.'

'Right,' said Callum, his colour fading a little. 'Only, it's a shock. To see her after all this time. Put a face to her.' I thought his hand might be trembling slightly, but then he laid the picture down, grinned broadly, and leant back in his chair.

'Does she look like your mum?' I craned to see the figure again, even though it had been etched on

123

my brain for years; in case seeing it here, now, might somehow have changed the detail.

'Hmm. A bit.' He still had this massive smile on his face. 'It's so nice to have found you, and this branch of the family. You know? Can you understand? It's always been the two of us, Mum and me, so it's amazing to discover all these other people in the bloodline.'

'I can understand that.' The tiny pale woman still leant against the scarlet Metro, still held her bump shyly. 'I must get my dark hair from Dad, although Poll says I was blonde at birth and it all dropped out, typical. I wonder how many months pregnant she was there. It's so strange both our mums, both sisters getting caught the same way.' Except your mum kept you, lucky bugger.

'Yeah, and both not having dads; I know. We're sort of, linked.' He rubbed his hands over his face as if he was washing, then dragged his fingers through his hair at the sides. 'Look, Kat, I know I can't take this—' He held up the photo between his thumb and forefinger, and I thought his gaze would scorch the paper.

'It's my only one,' I said. 'I haven't the negative or anything.'

'Of course, yeah. Here. But I wondered, since we're in a library, can I have a photocopy? A black-and-white one'll do.'

'I suppose so.' I wondered if it was all right to let him share the picture that no one else in the world knew about. 'You're very serious about all this, aren't you?'

'It's family,' he said simply. 'It's important to me to know where I come from. And I honestly *don't* know where your mum's living, if that's what you're

124

thinking. You have to trust me, I'm not about to track her down. Unless—'

'What?'

He leaned towards me and spoke quietly. 'Unless you want me to. I could have a go. Electoral rolls, the Internet; it's how I found your grandma. I couldn't promise anything, but there are Web sites where people leave messages . . .'

For five seconds I felt as dizzy as I did when Callum first presented himself. My God: to ask her, to tell her, to see what she was like, see where I came from. But then anger flashed through me like a fireball and burnt every other emotion away. It always does. My mother *is* anger. To remember her existence, and what she did to me, is to throw me into instant rage. 'God, no. *She* left *me*, why should I go running after her? I don't care where she is. She stopped mattering to me the day she walked out.'

I paused and lowered my voice again to a more normal, appropriate-for-a-library pitch. 'Sorry. I actually don't care, she's nothing. I only keep this photo to spite Poll. Do you want two copies, one extra for your mum? Or aren't you going to show her?'

'Haven't decided,' he said, retrieving his backpack. 'Play it by ear.'

No one is allowed to even breathe near Bank Top Library photocopier, much less lift the lid and press the red button. Terrible catastrophe will ensue if a member of the general public runs amok and attempts his own copying. Besides, it's 5p a sheet and Miss Dragon won't have anyone swindling the system. She likes to be there to count you down. But Miss Dragon was now with the computers, helping a young man type out a letter of application; we went and hovered by his machine but she was pretty engrossed. We had a hunt round for Miss Mouse, and tracked her to the office.

'Shall we knock?' asked Callum.

'I don't think we should, no. She might be on her lunch break.'

'Some lunch,' said Callum, blocking the glass square with his head. 'That is well odd. Oops. Come away.'

'Why? Let me see.'

'No. Shift.'

I let him lead me back to the photocopier. 'What was that in aid of?'

'Because she saw me looking in and she seemed a bit pissed off about it. Have you ever seen anyone eat a banana with a teaspoon?'

'A teaspoon?'

'Yeah, cutting teeny weeny slivers and sipping them off the end of the spoon. Like this. Really dainty. She must be sweltering as well, a long-sleeved jumper in this weather.'

It was true; even I had a blouse on. 'I've never seen her in anything other than baggy tops and long skirts, now you mention it. I get the impression she'd like a big shell, along the lines of a tortoise, that she could creep into when threatened. She always looks happiest in a cowl neck—' But I got no further because Miss Dragon was marching over, a nasty frown disfiguring her face. Surely it couldn't be for us?

'I'd rather you *didn't* spy on my staff when they're on their break,' she snapped, using the scary voice she uses with ordinary customers.

'What is it you want that's so urgent?'

'Photocopy.'

Callum tried a dazzling smile on her, but she took no notice, just whipped up the lid of the machine and slapped the picture face down.

'Two, please.' My voice was nearly a whisper.

She sighed heavily and pressed reset, then dip-dip for Number, then Start. The machine whirred, lit up, and two sheets skimmed out into Callum's waiting hand. His attention captured once more by the grainy lady, he could only hold out a ten-pence piece in Miss Dragon's general direction. She snatched the coin out of his open palm and stalked off to the till.

'That was awful,' I said. Out of all proportion I felt lousy. Poll could carp round the clock and it all rolled off me, by and large; but Miss Dragon was special. *I* was special. 'She's never cross with me. Why's she in such a mood?'

Callum didn't care about Miss Dragon. 'She's just an old bat. Never mind her. Bad day at Menopause City.' He folded the pages carefully so the crease went around the edges of the image and not through it, then pushed it into a pocket of his backpack. 'Right, come on, I've had enough of this place. Stop moping now and tell me where I can get a proper coffee. Because you were going to tell me about your dad, if you remember.'

'Was I?' I said miserably. 'I'll need to get my carrier bag.'

'Go on then,' he said. 'Scoot.'

*　　　　*　　　　*

One day they'll invent a drug that can locate and

127

destroy specific memories. Or they'll learn to shave bad times off your brain with a scalpel like slices of truffle.

I could have taken a chainsaw to my head. 'That's shock,' the doctor said somewhere in my subconscious. 'Or maybe concussion.' Total shut-down, I'd have called it; walking around the ward, blank-eyed. Two days later they shone a light in my face and I came to screaming. Tak-tak-tak went the doctor's shoes on the lino as he came to see me. He was pleased with the tears. 'That's healthy,' he said. 'We might be able to let you go before too long. Maybe when your hand's healed. We'll see.' Clang went the chart at the end of the metal bed. Tak-tak-tak.

I looked at my hand, which was bound up in a fat white bandage. I remember that, I thought. I put out my hand to grab the steering wheel back and pull us back out of the way. Something sharp cut me. I did try to save him.

A nurse came later to change the dressing. 'We've disconnected that hot drinks machine now,' she said. 'We don't want any more patients sticking their fingers under boiling water. Whatever were you thinking of?'

Then Vince turned up, looking like a corpse.

*   *   *   *

As we walked out of the library I glanced up at the sky, and directly above us was a cloud-placenta with a trailing umbilical cord. Callum said, 'Look at that cloud up there. It's exactly like a tree, isn't it? Freaky.'

'My dad,' I said, 'was handsome and clever. He'd

128

have been a doctor if he hadn't died.'

'I fancy being a doctor,' said Callum. 'Bit late now, though. Have you any pictures of him?'

I laughed. 'No shortage there. We've got about two hundred stashed away in albums, and we'd have them all out on display if Poll's eyesight was up to scratch. The best one's in my room, him in his suit before he went up to uni for his interview. It makes Poll cry if she looks at it for long enough.'

'And you? Does it make you cry?'

'It's not the same for me, I never knew him. But I wish nearly every day he was still around. He'd know what to do, about . . . the future and things. Do you fancy being a Methodist for half an hour?'

'A Methodist?'

'Their coffee's only instant, but they do make exceedingly good cakes.' I pointed at the poster outside the church. 'In aid of Lifeboats, 10.30 till 12.30. We're just in time.'

Callum looked doubtful. 'Don't you have to be religious to go in there?'

'Don't be daft, they only want your money. Just *look* holy. Don't start swearing at the top of your voice.'

It's a modern building, square and functional, with thin grilles over the windows to stop kids chucking bricks through the panes. There used to be a lovely old Gothic chapel, built in the 1800s, further down the main street; there are prints of it in the library. But the chapel got knocked down in the seventies to make way for a mini housing estate.

The new place was light, full of blond wood, and the metal grilles didn't stop the sun from flooding into the large foyer. Through a glass-panelled door you could see the church proper, a wall-hanging of a dove vomiting a rainbow, pews, a small plain altar covered with a white cloth. Here in the entrance there were children's drawings, posters and leaflets advertising community events, and small tables dotted around with plastic stacking chairs. Most of the tables were now empty but there was a tray piled with dirty crockery in the corner.

'Two coffees and two pieces of sponge cake,' I said to the old bid behind the table.

'My mother's favourite hymn's "For Those in Peril on the Sea",' said Callum piously behind me.

'Go and sit down,' I hissed. 'I'll get these.'

Beautiful World said a poster behind the counter, featuring two little girls, one black, one white, picking buttercups in a field. Old Bid collected all the components slowly, but did the sum in her head like lightning. 'Two pounds forty, and you're Pollyanna Millar's granddaughter, aren't you? Little Katherine.'

I dropped my head and spoke to my shoes. 'Yeah.'

'You'll not remember me, will you?'

'No.'

'Janey Marshall. I used to come round collecting catalogue money, d' you not remember? And you once fell while I was there and split your lip on t' step, and I gave you my hanky till it stopped bleeding? Are you sure you don't remember? Mind, you'd only have been about six. You were in a state. And you're getting a big girl now, aren't you? A big bonny girl. How's your grandma?'

'Fine.' I turned rudely away with the coffee but she came after me, passing *Let there be no strife For we be brethren*: picture of a happy football crowd, some wearing red, some wearing blue.

'I'll bring these plates for you, save your legs. And oh, who's this young man?'

It's at times like this I resolve to go and live in Australia. I'd write to Aunty Jean tonight about citizenship.

'I'm—' began Callum.

For a moment my heart stopped.

'—a friend from school.'

Old Bid Marshall put the plates down and looked at him over her glasses. 'I thowt as you went to a girls' school. Have they gone co-educational now?'

You cunning old bag, I thought. 'Only a bit in the Sixth Form. But he's my best friend's brother.'

'Kat's helping me do a history project,' said Callum. 'Do you want to see?' He started to pull open his backpack. Old Bid Marshall stepped forward. 'It's about prostitutes in nineteenth-century Lancashire,' he explained, drawing out a folder and making as if to open it. 'We've uncovered some fascinating facts. Here, take a look.'

'Well, well. Eeh, very good.' She stepped back with the expression of a woman who's been handed a cobra to nurse. 'They do some stuff in schools now. Eh, I don't know.'

'Go on,' urged Callum, pushing the folder towards her. 'Really. Be my guest.'

She gave an unhappy chuckle. 'I've no time to be looking at projects. That won't get the washing-up done, will it?' And she scooted off back to the counter and started putting cups into towers.

'What the hell did you say that for? God. That'll be all round the Over Seventies by teatime. Why

131

prostitutes?'

Callum pushed his chair back so he could tip it against the wall. 'Why not? It came into my head and I said it. Got rid of her, didn't it?' *I shall light a candle of understanding in thine heart*, said the poster behind him: photo of candle.

'What'll I say if it gets back to Poll? What if she asks who you are?'

'Say what I did. Friend's brother. You bumped into me at the library and you were only being polite. You had no idea what my project was about when you agreed to help.' He put his hands behind his head and looked pleased with himself.

I huffed a bit and ate my cake while he rolled a cigarette for later.

'So go on, tell us about your dad. He looked like you, you said?'

I gave a hollow laugh. 'I said he had dark hair like mine. Although he started off blondish in the baby photos. I'll bring some along next time. My grandma was enthusiastic but terrible when it came to taking photographs, so a lot of the pictures we have are out of focus or too dark, or he's missing body parts. And a lot of them are from the seventies so he's got this girly hairdo. But there's a nice clear close-up of him on the beach when he was ten, in a Cresta T-shirt; it's good because he doesn't know it's being taken, he's watching a crab die, so he looks serious. In every other photo we have he's flashing his teeth and striking a pose.'

'I'd like to see him.'

'Yeah, well, we'll sort something out. I wish I could tell you more about your aunt.'

'Hmm,' said Callum. 'Never mind.' He opened his folder and took a biro out of a side pocket in his backpack. 'Do you mind if I jot some of what you say down? I'll forget it otherwise, and it's important.'

I felt a bit shifty about that, but what could I say? 'If you really want to. What's actually in this notorious folder? Apart from prostitutes.'

He held it out across the table and flicked some pages quickly in front of my eyes.

'Mainly private stuff. Me. Some poems I wrote, my top-ten films and books, fantasy governments, a letter to my MP I once drafted. The start of a novel. A few diary entries. I take this folder around with me in case I have an idea for something. I'm going to stick that photocopy of—your mum into it, and I'd like to make a list of things about your family. Like, say, your mum's birthday and your dad's favourite bands; just, you know, trivia.'

I picked up the black ring binder and turned it over to see the front. 'Oh, wow.' Callum had covered it with photo-graphs of clouds, some of them really dramatic. There were wispy cirrus, stripy cirrocumulus, glowering cumulonimbus, plus two fantastic sunsets that could have been scenes from heaven, or hell. 'Did you take these?'

'Uh-huh. I love skies. Mum does too. She likes the sky at night best though. She reads the stars. She can draw up charts and things; it's not rubbish. People come to her for readings.'

I was still studying the photos, trying to make them out as picture-messages. 'Why did you take these particular clouds, though?'

'Dunno.' He tipped his chair back onto solid ground. ' 'Cause they're interesting. No reason, really; sky appreciation. Everyone goes round looking downwards when they should be looking

133

up. Do you ever look at the sky through Polaroid lenses? Fantastic definition of all the light and dark, like an oil painting or something.' He paused, half-turning the folder on the table, admiring his own work. 'These ones are all enhanced with filters. You don't ever get proper lavender skies. That sunset, it wasn't so amazing in real life. You can do all sorts with filters; every sky can be a sunset, if you want; you can turn a summer day into a thunderstorm just by fitting the right attachment over the lens. You feel like God.' He pulled the folder back and opened it again, leafing through for a blank page. 'OK.' He clicked his biro into action. 'Hey, I tell you what, though, I'm getting desperate for a fag now. Another five minutes and we'll make a move, shall we?'

I shrugged.

'I'll make these notes first.' He scribbled for a while and I finished my coffee. I could have taken the cup back to the counter in a helpful way, but I didn't. 'What sort of music did your parents like?' he asked finally.

'I don't know anything about my mother, I said. 'I'm not interested, and Poll wouldn't tell me if I was. Now Dad liked classic eighties stuff, the Jam, Pretenders, Debbie Harry, Adam Ant. I've got all his tapes and LPs; some of them are really good. I reckon one of his favourite albums was *Dare* by The Human League, because the cover's so scruffy. It looks like it's been played to death, and he's given some of the songs on it star ratings in red pen. "Love Action" gets the highest, he's written "I believe in the truth though I lie a lot" along the top, and "You know I believe in love" on the flyleaf of his chemistry textbook. It's a great song. Do you know it?'

'No. But I'd like a copy. Can you get me one?'

There was no way he was borrowing the original. 'I don't know.'

'Give us a list and I'll download them off the Internet. Do you know what films he liked?'

'Haven't a clue. Poll's keen on Ronald Coleman, Errol Flynn, David Niven, anyone with a tiny 'tache. I quite like some of those old black-and-whites myself, although having to explain to Poll what's going on all the time's a pain.'

Callum had stopped taking notes. 'Listen,' he said, not meeting my eye properly, 'I don't suppose your dad left any letters, did he, in with the photographs?'

'Letters? Who to?'

He turned in his chair and began lengthening the straps on his backpack. 'I don't know; your mum, maybe. Or her letters to him.' He cleared his throat. 'All it is, I reckon you find out people's true personality in letters.'

My heart started to beat fast. 'I don't get you. You're asking me about private letters, to see private letters? Even if there were any, I wouldn't show you. I wouldn't read them myself. They'd be love letters.'

He had the grace to look ashamed. 'Sorry, you're right. Don't know what I was thinking of.'

No, neither do I, I thought.

'I need a fag,' he said. 'Come on.'

*   *   *

We were in a house that was Poll's, and not Poll's. The same porch, leaded windows, stairwell, back kitchen,

135

but none of the detail right. Hardly any furniture. I wondered at first if they'd decorated, but this was all old with dirty carpets and marks on the walls. Vince took me up to the bedroom and I thought, aye-aye, but all he did was show me the camp bed with one of Poll's bedspreads on it. He'd brought some books and a radio. 'I thowt as you'd want to come reahnd a bit, befoore I fetch y' 'ome,' he said.

I slept and slept.

Next day when he came he stood and looked at me for a long time, then he hauled me up and steered me through to the bathroom. He started taking my sweater off, lifting my arms up like a child. I remember my heart plummeting, but not being able to resist.

'Can you wesh yoursen?' he said. I didn't say a word. So he went back to the bedroom and brought a sponge bag. First he cleaned my teeth. Then he wet a flannel. 'Tek your blouse off, love. Come on.' I unbuttoned slowly. 'Now, lass, what hev you bin doin' to your arms?' he said when he saw the marks. He shook his head as though it was very heavy on his shoulders, and went out of the room. I heard his steps on the stairs, and the front door shut, but I didn't move.

'I don't know,' he muttered when he returned. He smeared the little oval wounds with Savlon and then papered me over with plasters. 'This'll hev to stop.'

He left me alone to wash my bottom half and when I came out of the bathroom, he'd gone. There were some jam sandwiches on the floor and a flask of tea. He'd left some of my clothes too, clean. The nail clippers had disappeared, though.

Chapter Twelve

Poll was swanning about covered in fence mould. I didn't enlighten her. It was right down the back of her blouse, a great green smear on the white polyester. I saw from the kitchen window, first thing, but I didn't say anything. Her bed sheets are often marked all over from the washing line. So what, I say. She's damn lucky I launder them at all.

I was in her bad books already that day because she reckoned I'd broken her toe with a packet of fish fingers. It was true I had stacked the freezer in a rush, but it was her own fault for going in there, especially in her stockinged feet. Unluckily, you can't die from a squashed toe. 'What did you think you were after?' I said. 'You can't see the labels.'

'I just wanted summat cowd to put on my head where I bumped it,' she snapped.

Now that was my fault; I had left the kitchen cupboard open. I'd been selecting goodies for a binge later on, because the thing about bulimia is that you can actually plan round it. This is what bulimia looks like as a mathematical model:

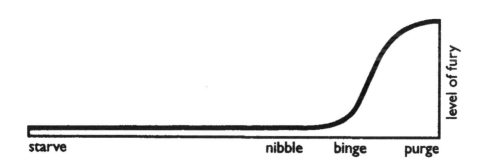

starve   nibble   binge   purge

So it's easy to fit into even a busy lifestyle. I felt in total control, for once, and as a bonus, my teeth were the cleanest they'd ever been. Poll shouted of me one evening in a panic. 'What's Winston got fast round his mouth?' We watched as the dog did a good imitation of a rabies victim, rolling around on the carpet and spitting. I bent down to peer between his black lips.

'Hell, it's my dental floss,' I said, holding his head while he wriggled insanely. 'You get his back end.' So Poll got his haunches in a wrestler's grip while I unwrapped his muzzle. It's just as well he's a nice nature. 'Christ knows how he got hold of it,' I said as the last length came free. I traced the line back. 'Look, he's trailed it down the stairs like the Andrex puppy. Yuk. You wouldn't think he'd like the minty taste.'

'He eats the bread we put out for the birds even when it's gone blue,' Poll reminded me. 'And cowpats.'

For a moment there, grandmother and granddaughter were nearly getting on, but by bedtime it had all gone sour again. The same mathematical model can also be used to demonstrate why Poll and I will always essentially be at war.

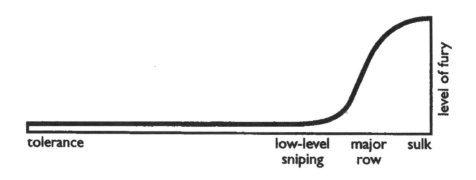

This time the argument had been about hair. I'd happened to say a woman on a TV news report looked a sight with short spiky hair. Poll had said she'd been in an earthquake so that was the least of her worries and at least you could see this woman's face when she talked. I said the reason my hair was so bushy at the moment was because it had been raining, so whatever else evil I was responsible for, Poll couldn't hold me accountable for that. Poll said, 'Yes, but you could wear a rain-hood. Why don't you wear a rain-hood? Maggie's given you dozens over the years. Slip one in your purse. You carry on like you're still seven. Why can't you act like a grown-up?' So I'd gone to the top drawer of the sideboard and got a rain-hood out and made as if I was going to garrotte Poll with it, but she turned and saw me, and twigged what I was doing. 'You're going all wrong, you are,' she shouted. 'You're going twisted like your mother.' Then she snatched the rain-hood off me and told me it was too good for me, and I grabbed it back off her and shredded the plastic in front of her face. I threw it on the floor and she screamed, 'Pick that up. Pick that up, lady!' But I just walked off and slammed the door.

Afterwards I sat in my room and thought about Callum. I didn't even know whether I was going to see him again. Being with him was like a sort of dance; when we met up I'd start off cool and awkward, then he'd say something which would make me feel as if he really understood me and I could tell him anything; then there'd be a split second when I suddenly lost confidence in him and became uncomfortable. Because who was he? What did I know about him, actually?

'I still feel terrible about Miss Dragon having a go at us,' I'd said as we walked towards the station. 'I don't even know what we did that was so wrong. Did Miss Mouse seem angry too?'

Callum took a drag of his cigarette, held the smoke in his lungs, then breathed it out smoothly through his nose. 'Forget about it. You want to stop worrying about that pair. Couple of old lesbos.'

'What?'

'Lezzies. Ladies of the Sapphic persuasion.'

'My God, do you think so?'

'For definite. They're neither of them married. That Miss Mouse never wears make-up, has her hair short like a boy. And Miss Dragon's your archetypal bull-dyke.'

Behind him, a bank of rosebay willowherb waved in the breeze; far off I heard the hoot of a train.

'I'm surprised you never noticed,' he said.

*   *   *

We sat in rows and you could smell the polish. I wanted to lean forward and bite the wooden back of the seat in front; instead I chewed at the inside of my cheek. I thought there'd be a jury like you see on Crown Court, but there was only a handful of us and the coroner in his dark blue gown.

'An inquest is not about establishing blame,' the coroner's clerk had said before we went in. The coroner was saying it again now from the bench. Tell Poll, I nearly shouted out. She wants me strung up.

The coroner went first with Name of the deceased and Time of death, then the pathologist gave the Cause of death which was trauma to the head and then we sang 'There is a Heavenly Land' while Poll

140

choked and sobbed into her service sheet. The place was packed with people from the village and students.

I had to go up and swear on the Bible.

'Try to answer as clearly as you can,' said the coroner to me.

I wanted to tell him, straight out. I killed Roger. It was my fault. I jerked the steering wheel in temper and pulled us across the road. I did try to say that but he asked me lots of questions about what I said and even as I was talking I could hear I didn't make sense. At this point, he said, I should warn you that you do not have to answer any question which you are asked in this courtroom by me or by any other party if you feel that the answer to the question would implicate you in a criminal offence. Do you understand?

I told him maybe I didn't touch the wheel, maybe I only hit the glove compartment with my fist.

After me, the lorry driver gave evidence. He was a Welshman, and thin as a rake. His eyes behind his black-framed glasses bulged with stress. 'The car just drifted across into my lane,' he whispered.

'I'm sorry,' said the coroner, 'but you'll have to raise your voice a little.'

The lorry driver wiped his glasses with a handkerchief and went on, clutching the sides of his chair. 'He was drifting. I saw what was going on and I tried to move out of the way, but I just wasn't quick enough. Lorries are heavy in the handling, they're not as responsive as cars are.'

'There was no sudden swerve on the part of the other vehicle?'

'No.'

'Are you sure?'

The lorry driver closed his eyes. 'Totally sure, good God.'

I kept quiet and watched the coffin which was pale wood with a huge wreath on the front in the shape of a heart. I thought, what did they do with his head in the end? Did they try and wrap it up in something? All that silk lining spoiled.

Another man, elderly, took the oath and said he'd been behind us at the scene of the crash and he'd seen the car drift in the same way. 'He'd been weaving for a while, a good few miles. To be honest, I thought he might be drunk.'

'Man that is born of a woman is of a few days and full of trouble,' said the coroner. 'He cometh forth like a flower, and is cut down. PC Whittle, could you give us your report on the crash scene now, please.'

PC Whittle talked about the pattern of tyre marks on the road, and the damage to the front and side wings of the car. The policeman said the physical evidence of the crash was consistent with the car having been struck a high-speed glancing blow to the extreme front offside wing, then having spun round on the road so that it was next hit squarely on the driver's door, which had caved in to some considerable degree. This suggested, he said, that the car had not swerved wildly into the lorry's path, but had been moving gradually over to the point where it was first clipped.

I imagined the coroner asking me again if I'd really grabbed the wheel. This time I'd say no, for definite. It made no difference. Roger was still dead. In my head we would always be crashing and he would always be dying; there would never be any room for anything else.

But the coroner didn't ask me again. He climbed up behind the lectern and gave his verdict. 'Without doubt, as we have heard from the pathologist, a contributory factor to Roger Millar's death was his failure to wear a seat belt. I note that his girlfriend, Elizabeth Castle, who was wearing hers and sitting alongside him, avoided sustaining any serious injury. Miss Castle feels she may have been personally to blame for the accident, but I have heard the evidence of Miss Castle and rejected it, because I believe she is confused about the details of those last few crucial seconds. She seems consumed by guilt, to a degree where her reliability as a witness is actually undermined. If she had really pulled the top of the steering wheel as she thinks she might have done, then the car would have swerved the other way, onto the left-hand verge. The weight of evidence from witnesses at the scene and from the Greater Manchester Police Traffic Department clearly suggests that Mr Millar allowed his concentration to wander during the discussion with Miss Castle, and it was this that led to the fatal collision. I therefore record a verdict of accidental death. Will the congregation now rise.'

The coffin began to move forward on the conveyor belt and the theme from *Chariots of Fire* was piped through the speakers. My mouth was so full of blood I had to swallow. The curtains closed and he was gone.

Outside the crematorium, Poll's friend Maggie was holding Katherine in her arms and jigging her up and down. She was singing, 'Andy is waving goodbye, goodbye,' under her breath. When she saw me she smiled and held Katherine out for me to take. But as soon as I touched her, the baby began to cry and I knew then she hated me.

*   *   *

143

I was skulking about outside the library, trying to decide whether or not to go in, when Miss Dragon pushed open the swing door and beckoned to me.

'I've got something for you.'

Bloody hell, I thought. I followed her past the video rack and the Books for Sale table to the counter.

'Here,' she said, bringing a postcard out from the shelf underneath. 'It's from your friend. He sent it here.'

The picture on the front was Glastonbury Tor by sunset, and on the back Callum had written: 'Staying with Mum's mates for two weeks in their Mediaeval barn. When I get back, I've got a present for you. Wednesday 28th OK? Late am, among the books. Cheers, Call.' Any other time I'd have been tickled by 'Kat Millar, Care Of the Library', but Miss Dragon wasn't smiling.

'There's no contact number,' I said, half to myself. 'So how can I let him know either way?'

Miss Dragon pursed her lips. 'You watch yourself. Timmy O, Danny S,' she said sternly, tapping the card with her finger. Then the phone rang and she turned away to answer it.

Timmy O? Danny S? Who where they? I hung around for a few seconds to ask, then decided I didn't care anyway and wandered back outside. I felt so lonely I almost went home and phoned Rebecca, but after a mooch round the newsagent's and a flick through some glossies, I came up with a better plan. Twenty minutes later I was on a bus to Bolton, nose in a fashion mag, a tenner filched from Poll's purse in my pocket.

De-Fuzz for Summer Fun, I read. *Nothing ruins a beach babe's look like a couple of coconut-style shins*

144

sticking out from under her sarong. You can forget the golden tan, the toned abs, the hot-label bikini. Furry legs say you just can't be bothered.

And the guys agree. 'If there's one thing that puts me off a woman's body, it's little black hairs poking out everywhere,' says Dave, 22. 'It may be OK for the Continentals, but it makes me feel sick. I wouldn't touch a hairy girl with a bargepole.'

Mind you, boys, it's only fair to tell you, we all loathe bristly backs on men, so if you're thinking about stripping your shirt off this holiday, you'd better sort yourselves out too!

Stubble Trouble

But with the vast range of depilatories now on the market, what is the best way to get those crucial bits smooth, sexy and strokeable? The Chique team have been road-testing the top brands and gadgets that promise no-fuss silky skin, and they've come up with some surprising results . . .

In Boots, I took so long assessing all the products that I attracted myself a store detective, or it might have been another pervert, I'm not sure. He was definitely having a good look at my bottom. I went to stare at the tampons for a while—that got rid of him—and then came back and bought a box of wax strips. Donna used wax strips; what had she said about them? I found where the electric straighteners lived, but they were way too dear. Then I went along the hair-dye aisle and imagined what life would be like if you looked like some of these women on the boxes.

I paid for the strips and went to check out clothes.

Our whole sixth form was out that sunny Saturday. In Dorothy Perkins I saw Emma Pearson

145

from my English set, and Surinder Badat from general studies in Woolworth's. Lissa Hargreaves was in the ladies' at Debenhams, wetting down a new perm and cursing. Serving behind the counter in W. H. Smith's was Nicky Hunter, while Donna French was pretending to browse DVDs next to her and sighing every time a customer interrupted their chat.

'Hi*ya*,' cried Donna when she saw me. 'Hey, Nicky, it's Kat.'

Nicky looked a bit sick but managed a smile. 'Hey.'

Someone came up and asked for stamps, so Donna waltzed over to me. 'Whatcha got there, then?' I opened the bag slightly for her to peer in. 'Ooh, yikes, rather you than me. Not going for a Brazilian, are you? Yow-ow-ow. Nasty. I'm saving up for laser treatment. For my legs, I mean.'

'Right,' I said.

'Nicky's being boring,' she said loudly over her shoulder. 'Working.'

'Earning money,' said Nicky.

'It's a drag. Anyway. You're coming, aren't you? To my do?'

'Oh, yeah.' Poll had taught me it was simplest to lie about these things.

'See?' Donna called over to Nicky. 'Kat's coming. Everyone's coming in the world, except you.'

Nicky was giving an old man some change, but when he'd gone she said, 'It's not my fault my stepdad's booked us a fortnight in Florence. I don't want to go.'

'Well, don't, then.'

'It's not as simple as that.' Nicky broke off to

direct a woman to the printer cartridges. Her face was like thunder.

'Come on,' said Donna to me. 'Nicky's too busy. Let's go and have a coffee, or something.'

I didn't look in Nicky's direction as we walked away.

Anyone watching us trailing round the shops, picking clothes off the racks and holding them up against ourselves might have thought we were proper friends. She looked completely fantastic in everything she chose. I wanted to tell her that, but I couldn't because it would have sounded crap. I just looked like a barrel. At last, in Blayz, we found a really good Plus section and she pulled items off the rack for me to examine, and tutted when I rejected them.

'I don't know why you won't try that one on, it wouldn't half show off your cleavage.' She passed over a scoop-necked white top with a ruffle down the front. 'You've got bosoms to die for. You'd be causing traffic accidents if you wore this in the high street. See.' She stepped close and unbuttoned the top of my high-necked pale blue blouse and pulled the collar apart. My heart was beating somewhere up in my throat. 'Undo a few more yourself. Loosen up. That's it. Till you can see a bit of lace off the top of your bra. That looks loads better.'

We stood in front of the mirror together, then she did a neat side-step out of the reflection. I knew why she'd done that; so I wouldn't compare our figures. She's only being nice to you out of guilt, said Poll's voice, why else would she be bothering?

'Thing is,' Donna was saying, 'we've all got bits of our bodies we hate. Everyone. I've got this

147

stupid scar on my belly button from an op I had when I was a kid. I can't stand anyone seeing it; not unless I know them very well, if you know what I mean.'

I was smoothing the white top against myself and squinting, trying to imagine it on.

'So I wear stuff that covers it up. Like, I'd never wear crop-tops with hipsters. Which is a fucking drag, actually. I never used to bother about it when I was little, until a girl at my primary school said it gave her nightmares. Katie Ainsworth, evil little cow. When we went swimming she made sicky noises in the changing rooms at me.'

I hung the top back on its rail. 'God, that's awful.'

'I got her back. Majorly.'

'How?'

Donna pursed her lips as if considering. 'Well . . . promise you won't be grossed-out by this? Because it is *pret*ty gross.'

'Go on.'

'OK. What I did was, I secretly dropped a handful of aniseed balls into the swimming pool at the shallow end where she always was, 'cause she couldn't actually swim for toffee, just mucked about with a float all the time and hung onto the edge. Within about two minutes there was a red slick all round her, it looked exactly like blood. I knew it would because a little boy in Greece last year had done the same thing in the hotel pool, and the lifeguards went mental trying to find the swimmer with the terrible injury.

'The instructor got us all out and sent us off back to the changing rooms, and while we were there I told everyone it had been Katie's period.

148

All the other girls started screaming and trying to get under the showers, and she ran into a cubicle and wouldn't come out. The more she denied it, the more everyone believed me. By the time the instructor came in, she was hysterical. And it became one of those school legends, you know, so that whenever anyone mentioned Katie Ainsworth, it was, "Oh, she's the one who had her period in the swimming pool." '

I had my mouth open and my hand to my lips. 'Wow.'

'Told you it was gross. I don't care though, she deserved it.'

'Oh, she did.' I was so happy, to be here, in this normal clothes shop, talking about periods with Donna French..

'Are you going to buy this groovy garment, or what? For the record, I think you should.'

I shook my head. 'I haven't got enough money left.' That was true. I was relieved too, because although the top was really nice, I couldn't have faced the thought of going into a communal changing room with Donna.

'Don't be wet. Open an account,' said Donna airily, biting at a hangnail and managing to make the action look cool and provocative.

'I don't know how you do that.'

'Go over to that counter there, tell them you want to apply for a Blayz card, and I guarantee they'll be doing triple somersaults around you. Take the top. You get ten per cent off, it says on that sign.'

I wanted to say, I don't know what size I am any more, but I didn't dare. I wanted her to say, Give it to me, I'll take it for you, I'll sort you out a card. I

149

wanted to drop the top on the carpet and run away.

She came up to me as I was still queuing. 'Are you sorted? Because I've got to go now, got to meet Nicks while she's on her lunch break. If she's speaking to me. Yeah? So, see you around? See you at my party, won't I? And on results day, oh God.' She made an unhappy mouth. 'See you.'

'Yeah,' I said, feeling suddenly flat. I looked down at the top again. There was no way I was going to be taking it home with me.

*   *   *

'She's going to have to come back with us,' I heard Vince say to Poll, over Katherine's squalling. 'She's its mother. Where else would she go?'

'Hell fire,' said Poll.

The baby carried on screaming.

*   *   *

I did it. I bought the white top, spoke to the scary girl behind the counter even though she had black nail varnish on and looked as if she could have gobbled me up for dinner. I had my library card on me, plus my Oxford letter I always carry, so that was two forms of ID. I thought everyone was watching me while I was standing at the counter, but when I turned round, they weren't. After I'd signed everything I went and tried the top on in Evans' changing rooms, which I know is a cock-eyed way to go about it, but it did fit so I didn't have to take it back. Came home to Poll's with the promise of unhairy legs and a killer cleavage, and even Dogman perched on one of the kitchen tops

150

didn't dampen my spirits.

Poll was sitting with her elbows on the table, troughing her way through a pack of party rings. 'Dickie's brought you summat.'

'I've fetched you some chocolates,' he said. 'They've a bit of a bloom on but they taste OK.' He was drinking a bottle of cider and making a performance out of it, sticking his lips out to the neck, tonguing the rim, gasping after each swig.

'Gee, thanks,' I said as sarcastically as I could get away with.

'He's good to you, is Dickie.'

'I am,' said Dogman, and belched.

There's a pay-off, though, I felt like saying. These rubbishy gifts all came at a price. I had to put up with his weaselly eyes doing a constant body-search on me, his pathetic stream of innuendo and no-brain political commentaries, his smell. And the fact he was always in our house, winding up Poll against me, making me feel like the interloper. Mouldy chocolates were no kind of compensation.

In my head I heard Miss Dragon's voice again. 'Timeo Danaos,' she was saying. Timeo Danaos. Not Timmy O, Danny S. Timeo Danaos et dona ferentes.

'Beware of Greeks,' I said out loud, very pleased with myself.

'Beware of Greeks?' said Dogman, wiping his mouth on the back of his hand. 'I should bloody well think so. They had my wallet off me when I was in Cyprus two year ago.'

*　　　*　　　*

151

For days I sat like an old lady, looking out of the window in Roger's room. I shall die in this chair, I thought. Vince brought meals up, and sometimes my baby, though I don't think it did either of us any good, me or her. One of us would be in tears within minutes. No one tells you how much screaming there is, do they? You expect newborns to scream sometimes, but Katherine never stopped. For God's sake! I shouted at her. Once I tried screaming back. That brought Vince running. Afterwards he came up with a brandy. 'I don't want that,' I snapped at him. He drank it straight down and left.

Sometimes, when Poll and Vince went out, I shuffled downstairs and prowled around. I brought back books, Reader's Digests and tatty, old-fashioned children's stories. *The Inquisitive Harvest Mouse* was the best one. I wanted to climb into the pages and make friends with the little girls, swap daisy chains. I wanted to share their sunny, Fifties picnic. It looked like a warm world.

Poll's house was like ice. Most evenings there'd be shouting and thumping coming up from below. Then Vince would go out the back and chop wood with a big axe.

I knew this other girl would turn up, it was just a matter of when.

I spotted her before anyone. A brown Triumph Toledo drew up, and after a few minutes, a fair, plumpish woman got out. I pressed my face right against the glass to get a good view. She had on a denim skirt and a high-necked white blouse with a pink cardigan over the top. Nothing special. I wondered if I'd seen her before.

She stood and looked at the house, then turned and opened up the passenger-side back door. Her head disappeared as she bent to something—I knew what that was going to be—and the bottom fell out of my stomach when she straightened up and there it was, this baby. This baby in blue shorts.

Then, instead of walking up Poll's path, she started off along the pavement, towards the top of the hill. I went dizzy with relief. After a hundred yards, she turned round and came back again.

Now the wind was getting up and the clouds were rolling across the sky like speeded-up film. It was spitting with rain as well. She shivered and I saw the baby wriggle in her arms and open its mouth to cry. She opened the car door again, peered inside, then slammed it, crossly. I watched her take off her cardigan and swaddle the baby tightly up, so only its head was poking out, and kiss it, and hold it close. She looked perished. I'd never do that for Katherine, I thought. I'd hang on to my cardi and let her freeze.

I knew that next she would come through the front gate.

I went over to the bedroom door as the bell was ringing. I heard: 'Oh, hello, my name's Jude and I've come all the way from Wrenbury.'

'Oh aye, wheer's that, love?'—Vince's voice.

'Who is it?'—from Poll.

'I've come to see you about Roger.'

The front door slammed shut. I slid down the wall till I was sitting with my back against it, and waited.

It didn't take long; about ninety seconds. I heard Poll shout, and a crash like broken glass. A scraping noise, like furniture moving, a yelp of protest. I came out of the bedroom and started down the stairs.

'I'm not having it, get out! I'm not having another one in the house. You can't prove owt, we've only

153

your word. You're after money? Well, you've come to t' wrong house. Can't you see this is a house of sorrow? What do you think them drawn curtains mean? How dare you.'

I ran back up and got to the window in time to see the girl stumbling down the path. The rain spattered hard against the pane now, distorting the detail, but I still saw Poll's Negro-lady money box smash on the brick behind her heels. The cast iron shattered apart like a bomb.

'I'll lame you!' screamed Poll, her voice almost unrecognizable. 'You've no respect—filthy liar—you ever come back here again—'

The girl almost threw her baby into the back seat. When she turned to get in the car herself, there was dark on her forehead, could've been blood, could just have been a shadow. I hoped it was blood.

As the car pulled away, tyres squealing, Katherine started to cry again.

Chapter Thirteen

I waited till the day I was supposed to meet Callum to do the wax business.

SILKEE Sensitive with Aloe Vera. The gentle and effective way to remove unwanted hair. Do Not use on ears, nose, eyebrows, breasts, genitals or perianal areas. Not suitable for the elderly.

What you had to do was rub the strips of paper between your palms, as if you were praying. Then you peeled the layers of paper apart and there was a coating of what looked like earwax on each one. You pressed this to your skin, did a bit more

154

rubbing, then dragged it off, yelping. It left a clearing of baldness in amongst the forest of shinhair, together with some patches of scabby yellow wax. It looked as if my leg was going septic.

I tried again round the back, on my calf. Yaargh. Another smooth bit. But now I saw that if I wasn't careful I'd end up with a sort of patchwork effect, hedgerows of fuzz. So, despite the pain, I set to and pursued those remaining clumps of hair. They got smaller and smaller, till I was using a whole strip for about three of the buggers. Finally I was done. One leg was completely depilated. Then I realized I'd run out of strips.

They made it look like fun-fun-fun on the TV advert, group of model types falling on the bed together, laughing, stroking each other's limbs. Nowhere in the proceedings does anyone cry with pain, howl, sweat or pee themselves in agony. 'With practice,' the leaflet said, 'the technique becomes easy and painless.' I could not *believe* they had been allowed to print that.

I swore a bit, then hunted out the instructions. *Each strip can be used up to three times*, it said. But when I checked the pile of discarded ones, a load were stuck to the carpet where I'd thrown them, and the ones that had made it into the bin were now covered in pencil shavings and hole-punchings. There were about four usable ones left. I picked up the bin and chucked it at the wall in temper, daft really because it would be me who'd have to clear the mess up.

It was at this point someone knocked on the bedroom door.

'Go away,' I shouted, assuming it was Poll.

The door opened a crack and Maggie peeped

155

round. 'I'm sorry, love. I just wanted to check you was OK. I thought I heard you crying. And then there was that thud, and I wondered if you'd fallen down, or summat. But I'll leave you in peace. Sorry to disturb you.'

Now why couldn't she have been my grandma?

When I got downstairs, Maggie and Poll were getting ready to go out, Maggie discreetly removing a truly disgusting hanky from the table and swapping it for a clean one from her own pocket. She nodded at me, and I hooked the thing with the kitchen tongs and dropped it in the washer.

'Bingo,' said Poll as she wrestled to find the arm hole of her raincoat. Luckily they've started using huge cards that even her mole-eyes can see.

'So we'll be back about four. And we're having our dinner at the Working Men's. What are you going to do with yourself?'

'Dunno,' I said, kicking the washing machine with my toe. Bugger off and leave me alone, I wanted to say. 'Might go down the library.'

'That cupboard under the sink wants clearing, if you've nowt else to do,' said Poll, stuffing the clean hanky in her bag. She made a face at Maggie. 'We had a leak, you know.'

'Oh, heck, was it your pipes?'

'No, it were one of these pouches of washing liquid. It bursted, and we didn't know till it had gone all ovver. I kept coming in here an' sniffing. Spring Fresh; by God, it did pong. Then Katherine went to get some bleach an' t' bottle were stuck to t' bottom of t' cupboard. It all needs swilling out properly.'

'That's my day sorted, then,' I muttered.

'I'll give you a hand if you wait till we get back,'

156

said Maggie. 'You get yourself off out. You're only young, you don't want to be stuck indoors at your age. Go to the library and have some fun. Ooh, look, your belt's twisted. You must be in love.'

'That'll be the day,' grunted Poll. 'Love. Pigs might fly. Are we going, or what?'

Maggie gave me a cheeky pinch on the arm as she went past and tapped the side of her nose.

'Bloody hell,' I said under my breath.

After they'd gone I let Winston out for a totter round the garden and went to put some lipstick on. It felt peculiar, as if I'd not wiped my mouth after eating a cream cake, but I resisted the urge to rub it straight off. I brushed my hair and tied it back in a low ponytail. Then, at the last minute, I noticed through my tights that my legs had come out all spotty, so I changed into the birthday tunic top and pants. A check in the mirror showed I looked quite smart. The effect was almost ruined by a wax strip which had attached itself sneakily to my heel, but Winston saved the day by limping back in and trying to eat it.

Up at the library Miss Dragon and Miss Mouse were busy dealing with the holiday influx of schoolchildren, and I couldn't see Callum anywhere. I took myself over to the Returned Today section and was just about to start trawling through when I spotted him in Newspapers, reading the *Guardian* Media supplement.

'You look different,' I said.

'So do you.'

'No, I mean you look *really* different. Why did you cut your hair?' He'd had a clipper cut, not skinhead-short, but short. He was wearing black framed glasses and a light coloured jacket.

157

'Felt like a change. And it's cooler on my scalp.' He ran his hand over the top of his head, feeling the fuzz.

'And the glasses?'

'Got sick of contacts. I'll go back to them, sometime. When I get bored with specs.'

'You're like Sherlock Holmes, master of disguise.'

He pretended to be peering at me through a magnifying glass. 'The Mysterious Case of the Missing Mother. Where did Elizabeth Castle run off to when she ducked out of Bank Top?'

'That's not funny.'

'Sorry. Hey, cheer up, I've brought you some stuff you might like.'

He pulled his backpack out from under the table and flipped it open.

'Here you go.' There was a small paper bag and a brown envelope. 'This one first; this is the proper present. From my holidays. She makes them, Mum's friend, the one in the barn. Shona. She used to live on a boat in France but somebody tried to set fire to it, so she came home.'

I unpleated the top and put my hand inside. I touched something cold. It slid out into my hand like a coin.

'A wasp?'

'No, you noggin, it's a bee. She does them in enamel. You can put it on a chain if you don't like the thong.'

I was staring at it. 'Are you sure it's not a wasp? It's on the skinny side for a bee.' The back was blank metal.

'Don't be silly, that's just the style. Who'd make wasp jewellery? Bees are cool, they make honey and royal jelly, they pollinate fruit trees. And they don't sting you unless they absolutely have to. Wasps, on the other hand, are pure evil. They live in litter bins and eat carrion.'

'They're not all bad. I'll tell you something really important about wasps.'

'What?'

'Not now. Later. Maybe.'

Callum scratched his head and frowned at me. 'You're being very enigmatic today.'

Miss Dragon walked past, scanning our table as she went. 'Everything all right?'

We nodded. I held up the necklace for her to see.

'Hmm,' she said. 'A median wasp.'

'It's a *bee*, for God's sake,' laughed Callum.

'Wrong shape,' said Miss Dragon. 'The abdomen's too narrow. And the bands of black are too wide.'

'Oh, have it your own way. It's two against one. Clearly I'm in the wrong.'

Miss Dragon gave him a searching look, then went away to deal with the queue at the desk.

'God, I wouldn't like to be late returning a book here, I tell you. Scaree. Anyway, these photos, I thought you might like to see them too.' Callum nudged the envelope over towards me. 'It's written on the back who they are.'

The first was a blurry picture of what looked like a horrid red doll with an oversize head. Its legs stuck out like a frog's.

'That's me,' said Callum proudly. 'I was really premature. Mum was so ill before I was born, they thought she might die. She had pre-eclampsia and the doctors had to get me out before I died too.

She wasn't allowed to move for weeks. She just had to lie flat all the time.'

There were four others of Callum; one as a toddler in a hooded suit with ears; one in his school uniform, aged about four ('I only went for two or three years, it was rubbish'); one where he was sitting on a motorbike dressed as a Cavalier and one with him standing in front of a huge unframed painting. 'I did that,' he said. 'It's in oils. It was exhibited in Nantwich museum for a couple of months 'cause it won a competition. Mum's got it in her bedroom now. It's clouds.'

'Yeah, I can see that,' I lied. 'Wow. Really good.'

'And this one's Mum.' He pointed to a photograph of a middle-aged woman with longish dull blonde hair and a round, friendly face. She was wearing a black top with an embroidered neckline, and dangly earrings. 'One of her would-be boyfriends took that last year. She doesn't like it because you can see some wrinkles, but I think it's a good likeness.'

'She has a look of her sister.'

'Yeah, I thought so. Now this one, this is the first cloud picture I ever took. No filters or anything fancy, I just pointed the lens and snapped. But the strange thing is, I took the photo because I thought it looked like a dolphin leaping out of the water, only when I got it developed, it had changed and now, can you see, it's a face. Look. Turn it round. The eyes there, and that's the mouth. A sad face.'

His finger traced the outline for me.

'Then there's this one I took at Avebury, which is through an orange filter. It's as though there's a giant finger pointing to the tallest standing stone. Like the finger of God, except it was really an aeroplane trail.

'This next one's a place called Mow Cop, a sort of folly, and when you stand on the top you can see for miles. What I did here was to frame the section of cloud I wanted to highlight inside the stone arch, can you see? And I used a filter to give a kind of subtle rainbow effect.'

'Like petrol in a puddle.'

'Yeah, exactly. And these last two, I took them over water, Lake Coniston, so you got the light reflecting back up to the clouds and kind of illuminating them from underneath. The filters here add some depth to the shadows, that's all.'

He changes when he talks about his photographs, I thought.

'I like this one the best.' I put my fingertips on the Mow Cop one.

'Do you? I'll make you a copy. You know, you could come down some time and see the place for yourself, bring your own camera. I might even be able to drive by then.'

'Yeah, that'd be good,' I said, knowing it would never happen but really pleased he'd asked. I could imagine us up there, staring out across the fields and towns under a lowering sky. Suddenly my empty stomach dipped, gathered itself up, then let out the most enormous whine. I froze, mid-cringe.

Callum turned his head from side to side, brows furrowed in confusion. 'That's strange. I could've sworn I heard a cat. Did you hear a cat mew?' He bent to look under the table. 'Here, puss puss. Tch-tch-tch. Nope, can't see anything.' He sat upright again and his grin started me giggling.

'Stop it.'

'It must have nipped behind the desk. Probably

after a vole. Oh, wait, did you see its tail poking out then?'

'*Stop* it.'

'I think we'd better get some lunch before we both starve to death. Any minute now our intestines are going to break out into a duet, and I tell you, mine sings a lot louder than yours.'

I nodded gratefully. 'Right, well, we could get a sandwich at . . . ' My fingers touched the pendant's leather thong and I drew my wasp towards me. I would wear this. 'We could go home. Poll's not in.' I felt myself blush, but carried on. 'So she can't get cross, she needn't know. Come and see our house.'

'I thought you'd never ask,' he said.

As we walked the mile down the village to Poll's end, I pointed out Bank Top's invisible highlights. 'That's the site of a Tudor tithe barn.'

'What, that hardware shop?'

'Yeah. They bulldozed the barn in the Fifties. And across the road, all down that side, there used to be a row of stone cottages that dated from 1585. The walls were two feet thick and they had flagstones on the roof instead of slates.'

'Where those Sixties bungalows are? God, what a waste. How do you know all this?'

'School projects, and also they have some pictures in the library, have a look next time. Miss Dragon's a big fan of local history. Now, coming up, on our side, there used to be a pub called the Brickman's Arms, and when they demolished that in the early Seventies they found a wattle-and-daub wall which dated from the end of the twelfth century. And there used to be a cock-fighting pit at the back too, although I'm glad that's gone. Oh, mind that sick on the pavement.'

As we pulled level with the big council estate, I nodded towards the road leading onto it. 'That used to be called Four Lanes, but it's been renamed School Road because they built a new primary school at the end.'

Callum crossed over and walked a few paces along the pavement, trying to make out the detail of the grey Eighties building with its red tarmac playground.

I followed him across the road, even though I didn't want to, and stood next to him. 'It still makes me feel ill, just looking at the place. The number of times I've willed a bomb to drop on it.'

There was dog shit and fag ends mixed in with the grass at the edge of the pavement, just as there had been nine years ago, when some girls had bent me over this metal street sign one afternoon, and told me I was in the stocks. Then they'd pulled up my skirt so everyone could see my knickers and Julie Berry shouted out that they were dirty, which wasn't true. Then Clare Greenhalgh had whacked me on the backside with a tennis racquet, really hard, so it left a bruise along the top of my legs. When they'd got me crying, they ran off. Obviously I wasn't going to tell Callum about that.

He turned back, and we walked slowly on. 'So is that where your dad—and your mum went?'

I shook my head. 'Don't know where my mother went. Somewhere in Bolton, I think. And Dad was at the old Victorian school, we passed where it used to be a while back. Do you remember that cluster of orange semis near the church?'

'Not really.'

'Well, that's where it stood, originally, I should've said while we were walking past. It was

163

stone, with a nice gable in the middle of the roof. I've seen it in the background of Dad's Year 6 photograph. I can show you, if you're interested.'

It was a bright day and warm; above us, cumulus clouds lay on their backs like dogs waiting to be tickled. I felt so confident I was doing the right thing, taking him home. 'There's the cemetery. I'll take you in there one day.'

'Is it where your dad's buried?'

'No, but it's a good place, quiet. There are these fantastic red-hot pokers all along the front in June but they've gone over now.'

We reached the bottom end of the village, the top of the Brow. 'Nearly there,' I told him. 'The council put a Christmas tree up every year, on that traffic island. Then there's this village tradition called Stoning the Lights. All the youngsters from miles around join in. The bulbs last, oh, three days maximum. Last year some of the kids got ambitious and stoned the Rotary Santa as he went round the council estate. He's said he's not coming next time.'

And I could swap all this soon for Gothic quadrangles and spires, if I wanted, I thought.

I couldn't read Callum's expression as we finally stopped outside Poll's house. I tried to see it through his eyes; the low wall and the tiny patch of grass too small for a mower, that Dogman has to clipper into a rectangle for us; the stone windowsill marked streaky green; the peeling black door.

'Nice fanlight,' he said, looking up at the last piece of leaded light above the door frame. 'I notice next door's have had theirs taken out. Big mistake. Some people have no soul.'

I hurried him through the front room with its nasty wallpaper and swirly carpet, and into the back where Poll and I eat, watch TV, argue and sulk.

'You've a lot of lamps,' he said, looking round. 'It's like a lighting shop in here.'

'Has to be,' I replied, thinking of Poll squinting through her super-magnifier at her large-print thrillers. 'They could probably spot this house glowing from outer space.' I saw, now, the sheen on the walls where Poll trails her hand as she navigates the room. I'd never spotted it before. Ditto the cobwebs up above the picture rail, and the layer of grey fluff on the carpet underneath the gas fire. I do clean, but there's no point in running yourself ragged when Poll can't make out the dirt and Dogman doesn't care. Suddenly the house looked a tip.

'Come upstairs,' I said quickly, before I got too shy to say the words.

He was still gazing round like he was at some sort of an exhibition. 'OK. Great. Lead on.'

*   *   *

That last night, Poll hit Vince. There'd been shouting, but that was normal. I'd gone downstairs for some milk and I saw it happen. I don't know what the lead-up had been, she just went for him with the iron. He grabbed her hand and shoved her over so she fell against the sofa. The iron dropped out of her hand, hit the wall, and the base came away from the plastic casing.

She scrambled straight up again and ran at him. It was like watching a dog or something, she was wild. He got hold of one of her wrists but she clapped the other down hard over his ear. I could see it hurt from

165

the expression on his face.

She started slapping him repeatedly round his head and he was trying to hold her off. I'd have belted her back. After a minute, she stopped struggling and threw herself face down on the sofa. She pulled a cushion over her head and held it there. I tiptoed back up the stairs. Katherine was screaming so I sat on the landing for a while.

Later that night, it must have been around two, I woke up and Vince was in my room. He came over to the bed and looked at me. It was too late to pretend I was still asleep. I thought, this is it, he's going to rape me. ⌐ He leaned over and touched the covers. 'I don't know about you, lass, but I've hed enough. I'm flittin',' he said. 'Are you comin'?'

Chapter Fourteen

Winston was snoring on my candlewick bedspread, so I scooped him up, carried him across the landing and dropped him on Poll's. 'Pee there, if you want,' I told him.

Then I nipped back down to the kitchen and stuck the kettle on. While the water was boiling I made some inelegant cheese butties, but trimming off the blue-mould edges which is more than I do for Poll. I shoved the sandwiches on two Royal Albert side plates, brewed up, and plonked everything on a tray to take upstairs.

When I returned, Callum had taken his jacket off and was fiddling with something in the inside pocket. I'd have thought nothing of it but for the way he jerked his head up guiltily as I came

166

through the door.

'Dinner is served,' I said, pretending not to notice. 'I've had to sack the butler.'

'Oh, excellent.' He left his jacket alone and took the tea off me. 'I am so ready for this.'

I settled myself on the floor with my back against the wardrobe, because there was obviously no way I could sit next to him on the bed, but he got up then, sandwich in hand, and started wandering round the room touching things. He traced the diamond shapes on the bed frame with his fingers, set the little drop-handles on the chest of drawers quivering, bent sideways to check out more book spines. Then he stopped near the photos and stood for ages, while I tried to wipe some dust surreptitiously off the bookcase with my sleeve.

'Are all these your dad?'

'Yeah. Can you see the school in that one? Wasn't it a nice building? Poll went there too, when she was young. She says there were stuffed birds in cases on the wall, and a platform for the teacher's desk. And she got the cane for being naughty, although when Dad was there the Head just used a slipper.'

'He hit the pupils with a slipper? Sicko.'

'Weapon of choice for Primary headmasters in the Seventies. Dad got the slipper every other week.' Cissie had told me that, not Poll. 'He used to make a lot of stuff up, and they didn't like it. Nowadays you'd say he was being creative, using his imagination.'

'That's school for you, bunch of Fascists,' said Callum, kneeling to flick through Dad's old LPs. 'I more or less got chucked out in the end. They could have slippered me into oblivion and it

167

wouldn't have made any difference. I wouldn't do what the others were doing. I didn't see why there had to be set times for painting, and set times for maths, set times for Plasticine play and sand expression. I mean, why not let the kids follow their impulses? That way, you'll get real impetus behind each individual child's work.'

'You told them all that when you were seven?'

'Oh yeah. Well, my mum did. They kept calling her in, for "interviews". She got more and more defensive, 'cause basically they were calling her a bad parent, inadequate single mother, till one day she marched me out of the building and said, "You're not going back there again." And I never did. It was great.' He eased out a record spine with his finger nail. 'Hey, here's that Human League album you were telling me about.' He rose, walked backwards to the bed and sat down, still holding the LP. 'And Mum was such a great teacher. She made learning fun, and if it was sunny we'd go outside, or take the day off. My dad sent us some money so she didn't have to work, although we were always a bit strapped for cash. It didn't matter, though, because we got by.'

I felt a pang of jealousy, hearing him talk about his mum like that. That kind of support must make a difference.

'Well, my Grandma took me out of school because I was being bullied,' I said. It was true; Poll had saved me from God knows what. Ritual burning, probably.

'Girls can be bitches,' said Callum, his eyes scanning the lyric sheet. 'They all have to dress the same, like the same music, that sort of thing. There's a girl at college, Lizzo, really funky, bit

168

Goth, and she said she'd had a terrible time in Year 9 because she stood out and wouldn't join in with all the trends.'

'They thought I was a witch.'

'What?' Callum put the album down and blinked at me.

'The other kids in my class. First they thought I was weird because of living with my grandma and having no mum or dad. And because I, because I didn't look like they did.' (*Oi, Pavarotti, Fatty-bum-bum. Look, she's got tits already!*) 'Then something happened. They thought I'd caused it, so I became a witch.'

There was a split second where I thought, Christ, I shouldn't have told him. Why did I have to fuck everything up by telling him what a crap person I really was?

'Oh my God,' said Callum. 'How cool is that?'

'Not cool at all, actually. A right pain.'

'No, no it is cool. Wow. A witch.' He leaned forward, encouragingly. 'So what was it exactly that you did?'

I thought of Donna's aniseed balls. 'Hell. I wish I'd never said. Look, you've got to promise not to make fun of me after, if I tell you.'

Callum offered up his palms. High above his head, a long furry cobweb wagged in the breeze. 'As if,' he said.

How could I not believe him? He'd come here, to this room from last century, with Vince's pictures of warplanes still up and dead people stashed away in corners, and he'd never flinched. He must have seen other girls' bedrooms, normal bedrooms, but he hadn't scoffed or made smart comments. Dad's jar was on the windowsill behind

169

his head. I knew Callum was OK.

'Right, then, are you sitting comfortably? Because it's a long story, if you include all the build-up.'

'You have to have the build-up.' Callum grinned.

'You do, don't you? OK, well, there was this boy. I mean, a lot of them used to hassle me and muck about with my books, my coat and stuff, but there was this one boy, Jason Roper, who was a year old for our class. I suppose they kept him back so he'd catch up or something. He was big and mouthy and he'd shout things from the climbing frame, and spit as you walked past.' (*You big fat cow, you're mental, you are, you still wear nappies and your grandma gets your clothes off the tip.*) 'So one day he was really having a go, about me not having a dad and my mum running off, and he was so into it all he overbalanced and fell right off, head-first. I was just standing there while he was writhing about and spitting blood; some moron had left their skateboard on the ground and he'd smashed his mouth against the edge of it. Then one of the girls suddenly screamed, "It was her, she did it. Katherine Millar hexed him." He pulled some strange faces, then looked at me and splurted, "Where's my tooth?" The dickhead had swallowed it. But I heard myself say, in this spooky voice, "I've made it disappear. You'll never get it back." ' (*You fucking evil witch. I'll have you, you're dead.*) 'I thought he'd try to hit me, but he ran off to the toilets, trailing blood down his shirt front.'

'Do it again, that spooky voice, it was really good. Really witchy.'

'Get away, you're putting me off. Where was I, oh yeah; I don't know why I came out with something like that, you know, against myself, because after that the other kids wouldn't leave me alone. I was Witchy-poo all afternoon and the next day too.

'Before, I'd been teased about my family and—stuff—but suddenly it got more serious. A friend of Jason's, Christopher Horton, wouldn't stop making evil-eyes at me, and he tried to throw salt at me in the dinner queue because he reckoned that it killed a witch's powers. That could've been the end of it, a two-day wonder, because within forty-eight hours Jason had passed the tooth and seen it go down the toilet. But then Christopher had an Accident.'

Callum's mouth hung open. 'Shit, what happened?'

'He got clipped by a bus, playing chicken. He wasn't badly hurt, just shaken up and bruised. But everyone blamed it on me, they said it was a curse I'd put on him.'

'Hang on, what's chicken?'

'You know, where you run out in front of a moving vehicle at the very last minute. Did they not play that round your way?'

'No, they didn't. So, let me get this straight, he blamed you for nearly getting run over while he was playing a game where the object is to nearly get run over? Durr. Was he as thick as his friend?'

I laughed. 'It wasn't a class full of geniuses, no. I started getting pictures of pentangles left in my desk, or I assume they were meant to be pentangles, a lot of them were those Jewish six-pointed stars because they're not so tricky to draw. One girl, Julie Berry, used to ask where my broomstick was every bloody playtime, it became a major nuisance. Then one day, while the teacher

171

was round the other side of the building breaking up a fight, this Julie announced to her friends that witches should be stoned and she threw a pebble at me.' (*Next time it'll be a brick, Witchy-poo. You better watch your back.*) 'So I lost my temper, 'cause it was just going on and on, and I shouted that Something Terrible would happen to her within fourteen days.'

Callum looked impressed. 'I bet that put the wind up them.'

'Yeah. They all went dead quiet. It's quite funny now, looking back, but it wasn't at the time.'

'Do you know, I'm seeing a whole new side to you. So go on, did she die horribly?'

'I wish. She had a rotten fortnight, though. I took in a doll I'd made out of bits of cloth, with some hair attached, and let her friend catch a glimpse of it. You know, like it was by mistake. I made sure she saw there was a big darning needle stuck through its middle.'

'And was it Julie's hair?'

'God, no, how would I have got hold of that? She never came within six feet of me. No, it was off Dogman's spaniel, Kylie. She had ears more or less the same colour as Julie's plait. And so there was a great debate raging amongst the girls, about how Julie should tell a teacher or her mum, or whether that would make the curse more potent, and whether it was worth looking up counter-curses on the Internet, and I had two of her mates come to me and plead with me to take the spell off. But I said that once a spell had been cast, there was no way of cancelling it out. It had its own momentum, I told them, like the laws of physics. I remember saying to them, "This isn't Mildred bloody Hubble you know, this is for real." They nearly wet themselves. If Julie herself had come and apologized for being such a cow, I might have pretended to sort it for her, but she hated me too much.' My heart was thudding as I thought myself back to that time. It was strange how fresh the feelings still were after eight years. 'The sad thing was, I was beginning to think I actually was a witch.'

Callum laid himself back on the bed with his feet hanging over the end. 'You and about a million others.'

'What do you mean?'

'How many people carry lucky charms round with them, or touch wood to ward off evil? Or have a special rhyme they use if they spot a hearse? Or walk round, instead of under, ladders? Personally speaking, I get spooked by magpies; never pass a magpie without greeting it politely, or you're asking for trouble, Mum taught me that. Everybody believes in witchcraft, to a degree.'

'You don't think I was being—abnormal?'

'I think you sound like the most normal person in your class,' said Callum calmly. I flushed with pleasure. 'Yeah, I really do. I thought my school was bad. What a bunch of fuckwits. What happened to Julie in the end?'

'Nothing much. It got to day thirteen and she was really wound up, and then day fourteen arrived and she was like, "Ha ha, I knew it was a con, let's get Witchy-poo Weirdo." When I realized how truly pissed off she was I scarpered, left the premises even though we hadn't even had morning assembly yet, and ran home. I told Poll I was ill, and she fed me cake and let me watch TV for a while before handing me the mop and telling me to wash the flags. She's always thought education's overrated. I thought what I'd do was, I'd stay off the rest of the week, then go back on the Monday when maybe Julie would have cooled down. Only, that very evening, her chinchilla died.'

'Dah-dah-daaaah.' Callum put his hands to his face and rolled his head about, imitating extreme horror. 'Oh, Christ, not her chinchilla.'

'No, stop laughing, it was a tragedy as far as she was concerned. She'd had it for years and she loved it more than her granny, she always said. She was way too distressed to come to school. I heard she made her family hold a funeral for him in the garden. And the fact that he was ten had nothing to do with his death, it was clearly my evil spell that had stopped his little heart beating. You can imagine how welcome I was at school, come the Monday.'

'Katherine Millar, chinchilla-killer?'

'Got it in one.'

'Jesus. And so you left school.'

'No, not then. No, you haven't heard the worst of it yet.'

Callum hauled himself up on one elbow. 'Bloody hell, what did you do? Set the place on fire?'

'Credit me with a bit more imagination,' I said, waving my hands at him in a witchy way.

He put his index fingers into a cross-shape and raised them in front of his brow. 'Oh no, you don't get me like that, you fiend. I am immune to your supernatural powers.'

'That's what you think. Listen, I only got the entire school banned from Chester Zoo. *And* they had to draft in an educational psychologist to deal with the fall-out.'

'I'll sit up for this,' he said. 'Go on.'

'Well, I got the idea from Dogman, he was my mate in those days. I used to go for walks with him and his dogs, he had three then. One of them was an ex-rescue greyhound bitch, Mollie, very nervy, she never stopped barking. He said the neighbours were getting sick of her and he was going to have to do something before they contacted Environmental Health. So he bought a dog-dazer.' I held up my hand. 'Before you ask, it's a little electronic device about the size of a matchbox that you use to subdue troublesome mutts. Press a button and it emits an ultra-high-pitched sound that only doggies can hear. They hate it, it must be like nails down a blackboard, and you use it to train them out of bad habits. You know, woof—zap. Or chew—zap.'

'Or hump—zap.'

'Dunno, probably. I had charge of the dog-dazer and I trained Mollie myself, although she had to be put down in the end because she kept attacking men in uniform. Afterwards Dogman let me borrow it so I could stop Winston eating the fence, and that's when I decided it would be a laugh to take it on a school trip.

'The girls at school were being totally horrible now and they were particularly shitty that day. I wanted to go round on my own but the teacher reckoned we had to stay in groups. All the bitchiest kids were in with me, Julie, Clare, Christopher, Jason, the whole brigade. I'm sure the teacher did it deliberately. Because she could hear them going on at me but she never stopped them. So we did the elephants and giraffes, the boring stuff, then we all trooped over to the Bat Zone. It's a huge mock

175

cave containing the largest collection of bats in Britain, and you had to push your way into it through some heavy plastic bat-proof strips hanging down like creepers, which kind of slithered over your neck and shoulders. That alone was freaking some of the girls out, that and the darkness inside.

'Jason said to me as we walked through the entrance, "This should be right up your street, Witchy-poo." So I said, "Yeah, I love bats, actually." And he said, "Yeah, well, you are a bat. Fat bat," and I said, "I can control these bats. I can make these bats do whatever I command." Just as I was speaking, a bat flew low over him and he didn't half jump. Clare, who was standing next to him, gave a little scream and we all began to realize just how many bats were in there; you can't make them out at first till your eyes adjust to the gloom, then they're everywhere. I took the dog-dazer out of my pocket but slyly, so no one saw, then I turned to Jason and said, "Right, are you watching? I'm going to say a magic spell and *all the bats will take flight simultaneously*." Jason goes, "Like fuck they will. Who do you think you are, Vampira?" but he sounded worried. Clare said, "Oh, don't, Katherine, wait till I get out, please." I laughed in her face like a madwoman and she screamed again, then she tried to make a dash for the exit but you couldn't run because there were so many people there and the pathways were too narrow. That's when I pressed the dog-dazer.

'Maybe it was coincidence, I don't know; maybe the bats picked up the scent of human hysteria, but suddenly it was like a black storm. Every bat in that cave left its perch and began swooping round. The air was thick with bats in an instant, I swear there must have been two hundred, and some of the tropical ones were the size of briefcases. All the kids and most of the adults were totally spooked; a lot of them were standing still with their heads bowed, but a lot were struggling to get out of the cave. I spotted Julie cowering in a rock crevice, her eyes closed, so I went up and ruffled her hair, shouting, "Oh my God, there's a giant bat on your head. Look out, it's biting your neck." She went ballistic and started hyperventilating. After a minute, an alarm sounded and some extra doors were opened to one side, and zoo staff rushed in to try to get everyone out and calm the bats.

'When we got outside everyone was in a state. Christopher was squirting Ventolin down his throat and Clare had wet her nice turned-up jeans. But Jason was a burning flame of indignation because, for once, it wasn't him in trouble. He was literally jumping up and down and pointing at me, shouting, "It was *her*. *She* did it. It's her fault." Some of the other kids joined in, those that weren't weeping or traumatized into silence. Mrs Kirtlan hauled me off to the side and looked me straight in the eye; I mean, I was smirking from ear to ear while everybody else was in shock. She said, "Are you in some way responsible for this mayhem?" And I said, "Yes," because at that moment I felt really proud of myself. "How?" she asked. So I showed her the dog-dazer.

'I had to spend an hour in the zoo office explaining what I'd done—I think they were worried I'd start a trend, because they'd had some trouble with sickos pointing laser pens at the big cats' eyes. I kept saying I was sorry if I'd hurt the bats but I don't think anyone believed me. Then the Deputy Head arrived in her car to take me home separately.

'And that was it. On the Monday, the Headmaster had my grandma in for a "chat" and told her the other parents were up in arms about me, Clare couldn't sleep for nightmares, Julie had hung garlic all round her bedroom, that sort of thing. He probably wanted to say a lot more but Poll never let him finish. The funny thing is, she criticizes me herself all the time, but she wasn't going to take it from him; at one point she threw a paperweight at him. I wish I'd been there. And the result was that I had a year off.'

'Fucking hell. So Poll tutored you?'

I laughed out loud. 'Poll? You must be kidding. I taught myself, more or less.'

'What, and Social Services let you?' Callum looked incredulous. ' 'Cause they were always on my mum's case, checking up.'

'Well, Miss Dragon helped me draw up a programme of work for the Support Officer to see, and provided me with some answers-in-the-back-type textbooks. She set me a few projects and did a spot of marking here and there. Mainly, though, I cribbed up on old Ladybirds.' I pulled *The Public Services: Water Supply* out of the bookcase and passed it to him. 'By the end of the year I'd the History series off by heart, all of Nature and Conservation, and my knowledge of Sixties technology was second to none. The Support Officer who interviewed me had his doubts, but I reckon what clinched it was when we went out into the back garden to look at my home-made rain gauge, and he commented on the spectacular

178

mackerel sky there was that day. I said, "I think you'll find they're cirrocumulus clouds, actually." He scribbled something down on his clipboard and left. The next year I started at the grammar school where, I can honestly say, I haven't touched a bat since.'

Callum rose to his feet and applauded. 'Jesus. Kat Millar, that is one hell of a story. You are so . . . ' He didn't finish, just shook his head at me, smiling, and sat down again. 'I take my hat off to you for sheer surreal inventiveness. Dog-dazer! The only times I've tried to get revenge on someone it's been pathetic, small-scale stuff. Prittstick on a chair, dropping someone's folder down the back of a cupboard. A rank amateur. Though I did once leave a king prawn in a glove box.'

'A prawn? What kind of cruel bastard does that to an innocent shellfish?' I felt so high now I'd told him and he'd been OK.

'It was *dead*. It was supposed to smell terrible after a while and send the owner of the car crazy. But he found it immediately and threw it out the window. Then I got called Prawn-balls for a while, but it wasn't serious, he was a mate.'

'*Prawn-balls?*'

'Uh-huh. Mary Prawn-balls. It doesn't do much for a guy's image.'

'I can imagine.'

'You've gone all pink.'

'I know, I do. After you with that hanky.'

When we'd sobered up slightly, I decided I knew him well enough to ask whether he wanted to help clear out the sink cupboard.

'Well, shit, you sure know how to show a lad a good time,' he said, starting to laugh again. 'OK,

179

then. On one condition.'

'What's that?'

'That I'm invited to this birthday do next week.' He pointed to Donna's invite, which I'd stuck in the wooden frame of the oval mirror that hangs above the chest of drawers.

He completely threw me. 'Oh, that. I didn't know what you—I'm not going, to be honest . . . ' A happy thought struck me. 'And even if I was, how would you get back to Nantwich? It goes on till one in the morning.'

'Oh, yeah. You've got a point. Forget it, then. I'll still help you do your sticky cupboard, though.'

'Good man.'

'I might have to have a slash first. It was a big mug of tea.'

'Straight across the landing, the door without the disgusting ceramic Westie plaque on it.'

The second the toilet door shut, I stopped grinning and made a dive for Callum's jacket. In the inside pocket, carefully folded into a tiny square, was one of Dad's early biology drawings: <u>Cockroach:</u> *A) Dorsal View B) Ventral View 1. Head 2. Thorax 3. Abdomen 4. Antenna 5. Wings 6. Veins* or

nervures 7. Segment 8. Spiracle 9. Trochanter 10. Coxa 11. Femur 12. Tarsus.

I turned the note over but there was nothing obvious on the back. The toilet flushed so I folded the diagram back up again and stuck it in the pocket. What on earth did he want with that? I so wanted to ask him, but I didn't want to admit I'd been rifling through his clothes.

'I've been thinking about all you've just told me,' he said as he walked back in. 'Amazing. And you're so modest about it.'

'It didn't occur to me there was anything to show off about,' I shrugged. In truth, it had always been a millstone of shame around my neck.

He smiled. 'You're a dark horse, you.'

You took the words right out of my mouth, I nearly said.

*　　　*　　　*

Are you tekkin' Katherine's pram? Only I'll hev to put t' back seats deahn,' Vince whispered from the doorway.

I jumped. 'No,' I said. He went away for a bit but then he came back with a bag full of clothes.

'What about her sterilizer?'

'No,' I hissed. 'No, none of it.'

He stopped trying to zip up his holdall. 'Well, how're you goin' to manage?'

I just looked at him.

'Oh,' he said. 'Reet.' He wandered off and everything went quiet. After a minute or two, he stuck his head round the door and said, 'I'll go and unclip t' baby carrier an' bring it in again, then, shall I?'

I went over to the cot to say goodbye but I didn't kiss her in case I woke her and the screaming started up once more. I didn't want to leave to the sound of that. Anyway, we were trying not to alert Poll. I can honestly say I felt nothing except relief that I was leaving my baby.

In the car, before we set off, I tried to explain to Vince how I felt. 'Do you know that story about Sinbad, where a little old man tricks his way onto Sinbad's shoulders and then won't get off? And he rides him like a horse, and turns Sinbad into his permanent slave? And when Sinbad gets angry, the old man beats him with a stick and throttles him with his thin little legs? And Sinbad has to get the old man drunk to escape?'

Vince was staring at me as if I was mad. 'You can always go back for her when you're feeling more yourself,' was all he said.

He turned the key in the ignition and we drove off into the night.

Chapter Fifteen

The phone on the sideboard rang at eleven the next morning.

'Kat?'

'Yeah?'

'Guess who.'

'God, I don't know.' I didn't either, not straight away. How was I to know Callum would phone me at home. Then light dawned. 'Oh. It's you, isn't it?'

'I can't deny it, it's me.'

'How did you get my number?'

'Rang Directory Enquiries, bozo, how do you think?'

'Oh, yeah.' Obviously. 'What is it?'

'I can hardly hear you, you're very faint. You sound like you're in outer space. Can you speak up?'

It was force of habit. Even when Poll wasn't in, as now, I still felt I needed to whisper if I was up to anything personal. Not that I had a lot of intimate phone calls to my history. 'Sorry. Is everything OK?'

'Yeah, fine. I thought I'd let you know, I've been doing some research and there's a train goes from Bolton at half-past midnight.'

Standing where I was, I could see straight through to the front-room window that looks out onto the street. Some boys of about ten were walking past up the hill, throwing gun caps on the pavement and shrieking when they exploded. I heard a dog bark from a distance, and some adult voice shouting, then the boys' jeering and swearing and more bangs.

'Well done, that's terrific,' I said to Callum. 'Goes where?'

'Crewe.' He sounded impatient.

'And the reason you're telling me is?'

There was a rapping sound from down the line. Then Callum came back on again. 'That was me banging the receiver against my head. Listen, I mean I can go to that party, I'll just have to leave early. Probably about ten past, quarter past twelve, depending on how far away the station is from the club.'

'It's pretty close,' I said before I could stop myself.

'Great.'

'But, Callum, look, I'm not going.' I leant against the sideboard and knocked a piece of paper to the floor. When I bent to see, it was a postcard from Rebecca that Poll must have picked up and neglected to tell me about.

Having a great time checking out National Trust properties. Going to see a garden tomorrow landscaped by Capability Brown! Counting the hours till Results Day!!! Becks X

Becks?

'—thought it might be a laugh,' Callum was saying. 'I'm always up for a party.'

'I don't like clubs,' I said, hoping he wouldn't guess I'd never been in one. The front of the postcard showed blank-eyed Poseidon in marble.

'Shame. It would have been a laugh.'

'So you said.'

'Hey, is Poll there?'

'No. She's—' I thought quickly; 'having her dinner at the Working Men's with Dogman.'

Poll doesn't go visiting much, because in general people put furniture in stupid places. But the truth was, Poll had gone round to Maggie's with a bunch of magazines and some bottles of Guinness because Maggie had fallen in our kitchen and sprained her ankle. The reason I didn't want to tell Callum was that Maggie had slipped on one of my Poll-traps, which he'd seen me setting up. 'Why, exactly, are you trailing a line of wash liquid across the doorway, Kat?' he'd asked, sliding the last box of antique Robin starch back in the cupboard for me. 'Mice,' I'd told him. He didn't ask again, so I suppose he believed me. Well, he'd effectively lied to me about the cockroach drawing.

'Dogman?' Callum snorted. 'What a name. I'm going to have to see this bloke some time. Does he actually look like a dog?'

'No, he smells like one.' And given half a chance, he'd clamp himself to your leg.

'Nice. So, you're definitely not going on Saturday?'

'No.'

'OK. Well, I'll, er, I'll be in touch. Is it all right to

184

ring you here?'

'Not really. If Poll picked up the phone and it was your voice, a male voice, I'd never hear the last of it.' I could just imagine the sort of things she'd say, my life wouldn't be worth living. And if she found out who he really was, my God.

'And you've not got a mobile, have you.'

'No.' No point: no one to ring.

'Have you got a Hotmail account? I could email you at the library.'

'Sorry.' How crap is she, he must have been thinking. 'It's OK to send messages through Miss Dragon. So long as you don't call her Miss Dragon.'

Callum made a noise that might have been a sigh, or simply an extra-large breath. 'Right. Fine. I'll be sending you a message, sometime.'

After he'd rung off I felt utterly flat. I went upstairs and tried on the basque again—now too loose—and the black skirt, with the boots. Then I put some make-up on and wetted my hair down so it wasn't quite so sproingy, then I twisted it up and fastened it with a jumbo slide and teased some strands down on either side of my face. I got the nail clippers out and snipped off some of the madder hairs from my eyebrows. Before I took it all off again, I pulled the curtains to, so the bedroom was in semi-darkness, and tried to imagine what I'd look like in a club. Stupid, was the answer, so I drew the curtains and put everything away. I left my hair up, though, and also I did put a couple of stitches in the back seam of the basque, because it seemed a pity not to. I could still detect Callum's male scent lingering by the bed.

'Hoy, Katherine.' I heard the front door bang

185

open and Poll clatter in. 'Are y' up there? Katherine?'

'Katherine,' shouted Dogman in a particularly stupid voice. 'Katerina!'

She reached the bottom of the stairs and yelled, 'Are we gettin' our dinner on? Dickie's fetched a big box o' beefburgers, and Maggie's sent you one of them giant

Toblerones. Next door brought it her off their holidays but she says she han't the teeth to cope with it.'

Dogman started up, I don't know who ever told him he could sing.

Well I was there, so were you
The mayor and the vicar and the council too
All the wives and ladies on full view
The night John Willie took his ferret to a do.

I checked my watch. Time for a binge.

*   *   *

The night before Donna's party, I had a funny dream. I was in a stone tower, I saw it first from the outside and then I was in it, trapped on the top floor. I'd laid an egg, and Callum was there. He said, 'I'll look after it, your egg. Trust me.' He put it inside his underpants to keep warm and then started to climb out of the window, holding on to my hair to stop himself falling. My head was hanging over the sill and I heard him say, 'I know a great recipe for Spanish omelette.' Then I woke up and found my plait was fast down the side of the headboard.

So I was in a foul temper all day and Poll, for once, insisted on coming late-afternoon shopping,

186

and that was probably why the Great Row happened. We'd been sniping most of the morning, through dinner, and all the way up to Spar. Then, round the aisles, she kept putting daft things in the basket and I kept taking them out again and slamming them back down on the shelves. It was like taking a naughty toddler round.

'We don't have a dishwasher, well we do, it's me, but we don't need dishwasher tablets,' I snapped, snatching them out of her wrinkly hand.

'They're for t' washin' machine,' she argued. 'I've seen 'em on t' telly, big white tablets. You know nowt, you do.'

'At least I can read,' I said nastily. An elderly woman I didn't recognize glanced across the freezer cabinet, saw Poll's white stick and frowned at me. Heartless teen attacking disabled grannie. 'Who put these crystallized violets in? As if I didn't know.'

'They looked like cotton buds,' she said, glowering. 'They're in t' same sized container. And you've finished t' others off and never towd me.'

'I did not. I never use cotton buds.'

'Well, you've shifted 'em, then. You know how important it is for me t' have my toiletries in one place. Otherwise it could be disastrous.'

It was Maggie who'd once stopped Poll at the last minute from rinsing her hair with Toilet Duck.

'Yeah, but how am I supposed to clean when there's clutter everywhere?' I threw two bars of Galaxy in the basket, and a multi-pack of Milky Ways. 'You can't stick a pin between the bottles on that bathroom ledge. Sometimes I have to move your bits and pieces because they're thick with dust. There's all dead flies and moths behind them

187

on the windowsill. *Don't* put that packet of baby food in.'

'It's rice, it says; see.' Poll shook the yellow box aggressively in my face.

'*Baby* rice. Not proper rice, Put it back.'

She did, and knocked a load of rusks onto the floor. 'Now see what you've done,' she said.

'God.' I scrabbled the rusks up and shoved them back where they'd come from. 'Can we get a move on? Because I'm really beginning to get fed up.'

Poll turned to me, her mouth small and pious. 'You're fed up? You are? You should try going blind. It's a ruddy picnic.'

She pulled away from me and tottered off down towards the checkout, only she went off at a tangent and crashed into a revolving stand of cards. I saw her keel over, and birthday greetings spill across the tiled floor. Several customers ran to help.

'Can you stand, love? Are you feeling dizzy? Did it knock your shoulder? Daft place to put a carousel, in't it? You could sue.'

I let them rush in, do their St John's Ambulance routine, while I leant against the chilled desserts and tried to take some of the weight off the wire handles that were digging into my arm. Watching her being pulled onto her skinny legs, her headscarf askew, I thought how harmless and pathetic she must look to an outsider. The manager came out from the back and offered her a wet wipe.

She mopped her brow bravely and made to hand them back.

'No, no, keep them,' he said, staking a £1.59 packet of moist tissues against a call from the

Accident Helpline. I knew, by the glee on her face as she stowed them in her bag, that she was perfectly all right.

'Eeh, I think I could walk if I had a sip o' Bailey's,' she said hopefully.

Once outside she dropped the dying duck routine and laid into me.

'Them people in there, they care more about what happens to me than you do. Standing there like you're simple while your own flesh and blood writhes in agony on t' floor. It's not on. And you can stop pulling faces. Just because I'm blind doesn't mean I can't see.'

'Tell me something I don't know.' I gripped the carrier bags tightly and the Bailey's chinked against a jar of pickled onions.

'If you brek that bottle—'

'Oh, give it a rest.'

'Don't speak to me in that tone of voice, lady.' She wagged her stick at me.

'It's not like you're my mother,' I said, and waited for the thunderclap.

We were passing the church where the pavement's really narrow. Poll stopped dead in her tracks, so I ran into her. 'Oof! Your mother?' She steadied herself against the wall and glared into my face, breathing hard. 'I should damn well think I'm not. I'm sane, for a start. I haven't run off and left a helpless infant to fend for itself. I haven't wrecked a marriage. I haven't—' pause while she pulled out a hanky from up her sleeve—'I haven't tekken anyone's son away from them.' Blowing of the nose, dabbing of the eyes. 'So, no, I'm not your mother, and you should be bloody grateful for it. God only knows what sort of a mess you'd be if she'd had owt to do with your upbringing.'

I'd heard this speech before over the years so it didn't have the force it should have had. I gave her a little dig in the small of her back to start her moving again and pushed in front of her, desperate to get home. We were still in the public High Street and, yes, there was Mrs Threlfall across the road, waving. Too late to pretend I hadn't seen her.

'Maud's out of hospital,' she shouted to Poll, in between traffic. Poll swung her head round to locate the speaker. 'Maud Eckersley. She's to wait on some test results.'

'Did you hear that?' I grumbled, half-turning.

Poll ignored me. 'Tell her Get Well Soon from me,' she yelled in Mrs Threlfall's general direction. Much nodding and waving, but we managed to carry on moving down the village.

Where the footpath widened, by the Indian, I slowed so I was level with her. We walked in silence for thirty seconds while I tried to get the words sorted out in my head. 'Yeah, well, you say all that about my mother—'

'Because it's true.'

'But you've always told me what to think, you've never let me decide for myself.'

'Decide what? What's to decide? The woman killed your father, oh, hell fire.' She got out the hanky again and stood still while she wiped under her eyes. Now we were almost outside Porter's Newsagents and I just knew someone was going to come out the door and march straight into the melodrama. I touched her arm with the intention of pulling her along, but she jerked it away irritably. I'm not going to let this conversation drop, I told her silently; doesn't matter what sort of feeble pose you strike.

'It's not that simple, though, is it?' I went on. 'Up till now, I've always swallowed your version of events. No one's ever told me the story except you, so I've only ever had your side. But I've been thinking recently, and some things don't add up. Like, if my mother really was a murderer, an actual murderer, how come the police didn't arrest her straight away? How come she isn't mouldering in prison somewhere?' I suddenly remembered a book I'd read as a child where that had been the twist. 'Oh my God, she's not, is she?'

Poll spat against Porter's wall, all tears gone, and wiped her lips on her cuff. 'Don't be soft. Of course she's not.'

'So is she on the run? Did she have to change her identity to escape the law?'

'Escape? That's the right word for it. No, she feigned madness so they let her be. She should have been put away, anyroad. I'd have had her strung up, a life for a life.'

I stared down at the top of Poll's headscarf, at the little interlinking horseshoe pattern round the border. 'Look at me, Poll. Look at me, this is important.' She raised her chin very slightly so I could see her sour mouth, but not her eyes. 'I thought you said she *was* mad. Are you telling me now she was putting it on?'

'Hello, ladies,' said a cheerful voice. Oh bloody hell, now it was Mr Ashcroft from the Over Seventies, stepping out of the newsagent's with a *Chronicle* and twenty Player's. 'Nice to see a bit of sun out.'

'Aye, it is,' said Poll without enthusiasm.

'We were due some.' He checked me up and

191

down and shook his head slightly, but I'm used to this treatment. I gawped back rudely and he turned to Poll. 'Where's your little dog today? He's not poorly, is he?'

'He's resting at home. He gets tired.'

'Don't we all?' Mr Ashcroft chuckled. 'I say, don't we all?' He stopped laughing when I scowled at him. 'I'll let you get on, then; I bet them bags of Katherine's are heavy, aren't they? Just as well you're a big strong lass.'

He may have sensed some violence in me because he shuffled off pretty quick, considering he's got emphysema, and Poll and I plodded on.

'So are you saying my mum wasn't really mad?'

Poll shrugged. 'Do I look like a doctor? All I know is, she went mental when it suited her, that's all. She recovered fast enough, after.'

This was good news, because I'd always worried she might have passed insanity on to me.

'I don't know why you're smiling,' said Poll. 'It means she was sound of mind when she decided she didn't want you any more.'

Poll's the sort of woman who enjoys dropping salt on slugs. I wish you were a slug, I thought; I'd season you to death. As we hovered to cross the road, the temptation to guide her into the path of a speeding van was enormous; to sing out, 'All clear,' and watch her get splatted against the tarmac. Her bloodstained headscarf left flapping in the gutter. Then the van and the moment passed and the road was empty except for Mr Boardman's electric bicycle, and no good pushing her out in front of that. I made sure she walked through some dirty great puddles on the way to the other side, though.

'I still want to know more about her,' I persisted

as we turned down the Brow. 'Whatever she did to me. I want to know, *things*, like, where she went to school, what sort of music she liked, her favourite film. I've never even seen a photo.' (Fingers crossed behind my back.) 'It's crazy, she's my mum.'

Poll stumped on with her head down. 'She doesn't matter, I've told you. You're better off without her, you always have been. Forget her.'

'But that's for me to decide. Isn't it? My right? I'm her daughter.'

A car horn blaring feet away made us both jump: Maggie's Dawn sweeping past in her silver Jeep, waving like a lunatic.

'Godfathers.' Poll clapped her hand to her chest. 'Who were it?'

'No one. A dog ran out. It's all right, though. It's gone in Aspull's garden.'

'That's a relief. Listen.' Poll stopped again and drew herself up straight, facing me. 'Let me ask you summat. Think back. Who was it sat up with you all night for weeks when you had croup and couldn't breathe? Filling bowls of boiling water for the steam and putting them all round? Who was it went trailing up to school that time they took you over t' fence and rolled you in a cowpat and you needed a change of clothes? Who was it gave that headmaster a good hiding, and convinced the education officer to leave you alone for a year? Who's shelled out for your fancy uniform all these years, blazers sixty pound a time, and we can't get second-hand because there's no one in your size?'

Yes, and I've paid you back for it, every penny, haven't I? Waiting on you hand and foot, your unpaid servant. I just gritted my teeth and said, 'I

193

know. But I still wish I knew where she was.'

'Well,' said Poll, flashing me an angry glance, 'I'll tell you what I think. The sort of creature she was, she's almost certainly at the bottom of a canal somewhere, or tekken an overdose or thrown herself off summat high. You go rooting about, you're going to find stuff you wish you'd never known. Sometimes it's better to live in ignorance.'

'Oh, well, this is the place for it, then. This whole damn village is founded on ignorance. I'm getting sick of ignorance!' I erupted. 'I'm sick of your take on the world, this hide-under-the-table attitude. I'm eighteen now, for God's sake. I could be married, all right, stop sniggering, I could be moving out and living in a place of my own with a job and everything.'

'You? You'd never cope, not on your own. It's dangerous out there, I've told you often enough.' We'd reached the house. 'Life's all about tragedy; you don't believe me now, but you'll know about it when you get to my age.'

Like age means you're wise. You are so full of shit, Poll Millar.

I badly needed something sweet so I hauled the shopping through to the kitchen and located the Milky Ways. I unwrapped two to be eating while I threw the duller items in cupboards, so my mouth was crammed with chocolate when I heard the cistern flush upstairs.

'Poll?'

'What?' she snapped, and her voice was too close.

I put my head round the kitchen doorway and she was sitting on the sofa trying to lever a shoe off.

'Hang on.' I gulped the chocolate down. 'There's

194

someone upstairs, using our toilet.'

'Oh, aye, that'll be Dickie. He said he was coming round.'

'Did you leave the door open?'

'No need,' grinned Dogman as he walked into the room, cool as you please.

'Dickie has his own key now,' said Poll, in a kind of Go on, I dare you to say something tone.

'I have,' said Dogman, holding up an enormous bunch of keys and rattling them smugly. 'Well, your grandma thought it made sense. I'm always round here.'

You can say that again, I thought. Fucking hell. 'How come you've got so many keys?'

But Dogman just laughed.

'Are you puttin' t' kettle on, or what?' said Poll.

When I came back, Dogman was jiggling a cardboard box in his arms and looking pleased with himself. 'There you go,' he said to me, holding the box out. 'One man's shit is another man's gold.'

I peered in. A load of old tat, how kind, you shouldn't have. 'What is it?'

'Women's things. Poll's had a root through earlier, but there's nowt she fancies. Here, tek it.'

Out of curiosity I did, dropping the remaining Milky Ways in too. When I got upstairs I tipped the box out on the floor and knelt beside it. A bunch of used cosmetics fell out; it looked for all the world as if Dogman had gone into someone's house and just cleared their dressing table while they were out. Even the brush had hairs wrapped round it; that went straight in the bin. The lipsticks were worn to chisel tips and the eye shadows starting to spill from their containers. But, bless the smelly old bastard, he'd scooped me a hot tong thing that

195

looked like it might, at a pinch, go some way to taming my hair. It was dirty round the handle and the barrel was covered in a layer of sticky brown, which I assumed was baked hairspray. I plugged it in and a red light came on to show the thermostat was working. While it heated up, I sat cross-legged in front of the wardrobe mirror and tried some of the new lipsticks.

In the end, I didn't make too bad a fist of things. There were a couple of dodgy moments when the burning barrel caught my scalp, but the final effect was worth it. For the first time in my life, my hair hung down rather than frizzed out. I shaped a curl at the ends, and twisted the sides in like I'd seen them do at school. I remembered what the make-up counter girl had said, and wondered about cutting myself a wispy fringe. Betty-the-Mobile usually trims my hair for me while Poll's perm is cooking; she's all right, but she only knows how to do pensioner styles. See, if I had a job and money, I could go to a swanky hairdresser's and have a consultation, investigate having the kinks relaxed, maybe have some layers razored in, or highlights. Except they were very scary, those salons, and the assistants all wore tiny skirts and looked like models, and they'd probably burst out laughing when I lumbered in. I wondered where you could have your eyebrows professionally tweezered.

I put the basque on, for devilment, and the long skirt and the boots, and stood in front of the mirror. What if I did go to Donna's party? I tried a mysterious half-smile at myself. Then, like victims do in horror films, I peered into the reflected room and spotted something nasty behind me.

On my bedside table, an open tub of Vaseline,

which wasn't mine or Poll's. And, eugh, gross, now I looked properly, a definitely-Dogman-shaped depression down the length of my bed.

I suppose there could have been a DIY, household-type explanation, Poll had him lubricating the sash window or something, but how likely was that, really? Sometimes, especially when I was younger, I'd imagined my dad lying there, listening to his records or reading his books. Now the picture would always be Dogman, greasing his privates.

I put my hands over my face and screamed quietly into my palms for a minute or two. Then I went over to the record player and put Ultravox on, very loud. I plugged in the phones and then lay down on the floor with my arms over my eyes, till I saw sparks. Oh, Vienna.

*   *   *

He drove me into the centre of Chorley, I saw the road signs in the headlights. We finished up on a cobbled side street, in front of a mid-terraced brick house.

'Have I been here before?' I asked as we got out of the car. Because it looked familiar.

'No, not to this one,' Vince said, leaning on the doorbell. His face was like a skull in the shadows.

After a minute, a scrappy little man in a dressing gown answered, rubbing his face. I thought he'd shout at us for waking him, but when he saw Vince he opened the door right up and we both walked in. 'I'll just go and put some pants on,' he said, and disappeared up the stairs.

It smelt like a dirty place. The man came back

197

down wearing jogging bottoms but no top, and his ribs stuck out like he was starving. I sat in the living room and Vince and the man went into the kitchen to talk. I heard Vince say, 'Are you sure it's still all right?' and the man reply, 'Yep, it's no problem, I owe you one.'

'You owe me several,' said Vince. 'July, August, September . . . '

'What can I say?' said the man. 'You're a saint.'

'I'm a fool,' said Vince, but in a nice way, not getting at him.

The man brought me a glass of brandy through and we all sat round the electric fire. 'My name's Stu,' he said. I was past caring. I drank the brandy down and asked for another.

'We can stay here for a little while,' said Vince. 'Stu's on holiday next week.'

'Lanzarote,' said Stu. 'You can have the couch for a couple of nights, Vince, till I go. I'll show you your room, love. Come with me.'

He led me up to the back bedroom and I had that déjà vu thing. 'I think I've been here before,' I said. 'Although I don't remember all this.' The walls were covered in Thin Lizzy posters and album covers, and there was a table with piles of paper and a BBC Model B computer on it.

'You've never been here, I promise you, love. Honest.' He waved his hand at the computer. 'I run two fanzines from this room, it's my base. I don't normally let anyone round, in case they mess up my system. But I know you won't, will you? Good girl. Now, the bathroom's across the landing.' He pointed through the door.

'I know that already.'

He shook his head. 'You're thinking of somewhere

198

else. There's loads of two-up two-downs round here with exactly the same layout.'

'Like Poll's,' I said faintly. It had taken me till now to see it. This house was the twin of the one I'd just escaped from.

'That's right. Now, make yourself at home, but don't touch my picture discs, OK? Some of them are worth twenty pounds.'

I meant to put a sheet over the mattress, but the minute I lay down I was asleep. I wish I could say I dreamt about Katherine, but I didn't.

Chapter Sixteen

God knows how long I was there on the floor; certainly till it got dark out. Whenever the record finished a side, I got up, flipped it over and lay back down again. This happened five or six times until, as I was pulling my headphones off to put side two on again, I heard a tapping at my window. I dropped the phones in fright.

Tap tap tap. Wasn't there a film about a murderer who did that, just before he struck? Must be a bloody tall murderer, though; either that or he was standing on a ladder.

I pulled the corner of the curtain up a little way. *I'M A BURGLAR LET ME IN* said the handwritten placard pushed against the glass. There was the faint sound of cheering below, and the card was swivelled round on its pole. *MEET U AT BOTTOM OF HILL U HAVE 10 MINS*

I pushed open the sash and poked my head out. Callum waved at me from the front garden.

199

'Get out of there,' I hissed at him. 'Don't let Poll and Dogman see you.' I was praying they'd drawn the front curtains, or that they were watching TV in the back.

'Come down, then,' he grinned. He was wearing his contact lenses again, I noted.

'I can't.'

'You can. If you don't come down, I'm going to ring the bell. In fact, here I go now, here I am, extending my digit in the critical direction, I'm only centimetres away—' He stretched out his arm towards the door.

'Oh, for God's sake. It's not funny. Stop it.'

'Aw, just come down, for a minute, say hello. Pleeease.' He dropped his hand to his side and looked up appealingly.

For two pins I could have dropped my *Illustrated Dictionary* on his head, that would have shut him up. But that smile . . .

'Pleeeeeeeease?'

'Oh, hell. All right, then. For *one* minute. And you have to put Poll's clothes prop back where you found it, and pull all that parcel tape off the end. And take that cardboard with you; she could read that and have a fit.'

He did a smart salute and threw the prop onto the ground. I hoped to God there were no neighbours watching. At least it was night time.

'I'll see you in five, then?' He flashed a palm at me, fingers spread out.

'You said ten minutes.'

'OK. But don't waste time mucking about with your hair or anything girly. You look great already.'

I glowed for a second, then realized it was something he'd said simply to speed me up. Still. 'I

200

need to get a coat.'

'Nah, it's warm out here. Come as you are.'

I looked down at my near-bare bosom. No way could I be seen in the street wearing a basque. 'Well, something to cover up, then. Hang on.' I ducked back in but he called me out again. '*Will you stop shouting?* You'll have the whole street out if you don't quieten down. What is it?'

'Can you bring that party invite with you?'

'Christ, you don't give up, do you?' I muttered, shutting the window.

I yanked open the wardrobe door and pushed aside the woollens. Under my long navy cardigan was the white top I'd bought with Donna. I snipped off the price tag with my nail clippers and started to undo the basque. Then I thought, I haven't time, and anyway it'll only be like having a bra on. I buttoned up the blouse over it; you could see a hint of red through the white material but I didn't stop to worry. A few strokes with the hairbrush to smooth my hair at the back where I'd mussed it up, and I was ready. As a last thought I flicked the invite through the gap at the bottom of the window. I didn't see where it landed.

I crept to the bottom of the stairs and listened. *We know what you've been up to, Hastings. Your mate's told us all about it.* A tough policeman was interrogating someone at the top of his voice. I heard Poll say, 'Why don't they look in his car, there must be blood all ovver it,' and Dogman reply, 'They're daft, the police, they don't see what's going on under their noses.'

I so wanted to turn right, through the front room, and make a run for it. But my front door keys and peggy purse were in the fruit bowl on the

201

sideboard, which was in the living room, on the left. I'd have to go in.

I tried to keep the noise down, but Dogman turned round in his seat as soon as he heard the door swoosh over the carpet. 'Bloody hell, look at you,' he leered. 'You've been busy, haven't you? No wonder you've been so quiet all evening. I like your top-thing.'

Poll whipped round too. 'Where do you think you're going?' she said as she heard the jingle of keys.

'Out. So?'

'Don't cheek me, madam.' Poll pushed herself up from the sofa and came round to peer at me, putting herself between me and the door. 'Lord above, what have you done to yourself? You look like Bette Davis in that film where them sisters were foul to each other, what were it called? And one were a cripple, and t' other went mad.'

'I think she looks tasty,' said Dogman. 'I could eat her up. Yum yum.'

'I need to go,' I said. Before I vomit, I could have added.

'You've had no tea. I did shout of you but you never answered. It was bacon grill but we had to throw yours away, it went like leather.'

'Doesn't matter.'

'You can't go missing meals at your age. Don't blame me when you're stricken wi' gallstones. Where are you off to?' Poll stuck her chin out belligerently. 'Who are you meeting?'

'Rebecca. It's a birthday party for a girl at school.'

Do you expect me to believe that? shouted the TV detective in the background, thumping the table.

Poll relaxed her body language very slightly. 'Birthday party? Oh. Where?'

'Harrop community centre,' I said promptly. 'Where we went to see *Beauty and the Beast* that time. Rebecca's giving me a lift there and back. I don't know when it finishes, though, so don't put the deadlock on.'

Behind her, Dogman was licking his lips. 'You scrub up nice,' he said. 'You're a bonny girl.'

I dodged past Poll and made a run for the front door.

'How come you didn't tell me about it before? And where did you get them clothes?' I heard her screech. 'You've no coat.'

I slammed the door behind me and glanced round. The street was empty, so I started off down the hill, my purse banging against my chest.

Callum was standing in the lay-by at the passenger side of a small van. He was wearing combats and a jersey top with a hood.

'Hiya,' he called when he spotted me. 'Hurry up. We've been here for hours.' He opened the door for me. 'Hop in.'

I checked inside and did a double take when I saw a redheaded lad at the wheel. 'Hey,' he said, without turning his head. Cigarette smoke streamed out of his nostrils.

'It's all right.' Callum nodded into the van. 'This is Mitch from college, he's a mate. In you get.'

Panic began brewing in my stomach. Stranger Danger, I thought. Climbing in a van after dark with two lads. It went against a lifetime's instincts. I'd be front page of the *Bolton Evening News* tomorrow, Big Fat Girl Found in Ditch. Grandmother Says It Were Her Own Stupid Fault.

'But where are we going?'

'Bolton. Mitch has got some business there. I cadged a lift. Thought we could at least have a drink, you and me, even if we don't get to that party. Oh come *on*, Kat, have some fun for once.'

I bet this is how people end up taking drugs, I thought: not wanting to offend. 'I'm not sure.'

'Look,' said Callum, coming up close and lowering his voice, 'I promise if you change your mind halfway there, all you have to do is say the word and we'll turn straight round and come back again, no harm done. So you've nothing to lose. Go on. All we'll do is sit in the corner of a nice quiet pub for an hour or so. I think we'll have a really good time.'

'Is Mitch coming with us?'

Callum laughed. 'Well, it is his van, fair dos. But don't worry, he's dropping us off in the town centre and going on elsewhere.'

I took a breath, and hauled myself up by hanging on the sides of the door. 'Shove over,' he said when I was in. So I shuffled my bum across the seats to Mitch, who still didn't take me on. Who is he, exactly, I wanted to ask, and why is he wearing so many rings?

'Belt up,' chirped Callum, clicking his seat belt into place. 'We don't want anyone pulling us over tonight, do we?'

'We do not,' said Mitch. The ignition started up and the CD player began blasting out a dance track, all bass, that went right through my jawbone.

It all felt unreal, sitting in that smoky cab with the air throbbing and the streetlights flicking over us. I realized I was gritting my teeth with fear; tried to relax; failed. I looked over at Callum and he smiled back. He'd lit a cigarette too and the glowing tip bobbed around in the darkness.

'Mitch used to live in Bolton.' Callum tapped the dashboard with his free hand as though he was playing it.

'Oh.' *DUF-DUF-DUF* went the music. 'So you're back here to see your friends?'

'Yeah,' said Mitch. 'Sort of.'

'Whereabouts in Bolton?'

'You know where there was that IRA shooting?' *DUF-DUF-DUF*.

I nodded.

'More   or   less   next   door.' *DADADADADADADADA DUF-DUF-DUF*.

'Right.'

'But that were after I moved.'

'Oh,' I said. 'I expect Nantwich is a bit quieter, is it?' I gave a nervous snort.

'Well, it was till Mitch came to live there,' said Callum. I thought Mitch looked pleased at this, but it was hard to tell in the gloom.

He dropped us at the bus station, Callum leaping out like a dancer and me landing like a sack of potatoes beside him.

'We can't go to that party,' I said at once.

'I know; way too early. Let's find this nice pub first.' He strode off down the road and I trotted after him, hugging my purse to my chest. 'Know anywhere good?'

'No,' I said, but my voice was lost in the sound of some passing girls shrieking. The street was as crowded as a Saturday afternoon, but shoppers usually wore more clothes. Poll would have had a haemorrhage at the amount of flesh on show, Dogman would have drowned in his own saliva.

205

There were some hefty lasses among them, too.

We ended up in a tiny old pub off a paved square. Inside it was busy but not packed, and I found a seat near the fireplace and studied the beams while Callum got me half a pint of cider.

'Been here before?' he asked when he came back.

'No.' I wondered if he'd burst out laughing if I told him precisely how many pubs I'd ever been in; one, and that was only the Working Men's Club to pick up Poll's shopping which she'd left under the table.

'It seems funny,' he began, then stopped.

'What?'

'Nothing. How's your cider?'

'Fine. I have had alcohol before, you know.'

'I never said you hadn't.'

'What were you going to say?'

He pursed his lips and took a sip of his pint. 'Only that it seems funny, odd, to see you out of Bank Top. Out of context, out of your environment. It's like you belong there—'

'Christ, don't say that.'

Callum raised his eyebrows. 'Why, don't you like it?'

'Not much, no.' And yet I thought of the fields that stretched behind our house, the hazy moorland above Harrop, the quiet stones of the cemetery. 'Well, I like some of it.' Clare Greenhalgh, grown up and sleek, smirking at me from the top deck of the bus, nudging the boy beside her and pointing down. 'Not the people so much. But Bank Top's where I'm from, it's my roots. The place where you grow up is part of your identity, whether you like it or not, isn't it?'

Callum shrugged. 'Dunno. Is it?'

'I think so. It's just a shame my roots are in Bank Top.'

'It's not that bad. At least you don't live on a mafiacontrolled estate, or in one of these mega tower blocks where the kids drop bricks on passersby for fun.'

'No, but it's dull and rundown, and every bugger wants to know your personal business.'

The lights of the fruit machine played over Callum's serious face and I thought once again how great it was to have somebody who listened to me. The next time he came to my house I was going to show him Dad's ashes; he deserved to see them.

'I can take or leave Nantwich,' he said, 'it's OK, not a patch on Scotland, obviously. But I always got the impression you loved your village, really, and that was why you never went anywhere much. I reckon you're attached to Bank Top by a kind of spiritual bungee cord.'

'Oh, pur-leeeese.'

'Yeah, because you know all sorts about it, the history and that. I know you slag it off but I thought that was affectionate slagging, like the way kids moan about their mums. Sorry. Or their grans. Even though they love them.'

Good God, he thought I loved Poll.

'Well, I don't like Bank Top, for the record, and if there is any sort of bungee cord in existence, it's about to get snipped. I'm going to tell you something.' My heart started to speed up. 'A great big secret. Nobody knows this, or at least not all of it. Some people know bits, but nobody knows the whole picture . . . '

'Get on with it, then,' said Callum, taking his

207

tobacco out. 'I'm agog.'

'Well, I might not be living in Bank Top much longer.'

He paused, mid-pinch. 'Really? What, a job or something? Oh, I get it, you're off to uni. Where you going? I've kept meaning to ask where you were headed. I really need to get my arse in gear and go to some open days. I missed a load last term.'

'I'm going to Oxford.'

'Fucking hell,' said Callum, breaking into a huge smile.

'You kept that quiet. Oxford University? Fuck me. You must be well clever.'

As soon as the words were out, I regretted it. 'What I mean is, I have a place. To read English, at University College. But I can't go, obviously, 'cause I can't leave Poll on her own. For God's sake, she's seventy and disabled, it would be really cruel. And anyway, I might not get the grades.'

'Yeah, you will,' said Callum, rolling a cigarette. 'You'll get all As, I can feel it in my water. I've got some module results to come, but I'm only predicted Ds. I don't care. Mum says my education's rounded enough, and anyway, I might take a year out. Hell, Oxford, though.'

'But it's a secret,' I insisted, 'you've not to tell anyone.'

He looked at me, puzzled. 'So doesn't Poll know?'

'No. She knows they called me for interview but she thinks I got rejected; she told me I would before I went. The teachers at school know I was offered a place because the college wrote to them and said so, but they think I'm going in October. I

208

put it down on my UCAS as a firm acceptance.' I grimaced. 'Bit of a mess, really.'

'And has the school not told your grandma?'

'She never goes anywhere near it. In the seven years I've been at the grammar, she's never gone to a single parents' evening. She says they're too stuck-up.'

'Jesus. But why keep it a secret? I don't get this.'

'No, I don't either, to be honest.'

'Are you going or not?'

'Keeping my options open.' I dipped my head to swing my hair down defensively, but I'd lacquered it into place and it didn't budge. I knew how stupid I sounded.

'Drink up,' said Callum, 'and I'll get you another. I want to hear how you got yourself in this mess.'

'There was this wasp,' I said, as he walked away.

*   *   *

We stayed in that house for two weeks. Vince hardly talked at all, but that suited. I made little meals that neither of us ate. In the mornings he tried to reclaim the back garden, while I had a trip to the corner shop and then did a bit of cleaning. I found the local library was only three streets away so I spent my afternoons there. I don't know what he got up to then. And in the evenings we watched sitcoms and quiz shows. We always went to bed early.

After a fortnight, Stu came back. 'See my chest,' he said, pulling his shirt up. 'Good, in't it? Mind you, all my arms are peeling. Oh, hey, look at the garden, I never knew I had a lawn.'

Later, I saw him giving Vince a wad of notes in the

kitchen. Vince said, 'I think that's my cue to leave.'

Stu said, 'Only if it's convenient. I do need to do some work on my fanzines, though. I'm planning a special with a pull-out section on bootlegs.'

We went back to Poll's, but only to get some stuff I'd left behind by accident. The idea was to sit outside in Stu's car till we saw her go out with the pram, then sneak in.

'Get all your personal documents,' said Vince. 'You need to register yourself wi' a doctor, apart from owt else.' But I wouldn't go in, in case I saw something of Katherine's lying about. I'd had to shut my eyes while Poll wheeled her past on the other side of the road.

We went straight from there to Chorley again. I thought we were returning to Stu's, but Vince stopped outside a row of shops. 'I've a flat,' he said. 'Ovver th' hairdresser's. Come in and have a look.'

You could smell hairspray, I swear, but it was OK. A tiny TV, thin-legged chairs, saggy sofa. The bathroom suite was brown with palm-tree tiles. On the bare single bed was a pile of sheets and towels, still wrapped in cellophane.

'Will you be awreet on your own?' asked Vince.

'Are you not staying?' I said, then had a panic in case he thought it was an invitation.

'I've Stu's car to tek back. Then I've some business to attend to. I'll drop by wi' some groceries later. Are you sure you'll not get lonely?'

'I like being on my own these days,' I said. It was true, although the nights sometimes gave me trouble.

He appeared at tea time with some tins, a loaf, and milk. 'You've gone to skin and bone,' he said as he watched me unpack. Before he went he gave me a phone number. 'This is for emergencies. You can stay here as long as you want, but let me know if you're moving on. Get signed on tomorrow with the DHSS, and see a doctor. There's fifty quid to keep you going till your giro comes through.' He laid it on the table and put the salt pot on top of it.

It had been quiet before at Stu's, but it was quieter after he'd gone. That was all right. I just had to wait till the library opened next day.

Chapter Seventeen

While he was at the bar I watched a very slim woman in knee boots perching on a man's knee, swinging one leg sexily. I wondered what would happen if I sat on a man's knee; he'd probably never walk again. For a second I imagined lowering myself onto Callum's knee, oh God oh God, think of something else quick. He did a thumbs-up across the bar at me and I had to look away in shame. But by the time he came back, I'd got myself in order.

'So,' he said, shuffling his chair in, 'if it's not a daft question, why did you apply to university if you didn't think you could take up the place?'

'Fear,' I answered promptly. 'I only put my name down for Oxford because Mrs Law told me to. I do as I'm told, mostly, plus she's one scary woman, she makes Miss Dragon look like Shirley Temple. Then, when I got the letter inviting me down, I said to her I couldn't go because I didn't know what train to catch or anything. I'd never been on a train on my own, and it would be December, and dark at four. I also explained that Poll couldn't be left overnight. I thought that would put an end to it, but Mrs Law just said I ought to try and Sort

211

Something Out, and threatened to come round to our house and see Poll herself, which would have been like Godzilla versus King Kong. I was so petrified of Mrs Law that I went and asked Maggie to Poll-sit, which she said she'd do, bless her, but that still left the train problem. Poll said she'd been hearing about that route and apparently there'd been more fatal crashes on that line than any other, and also there'd been a rogue guard luring female passengers into his van by asking if they'd lost a Rolex, then showing them Japanese porn. I think she might have been making that up. But I was still completely rattled, so I went back to Mrs Law and confessed that I just didn't want to go.'

'Was she pissed off?'

'She wasn't very happy.'

She'd gone mental with me. She said I was one of the brightest students they'd had through the school in her time there, and what a total waste it would be not only of my own talents, but of the dedication and interest of the staff, if I ducked out of higher education simply because I lacked the wherewithal to read a timetable. I'd started to cry, which threw her, and her efforts to talk me round after that ended up with me sobbing hysterically. In the finish, she'd had to go and get matron to help calm me down.'

'But you were still too frightened to refuse?' asked Callum.

'No, I think I'd have bottled out of going even despite Mrs Law, but then I had this stroke of incredibly good luck. Because, at the last minute, Mrs Law said she happened to be travelling down that way to her brother's to drop off some Christmas presents, and she could give me a lift.

There *and* back. I mean, how lucky was that? Maggie said it was Fate, and I agreed with her. And although it was pretty weird sitting in the car with Mrs Law for all those hours, it wasn't as bad as I thought because she turned out to be quite funny one-to-one. She didn't expect me to talk at all, just told me stories while I listened.

'She told me about her childhood and going to a convent school where you had to curtsey to the nuns, and how kind they were to her when her father died suddenly. She said they were kinder to her than her own mother, who spent the wake leaning on men and drinking bourbon, and never even gave her daughter one hug. I kept glancing across and trying to imagine Mrs Law young; I couldn't, though.

'When she'd talked for a long time, she began asking me about life with Poll. I told her the practical things I have to do for my grandma, and how she can be moody with me. Then I went on to Dogman and Maggie; some of that made her laugh. Finally I found myself describing what happened with my parents. Just before I got out of the car, I asked Mrs Law if it was all in my confidential file at school and she said, "Only the basics." So I begged her not to repeat any of it and she said, in this haughty voice, "Do you honestly think I would?" and went straight back to Scary Teacher mode.'

'That's teachers for you. You can't ever make friends with a teacher, however they suck up to you. So what was it like then, the interview? Were they all dead posh?'

'I stayed in my room most of the time because I didn't know what to say to anyone. I did try, in the morning. I thought I'd go down to breakfast and listen in to what the others were saying, see if I could pick up some tips. So I went down and it's all dark wood panelling and narrow little stairs, into this sort of ante-room with a wall of carvings and a door cut into it. A sign next to it said *BREAKFAST*. Students were going through the door, so I waited a minute and I went through too. But when I got on the other side, it was pitch black. The door was on springs behind me and once it had closed, I couldn't make a damn thing out. I thought it was a joke, or a test. Like, they might be watching me with infrared cameras to see if I panicked.'

'And did you?'

'Oh yeah. I put my hands out in front of me and felt around but I couldn't make anything out and my chest started to go tight as though I was having an asthma attack. It was dusty, like a secret corridor. Then, I suppose it was only a few seconds later, another door opened right in front of me and there was the dining hall, and this young man peering in at me. I barged right past him to get out into the light. When I looked back, I could see it was a sort of double wall with a space between. I don't know what it was in aid of, but they could have done with a few candles in there or something. So by the time I sat down to breakfast I wasn't in any state to listen or eat. I thought, if there's any dons in here having their Weetabix, they'll have been watching me and thinking, Christ, she's too gormless even to walk though a door.'

Callum was smiling as he took out his tobacco tin again. 'Trust you.'

'I know. If there's a way to fuck up, I'll find it. Then what happened at the interview itself, that was bizarre and surreal too.'

'Bizarre and surreal? That doesn't sound like you, Kat.'

I kicked him gently under the table (me! kicking a boy! in a pub!).

'I'll ignore that. What happened was, I got taken along to this old room full of books and there were two academic types sitting behind a huge desk, a man and a woman. The woman had a look of Honor Blackman, and the man was the spitting image of our newsagent, Mr Porter, but without the tattoos. I was pretty strung up with nerves, not because I especially wanted to get into Oxford, because I wasn't sure I did. I just hate talking to people I don't know.'

'You talked to me all right the first time.'

'Yeah, but that was different. You were family, we were on home territory.' And there was something special about you from the start.

I looked across at him playing with his pendant and wondered what would happen if he could read my mind.

'Go on, Kat,' he said. 'Give.'

'Yeah, so, anyway—' I took a long drink and tried to gather my thoughts again—'I hadn't been sitting down two minutes, I think they were asking what texts I'd been studying for A level, when I felt a tickling behind my knee and when I checked, there was this massive wasp crawling up my leg. I whooped and jumped up, and Honor dropped her glasses under the desk. The wasp buzzed off and we all watched it fly over to the window, head-butt the glass a few times, and settle. Honor goes, "I've told Mr Bowman the heating's on too high, it's ridiculous. And the Porter man goes, I believe there's a nest in the boiler room, Hadrian was

215

telling me last week, though I don't expect anyone will actually *do* anything about it." Next thing, I found myself reaching down for Honor's glasses; I'm so used to picking stuff up for Poll it's automatic. I passed them across the desk to her and she said thanks, and we had a little laugh, although I was fighting hysteria. So I went to sit down and—oh, God, it was awful.'

'What? *What?*'

'I felt something sting my side.'

Callum winced. 'Yow.'

'I shrieked at the top of my voice and bolted for the door, quickly followed by Honor who caught me outside and bundled me down a corridor into a toilet. Only when I undid my clothes—' I leaned towards him conspiratorially—'because when I said "side" I really meant "bottom"—there was nothing there, no red mark or anything. So I flapped about a bit, in case the wasp had got trapped inside my skirt and was getting ready to do a proper sting.' I didn't tell Callum but I'd also pulled my knickers down, to be on the safe side. 'And that's when I spotted the plastic tag. You know when you get new clothes and the labels are attached with a plastic thread that you have to cut off, otherwise you pull a big hole in the material? Well I'd had a new skirt.' (New knickers, really.) 'And although I'd clipped the long end of the tag off, I'd left the other stuck in, and it was that that had pricked me. Not a wasp at all.'

Callum was shaking his head at me.

'I know, I know. Trust me. So I came out of the toilets hyperventilating, and Honor assumed I had been stung but that I was trying to be brave. I didn't enlighten her because that would have made

216

me look even more stupid than the fight I had with the door. She was all for sending for some antihistamine cream, or at the very least, some vinegar, but I told her I'd put a wet tissue on it and I'd be fine. She sat me in a side room, very plush, waspless, and gave me a glass of water to sip. Then she said, had I heard of the Bach Flower Remedies? I didn't know if the question was part of the interview, so I tried to sound noncommittal. She scuttled off and came back half a minute later with her handbag. "Here you are," she said, and brought out a tiny dark bottle with a bulb on the top, like a dropper. "It's totally herbal," she told me, and squirted a dose into my cup. I said, all suspicious, "How come it smells of brandy?" '

'You're seeing that cider off no problem, I notice,' said Callum drily.

'Yeah, well, it's only like apple juice, isn't it?' I took another huge swig to show I wasn't fussed. 'Anyway, Honor maintained it was only the smell, it wasn't alcoholic, and the stuff would help calm me if I sipped it slowly.'

'Did it?'

'Oh, and how. She left me on my own, which was exactly what I wanted, and said she'd be back in fifteen minutes. Then, and this part is weird as well, a little boy appeared.'

'What, like you were hallucinating?'

'No. I think he was somebody's son or something. He wasn't supposed to be there, I suspect, but then I wasn't either, technically. He sneaked round the door and just stared at me for ages, the way kids do. White-blond hair, Spiderman sweatshirt. I reckon he'd have been about four, five. Then he goes, "Does a goat wear a coat?" The

217

Flower Remedy must have been working because instead of ignoring him, I heard myself say, "Does a bat wear a hat?" Then he said, with a dirty laugh, "Do ants wear pants?" and I said, "Do kittens wear mittens?" '

'I see a pattern emerging.'

'So we carried on like this for ages, Does a fox wear socks, Do mites wear tights.'

'Does a fly wear a tie.'

'Do shrews wear shoes, you've got it. He was sharp, I'll give him that. I started saying silly stuff—'

'As opposed to the sensible stuff you'd been saying before.'

'Yeah, and when I couldn't think of any more rhyming clothes we made up nonsense phrases, Does a hog live in a bog, Is a dove in love, Is a cheetah neater. Then Honor returned and he nipped off up some stairs. I was taken back to the interview, only by now I was high as a kite. Instead of being tongue-tied, I couldn't stop blathering.'

'You didn't try the goat–coat routine on them, did you?'

'Oh no, it all made perfect sense, what I came out with, thank God.' I'd been inspired. I could tell they were impressed, and that had made me want to talk even more.

Callum's lips made a little popping sound as he took his cigarette away from his mouth. 'So they offered you a place.'

'I got the letter three days after Christmas. Mrs Law said they're trying these days to give people from, ahem, deprived backgrounds a leg up. So the fact no one in our family's ever got a university degree will have counted in my favour. I've still got to get two As and a B, though.'

'You've got to go. I mean, Oxford. You have, haven't you?'

'Sometimes I think, how can I not? That wasp was an omen, I'm convinced of it. You don't get wasps in winter. It was sent to get me through the interview, because I'd never have managed it on my own. Then I see Poll, stumbling around the place, scraping chutney on her toast instead of jam, and I think, how could I even contemplate leaving her?' I wondered what she was doing at that moment; whether Dogman was still with her or whether she was sitting on her own in the dark.

'Mmm,' said Callum, noncommittally. 'Tough call. Can't social services sort something out?'

'Not twenty-four/seven. And there's all kinds of rules and regs, it's incredibly complicated to apply, which I suppose is the idea. It's too depressing, I don't want to talk about it.'

We sat in silence for a while. Smoke curled up between us; in the saloon next door, someone was singing 'Lady in Red'.

'Still,' said Callum at last, 'you got a place. That's so impressive. You don't half hide your light under a bushel. You're funny, you're clever . . .'

I'm fat, I thought.

To stop myself blushing I said: 'I'm broke too, I'm afraid. I can get one round in, that's all. Sorry. I thought I had more in my purse.'

'It's OK.' Callum got to his feet. 'I got paid today, and money always burns a hole in my pocket.'

He took himself off to the bar and I went hunting for the ladies'. In the mirror I saw that my hair was still where I'd moulded it, and my face still

219

matt. I touched up the lipstick and, unbelievably, undid two buttons on my blouse. I thought I looked nice, till a skinny girl showing her stomach came and stood right next to me. I could see the thought bubble over her head: Eugh, what a lump. But when I turned to go, I could see she was intent on fiddling with a contact lens, tears streaming down, and probably hadn't even noticed me. 'Shyness is a kind of vanity,' I remembered Cissie saying. 'I read that in the *Reader's Digest.*'

When I came back to our table, someone had taken our seats so we moved over to the side door and stood in the breeze. We started talking about teachers, and the worst ones we'd ever known— Callum had quite a lot to say on the subject—and then he outlined his plans for a year off, and which university he'd like to go to when he came back from travelling the world (Newcastle). He told me about a holiday he and his mum had spent in Thailand, and how she'd once told someone's fortune and they'd paid her with an antique necklace but his mum wouldn't wear it because she said it had sad vibes about it. He described life on a croft, and how he'd have a state-of-the-art photographic studio constructed without ruining the character of the building, and how, at night, he'd play his music at top volume because there'd be no neighbours to complain. 'That's the one thing I hate about where we live now,' he said, leaning sideways to stub his cigarette out in someone else's ashtray. 'It's a terrace and it's over a shop. That's three separate lots of people to moan about noise. I wouldn't mind, but the old woman on the left reckons to be deaf, so how does that work?'

'It's the natural state of the old, to be hacked off.'

'Do you reckon? My grandad used to be nice. Before he died. Mum was always complaining he spoilt me.'

I heard that a lot, about grandparents spoiling grandchildren. I wondered what had gone wrong in our house.

'How are you feeling?' he asked suddenly.

I shifted my weight from one leg to the other. 'OK. My back's stiff, I could do with sitting down. Shall we go into the beer garden and find a table there?'

'Or—' Callum grinned. 'We could go along to that party.'

'For God's sake. I thought I'd said I wasn't going.' I couldn't help but laugh at him. 'Ten out of ten for persistence.'

'I know, I'm very persuasive. I might go into politics if the croft falls through.'

'But I haven't got the ticket any more, so it's academic.'

'No, I've got it. You threw it out of the window; I caught it. I had to chase it right across the road.' He reached into his pocket.

'Well, you'll need to go on your own because I've only got one ticket.'

'Aha, Kat, but that's where you're wrong, because it says here, "Admits two".' He waved the ticket under my nose. 'So, are you up for it?'

I grabbed the ticket off him to check although I knew he was right, held his wrist briefly. 'Tell me why you're so keen to go. You won't know anyone.'

'Those are the best sort of parties,' he said. His face was half in shadow, his cheekbones outlined.

221

The short hair had made his eyes look much bigger. 'I just love clubbing.'

'How does that square with wanting to live on a croft?'

'I'll be old by then, I'll have got it out of my system. Oh, go on, Kat, now I've come all this way.'

I didn't ask you to, I thought.

'Tell you what; how about we go along, see what it's like, then if you're not keen we can leave.'

And go where? The pubs were ready to close.

'Please?' He held up an imaginary microphone. *'Come with me into the night, You never know what's waiting there.'*

'"Stellar Days"?'

'Angelhunter.' He looked pleased with himself. 'I've been doing my own research into Eighties music. Was it one of your dad's favourites?'

'Yeah, it was; I mean, he had the single. I play it sometimes when I need cheering up.' Poll always complained the beat went straight through the floor. 'It's one of my favourites.'

'So,' said Callum, taking me by the arm, 'in the spirit of "Stellar Days", let's go for it, eh?'

Donna's face when I walked in with him by my side. *'And watch the ice catch fire?'*

'That's my girl,' he said. I let him take me by the hand and lead me to perdition.

Five minutes later we were outside the entrance to Steem. 'Are you cold?' he asked.

'No. Why?'

'I thought you were shivering. Oh, here we go.' He handed the ticket to one of the bouncers, who pointed wordlessly up the stairs. 'Come on.'

The people who'd come behind us were directed down, into a sort of cellar, and we began to climb the illuminated steps towards the thudding music. On the landing, a boy I'd never seen before was leaning his head against the flock wallpaper and groaning. A blonde girl was sitting nearby, scowling. We took no notice; Callum's eyes were fixed on the door ahead and his face was aglow. He was jerking his head already to the beat.

Then, as we walked through into the spinning lights, I heard a riff that sent a thrill down my spine. I gripped Callum's shoulder. 'It's "Cars", they're playing Gary Numan.' It was another sign, and my heart leapt with confidence.
But the riff slid away and the tune changed to something I didn't know, modern.

'It's a sample,' he yelled over the noise. 'Armand Van Helden. The track's called "Koochy". 'S good. Let's get a drink and go up on the balcony.'

The music was so loud it was disorientating; lights flashed in my eyes without any obvious sequence. I saw faces I knew, saw plenty of double-takes, which was good, unless they were saying, 'My God, what does she look like, silly cow.' Callum came back from the bar then went to dance, while I leaned on the rail and watched him. My head felt blurry but I didn't want to lose sight of him. Donna nearby, in the middle of the crowd, I waved but she didn't see me, somebody trying to snog her, somebody letting off a party popper over her head. A black-haired girl dancing close to Callum, waving her arms around in front of his face, showing her ribs, putting her arms round his neck. Callum laughing, throwing her arms off, moving away, moving away. The girl dancing on unfazed, turning to writhe next to someone else. My limbs had gone heavy but my brain was wired.

'What time is Mitch picking us up?' I shouted when Callum returned, stripped to the waist and soaked with sweat.

'Give us that glass,' he signed, and drank so fast that half of it went down his chin. 'Jesus. I'm fucked.' He sat down on the floor with his back to the railings. 'Come here.' He tugged at my skirt, so I lowered myself next to him. Alex and Sita sloped past, nudging each other when they saw me. Callum gave them the thumbs-up and they giggled, and gave it back.

'Why don't you dance?' he yelled in my ear.

I just shook my head.

'It's good. I'll request that "Koochy" for you, if you want. Hey?'

'No thanks.'

'Come down with me, next time something you like comes on.'

'No.' I sighed. 'I hardly look the part, do I?'

'You what?'

'Nothing. I don't want to dance, OK?'

'Suit yourself. You look fine, though. Really.' He smiled and elbowed me in the ribs. 'You should relax more. Come out more, get drunk occasionally.' His face tickled my cheek.

I felt strange; tipsy and anxious and excited and careless.

'Listen,' I shouted down his ear. 'Do you want to know another secret?'

'Bloody hell, what now, Woman of Mystery?'

I started to giggle. 'I'm gay.'

I watched him break out into a slow smile. 'Get away.'

'No, I am. I'm gay.'

'You're not, you know.'

'How come?'

The grin was very sure. 'Because.'

My heart felt like there was a live bat inside it, fluttering and swooping. He was right there next to me, his smell through the smoke, the stubble on his chin. So I kissed him.

He didn't resist. So I kissed him again, and this time he kissed back. All the blood in my body rushed upwards into my head; I thought I was going to faint. Then he pulled away, and put his palms against my shoulders to keep me back.

'No,' he said. 'This isn't going to work.'

'Sorry, sorry. I know, I'm too fat. I don't know what I was thinking—'

Callum stared at me as if I was insane. 'What are you on about?'

I started to talk in a rush, tried to stop tears of embarrassment forming; 'I'm too big for you to fancy. Everyone thinks fat people have no feelings but they do, it's not just thin beautiful people who have souls, is it—'

'Stop it.' Callum pulled me against him for a moment and I wondered if he was going to kiss me again. But he moved away again and put his hand up to show I should keep quiet. 'Kat, Kat, it's nothing to do with your shape. I think you're great. I think you're really fanciable. I—'

'What?'

'I can't fancy you, I mean, I do, but I mustn't. Shit.' He hit his forehead hard with his hand. 'Why did I get myself into this?'

I gazed at him in bewilderment.

'I'm so sorry. I should have told you from the first, but then you wouldn't have had anything to do with me.'

'Told me what?'

'Don't hate me, Kat.' He closed his eyes in pain. 'I'm your brother.'

*   *   *

I learned to live in that library. I was there outside the doors when it opened, and always the last one to be ushered out at closing time. They didn't mind because I was quiet and clean. Mostly I took out children's fantasy, Susan Cooper, C. S. Lewis, Andre Norton. But once a week I reread *Pride and Prejudice*. I wanted to climb inside that book and never come out. Wednesdays were bad because the library was closed all day, and Sundays.

It was a Sunday when I phoned Vince. I'd run out of books and it was dark outside. There were some drunks shouting outside the takeaway on the corner.

I was sitting on the sofa, holding a cushion on my lap, when I realized I was patting its back and rocking. That's mad, I thought, and put the cushion down. But my arms felt empty without it. I carried it round the flat for a while, shushing it, then I decided to call him. Just to hear a voice.

He was a long time picking up, and when he did he sounded weary. But he tried to make his voice more cheerful when he knew it was me.

'How're you gettin' on, love?'

I said I was fine. I'd got my giro, and some tablets from the doctor. I said I'd decided I was going to go to apply for college and learn how to be a librarian. He sounded happy when I told him. Neither of us mentioned Katherine.

Then I heard a baby crying in the background.

'Howd on a minute,' he muttered, but I don't know

226

who he was talking to, because there was a woman there. I heard her say, 'I think he might be teething, see his cheeks.' It wasn't Poll.

So I put the phone down, then I called Directory Enquiries. 'Where's this the code for?' I asked them.

'Sheffield,' they said.

I couldn't find my own nail clippers, my violin ones; Vince took them away. But I lighted on a pencil sharpener in one of the kitchen drawers, and managed to unscrew the blade with a coin-edge. So that did the job.

Chapter Eighteen

'Half-brother,' he'd said as he bundled me into a taxi and thrust a couple of notes at the driver. 'Only half-brother.' As if that made it less dreadful.

He'd steered me out of the room, 'where we could talk properly', and we'd become the rowing couple on the stairs.

'I don't get it,' I kept saying. 'You're my cousin.'

'I lied,' he said. 'Your dad was my dad. Different mums.'

I had to think about that for a few seconds, it was all cock-eyed. Then I rounded on him. 'That's crap. My dad was only eighteen when he died, how could he have had time?'

'He just did.' Callum was pulling at his necklace. 'He met my mum at uni, he met yours at school. Christ, I'm sorry—'

All right being sorry now.

'But someone would have told me—Poll, Cissie, someone in the village. You are so making this up.

It's *total* bollocks.'

Callum winced, but went on. 'My mum says she went to Poll, but Poll refused to believe her, threw her out of the house. Actually tried to kill her.'

'Don't talk wet. Poll's moody but she's not a bloody murderer. For God's sake. I reckon your mum's got a mental condition. Does she know you're here, did she send you, to make trouble?'

'No.' He hung his head. 'She's got no idea. I lied to her too.'

'So the only reason you hung around me was to find out about your—' I could barely get the word out—'dad.'

'No.' He jerked his head up. 'No. It was at first, I admit, but I didn't know how things were going to turn out. I didn't know I was going to like you as much as I do . . .'

'But—eugh—that's disgusting. Think, think what you're saying. It's incest, isn't it? You can go to *prison* for that.'

Callum grabbed my arms and held them, looked into my face. 'I could run, now. I could run away from you and this God-awful mess, and never see you again. But you have to hear this. We've got a link, we're connected. You've felt it, haven't you? Haven't you?' He gave me a little shake but I didn't reply. 'Admit it, you can talk to me like no one else. Or you wouldn't have told me all those secrets. And the clouds, nobody else has been interested in my cloud photos except you. You're my sister, my only sibling, it's natural I should feel in tune with you—'

I wrenched myself free and clattered down the stairs to the entrance. Callum came after me.

'Get away from me, or I'll scream,' I called as we

landed on the street. One of the bouncers put his head round the doorway, watching.

'Will you just listen? Will you let me finish?' His top, which he'd tied round his waist, was starting to slide down his hips. He looked sweaty and dirty. I wanted to get away from him, fast.

'No. I'm going home.'

'How?'

My heart whirled round in a panic. 'With Mitch,' I said faintly.

Callum shook his head. 'At least let me hail you a taxi. I need to get you back safe, Christ, it's the least I can do.'

I let him follow me to the taxi rank, and sort things out with the cabbie. It made it worse, somehow, him paying the fare, but I had no choice.

I cried all the way home and, do you know, the driver never said a word to me. I suppose they get it all the time.

When I walked in, the house was quiet and the downstairs lights all off. I put my keys and purse in the fruit bowl and went upstairs to wash my face. As I passed Poll's room, I heard her call out.

I pretended I hadn't heard and went into the bathroom, locking the door. I wiped the make-up off as best I could, brushed out the hairspray viciously, then tied my hair back into a tight plait. The clothes I left in a heap under the sink. I'd deal with them in the morning; burn them, probably. When I came out, Poll was still shouting for me.

'Wait a minute,' I said. I went into my bedroom, rooted out my big smocked nightdress and pulled it over my head. It was so comfortable after the basque. I didn't look in the mirror as I passed it.

Poll was sitting up in bed, waiting, with only the

bedside lamp on. She wouldn't have been able to see a damn thing. Winston breathed somewhere in the gloom.

'Thank God you're safe,' she said in a quavering voice. 'I've been imagining all sorts.'

I bet you haven't imagined an incestuous entanglement, though, I thought.

'I'm fine,' I said. 'Back in one piece. What time did Dickie go?'

'About ten. What time is it now?'

'Getting on for one.' I wondered if Callum had caught his train, or if Mitch had turned up again. Callum. I must never think of him again.

'I were frittened.' Something gleamed on her cheeks. 'Winston started barking at nowt, an' he wouldn't be calmed. They've had a break-in at Spar, Maggie were tellin' me. There's gangs roaming about.'

'Well, I'm back now.'

'It's dangerous out there.'

'Yes, it is. But I'm here now.'

*   *   *

Who else could I go to but Cissie.

It was a buzz of activity when I got there. Freddie the manager was in reception, up a stepladder, fastening bunting to the steel beams, while the women at the desk were blowing up balloons. As I signed in, Ally trotted past wearing a fox fur round her neck. 'Hiya,' she sang, and waggled the head-end of the fox at me. Its little dead paws rolled on her huge bosoms.

'What in God's name's going on?' I asked Cissie when I found her in the lounge writing numbers on lolly sticks.

'It's our fete tomorrow, don't say as you've forgotten. I thought you and Poll were coming?'

'We are, we are,' I said hastily. Poll would be well cheesed off when I broke the news.

'Well, bring your pennies. There'll be a cake stall and second-hand books, and I'm in charge o' t' treasure hunt, you'll have t' have a go at that.'

'Smashing.' I hate fairs, actually. When we had one at Bank Top Primary once, somebody stuck a label on my back saying I was the bouncy castle. I wore it all afternoon, till Mrs Kirtlan spotted it and pulled it off.

'And a dialect poetry recitation with a hamper for t' best performance. Only open to residents. Mr Poole's going to do an Edwin Waugh medley. I s'll have t' have my hanky out for "Willy's Grave".'

'I can't wait,' I said. 'What's Ally's fox fur in aid of?'

'No idea, unless it's come in a bag of jumble. She's a card, she really is. Now, where was I up to with these?'

I helped her finish her lolly sticks and then we went back to her room. While she was shifting Beanies off the armchair, I hung the Do Not Disturb tag on the door, and shut it.

'I've got something to ask you,' I blurted out, the minute she was settled.

She saw by my face it was serious. 'Ahh, love, is it Donny?'

Donny? I was thrown for a moment. 'Oh, no. It's Dad.'

That made her sit up. 'What about him, love?'

'I know,' I said.

'Know what?'

'About his other woman. The one he had on the go when he died.'

Her wrinkly lips pressed together and she sank back against the chair.

'And his other baby,' I went on. 'So it's no use trying to pretend it never happened. Too late for that. But I want to hear your side of it.'

'Dammit,' she said. 'I knew this would happen, one day. How have you heard? Who's been talking? 'Cause you've not to believe everything you hear, you know; there's some wicked folk out there who only want to mek mischief.'

'That's why I came to talk to you.' I leaned towards her. 'I know I can trust you to tell me the truth.'

'Oh aye, the truth. It's a slippery beggar, truth. My truth, your truth,' she gave a great sigh, 'it all blurs. Have you got this off Poll?'

'No. She's no idea I know anything.'

'So, who?'

'Look, tell me your version of events, then I'll tell you how I came to hear.' Callum's face flashed up before my eyes and I felt a twisting sensation in my chest. Not to think of him.

Cissie sagged. 'I suppose you had to know sometime. You're, what, eighteen now. But it wouldn't have done any good before, telling you your father's failings. He's been everything to you, your dad, whatever his faults were. How could anyone have tekken that away from you? I never rated him so much, but I wasn't going to say owt as'd upset you.'

'But I need to hear about him.'

Her face was working, as though she was fighting back words. 'As long as you aren't angry with me.

232

Don't go shooting the messenger, as they say. I've always tried to protect you, as much as I could, stuck in here. You've been like a daughter.' She reached out her hand and I got up and went over, to kneel by her chair. She took my fingers and held them tightly. 'You're very dear to me.'

'It's OK. Tell me what you know.'

Her voice sunk to a near whisper. 'Poll told me, a month or so after Vince had walked out. She was at her wits' end, looking after you—and you weren't an easy baby, bless you—and still overwhelmed by her son's death. Then her husband deserting her. And, you might as well know it all; it was your mother that Vince ran off with. Can you imagine? Not that we broadcast the fact. I tell you, the moment Elizabeth Castle walked into this family, she started to poison it. Evil.

'Anyway, Poll came to see me, I was still at home then, and we opened a bottle of sherry. We talked about the past, when her younger sister Mary died of polio, she was only seven, and Poll had done everything for her with Florence being ill so often. Dressed her, made her meals. They'd been very close, so it was a terrible blow for Poll when little Mary died. Jean wasn't so cut up; she was always the odd one out. I wasn't surprised when she emigrated.

'And we remembered her dad dying so suddenly of peritonitis, he was only fifty. Everyone else was celebrating the Coronation, it seemed very hard at the time. Poll thought the world of her father. Then she lost her mother in '79. It was one blow after another.

'We were putting this sherry away and she got

233

pretty drunk. She said to me, "Cissie, I shall never care about anybody again. All that happens is, you get hurt." Because she'd worshipped Roger, absolutely worshipped him. And she thought, after his death, that things couldn't get any worse, but then this madam turns up out of the blue, with a baby girl, claiming it's his and that he got her pregnant during Freshers' Week, whatever that is.'

'Baby *girl*?'

'Oh aye, that's why Poll was so hostile. It might have been different if the baby had been a boy. She pined for a grandson. Not keen on women, in't Poll.'

Now I was really confused. God, was there *another* baby out there that was my dad's?

'So Poll told me she threw this young woman out of the house straight away because she was obviously lying, she'd got herself in a fix and was just after money, and she must be scum to go bothering a bereaved mother like that. Roger would never have two-timed like that, Poll said. But even while we sat there shaking our heads, we both knew he would. He'd been spoilt, that was his trouble. Own way and a bag to put it in, from day one. I didn't say that to her, of course. I went along wi' it, and vowed to keep it a secret. Partly I felt really sorry for her, partly I knew it was the drink talking and she'd wake up next morning regretting having told me. We've never spoken about it since.'

'But a baby girl? Cissie, it doesn't make sense.'

'How do you mean, love?'

So I started to tell her about Callum. I told her how he'd first appeared at the bus stop, then at the library, and what he'd claimed to be. 'He said he'd found me on the Internet,' I said, remembering

234

how happy I'd been that day in Miss Dragon's office, and now it was all spoiled. 'He told me about his life and his interests, that he was "straightforward"—I remember that. Of course, I can't believe a single word in retrospect. He could have been anybody, lived anywhere. And right from the word go it was all about Dad, what sort of music he'd liked, could he see a picture, that sort of thing. Pretending his real focus was my mother.' I recalled the way he'd pored over that photo of her; God, he was a good actor.

'And you had him in the house, on your own?' Cissie looked grim. 'Eeh, I think you've had a lucky escape. He could have done anything at you.'

I remembered him palming the beetle diagram. What else had he nicked while he was there? 'He seemed nice at the time.'

'Well, they do. Have you been in touch with the police?'

For all the misery of the situation, I couldn't help smiling. 'And what would they charge him with, exactly? Impersonating a cousin?'

Cissie huffed. 'A phone call wouldn't hurt. They might have his details on their records.'

I shook my head. How to explain that, despite all the lies, he'd felt like the best friend I'd ever had and I still missed him like crazy. The summer of Callum. It had been my best time of my life. I could never tell Cissie about his smell, his laugh, his eyes. That kiss. Oh God, that awful, awful kiss.

'Are y' all right? You've gone a funny colour.'

I swallowed. 'I was still trying to work out how the two stories fit together. You say it was a girl, then this son turns up. Either Poll got it wrong, and the baby was a boy, or there's another one out there, a half-sister, by someone else again.'

I loosed my hand and stood up, feeling as heavy as if I'd stepped out of water. *Don't tell me to relax* said a poster next to Cissie's bed, picture of a hairy terrier; *It's only my tension that's holding me together.*

'Either way,' I said at last, 'my dad wasn't very nice, was he?'

'I think he loved *you*,' said Cissie, looking up at me anxiously.

'Yeah,' I said. But I thought, she could so easily be lying, couldn't she? It's all just words, in the end.

I felt as though I'd lost two people. Back in my room I stared at Dad's portrait, willing him to explain. The grin, the floppy fringe; you'd think he hadn't a care in the world. I looked for Callum's face in his features, saw as if for the first time the long-lashed eyes, though the jaw was different. Or was it? I wasn't sure any more. Through the window, the sky was mostly clear and blue, with some indefinite wisps hanging over the Pike. I watched them for ages, still holding the photo frame, but in the end they melted to nothing.

It was your mother's fault, I imagined him saying. *She drove me away, with her mad behaviour.*

Was it my fault too, for being a difficult baby?

No, absolutely not. You were great. You were my little girl.

Poll calling from next door evaporated the fantasy. 'I need a hand,' she was shouting. She sounded upset.

I went through to her room and found her with her sweater up round her neck and her bra tied in knots. Her old breasts sagged down over her blown-out stomach.

'Blasted thing,' she said. 'I don't know what I've done.'

I tried not to look as I pulled the sweater off and turned my attention to the bra. I'd never done anything so intimate for her before and we were both ratty with embarrassment.

'What the hell have you done to it?'

'I don't know. I can't flamin' see, can I?'

Normally she's good with bras. At the market she chooses ones with silk rosebuds on the front, so she can still cut the scratchy labels off but she doesn't get them inside out; or, in the event of no rosebud style being available, I sew a shirt button between the cups for her to feel. Glamorous it isn't.

'You've managed to twist every damn strap there is. God. And you've bent the hook, so it won't fasten any more. That's with yanking it. I'll have to cut it off and sew another on, unless I can force it back into shape with some pliers. Look, take this one off and start again with another.'

I wrenched open the bra drawer and threw a new Playtex at her. She caught it as it hit her chest, and started to unravel it, feeling for the button. I went round the back to help.

'I'm all right now,' she snapped. 'Go and get t' kettle on, do summat useful.'

I thumped downstairs and made two mugs of tea, then took mine to the settee so I could sit next to Winston. I stroked his bony brow but he didn't wake up.

'All he does is sleep these days,' said Poll, peering over the back of the settee as she walked past. 'Mind, it'll do him good. He dun't cough while he's asleep.'

She came in with her tea and sat in the armchair

237

nearest me. 'Dickie says, if he's still coughing by Monday, we should tek him to t' vet's. He might have got a piece of bone fast in his throat. Or it could be furballs; he does chew hisself a lot, so it's likely. Dickie's been putting Vaseline on his nose to stop him getting bunged up; apparently it works a treat for cats. They lick it off and it lubricates their insides, he saw it on *Pet Rescue*. I'd have put it on Winston myself, except I'd probably have greased his back end by mistake.' She laughed wheezily.

'Or used Vicks, and had his nose on fire.'

'Aye, well.'

'I know; I should try being blind.'

'Well, you should. Then you'd have more patience.' Poll sipped her tea virtuously.

'That's the pot calling the kettle. You're the shortest-tempered person I know.'

'I've a lot to put up with.'

'Haven't we all.'

Winston let out a huge shuddering sigh. We held our breaths to see if he'd cough, but he only yawned and smacked his chops.

She mumbled something into her mug and got to her feet.

'You what?'

'I said, I'm sorry if I was a bit sharp with you upstairs. It's frustrating, though.'

I nearly dropped my tea on the carpet.

She went on: 'Are you having some malt loaf? I could just do with some.'

'Let me come round a minute, I feel quite dizzy.' She missed the sarcasm completely. 'Yeah, all right.' I balanced the mug on the arm of the settee and stood up. 'But I'll cut, you can butter. I'm sick to death of blood on my cakes.'

*   *   *

A week later I paid a visit to Dad's. I had no key any more and there was no answer when I rang the bell. All Mum's pots were dead, and there was post on the mat behind the letterbox. I got in through the kitchen window at the back.

I could see straight away things weren't right. It smelt. There was food on the floor round the bin and you couldn't see the drainer for pots. And it was a shock, because Mum always kept everywhere beautiful. I thought, he's died. I'll go through and find him full length on the rug.

He was lying on the sofa and he wasn't dead. He wasn't even asleep. He rolled his eyes when he saw me. I said, 'I'll make a start on the kitchen.'

When I went back in the lounge he'd gone upstairs, so I tidied round the sofa too. There was a bottle of Lucozade by one corner, except, when I sniffed it, it wasn't Lucozade at all. I poured it down the toilet and threw the bottle in the bin.

After half an hour he came down again, and he was in fresh clothes. I carried on washing up, didn't say anything.

'I wouldn't have recognized you,' he said. 'You've gone that thin.'

'Have you any milk?' I asked.

He just looked at the floor.

'I'll pop down to Haslet's and get some. Is there anything else, while I'm there?'

I could have been a Martian, the way he kept staring.

'I heard about your feller. Where's the baby?' he said finally.

239

'I lost it,' I said. Which was true in a way.

He nodded. 'We're out of bread and lavatory paper,' he said. 'You'll want some Shreddies. I'll make a list. Do you have a car? You could have a run to Tesco's.'

'No car,' I said. 'And I'm off Shreddies at the moment.'

'Whatever you want, then,' he said, and shuffled out. And just like that, I was home.

Chapter Nineteen

I didn't want him near me ever again, but I wanted an explanation. Every day that passed and I hadn't heard from Callum, I thought about destroying the wasp pendant. I imagined hurling it in the River Douglas, or burying it somewhere in the cemetery. Or laying it on the railway line so it got bent out of shape the next time a train passed. Poll used to do that with pennies when she was a girl; other children's, not her own.

Two things stopped me getting rid of the pendant, though. One was, it was the only physical reminder I had of my brother, and if I threw it away, I might as well have dreamed him. And the second was to do with my place at Oxford, in case the wasps were somehow related by luck, and junking the pendant meant forfeiting the grades. I thought I'd hang on to it till after the results came out, at any rate.

The night before, Rebecca phoned in a state; said she'd had a dream that she'd sat the wrong paper, and did I think it was too late to call Mrs Clements to check? I'd been pretty cool about results day till then, but afterwards I was like something on springs.

'For God's sake, sit down. You're mekking me weary just watching you,' moaned Poll as I hovered painfully between the living room and the kitchen.

'Leave her alone, she's on edge,' said Dogman over his shoulder. 'Hey, Katherine, while you're up can you do us some cheese on toast?'

I made it without grumbling, ate half a packet of Fig Rolls while I watched the grill. After all, he was harmless; there was no mystery about Dogman. He was disgusting, but he wasn't about to come out with any jarring revelations. Better the Dogman you know.

That night it took me ages to get off to sleep, and when I did I dreamed I was back in the interview room with Honor asking me about my AS texts. The questions weren't difficult, but every time I tried to answer, I found my mouth was full of chewing gum. I tried to pull it out but there was more and more, great long strings of it, until it was all over my hands and blouse, and my mouth still full. Honor looked totally pissed off with me and I knew I'd failed.

Winston woke me, hawking in my ear, at six, so I went downstairs in my dressing gown to wait for the post. Two hours later, Poll made an appearance.

'Have they come yet?'

'No.'

'You've to phone Maggie when they do, remember.'

I went back up to have a wash, straining my ears all the time for the letter box.

'Summat's come,' I heard Poll shout up. I threw

the towel on the floor, pulled the dressing gown on again and thundered down the stairs.

YOU HAVE PAST, 10/10 said the note she was holding. It had been written on a piece of cereal packet. Bloody Dogman.

'What's it say?' asked Poll.

Dogman tapped at the front window. 'I've a doctor's appointment at nine, can't stop. I'll see you later,' he mouthed through the glass. He took a good long look at my cleavage before backing off down the path. I was delighted to see him smack into the edge of the coping stone and wince in pain.

'It's a good-luck card,' I told her. 'I'm going to get dressed now.' But as I turned to go, I spotted the postman way off near the top of the brow. I could have run out naked, I was so desperate.

At last the letter box clunked and there was my future on the mat. I ran to open the envelope.

'Is it here?' asked Poll, somewhere in the background.

I let out a howl of grief and collapsed on the chair. 'I've failed! I don't believe it, I've failed. How? How did that happen? Oh bloody, bloody hell.' I buried my face in the cushion while Poll swiped the bit of paper off the arm and went to get her magnifier.

I raised my head to see her standing by the window, frowning. If only she could see something different printed there.

'I can't mek it out, it's too small.'

'It's two As and two Bs.'

'Two As and two Bs? How is that a fail? You told me it was a U if you didn't pass. Honest, what are you like? Histrionics over nowt. You want summat to skrike about, you do.' She threw the scrap of paper at me and it swooped to the floor.

'But the A in General Studies doesn't *count*. God. I was supposed to get AAB, at least. How have I got a B in English, for God's sake?'

'What do you mean, you were "supposed to get"?'

I buried my face in my hands. 'You might as well know now, 'cause I'm not going. I had a place at Oxford. I didn't tell you because there didn't seem any point. Well, there isn't now, that's for sure.'

As Poll stood and scratched her head, I ran back to my room to get dressed. I had to get out of the house, and quickly.

I must have sat for an hour or so on the war memorial. Why was my life so crap? Why couldn't just one thing turn out right for me? I knew I was clever, and that wasn't boasting, that was empirical fact based on years and years of exam results and coursework and reports and what Mrs Law had said to me, and God knows, I'd lived with the swot label for years and I wasn't even going to reap the reward, it was so BLOODY unfair.

—But you weren't going to university anyway. You know you couldn't leave Poll on her own. You always knew that. You should never have applied in the first place.

—I could go. I could! Now the place at Univ had been taken off me, I realized I'd never wanted anything else so badly. Poll would have sorted something out with Dogman or Maggie, or I could have had a proper go at the council to see about a home help. Just because her life was restricted was no reason for mine to be as well. I'd have done it somehow.

—That's a fib and you know it. Never mind

243

worrying about Poll, that's a smokescreen. You're too scared to leave. That's the truth. You think you'd never cope on your own.

—I would cope, I really would. They have college rooms for you to live in, and college parents to look out for you, and there are clubs to join, and tutors to talk to if you're feeling low. And you get three meals a day but I know how to cook and clean anyway, that side of things. Thanks to Poll, I can wire a plug in seconds.

—*And how good are you at speaking to strangers? Finding your way round new places? Have you really thought through how complicated adult life is? There are trains and buses to catch, maps to read, bank accounts to manage, doctors to register with; there are relationships to form and maintain and finish, all sorts of social events to attend. At some point you'll have to learn to drive, apply for jobs, rent a house. Can you honestly imagine yourself doing these things?*

—I can't be the only one, though, there must be other students feeling scared about leaving home. I thought of Rebecca, Donna, Nicky, Alex, whatever our results were today, all of us peeling away from our old lives and spinning off into the unknown. Terrifying. But people coped, didn't they?

—*You don't have to go anywhere. Clare Greenhalgh has bought a house two doors down from her mum and goes round every night for her tea. Better to be dull and safe. And how would Winston feel if you walked out on him? You can't explain a degree to a dog. He'd probably pine to death, and it would be your fault.*

Rainy afternoons with Winston on my lap and a box of chocolates between me and Poll on the sofa. Was it such a bad life? Being a carer was an important job, that's what the Rehab officer had told me. The world couldn't turn without carers. I'd never have to justify my lifestyle, leading Poll on my arm.

Then Dogman popped into my head; Dogman taking us to a cafe in Bolton once after a big win on the horses, me pointing out that other customers were leaving tips, Dogman shouting out, 'Tip? They want a tip? I'll give 'em a tip. Never wipe your arse on a broken bottle.' Everyone turning round to stare while he guffawed at his own wit.

I had to get to Oxford. I had to get to Oxford, or I'd die.

There were quills all across the sky as I walked home. There's irony for you, I thought, now trying to pick over the exam questions where I might have slipped a grade.

They were sitting round the table when I got in; Maggie, Dogman and Poll, sharing a Swiss roll.

'There's a Mrs Lord been on t' phone for you,' Poll piped up. 'She says summat about your "insurance", is that right? Anyroad, you've to ring her, she says.'

I knew what that would be. Did I want to take up my reserve offer at Aberystwyth. No, was the answer. I only stuck it down because we had to put something, and it happened to be the first one on the list.

I dialled the school number with shaking hands but only got the engaged tone.

'Well, Vince was a clever man, you know,' Poll was saying. 'Brilliant wi' figures. He should have been an accountant, really. Not stuck at t' loco works all them years.'

'And your Roger.' Maggie nodded

245

sympathetically.

'Oh, now he was sharp as a tack. Mind you, I went in for th' Eleven Plus, and there were only six of us sat it.'

'Aye, I remember that,' said Maggie. 'Were it a clerical error?'

'I don't know. Unless my father demanded I sit it. He were a bit of a mard, that headmaster, he might have put me in for th' exam just so he could have a quiet life.'

'Didn't you have a funny turn, though?'

Poll laughed creakily. 'It were t' statues. All these naked statues round the room.'

'Where was it? The Mechanics'?'

'That's right. I'd never seen owt like it. And they put me bang next to a marble man, all his tackle hanging out. So the first thing I do is, I knock my inkwell ovver and there's ink everywhere, on their nice parquet and down t' table leg. I was never going to pass after that.'

Maggie tutted and took another slice of roll. 'I weren't clever at school. Do you remember the time Miss Eavis asked us which window we should shake a duster out of? She wanted me to say, it depends on the way the wind's blowing, but I said the back window, in case the neighbours see how dusty your house is. She thought I was being cheeky. And I got the cane once off Mr Marsden, for saying the Equator was an imaginary lion that ran round the world. They weren't nice like they are now, teachers.'

'I'm dyslexic,' said Dogman.

The phone rang under my hand and I jumped a mile.

'Hello? May I speak to Katherine Millar please?'

246

My heart rejoiced to hear Mrs Law's stern tones.

I started to gabble about Aberystwyth and having a re-mark, but she stopped me.

'I've been onto the Admissions Tutor at University College and they're going to call me back. There's nothing you can do at the moment but wait. Would you be prepared to accept a deferred place, if one were offered?'

'I don't know. I'm scared that if I don't go this year, I'll never go. Do you understand what I mean?'

'Yes, I think I do.' Mrs Law was brisk. 'But you'd take it if it was the only option?'

'I suppose.'

'Good. I'll get back to you as soon as I hear from them. All right?'

After I put the receiver down I had to face Poll.

'So, did you get in, or what?' There's something about Poll's eyes; even though she can't see very well, it feels as though she's staring into your soul. Maggie and Dogman turned to look at me.

'They're going to let me know. But if I do get a place, I'm going to take it, Poll. I have to.'

Poll's face fell. I could tell she was totally shocked. Maggie reached across and patted her on the arm. Dogman shrugged and took an enormous bite of cake.

'Cross that bridge when you come to it,' murmured Maggie, still patting away.

'I'll be upstairs, then,' I said, like the coward I was. 'Can nobody use the phone till Mrs Law calls back?'

'Now don't get yourself in a state. It'll probably come to naught,' I heard Maggie say as I left the room.

It was past dinner time when Mrs Law called back. I went to tell Poll straight after. She was in the kitchen with Maggie, Dogman having gone off to the betting shop. Maggie was watching her make a cup of tea; pick up the cordless kettle with one hand, find the tap with the other and turn it on, feel up the side of the kettle for the spout and, keeping her fingers there, move it across the sink till it was under the stream and she had water splashing over her fingertips; then take her fingers away whilst keeping the kettle totally still. I saw her listening for the sound of it getting full and testing the weight of it through her wrist. Then she turned back and felt around for the little contact knob on the kettle base, and slotted it home. Her fingers crawled up the handle to the switch at the top, and she flicked it on. I slipped over and turned the tap off for her.

'Well?'

'I've got in. I've got a place at Oxford for this October,' I said, feeling queasy with fear and happiness.

'That's smashing, love,' said Maggie, uncertainly. 'Fancy. We s'll have to start talking posh now, you and me, Poll. Holding our little fingers up when we sup our tea.'

Poll's expression was one of utter dismay. 'So are you going?'

Maggie held her breath.

'I don't see how I can't. It's a once-in-a-lifetime opportunity. Some people would give their right arm for a place.'

'That's right,' said Maggie. 'You've to mek the most of your education. Although Manchester University's very good, and it's close to home.

Dawn's Paul went there and he works for Marks and Spencer's now.'

'But I haven't got a place at Manchester. I've got one at Oxford. Don't you see, being clever is the only thing I've ever been good at. It's the right place for me. It'll give me time to think what to do with my life. I'll come back.'

'Aye, but will you?' wailed Poll. 'Will you come back to your blind old grandma once you've tasted the good life? Or will you be off to London or somewhere, doing some high-powered job with no time even for a visit?'

'Of course she'll come back,' said Maggie. 'Won't you, love? Yes, look, she says she will.'

'But how am I going to cope without you?'

The kettle clicked off. Poll reached for it angrily and, before either Maggie or I could stop her, she'd snatched it up and poured boiling water over the kitchen top and down her leg.

'How am I going to manage on my own?' she kept saying as we cut her tights off and bathed her shin with cold water. 'Is it blistering?'

'No, it's just red, that's all,' said Maggie.

'Well, it stings like the devil. I should see a doctor.'

'I don't think there's any need.' I left them while I went to mop up the mess in the kitchen.

'What if I'm in shock?' she shouted after me.

'I'll ring the surgery, ask Mrs Ashburner at reception, if you like.'

'Aye, do that. Tell her I'm in terrible pain.'

I'll tell her you are a pain, I thought. She's tipped scalding water on herself deliberately, Mrs Ashburner. What would you do with her?

'Tell you what,' I said from the doorway, 'I'll go

up there and ask if there's anything I can get from the chemist. Are you all right to stay, Maggie?'

Maggie nodded. But she followed me to the front door.

'You have to understand, love, she lost her son when he went away to college.'

Do you think I'm stupid, I nearly said. 'I know. But that was different.'

'I'm just saying.'

I backed out, pulling the door to sharply. I needed to go to the library and see Miss Dragon.

*　　　*　　　*

'It wasn't exactly *The Corn is Green*,' I told Miss Dragon. No one to lift me shoulder-high and carry me in triumph down the street: nobody strong enough.

'I expect your grandma's proud, really, she needs some time to get used to the idea. Anyway, never mind that. You've got in, that's what's important,' she said, giving me a hug unexpectedly. Miss Mouse, standing by, touched my arm and smiled shyly. This was more like it. I hadn't felt so happy for ages.

'We've got you this, for your studies,' Miss Dragon went on, bringing out a Waterstone's bag from under the counter. 'I'd have given it to you whether or not, because I know you'll use it.'

It felt like a brick, but it turned out to be *The Oxford Companion to English Literature*. Both women had signed their names under a Best Wishes for the Future message on the flyleaf. I glanced round to see who might be watching, but there was hardly anyone in; Thursday afternoon, a quarter to two. Come half three it gets busier, when school comes out.

'I feel I have a vested interest in your education.' Miss Dragon picked up a pile of leaflets from the desk and shuffled them like cards till they were edge to edge neatly. She lined them up with the corner of the counter. 'We think you'll go on to great things. It's about time you left us behind, spread your wings.'

Then the phone rang and Miss Dragon picked up. I stood for a while, in case it was going to be a short call and there'd be more time for singing my praises. Miss Mouse waited too, smiling all the time.

'Well done,' she whispered, twice, before drifting away.

I watched her thread her way between revolving book stands to work at the table Callum and I had used, last time we'd been here. Callum again. When was he going to stop invading my head? But I ached to tell him my news. *Fan-fucking-tastic*, I could hear him saying. I wished to God he'd call, even if it was only so I could tell him to get lost.

I looked back at stout, lovely Miss Dragon tapping the notepad with her blunt-ended fingers, her mouth showing impatience with whoever was on the other end. She was stretching herself up straight and pulling her cardigan round her. I could tell she was cross with someone. But she liked me. And whatever I'd been thinking, even if she was a lesbian, there was no gayness in that hug. It had been warm and kind, happy for my happiness; maternal.

*　　　*　　　*

251

It wasn't long before Vince caught up with me. I wasn't sure what you did when you left a rented place, so I'd taken the keys but left a note of my dad's phone number on top of the TV. Daft really, but I wasn't thinking straight.

We met on the Town Hall steps; I told him where I'd be. When I handed over the keys, he said, 'If you're sure. You could have stayed there longer, if you wanted.'

'Will you be coming back?'

'No,' he said. 'I've to look after her now. She's been pretty poorly.' He scratched his head like he was embarrassed. 'She took some finding.'

'Who?' I asked, because I wanted to hear him say it.

'Judith.'

'And the baby.'

'Aye; and t' little lad. Little Callum.' He'd smiled fondly and I'd wanted to slap him in the face.

'I don't need you any more,' I said rudely.

'I know,' he said. 'But I'll still send you money.'

In films they always say, 'I don't want your money', but I kept quiet. The packets came for years, all the time I was at college, and I spent them all.

Don't think I loved him, because I didn't. I realized long ago he wasn't father material; Katherine's or mine. He was just useful for a while.

Chapter Twenty

Rebecca got her place at Bristol, Donna was off to Lancaster by the skin of her teeth. For two whole weeks I was leaving Bank Top to go to Oxford, till Fate poked me in the eye once again.

At home, Poll, Maggie and Dogman had been mounting a three-pronged attack to dissuade me from going.

'You'll have to completely change the way you talk, you know. They'll never understand you like you are. They'll think you're mentally deficient.'— Poll.

'I've brought you a brochure on Manchester University. It's six year owd, but I don't suppose t' place has changed that much. Dawn says Paul was home every weekend, and he could have stopped there if he'd wanted, and travelled in each day. It would save you a stack of money. Otherwise you end up in terrible debt, for years.'—Maggie.

'I've brought you a video, about some college girls who all get murdered one by one. Killer's in t' roof space and he comes down at night and chops bits off 'em.'—Dogman.

I spent every hour I could at the library, where Miss Dragon was compiling me a reading list while we waited on the official one turning up.

'Some of these I've had to order in from Manchester Central,' she said, scrutinizing the column of titles. 'Of course, you'll soon have access to one of the finest libraries in the country.' She looked at me over the top of her reading glasses. 'You're a lucky girl, you know.'

253

'I appreciate that.'

'How's your grandma?'

'Livid.'

Miss Dragon sighed and leaned her forearms on the counter. 'I gave up decades of my life to look after my father. And after he died, what was there left?'

'I don't know.'

'A bungalow in Harrop, to myself. Of course, I had my qualifications and my job, one keeps busy, there's the RSPB . . . But I like to think I could have got a little further, had I made different choices. So let your grandma be livid. You have a life to lead.'

'I've got an interview with the Rehab Officer next week, to talk through care packages.'

'Well, that's splendid. Taking practical action; good.'

'Yeah. The trouble is, she's so stubborn. They have people to train you, show you how to do ordinary household tasks with limited vision, but she won't let them in the house. She says they'll snoop. And they have all sorts of gadgets, talking clocks, embossers, brilliant stuff, but she's really choosy about what she has.'

Miss Dragon frowned. 'Why is that? You'd think she'd want to be independent.'

'Oh, she does and she doesn't. One minute she's wailing for help, the next she's shrugging you off. I can't do right for doing wrong. The objection to the gadgets is that they cost money.'

'Doesn't she get them free? She should do, a pensioner with . . . Sorry, I'm assuming she has no assets. None of my business, of course.'

'No, you're right. She's as poor as a church

254

mouse, she's always telling me.' Which is why no computer, no mobile phone, charity-shop clothes, I could have carried on. But I didn't want Miss Dragon to think I cared about things like that.

'So what's the problem? Are social services being awkward about it? I've heard some dreadful stories about means testing.'

'Social services are fine. Well, they did lose a form once and we were waiting for ages, but mainly they're pretty helpful. It's Poll who's the obstruction. She says she won't have them going through her private documents. She says she came from a generation where your personal finances were nobody's business but your own, and she doesn't see why total strangers should see how little money she has and make mock.'

Miss Dragon tutted. 'People of your grandma's age are often fiercely proud. I don't suppose she approves of credit either, does she?'

'God, no. Not least because to get yourself a credit card you have to give all sorts of information about yourself. She's spitting fire when these researchers stop her in the street and ask what brand of cooking oil she prefers. She hit a woman once. It was so embarrassing.'

'I can imagine it was.'

Miss Mouse floated by and smiled sideways, without raising her head.

I felt like I was back in the fold again.

*   *   *

Walking back down the village, under a sky that threatened drizzle, I tried to see Bank Top as though for the first time. Imagine not living here

255

any more. Would I miss the place? Past the doctors' surgery, with its nosy waiting room, always someone calling out some awkward question or other when you went in to collect a prescription. Past the church where I'd had to go every Easter, Christmas and Harvest, on account of attending a church school, and where Revd Rowland had once given a really good talk on bullying, which had had no effect whatsoever. Past the sweetie shop, the Methodists', the road leading to Bank Top Primary Hell. It was impossible to see this long street as just a road with buildings on it. Everything was filtered through memories.

That led me to thinking about Oxford, and what it would actually be like starting university. Would I get a room to myself? With a sink? What if there was nowhere to be sick in private, and I put on *stones* in weight?

What if I got lost on the way to a tutorial? And the don thought I was messing about, and assumed that I was lazy? What if everyone turned out to be way cleverer than me? If it came out that I only got a B, while all the other students had As? And they decided I was only let in because I was from a lower-class background? Did you have to write your grades down anywhere, so people could see? Maybe they got read out at the first tutorial.

What if all the other students had loads of money, and did expensive hobbies that I couldn't join in with? Or they all had dead posh clothes? What if they really *couldn't* understand my accent?

What if the door had been the omen, and not the wasp?

I don't know what I'd been thinking. Leave home, me? Two minutes, I'd last.

I wanted to call in at the cemetery, but I'd already been longer than I'd said and there was Winston to walk so I carried on down the Brow, feeling thoroughly depressed. As soon as I got in, I'd find Poll's tea tray and hit myself over the head with it a few times.

I felt in my peggy purse for the key, then realized I'd left it on the sideboard. I rang the bell and waited. Normally you get a scratching of claws on wood, some snuffling or a bark, followed by old-woman swearing in the background. But today all was quiet. Poll must be round at Maggie's, or in the garden. So I went down the ginnel at the side of the house and through the gate. The garden was empty and the back door locked.

In the outhouse, where Poll once used to keep coal and which currently houses a broken washing machine that Dogman's going to fix someday, I felt above the lintel for the spare key. Then I let myself into the kitchen and pressed the kettle switch as I walked past. I flipped up the lid of the bread bin, extracted a chocolate sponge slice from the plastic packaging, and folded it, whole, into my mouth.

I only found Poll when I came through into the living room.

It was like those TV murders, where all you see at first is a hand sticking out. I gaped down at her curled-over fingers for a second, then ran round to the other side of the sofa to see the rest. She was flat out on her back, one arm flung above her head, eyes closed. Her skirt was up above her knees, showing the top of her tights, and her forehead was bleeding where she'd struck it against the gas fire as she went down. One slipper was missing. For a second I thought she'd been attacked. Then I spotted Winston, also motionless, near her feet. I know it sounds mad but I went to him first.

I pushed his head gently up and it rolled sideways in my hand. When I let go, it just flopped to the carpet. His flank had a caved-in look about it; he reminded me of an empty nightdress case. I couldn't see breathing.

'Poll,' I yelped in fright. 'Poll? Can you hear me?'

I turned back and knelt by her head. I reached out to touch her cheek, my arms weak with panic. Her eyelids flickered.

'Poll!'

No response, so I heaved myself up and made for the telephone. Trembling all over, I dialled for an ambulance, listened to the choices, answered some questions. I was to keep talking to her, they said. Gather any medication she needed. Don't attempt to move her, or give her anything to eat or drink. Paramedics would be there within fifteen minutes.

I should have gone back to sit with her but instead I phoned Dogman's mobile. Maggie would have been nicer but she's no car and she's not allowed to lift anything heavy.

'I'm only at t' top of t' Brow,' I heard him shout through the swish of traffic. 'I were coming round anyway to knock a nail in that bit of carpet on t' landing. Get some Bailey's down her, that might bring her to.'

I ignored this stupidity and went to sit by Poll, who was now twitching her head and moving her lips like a dreamer.

'You're OK,' I kept saying, which was a huge lie but it's what you say to accident victims even when limbs are hanging off. 'I've called an ambulance and Dickie's on his way.' I wondered whether to lie about Winston too.

Then the door burst open and Dogman was there, two carrier bags full of crap in his hands as usual. He dumped the bags on the floor.

'Have you a blanket?' he said. 'We could put a cushion under her head too.'

'I don't think you've to move the patient,' I told him. I lowered my voice: 'In case you paralyse them.' I went to get the blanket, though.

When I came back he was prodding Winston while still talking to Poll. He made a slitting-throat gesture at me and pointed to the dog, let's hope he never goes in for bereavement counselling, then swivelled on his haunches and peered closely at Poll. 'What's this in her hair?' he hissed. 'It looks like mouse dirt.'

I leaned over. 'Chocolate sprinkles,' I said, like it was perfectly normal. I knew it was probably down my front as well as round my mouth. 'Shift out of the way then I can throw this blanket over her. Did you leave the front door open for the ambulance men?'

Just before they came to take her away, Poll woke up. We watched her eyes focus and unfocus a few times before she was really with us. 'I tripped ovver Winston,' she said weakly.

'I know, I guessed.'

'He's poorly, I think.' She tried to raise her head.

'No, he's fine. Just sound asleep,' said Dogman.

She drifted off again. Then, as the paramedics shouted from the hall, she squinted at me. 'You took your bloody time, you did.'

The paramedics were upbeat about the

259

situation.

'What's your name, love?' Pause. 'What's her name?'

'Pollyanna Millar. We call her—'

'Pollyanna? Pollyanna, can you hear me, love? You've been in the wars, haven't you? But we'll soon have you in safe hands. We'll have you break-dancing again before you know it. Can you tell us where it hurts? Can you feel this? Could you give my hand a little squeeze? That's smashing. Now we're just going to lift you onto a stretcher, so you might—'

While they got her onto the stretcher, Dogman saw to Winston, rolling him up tenderly in the blanket. 'I'll have him,' he whispered. 'You go with Poll.'

'Are you going to the vet's with him?'

'Do you think there's any point?'

'There's some money for bills in the top drawer. Take him, please. Just in case.'

'Aye, awreet, I will.' Dogman shifted the blanket against him as though he was carrying a baby. 'Give us a ring from th' hospital, will you?'

I nodded, and we all trooped out.

'Have you locked your front door, love?' said the lady paramedic as we stood by the back of the ambulance. 'Only there's scum who'll break in even at times like this.'

I ran back to check, even though I knew for certain I'd shut it with the latch on.

*   *   *

It had been a long day, but it was an even longer night. They sent me home about eight, by which time they thought Poll might only be suffering from concussion and a twisted ankle, but they said they still wanted to keep her in for observation. I wondered if her notes said, 'Pollyanna Millar: fell over dog'.

I had to get the bus back, in the dark, and I had no coat and only just had enough money for the fare. When I got there, the house was chilly and there were no lights on, and I was shaking with cold and nerves as I walked in through the porch.

I checked every room as I went round lighting the place up, in case a burglar had got in, hidden himself in the wardrobes or under the beds, or in the airing cupboard, or under the stairs with the vacuum cleaner, or behind the long curtains in the front room, or under the sink. I struggled not to think about the Killer who lived in the Attic, or rapists who shinned up drainpipes.

Our attic entrance was over the landing and, when I went to look, well covered with unbroken cobwebs, so clearly no psychopath was using it as a hideout at the moment. But the idea of a man scaling the walls and his face rising up against the blackness freaked me so much I had to go and make sure all the windows were shut tight. Then I re-checked the beds, wardrobes, etc. in case some-one *had* climbed in upstairs while I'd been downstairs. All the time I was thinking, this is so stupid, because even if Poll was here and an axe murderer broke in, what could she do against him?

Then I imagined Winston leaping to my defence against an intruder, in a feeble, miniature sort of way, and that made me feel so sad and lonely I started to cry. When I'd called earlier from the Royal Bolton, Dogman had said the vet thought

Winston had been run over. He must have hopped through the dog-flap and then nipped out illegally through the gate, although I'd not left it open. Maybe Poll thought she'd put the bolt on when she hadn't. Anyway, he'd probably seen something on the opposite pavement and gone hurtling across. Nobody knocked at the door and said, I think I've flattened your dog, but then the driver might not even have spotted him, he's so small. There was some blood in his poo, the vet said, so that meant internal bleeding, and his claws were frayed at the tips as if he'd been pushed along tarmac at speed. Dogman described Winston staggering home and dragging himself through the flap, across the kitchen and living room, to collapse between the sofa and the armchair, where he died. I saw it all as he spoke. How was I ever going to break it to Poll?

Poll, lying crumpled on the carpet; Poll under a white sheet on a metal bed with glazed eyes, this terrible gash on her forehead. Me standing there in turmoil, waiting for the doctors to tell me what was going on. What if they were wrong and it had been something serious that affected her balance? Maybe I'd go tomorrow and they'd take me off into a side-room, like they do on *Casualty* when they have to break bad news, and say, 'Are you next of kin?'

And now back at home, alone and upset, with no dog even. I never thought I could miss her so much. I hadn't spent a night on my own ever before. Dad was no help now, of course, smirking at me from his photos, the big deceiver. I wasn't speaking to him because when I'd gone to the cemetery to tackle him about Callum, all he'd sent was a cloud-trail of Morse code. 'Sackless bloody

262

symbolism,' I'd shouted up at the sky. 'Why do you have to talk in riddles all the time?'

I almost phoned Dogman again: I was *that* desperate, even though it would probably have been a frying-pan/fire situation. I could just imagine the sort of comfort he'd offer, given half a chance. My opportunity to see the glories that lay beneath his manky old coat.

Instead I called Maggie and brought her up to date, even though I'd in fact told her all the news from the payphone at hospital. 'Did I get you out of bed?' I asked, when I realized she had no teeth in. She said not, so I spun the call out for fifteen minutes. I couldn't tell half of what she said but it didn't matter.

After that I went to the kitchen, piled some food on a plate, did one more recce of the house and retired to my room with a chair against the door. I started on *Pride and Prejudice* because that's my ultimate comfort book, the one that always makes me feel better. The number of times I've hidden inside Mr Bennet's library. But the house was creaking and groaning as though an entire army of burglars was scouting the downstairs, and I couldn't get past the first page. I seemed to have forgotten how to read.

It seemed a long time till it got light outside again.

*   *   *

There's no drug like a book. If I couldn't read, I'd die.

Chapter Twenty-One

It took a whole week till Poll returned—some problem with her blood pressure and a suspected hairline fracture—and ten days to admit that I wasn't going anywhere. There was still a month and a half till term started but I knew the whole idea of leaving to become a student a hundred miles away had always been a fantasy. My instinct had been right. I would never, ever cope on my own.

Which was just as well, because Poll had turned really clingy.

'I don't know what they did to her in th' hospital,' whispered Maggie, as Poll took herself off upstairs, limping and sighing and clutching her chest. 'She keeps having these dos, panic attacks she calls them. Our Dawn had them after little Kayleigh was born. One time she couldn't go out of th' house and she'd run out of nappies. When I went round she'd put a sanitary towel on t' baby and taped it down with sticking plaster.'

I shrugged. I hated babies. Dawn could have wrapped it in Bacofoil for all I cared. 'How long did it last?'

'The sticking plaster?'

'No, having panic attacks.'

'Oh, well, she waited I don't know how long before saying owt in case they thought she were an unfit mother and took Kayleigh into care. But she went to t' doctor in t' finish, and he gave her tablets. Psoriasis, I think they were called.'

'That's a disease.'

Maggie narrowed her eyes. 'Eh, I don't know.

Summat-sis. I'll ask next time I see her. But Poll's got to get over losing her dog, that was a terrible shock for her on top of the fall. And with you going too . . .'

I got up quickly and went in the kitchen out of her way for a minute. I looked through the smeary glass at the long narrow garden with Winston's mound at the bottom, at the faint white shadows of Dogman's melted gnomes, at the saggy washing line beaded with rain. I could simply have said, I'm not now, I'm staying put. I don't know why I didn't come straight out with the truth. Maybe I didn't want Maggie to feel she'd won. Anyway, she and Poll would know soon enough I wasn't leaving for Oxford.

When the Freshers' Guide came through the post, it was with a kind of relief that I scanned it and then threw it in the bin. You had to have a medical and I always hated those, stripping off to your underwear, watching the nurse eye your rolls of flesh; the scales with their sliding bar that had to be tipped back, and back, and back till the doctor tutted in amazement. Also on the agenda were Karaoke, Bar Quizzes, Treasure Hunts, Ice-skating, all manner of crazy fun. Condoms were available in the toilets near the JCR, because who knows but in the middle of a barn dance you might not fancy a shag with someone you've only known ten minutes. My Freshers' Week would have been a hundred and sixty-eight hours of sitting in my room trying to avoid everyone.

I did pick the envelope out of the bin, though, after a while. I'd keep the guide, with the reading list and the original letter offering me a conditional place, in the pages of Dad's textbook alongside the photo of my mother. I figured it would be a good memory to have, proof that I could have gone to Oxford if I'd wanted.

'But,' I told Maggie as we washed up together, 'if I do stay, there'll have to be some changes round here. You know, more freedom.'

'Tell your grandma,' said Maggie, rubbing at a slug trail on the back doormat with her shoe.

'I will. I've been making a list.'

We went through to where Poll was sitting, hunched and miserable, in front of *Boot Sale Challenge*. 'All the fight's gone out of her,' Maggie had said earlier; it was true. A good time to tell her what was what, then.

'I've been having a think,' I said, settling at the end of the sofa nearest Poll's chair and muting the volume on the TV.

'Oh aye? What about?'

Maggie smiled at me encouragingly. 'Go on, love.'

I took a deep breath. 'Now I'm eighteen and I've left school, I want a bit more freedom.'

Poll turned and peered at me. 'You what?'

'I'll stay under this roof, look after you—'

Poll spluttered. 'It's me as looks after you, more like.'

'Keep going,' Maggie said to me.

'But there need to be some changes round here.'

'Oh, *do* there?'

'Yes, there do. Such as, I want to come and go as I please.'

'You've got a key,' Poll huffed. 'I don't know what you're moaning about.'

'Yes, but I still have to tell you everywhere I'm going, don't I?'

'I should think so too. That's manners. I don't want to be worrying where you are all t' time. What if you're abducted, and t' police go, "Where did she say she was headed?" and I have to tell them, "I'm sorry, officer, I don't know"? That'll look good on t' news, won't it?'

'Poll's got a point,' said Maggie. 'A quick phone call to say you'll be late. Just so's she knows you're safe.'

'But not twenty bloody questions every time I step over the threshold.'

'There's no need for bad language,' said Poll. 'All right. You tell me so I don't have to ask.'

I left the point and moved on. 'I want to be able to wear what I like, not just the things you get for me off the market. They make me look like, like you. Like I'm about seventy.'

That nettled her. 'You wear what you damn well please, then, if you don't mind all and sundry looking up your skirt and down your bust. And I'm not paying out for it, you've to fund it yourself. "Vest" is all I've got to say on the matter. Dress like a trollop, see what happens.'

'Well, they do,' said Maggie. 'It's what t' young 'uns want. They all do it, show off their bits and pieces, it's the fashion.'

'I've said all I'm saying.' Poll pointed a finger in my face. 'You'll find out.'

'That's up to me. And while we're on the subject, I don't want any sarky comments about boyfriends, if I bring somebody home.'

Poll didn't say anything but she started to laugh, which was worse. I looked despairingly at Maggie.

'She's a bonny girl,' said Maggie. 'She's a lovely curvy figure. If she'd tie her hair back a bit more so

267

we could see her face . . . ' She leaned across the sofa and lifted my hair away from my cheek. 'You want to mek the most of yourself, love. Lift your head up more, put your shoulders back. You're always trying to hide away, and you've no need. You've beautiful skin.'

Poll had carried on laughing but in a forced sort of way. 'If you say so, Maggie.'

'I want to watch more of the programmes I like,' I continued. 'I'm fed up of house-decorating and quiz shows. In fact, I want a TV of my own, in my room. Everyone at school had their own TV.'

'Everyone at your school had more money than us,' snapped Poll. 'I'm a pensioner, if you hadn't noticed—'

'Now, hang on, I think our Dawn might have an old one,' Maggie interrupted. 'She were going to put it in t' free paper, but I'm sure she'd let you have it for next to nowt. I'll have a word.' She beamed at Poll. 'So that's summat else sorted out.'

'Thanks, Maggie. Where was I up to? Oh yeah, at some point I want to do an Open University course. Miss Stockley'll help me apply, and I can use the computers in the library to do the assignments.' I had in mind a degree in librarianship, but I didn't tell Poll that. I was hoping madly that Miss Dragon would be so flattered by my career choice she'd forgive me for throwing away Oxford.

Poll just shrugged.

'And the last thing is, I'm fed up of Dickie being round here all the time. Can't we see less of him? It's as if he lives here, for God's sake. I'm nearly tripping over him. I don't like the way he lets himself in now without ringing the bell.'

268

She sat upright, her brow furrowed. 'Dickie's a friend. He's good to you, I don't know why you've tekken against him all of a sudden. You used go walking with him and all sorts. You used think he was marvellous. Well, didn't you? You'd moth-eat him every time he was round. Honest, Maggie, she did.'

'I know, I can remember.' Maggie smiled fondly. 'You were a bobbin when you were small. Allus into everything, doing your little projects. I remember saving you all that tinfoil once.'

'Aye, and do you not remember Dickie building you that bird table so you could do your survey for school? You've a short memory, you have.'

That was pre-breasts, though. I said, 'He's changed.'

'You mean you have,' said Poll. 'Bread etten's soon forgetten. You ought to be more grateful for what you have, not whining for more all t' time. Anyway, Dickie's like family. Well, he is to me.'

Family; now there was a word to conjure with.

'He is harmless,' said Maggie, nodding. 'You've not to tek him seriously.' She patted me on the knee. 'So, are we straight now?'

Poll and I scowled at each other.

'Well, then,' Maggie went on, 'I wanted to show you both this in the catalogue.' She pulled a rolled-up magazine out of her shopping bag and opened it up where the corner of a page was turned over. 'Get your magnifier, Poll. Move that light closer, Katherine. Can you see?'

'Is it a penguin?' Poll cocked her head.

'No, it's a stone dog; see, it's sitting up and begging. It's the spitting image of Winston. I thought you could put it in t' garden, on his grave.'

269

Poll dragged the picture closer. 'I see him now. In't he beautiful?'

'*This life-like canine companion,*' Maggie read over her shoulder, '*crafted from hard-wearing resin, will withstand the harshest of British weather. Rain or shine, Westie will always be ready to play. Price slashed to nineteen ninety-nine.*'

'Oh yes, we've got to have one of those. Can you fill in the form for us, Maggie?'

We've money enough for that, then, I thought.

*   *   *

I got the TV, though, within days. That made me feel a whole lot better, because I could go up to my room, shut the door and watch decent programmes without a background of non-stop grumbling. It was mean in some ways, because it meant Poll had to try and make out the shows she liked all on her own downstairs, without me to fill in the crucial details. But it gave us a break from each other.

I'd started to rearrange my room too. I bagged up half the clothes in my wardrobe; I was going to take them down to Scope. Some giant old lady would be glad of them. I moved some of the furniture round, just for a change, and took most of Dad's posters down off the walls. I was fed up of living in a shrine. In their place I Blu-tacked some posters of my own; one of Virginia Woolf, one for *The Lord of the Rings*, and a black-and-white study of some trees on a hill. Dogman had given me these six months ago and I hadn't even unrolled them because I assumed they'd be smut. They were tatty round the edges, as if he'd peeled them off someone's wall himself, but he swore they were

270

from a table-top sale in Harrop.

I also repainted my door cherry red gloss from a tin I found in the outhouse, and borrowed Maggie's steam cleaner for the carpet. It came up a different colour. With tea-lights all round, a joss-stick burning, and a black lacy shawl hung over the back of the chair, the room looked nice. I'd plans for a new lampshade and a throw for the bed, with velvet cushions. Maybe I could ask for them at Christmas.

Poll thought it looked like Santa's Grotto, but Maggie was impressed when I took her up and showed her.

'You've a flair,' she said. 'Our Dawn's keen on stencilling and she's done all gold butterflies round her picture rail. You could do summat like that.'

'Look at this,' I said, holding out my hand.

'Whatever is it?'

'Isn't it obvious? It's a tractor.'

'Oh. I thought it were an old cotton reel with a drawing pin stuck in.'

'Ah, well, that's where you're wrong.' I put the collection of pieces on the dressing table and started to assemble them. 'I found it when I was clearing out; Dickie made it for me out of the *Ladybird Book of Things to Make and Do*. I remember him cutting the end of a candle off and pulling the wick out, and hunting all round the house for the right size elastic band. It still works. See. You use the matchstick to wind it up.'

We watched together as the cotton reel crawled along the top.

'It goes over hills too.' I leant a book in the tractor's way and it clambered on, and up. 'Dickie cut notches round the edges to make it grip. Clever, isn't it?'

271

'Very good,' said Maggie.

'And I tell you what.' I scooped the tractor up and let the matchstick spin. 'I've decided to be nicer to Dickie. Make more of an effort. He's not going to go away, it's no good kicking against the pricks.'

'I think you're very wise,' said Maggie solemnly. 'Mek the best of things, that's the secret of happiness. Not money.'

We heard a thump in the porch followed by Dogman singing a burst of 'On Mother Kelly's Doorstep'.

'Talk of the devil,' chuckled Maggie, nudging me in the ribs.

'Hey, look what I've got.' Dogman was standing at the bottom of the stairs, holding up a dripping carrier bag and looking pleased with himself. A dark liquid was spotting the carpet by his feet.

'What've you done at your leg?' asked Maggie, squinting down the steps at the stick he was holding. 'Have you lamed yourself? There's blood on your trousers, did you know?'

Dogman snorted, and strode through into the living room. When we got down he'd made it to the kitchen and was holding the bag over the sink. Swirls of red were pooling round the plughole. He'd obviously murdered somebody and brought their heart in a bag to show us.

'Blackberries,' he grinned. Except he pronounced it blegbrizz. 'I bet I've two pound here. The bushes on t' station car park are full of them. I could have filled twenty carriers if I'd wanted. Only thing is, I don't really like 'em myself. So I thought Katherine could mek a nice plate pie out of them. Or jam.'

'Won't they be covered in chemicals off the exhausts?' I found a mixing bowl and tipped the berries into it.

Dogman winked at me, as if I'd just said something flirtatious. 'Soak 'em in salted water, get the maggots out. That's all you need to do. Do you like my bramble hook?' He tried to twirl the cane and dropped it with a clatter on the floor.

'Poll's out in the garden,' I said, to get him off my back. 'Her Westie statue's come and we planted him this morning.'

Maggie tottered through the back door and I stayed to wash my hands. 'They always remind me of Seamus Heaney, blackberries,' I said, thinking aloud.

'Is that your boyfriend?' leered Dogman. 'You're not courting a Paddy now, are you?'

'No and no. I think Poll's calling you.' I made to get past him but he blocked my way.

'I think it's a good thing you're not going off to college.'

'And why's that, then?'

'Load of ponces, students.' Dogman folded his arms. 'The ones at Oxford are the worst. You have to wear a gown all day, I've seen it on t' telly; swanking about. Then there's all the murders. It's one a week.'

'What, in Oxford?'

'Aye. All t' posh people busy knocking each other off, when they're not listening to opera.'

I shoved him away. 'Inspector Morse is a fictional character. You know, made up. He's not real, it's a cop show.'

Dogman only smiled and tapped the side of his nose sagely. 'Anyroad, you don't want to be a student 'cause they do nowt all day long.'

'As opposed to you, who works all the hours God sends?'

He grinned from ear to ear. 'I've a job, me. Very important.'

'Oh yeah; what?'

'Don't you know? I'm a rent boy,' he said, laughing at my expression.

I couldn't get outside fast enough.

Under the streaky blue sky it was warm, with clouds of midges hanging in the air. I went to stand with Maggie and Poll, who were chatting by Winston's grave.

'You wouldn't want him to have suffered, though,' Maggie was saying. 'And he'd had a good long life.'

'Do you remember when we got him, Poll? Off that wacky woman who lived behind the church?'

Poll sighed. 'I do. I think it were a lucky escape for him. She ran a filthy house. She had about six or seven dogs and they all had their dinners out of one big trough. Poor Winston could never get his share, I reckon. We thought he were a puppy he was so small, but she said he was at least two year owd. He did eat when he came to us, didn't he?'

We'd gone to get Winston after a particularly hellish period at school. I'd suggested a dog, never for one minute thinking Poll would say yes, but she did.

'What are the eyes med out of?' asked Maggie, bending down to see the statue in close-up. 'Are they glass? Very lifelike.'

'And what about that time his claws got fast in t' rug, and we thought his leg was paralysed?'

'And when he bit that little boy who was

274

tormenting him with a stick outside Porter's. And you told the mother, "Stop carrying on, he's learned a valuable lesson." '

'Well, he had. You've to go careful with dogs, till you know them.'

'Ooh,' said a voice at my neck, 'stockings.'

I whipped my head round and there was Dogman lifting up the hem of my skirt with his bramble hook.

'Jesus.' I leapt away from him in horror. 'What the *fuck* do you think you're doing?'

'Ooh,' said Maggie, who'd never heard me swear.

'Whatever's t' matter now?' said Poll wearily.

I took off up the path, feeling dizzy with disgust.

'That were a mean trick,' I heard Maggie say, above Dogman's laughter.

I went out through the side gate and down the ginnel to the road, where I stopped for a moment to kick the wall.

I'd thought I looked nice in my birthday purple sweater and a knee-length bias-cut black skirt that Maggie had brought me off Dawn. 'It's an elasticated waist,' Maggie had pointed out. 'Dawn says she's too owd for it. I thought I'd pass it on.' I'd been thrilled when it fitted. The stockings had been an idea I saw on a daytime makeover show. 'Black opaques really slim chunky calves,' the presenter had said, pointing at an embarrassed woman with over-highlighted hair. I thought it was worth a go, so I'd checked tights out in Boots but they were too expensive. Then I'd found some black opaques on Chorley market, except these were hold-up stockings. 'They're good, them,' the lady on the stall had remarked as she wrapped them up for me. 'Very *hygienic*.' I didn't know what she meant by that, but she was right about them being good. They stayed put and looked sort of funky.

Oh, the thought, though, of Dogman looking up my skirt. Years of him stretched ahead; poking, prodding, squeezing past, ogling. I didn't think I could bear it.

I'd go to Miss Dragon and she'd say, That's awful, I don't know how you coped with it for so long, move in with me while you train to be a librarian.

She'd say, Well, don't come crying to me, you had your chance to get away and you blew it.

I'd go to Miss Dragon anyway, whatever she said.

*   *   *

It took four years to get my full qualification. Dad offered loads of times to buy me a car so I wouldn't be mauling with buses, but I always said no. You can read on a bus.

I soon got the house nice again and, after a few months Dad started to do a little bit of gardening. That was the first sign he was on the mend. We kept ourselves to ourselves. It was a happy time.

And then, after I'd got my degree, I had this chance to be near Katherine again, and I found I wanted to take it.

Chapter Twenty-Two

I walked slowly, under a sky of fat white taproots. *It's only water vapour, it doesn't tell the future. You make your own future.*

Not really; not in real life. My life.

I pined for Dad and his messages which I didn't believe any more. Who was I to mock Cissie for her anthropomorphism, when that was exactly what I'd been doing all these years? I never knew the man. He was an invention of my head, a fantasy friend.

I wanted to tell all this to Miss Dragon, and try to explain again why I couldn't go to Oxford, and what had happened with Callum. I still looked for him when I went out, squinted into the distance to see if it was his figure coming towards me. I looked especially when I passed places we'd been together, like the Methodists', as if I could maybe catch up with the time that had gone. In a stupid way, it was a surprise *not* to see him sitting on the chapel wall, blowing smoke rings and watching the clouds. Of course he wasn't there. And if he had been, what would I have done?

I didn't hurry. I wanted to get to the library about fifteen minutes before closing, then I might have a chance to talk to Miss Dragon in private. I had this idea that she might see how upset I was, lock the front doors and take me into her office. I could maybe ask to stay at her house for a few nights, if she didn't offer first. Logic told me there was a thin chance of that in reality, but what else was there to try?

Even though the schools had only been back a

couple of weeks, the kids had been busy with autumn themes. Bank Top Primary had donated some cut-out squirrels to decorate the library windows, and some studies of leaves and poems about harvest for the notice board. Miss Dragon keeps her kingdom smart.

At first I could only spot Miss Mouse, talking on the telephone with her back to me. I slipped past her and settled myself into the children's corner, grabbing a Jacqueline Wilson and burrowing into the beanbags. You can't see this area very well from the front desk so I thought I was pretty safe. The place was empty anyway, apart from Mr Rowland, who was pinning up leaflets on the community space. Then Miss Dragon came out of the office looking glum.

The two women muttered together and I could see some kind of mild argument taking place. I wondered what they could possibly be disagreeing about. Miss Dragon looked the most upset. I was sure neither of them had seen me, so I took the opportunity to slide into my secret hiding place; that is, under the curtain which hangs down behind the end of the Early Readers' bookcase. I've used it before, when people have come in that I didn't want to see, e.g. Clare Greenhalgh. If you crouch down below sill level, then no one can see your back view through the window from outside either.

I put the book down on the floor and settled myself quietly against the wall. I knew I'd only have to wait five minutes or so till the library was officially closed, Miss Mouse went to catch her bus, and Miss Dragon would be alone and available for counsel.

I heard Mr Rowland make a poor joke about

daylight saving, then say goodbye. The doors squeaked open, shut. A calm settled.

'Go on, get yourself off,' said Miss Mouse's voice. She sounded quite authoritarian.

'But your bus,' came Miss Dragon's weak reply.

'I can catch the later one. Stop arguing, you're in no fit state.'

There was a pause and I caught the scrape of keys along the desk top.

'Are you all right to lock up? And set the alarm?'

'Yes. I'm fine. Now *go*.'

Another pause. Miss Dragon, sounding apologetic: 'I will, then, if you're positive. I must admit, I am in agony. It must be an abscess. They say bad toothache's worse than childbirth.' Feeble laugh. 'Not that either of us would know. Right, I'm going now.'

'Good luck,' said Miss Mouse. 'Hope you get it sorted.'

The doors squeaked once more. Shit, I thought. Is that not totally bloody typical. Thank you, Fate. And now, how was I going to get out without looking a fool?

There were movements across the room; books thumping into place, chairs shushing across carpet, newspapers crackling. Lights began to go out, click, click. I could say nothing, stay here all night. That wouldn't be so bad. Because if I emerged now, after staying silent so long, Miss Mouse would probably have some kind of fit. I heard the rattle of curtain along track and knew she was coming closer. Miss Dragon would have understood but Miss Mouse was nervy at the best of times; she'd freak. She'd think I was going to attack her, or something, steal a computer. She'd press the panic

279

button and the police would come. It would be in the papers. The whole village would read it. Dogman would rupture himself laughing, and Clare Greenhalgh would show her friends and say, I always knew she was screwy, that one.

My breath was coming shorter and my heart pounding, so I nearly died when a voice just next to me said, 'The lights are off. You can come out now.'

There was nothing for it. I pulled the curtain sheepishly to one side, feeling my hair crackle with static. She was standing six feet away, her arms by her sides and her cuffs down over her fingers.

'I was waiting for Miss Stockley.'

She nodded. 'Come in the office.'

I let her lead me there because I didn't know what else to do.

'Sit down. I'll make a drink.'

Callum was there again, in my head; sitting across the table, twiddling his pendant. It was too painful, so I turned instead to watch her. Her long skirt today was black, her baggy cardigan olive green. Her clothes always looked too big for her.

'We've no milk left,' she said, addressing the wall above the sink. 'Do you mind having black coffee?'

I thought that sounded yuk, but I didn't say so. I needed to talk to someone and scalding hot coffee guaranteed me at least quarter of an hour.

Finally she settled herself opposite me, but with her legs turned sideways as if poised for escape. She was terribly nervous, I could see. Maybe it was because I was seeing her close to; usually she had her back to you, or her head in a book. I thought I could detect darker roots at her scalp and wondered whether she lightened her hair, although that didn't seem likely for a woman who never wore make-up. 'It's me,' I felt like saying, 'don't be scared of *me*. We've never spoken much but we are friends, remember.'

'You seem—upset,' she said. 'You want to tell me about it?'

Yeah, why not, I thought.

'Oh, you know. Home life. It's not very easy living with my grandma. You don't know her, do you? She never comes in here. She thinks libraries are a waste of time.'

'Miss Stockley's talked about her,' said Miss Mouse. The surface of her coffee trembled between her hands. 'I gather she's—quite strict with you?'

'She was. Not any more, though. I've turned the tables, it's me in charge now. She used to tell me what to do when I was younger but I've told her, I'm an adult, I can make my own decisions.'

'Good on you.' She spoke quietly and carefully.

'Mmm . . . It doesn't work like that, though, does it?'

'What doesn't?'

'Life. Being an adult. You can't just do what you want. I thought you could, but you can't.'

Miss Mouse pressed her lips together and frowned slightly. 'What do you want—Kat?'

'To go to Oxford!' That was easy. 'I want to take up my place and do a degree. But I *can't* because Poll won't be able to cope without me, emotionally or practically. She poured boiling water down herself a couple of weeks ago, then a few days later she had a bad fall and had to go to hospital. And her dog died . . . I can't leave her. She brought me up. I couldn't walk out on her after all these years,

281

it would kill her, probably. There's no halfway house in these situations either. If you stay you're a saint, if you walk away you're a rat. Nothing in between.'

Miss Mouse didn't say anything to this. She just gazed into my eyes, and the lines at the corner of her mouth tightened.

'Thing is,' I went on, 'I've made my decision and I'm happy to stick with it; well, not happy but I've come round to it, to staying at home and looking after her. I could do correspondence courses in my free time. I wouldn't let my education slide, I'd keep it up. And I'd be doing my duty at the same time so it wouldn't be so bad. Except for Dickie, this friend of hers, he has his own key and he wanders in whenever he feels like it. It's as though he's the one who has a right to live there, not me. The thought of spending more time with him. Why he can't be her full-time carer . . . He reckons he's got a demanding job, but I've never seen any evidence of it. He's always down at the bookies' when he's not with us. He's basically a bum.'

I paused and waited for her to sympathize, but all she did was blow on her coffee.

'Do you know him? Dickie Knowles? Nasty yellow hair, he always wears a filthy beige coat? He's no reader, so you wouldn't get him in here, and I know you don't live in Bank Top, but you might have seen him slouch past.'

Miss Mouse shook her head.

'Oh. Well he's horrible. He *touches me up*. I've had enough of it.'

You were supposed to feel better after you'd got something off your chest. I wished it was Miss Dragon sitting opposite, she'd know what to say to make me feel better. I thought of a film once where a woman was crying and crying during a therapy session, and all the counsellor did was wait till she'd finished, hand her a tissue and say, 'Same time next week.' Perhaps that was the way to handle problems.

I said, 'Perhaps, if I'm being totally truthful . . . '

Her eyes burned into me.

'. . . it's not all my grandma's fault. Some of it's me.'

Miss Mouse raised her eyebrows.

'What I mean is, secretly I'm sort of glad I can't go—oh, for God's sake, promise you won't tell Miss Stockley this. Don't tell anyone. You won't, will you?'

'I won't say a word.'

'You know, when I was little I sometimes used to get invited to parties, and they were always horrible. I used to sit in the corner and watch the other kids race round doing stupid tricks with balloons and teaspoons, and wish I was anywhere else. Once I took a book upstairs and hid in a mum's bedroom while they did games. You had to do something with an orange, roll it through your legs I think, and I knew I'd be crap at it. When this mum found out, she was really cross because she said it was rude to go in people's bedrooms unless you were invited. She told me off in front of the other kids and they were in stitches. So the next time I got an invite—and it was only 'cause the whole class were going—I told them my grandma wouldn't let me out. I pretended I was furious with her, and they believed me.'

Now I'd started talking it was as if I couldn't stop.

'Then, every time something came up, something social, I got into the habit of saying I wasn't allowed to go. I used the excuse all the time at secondary school. And I made out that my grandma was a bit iller than she really was, that she couldn't be left, because there was no arguing with that, I just got sympathy from the other girls. I mean, they thought I was boring, but they never made fun.

'So really, the Oxford business is just an extension of that. And I think I could have convinced myself it would all work out for the best if it wasn't for Dickie and his wandering hands.' I took a breath, let it out slowly. 'God, sorry for going on, I didn't mean—'

'But you do want to take up your Oxford place,' she said. 'And I think you could, Miss Stockley was telling me, from a practical point of view. With a reassessment from social services, and your grandmother's friends helping out. And of course, the terms at Oxford being so short, only eight weeks. You'd be back before she realized you'd gone.'

She was making it sound so straightforward. 'But there's nothing you can do about my fear, is there? There was one night, when Poll was in hospital, I nearly went mad because I was in the house all on my own. I couldn't cope at all.'

'That's precisely why you *must* go away. Otherwise you'll end up on your own permanently. Do you understand what I'm saying?' Her pale cheeks were growing pink.

A vision of myself in my forties rose up in my mind's eye; stuck in Poll's house, the furniture and decorations all still the same but scruffier, Poll's ashes on the sideboard. I'd sit in front of the telly all day and eat till I was too fat to get through the door.

'Do you understand?' Miss Mouse said again, more urgently.

'I think so.'

'If you don't go, you risk becoming very bitter. You can't go through life saying, "I could have gone to Oxford," every time you meet someone.'

'I know.'

'Would it be too late to write and tell them you've changed your mind again, and you will be coming? Is that possible?'

I giggled with embarrassment. 'I never let them know in the first place. Never got round to it.'

'Well, then. That means you always intended to go, doesn't it?'

'It means I couldn't bear to write the words down.'

'Same thing.'

'Is it?' The room seemed to vibrate around me and I thought of Callum again, his surprise and admiration when I'd told him where I was headed. He was there again, at the sink, washing mugs and grinning. 'I think this office must be built on top of ley-lines, or something. Everything seems to happen in here. It's the place where my life turns upside down.'

I started a laugh that turned into tears. Miss Mouse reached out and touched my hair very gently, then let her arm fall to my sleeve. She stroked my cuff and I stared at her fingers, surprised.

'I did a good job when I chose this for you, didn't I?' she said.

I swallowed. 'That was you? That bag of clothes on the doorstep?'

'Yes.'

'God. It's brilliant, everything was. You've seen me wearing the tunic, haven't you? You don't know, you don't know what you started . . .'

Then I saw: it was like washing the mud away from a piece of ancient pottery and the pattern coming clear before your eyes.

'I think—' I began.

'I started it nineteen years ago. Nineteen years ago, my first mistake. I wanted to begin to put things right.'

She was leaning forward and her eyes were bright.

'Are you—?'

'Although I can never really make up for going. I understand that.'

'I think I might know who you are.'

All the random moments that had been swirling around us for years suddenly coalesced to form a new future. I could make out her nodding through my tears, then her arms were round me and mine round hers, her bony body. And even then I was thinking, don't touch her, she abandoned you! But the pull was too strong and I let myself be held while the room buzzed and my brain splintered apart.

After a long time I moved away and we sat back down, though she kept her hand on my wrist.

'Could you come back home with me tonight?' she said shakily. 'There's a lot to talk about.'

When I was a little girl, I'd rehearsed this moment. It had never been here, with her, though. It usually took place when I was a grown up successful something-or-other, sitting behind a huge oak desk, or in the hall of a posh house with stripy wallpaper and a bowl of roses on the table. She'd turn up unannounced, all apologetic, and I'd sweep her to one side. 'Life-wrecker,' I'd cry. 'Coward.' She'd slink away a broken woman with me shouting, *'Serve you right.'* I'd slam the door and draw a line under the whole business.

I'd had it all worked out for so long. Where were the words that I needed; where had they gone?

*   *   *

Please God let me have said the right thing.

Chapter Twenty-Three

The first thing I did, to my surprise, was phone Poll from the front desk and tell her I was staying overnight with a girlfriend. I didn't let her argue, although I could hear her chuntering on as I was talking. I *think* she heard me say I'd call back in the morning.

Miss Mouse—Mum—went round having a final lock-up, and set the library alarm, then we—Mum and I—had this surreal, spaced-out walk to the bus stop, neither of us talking, although my head was screaming with noise. *You've got no nightie, how could she run off like that, who'll do Poll's eye drops, dare I ask her if she killed my dad, does she know about Callum, where does she actually live, is Vince there, how* could *she run off like that, how* could *she run off like that?*

Some drunks called to each other from across the street. I said, 'I'll have made you miss your bus, won't I?'

'No, there's one every half-hour.'

I was thinking, whatever happens, I want a souvenir of this evening, something tangible I can put away in a box with Callum's wasp, the Oxford newsletter, her photo. I'd hang on to the bus ticket and keep it forever; if it came to it, I'd pick that manky old lolly stick up off the pavement and have that as my treasure. Anything to prove this had been real.

She was talking now, about Miss Dragon.

'My best friend,' she was saying.

'I thought so,' I replied. I didn't say I thought for a while they'd been lovers.

'She's done more than show me the ropes, she's understood my ways.'

I didn't really get that, but I smiled as if I did. 'Does she know? About you and me?'

'No. I've not told anyone. But she was very kind when my father died, last year.'

My other grandad. 'Oh,' I said, 'Miss Stockley's dad died as well, she was telling me.'

'That's probably why she was so good with me. Our households were the same.'

It was such a weird conversation to be having, not least because what we were talking about bore no relation to my loud, racing thoughts. It was like having the radio and the TV on at the same time. The bus came and we got on. I pushed my ticket down to the bottom of my peggy purse, and we sat at the front behind the disabled seats. Aside from us, the downstairs deck was empty.

'I mean,' she went on, 'that Dinah lived with just

288

her father, and so did I. They were much closer, of course; they did a lot together, while he was still fit. Dad and I were sort of semi-detached. We liked our own space.'

'So you live alone now?'

'Yes.'

Not with Vince Millar, then.

The central strip light hummed above us, you heard it when the bus was idling. Flick-flick-flick went the street lights past the window. I thought, I'm sure I shouldn't be sitting on the 575 having a polite conversation. It should be ranting and recriminations, and running off into the night and sobbing till dawn on the moors. Or hysterical joyous weeping and white-knuckle clasping of limbs, like the victims of *Surprise, Surprise*. Trust me to get it wrong. Bet Donna French would have handled herself with style.

'If I'm being truthful, I don't even really miss him.' Mum (*Mum*) was rolling her ticket into a long spindle between her mottled fingers. 'That probably makes me sound terrible, but we'd made our peace, and he went quite suddenly, without a lot of suffering. He had said a few times he was moving to Exmouth to be near his cousin, so I often pretend to myself that he's just gone there for a while.'

That sounded a bit mad to me, but everyone's got their own way of coping. 'So what happened to your mother?' Because if she ran off, that might go some way to explaining what you did, I was thinking.

'I lost her in my teens.' Mum had unrolled the spindle and was now pleating it into tiny folds.

'What do you mean? You got separated?' I said

289

stupidly.

'She died of stomach cancer,' said Mum. I looked away, watched the driver's hairy forearms for a while, counted his gold rings. I never know what to say when someone comes out with that sort of thing.

After a minute she said, 'It wasn't a good time. I was ill for a while after.'

I held my breath, waiting for baby Kat to come into the story. But she changed the subject.

'I live on Windermere Crescent. Off Chorley New Road. I get the bus in every day, well every day the library's open, because the stop's only a minute away from my front door. It's a nice house. When I was away and Dad lived there on his own, he really let it go. I had to do a lot of tidying up when I came back. You can have the spare room, it's quite a good size. I can wash your sweater and things, and tumble them for you in an hour, so you can wear them tomorrow. You'll have to wear Dad's old dressing gown in the meantime.'

Yes, I thought, because none of your stuff will fit. Why wasn't I that shape? And then a voice in my head immediately went, How can you be concerned with something as trivial as fat when this is your *mum* at last?

'You are definitely all right to stay, aren't you?'

'Oh, yeah,' I said, trying to sound as if I was in control of my life. 'It'll be fine.'

*   *   *

The house turned out to be a biggish Thirties detached with one of those porches shaped like a huge brick keyhole. A security light clicked on as

290

we went through the metal gate, showing a paved driveway edged with neat stone pots.

'You should have seen it when it was just my dad on his own. This was all grass, knee-high.'

Inside the long hall was an Axminster carpet and a white-painted banister. I could smell potpourri or air freshener. Everything looked very clean. I followed her through to the kitchen and watched her fill the kettle.

'Tea? I'll just nip up and put sheets on the spare bed,' she said, taking her coat off and hanging it in a cupboard under the stairs. 'Go through to the lounge.' She pointed the way.

I poked my head round the door to see a very ordinary sort of living room, a bit old-fashioned, tons of books lying around, then I went back to the kitchen to brew the drinks. While the kettle boiled I took stock. The surfaces were immaculate and, in the main, bare. Apart from the kettle, a radio and a toaster, nothing else was out on show. No mug-tree, no utensils, no jars, no cleaning fluids. No ornaments or plants on the windowsill, no fridge magnets. There was no evidence of pets. Only a calendar and a Constable reproduction hung on the walls.

I opened a few cupboards to see if I could locate the tea and only found lots of crockery and pans. At last, inside the cupboard above the fridge, I found some jars and packets, half a small loaf in a bag, and a pot of freeze-dried tea. In the gleaming fridge there were some diet yoghurts, skimmed milk, and a bunch of bananas; that was it. Not even any butter. She must be due a major shop.

'That's sorted,' she said, coming into the living room, where I'd settled with the drinks. 'I'll make

291

us something to eat in a bit.'

Like what, I wondered. Oxo on toast?

'Have you been watching me, then, all these years?' I burst out. 'All this time, have you known who I was?'

She'd been going to sit down, but at that she scooted away from the sofa and went to stand in the bay, arms clasped round herself.

'Yes.'

'Well, *why* didn't you say something to me?'

'I tried, a few years back. I did. I telephoned, and you told me to get out of your life. That's what you said. *Get out of my life.*'

My heart started to thud, because it wasn't true. 'No way. I didn't know anything about you phoning. When? What else did I say to you?'

Mum was twisting on the spot unhappily. 'I'd talked to your grandmother about meeting you— this'll have been about six years ago, a year or so after I started at Bank Top Library. I phoned her several times and she told me you didn't want anything to do with me. I said I didn't believe her, so she put you on and you told me to leave you both alone. It was you. I'd been going to speak to you about who I was, the next time you came to borrow a book, but I didn't dare after that.'

'I can't remember it at all. Poll never said you'd been in touch.'

'That I can believe.'

'And you told Poll you were working in the library?'

'*No.* I only said I wanted to see you. I didn't dare tell her where I was based. I honestly think she'd have tried to kill me if she knew. The woman's mad. She attacked her own husband, beat him up.'

292

That made me feel peculiar, her talking about Poll like that. 'She thinks you went off with him.'

'He helped me to leave, that was all. Then we went our separate ways. I don't know where he is now. Good God. He was ancient. It would have been like eloping with my father.' She put her hand over her eyes for a moment, and laughed unpleasantly. 'What an evil mind that woman has.'

So Cissie got that wrong too, I thought. But she had it from Poll, so no wonder. Perhaps Poll was mentally ill. It would make sense in some ways.

'So did you deliberately get a job near to me?'

Mum nodded. She kept looking up at the ceiling and taking deep breaths, as if she was trying to stop herself saying too much all at once.

'Well, wasn't it one huge risk coming back? I mean, didn't you think someone would recognize you?'

'It was a risk, yes, but one I was prepared to take. It had been ten years since I'd been in the village and I'd changed a lot. I'd lost a great deal of weight, I'd dyed my hair and had it cut short. Changed my name, obviously—and quite legally; I'm Ann Ollerton now, you must never ever call me Elizabeth. That was another life. And the only people who ever saw much of me when I was living in Bank Top were Poll and Vince because I was so ill I hardly ever left the house. Vince had disappeared—'

'—And Poll was going blind even then. Did you know that when you came?'

'I'd seen her with her white stick when I drove through once.'

Bloody handy for you, then, I thought.

'There was a woman, Maggie, Mary, I can't

293

remember exactly; she might have spotted me, at a pinch, because she used to come round sometimes when I was still at Poll's.'

'You're lucky,' I said. 'Maggie does read, but she favours inspirational books from the church library, or romance off the market, type of books where the heroine starts off in a shawl and ends up in Brussels lace. So she never bothers with the library.' And if you're not actually looking for someone, I was thinking, if you don't expect them to be there, you probably won't see them.

Mum only stared up at the ceiling rose. 'I never thought it through like that, I just needed to be there. You don't understand the pull I felt to be near you.'

'But not when I was a baby.'

'No. I told you, I was ill. Depression's been my baby.'

There was a silence. I wondered whether to ask her about Dad, and about Callum. It would be like blowing up mines in her face.

'Do you know what I think?' she said suddenly. 'I think we should have a drink.'

I thought so too. I needed a break. 'Can I use your toilet?'

'Up the stairs on your left. Sherry, brandy or Martini?'

I thought they were all vile. 'Martini, smashing.'

On the landing I paused and counted doors. The bathroom was on the left, what must have been my room in front of me with the curtains drawn, the light on and a dressing gown laid across the bed. Two doors on the right; hers the first one I opened.

I suppose I was hoping for a little shrine. The room was pine and pastel, unremarkable except for

294

the towers of books along the wall under the window. The dressing-table surface was clear, no cosmetics out, and even on the bedside table there was only a pair of reading glasses and a bottle of pills. But over the chest of drawers was me; two newspaper clippings, one of me winning a book quiz in about the third year at secondary school, and an older one of Bank Top Primary's Harvest Festival, with me holding a plate of onions. Both pieces had been laminated and pinned to the wall. There was also a colour photo that I remembered Miss Dragon taking, the day after I got the letter saying I'd got a place at the grammar.

I stood grinning for a minute, remembering. Then another memory popped up, of me screaming down the telephone while Poll held the receiver in such a way that I could only get at the mouthpiece. 'It's that flaming pervert again,' she'd said, shaking with temper. 'Don't listen to his filth. You just tell him, tell him to get out of our lives.'

I turned the light off and closed the door behind me.

When I got down there were two glasses of Martini sitting on the coffee table.

'I'm not a drinker,' said Mum. 'I can't remember when this was last out. But we should have a drink tonight. Shall I make us something to eat as well?'

That was weird, because all she had herself was two Weetabix, lightly sprinkled with milk so they held their shape, and this slug of Martini. I wanted to help her make the meal but she insisted I stay in the living room watching TV. Eventually she brought through a plate of cheesy broccoli pasta for me, the sort where all you do is add water, and we ate sitting on the sofa in front of *TOTP2*.

'I wasn't expecting company tonight,' she said, observing as my fork uncovered a little pocket of unmixed sauce powder.

'No no, it's delicious,' I said, and I wasn't lying either. I'd been ready to eat the kitchen sponge I was so hungry. On the screen in front of us Sting sang about being lonelier than any man could bear, but he didn't look it.

Afterwards she let me back in the kitchen to wash up; I felt we were making strides. The Martini was beginning to penetrate and I was feeling bolder.

I said, 'Was it awful when Dad died?'

'Yes. I was ill.'

I acted ignorant. 'From the car crash?'

'That wasn't my fault,' she said quickly. 'The coroner said so. It was a proper inquest and the verdict was accidental death. I've got the newspaper clippings to prove it.'

'Right.' I carried on swilling the sink, chasing particles of Weetabix down the plug hole.

'I'll show you.'

'There's no need.'

She put down the tea towel and took my hand. 'Yes there is. I can guess what you've been told.' Her grip tightened. 'I know you must hate me, I know that really.'

'I'm not sure what I feel,' I said, after a struggle. If we weren't honest here, we were lost. 'It was a mistake on the phone that time. I didn't mean to tell you to go away. I got confused and thought you were someone else.'

Tears started at her eyes and she began to pull me through the hall.

'I've never been far away. I wanted to help. You

296

liked the clothes, didn't you? That was something I got right. It took me weeks, months to get them all together. I only wanted nice things for you.'

'They were lovely.'

In her room I pretended surprise at the photos of me.

'See? I've only been able to put these up after Dad died, but I've been close to you for a long time.'

I sat on the bed while she brought out the coroner's report from a suitcase under the chest of drawers. I didn't feel comfortable reading it with her there, I'd have preferred it if she'd left me alone, but she clearly wanted to gauge my reaction.

'See?' she said when I'd finished.

It was true; according to the paper, she'd been cleared. It had been my dad's fault for driving like a maniac. I thought of Poll's lies and hated them, and understood them.

'He was so arrogant,' Mum began. 'He always had his own way, and his own rules, he never stopped to think about other—'

'Don't,' I shouted. 'Don't say anything about him. I don't want to hear. If you start slagging him off, I'll walk straight out of this house and never come back, I promise you. I did not come here to listen to bad stuff about my father.'

I stuffed the report back in its envelope and threw it back into the open case. She went out of the room and after a minute I heard taps running, over the sound of sobbing. I'm not going to feel guilty, I thought, I don't actually owe her anything. For a moment I wondered whether I should just grab my purse and go. But then I caught sight of the photo album. At the back of the case, half under a college scarf, a gold embossed maroon cover: *My Memories*.

And there they were. All the pictures that should have been round Poll's house: Roger and Elizabeth, Roger and Elizabeth. In Poll's back garden; sitting on a stone wall up on the moors somewhere; in my old bedroom; holding hands in the porch of this house. Mum with her long dark centre-parted hair, Dad with his devil-smile. And they did seem odd together, as if they were asking to be cut apart with scissors.

I sat for a long time looking at one of them in his Metro, smiling through the windscreen. The water was still running in the bathroom. It felt as if my whole identity was draining away with it.

I flipped over the last couple of pages and it was me, a fuzzy fat baby. First the three of us, then me and Mum, then me and Dad. Finally just me on my own, boss-eyed and chewing a teething ring. It was really me; Poll had the ring and the Babygro still in a bag under her bed. The strange thing was, in all the shots, everyone looked really happy.

I put the album open on the duvet and went to get Mum.

*　　　*　　　*

I leant over the sink and watched the water run away from me into darkness. I thought, what if I've lost her all over again?

298

Chapter Twenty-Four

It was still dark when I heard her get up.

She was out on the landing, laying my clean clothes carefully over the banister. All she was wearing was an underslip, and my eyes were drawn to her thin arms covered all over with small silvery scars, like stretch-marks. She caught me looking, and jumped.

'I didn't know you were awake.' She pulled my sweater against herself.

'Is the bathroom free?' I mumbled, wanting to get away as much as she did.

She nodded and we fled in opposite directions.

I washed and dressed quickly because I knew she'd have to be at work. Personally, though, I was in no rush to go back to Poll's. I started to rehearse the tale I'd tell her about where I'd spent the night. Tempting to be hung for a sheep as a lamb, and tell her I'd been at an orgy in Harrop, or mainlining heroin round the back of Porter's. Even that would be nothing like the shock of the truth.

'I'm going to tell Poll I've been with my friend Rebecca,' I said to Mum over my slice of dry toast. She was sitting opposite, sucking on a cube of frozen orange juice that dripped down her sweater cuffs every so often. I kept remembering the arms under those chunky sleeves, and tried not to stare. 'I don't like to lie, but on no account must Poll find out about you. She'd go berserk, and she's unstable enough at the moment.'

'All right.' Her voice sounded flat, disappointed.

Well, what did you think I was going to do? I felt

like asking. Shout it from the hilltops? Destroy my entire past at one fell swoop? I could have gone back to Poll holding the information like a flaming sword above her cowering form, and cut her version of my life into tiny parts. But what would that have done for me?

Here, in this kitchen, was a woman who had sat by and watched me struggle for years, who never even told her own father I still existed. It was in my power to take her apart as well, if I'd wanted; tell her I never wanted to see her again, that the embrace last night in the bathroom was only the product of Martini and confusion. Or I could confront her with the unmentionable, the story of Callum and his mother. Did she even know?

I wouldn't though. Hurting either of them would only be hurting myself. I'd keep the secrets, for now, while I decided what to do with them.

'We'd best run if we want to make the eight-twenty,' she said suddenly. I watched her load her bag with bananas and crispbreads, and felt sad. Why did she have to be so bloody fragile? Why couldn't she have turned out to be strong?

*   *   *

Poll was making a show of ironing when I got in, putting more creases in than she was taking out.

'Ooh, look who's showed her face,' she said. 'Finally. You'll get a name, you will.'

Instantly I wished I'd never come home. I said, 'How lovely to see you, Kat, have you had a nice time with your friend?'

Poll only pulled a face. 'Out till dawn. Well, I don't care. I've been managing fine on my own.' I watched as she deftly ironed a ladybird flat into the sleeve of her blouse.

'Good,' I said. 'Because I'm seeing her tonight as well.'

'What, *all* night? God Almighty.' Poll rested the iron up on its end. 'Out all night with a woman? That's not normal. Dickie says you might be gay. He says he's had his suspicions for a while. I don't know what to think; there's summat shifty about you at the minute, that's for sure.'

'Actually, I'm asexual.'

'And what's that mean, Miss Clever?'

'Look it up. Hey, have you seen that nasty stain on your blouse?' I pointed to the orange blob on the sleeve and she skutched it away to hold it near the window.

'Damnation. Is it brown sauce?'

'It *was* a ladybird. Give it here, I'll put some Vanish on it.'

Poll dropped the blouse across the ironing board and sat down on the sofa, looking defeated. 'I've been worried,' she muttered. 'I hate it on my own.'

'Didn't Maggie come round, or Dickie?'

She didn't answer, so I presumed they had. I put the blouse on a short wash and brewed us a hot chocolate each. Then I cut us two thick slices of parkin and brought them through.

After a few minutes chewing, she seemed happier. 'Dickie's left you a present. To say sorry, he reckons, although he were only having a bit of fun. It's a queer do, stopping out all night up to I don't know what, but then tekkin offence at one little joke. Anyway, he's apologized. It's in a bag on your bed.'

I left the parkin and went up to see. The

301

redecorated room still gave me a pleasurable shock when I went in. Wherever I went in the future, this would always be my home. I wondered if Dogman had managed to find me a throw or some velvety material for cushions.

But no, it turned out to be an apron. A full-length laminated apron with a cartoon picture of a scruffy dog on the front that would sit about level with your tummy. I thought perhaps if he'd got it me because it reminded him of Winston. I checked the ties and they were all intact, no dodgy marks or stains anywhere. I'd seen aprons you could get that looked like you were walking round in your underwear; thank God he hadn't got me anything like that.

I tried it on for fun and stood in front of the mirror. Something was written underneath the dog in swirly writing; I hadn't seen it before. I struggled to spell it out from the reflection: *S-N-A-T-C-H*. Dogman wanted me to wear the word 'snatch' written over my crotch.

'Whatever are you up to now?' Poll found me at the bottom of the garden two minutes later, with the apron and a box of matches.

'Watch,' I said, and struck a match. I held it against the offending word. There was a feeble glow, then the laminate burst into flames. I laughed out loud. 'Call that fireproof? How could you have worn that in a kitchen? It was a complete health hazard.'

'Is that Dickie's apron?'

'It is.'

'You're mad,' said Poll. 'You'll be put away.'

*   *   *

302

Come and live here,' Mum said that evening. 'You can have new furniture, decorate anywhere you like. I'll get you a computer if you want. I'm not short of money. Move in with me.'

'I can't.'

She looked upset. 'But you hate it at your grandma's.'

'I know, but it's home. I'm, I'm not sure how I feel.'

'About what?'

About you, I nearly said. 'Everything.'

'I suppose it's a lot to take in all at once.'

I thought, you don't know the half of it.

*   *   *

I told Maggie first.

'I've got to go,' I said. We were shelling peas in the kitchen while Poll had a nap upstairs.

Maggie seemed to know at once what I meant. 'I know, love, I think you have. Will they still tek you?'

'Yeah. I've to be in Oxford next Sunday, for Noughth Week.'

'Is that when they show the northern students round?'

'No. It's a week for the new ones from all over to settle in, sort out their accommodation, meet their tutors.'

'Ooh, hey.' Maggie nudged me. 'Tutors. You will be grand. You'll not want to know us common folk.'

'Don't be daft.'

Peas plopped into the bowl between us and the

303

weak autumn sun shone through the kitchen window.

'I presume you've not said owt to your grandma?'

'Not exactly.'

Maggie nodded. 'You will tell her, though? You won't just tek off? Because that would be very upsetting for her. I've a book she might find helpful.'

'I'm going to tell her this afternoon, when she wakes up.'

Maggie looked grim. 'I should have some Bailey's ready, if I were you.'

By the time Poll appeared the peas were shelled and Maggie and I were watching *A Place in the Sun*. Bob and Carol from Leeds were examining an apartment in an Italian village. 'It's all very well,' Maggie was saying, 'these foreign places might be warm but no one speaks English, do they? And all them steps up and down.'

We got Poll sitting with a drink, Maggie standing by with her lavender cologne stick, then I explained to her that this time I was definitely leaving home.

'Get away,' she chuckled. 'We've heard that one before. Shift out o' t' way, I can't see the screen properly.'

I stayed where I was. 'No, this time it's different, I've decided.'

She scratched her side and yawned. 'You're not capable of mekkin decisions, you. Well, you aren't, are you? Chopping and changing. I'll believe it when I see it.'

Maggie came in at this point: 'She is going, Poll. She's bought her ticket and I've seen it.'

I gaped at the lie. But it was a canny thing to say,

because it seemed to dawn on Poll that I was serious.

'But you wrote and told them you weren't coming, didn't you? They'll have given your place to someone else.'

'No, I never did.'

Poll was beginning to look really alarmed. 'You'll never manage. You're one of life's square pegs. It doesn't matter where you go, you'll never fit in. I bet you'll be back in a fortnight, won't she, Maggie?'

Maggie kept quiet.

'What'll happen to me? I'm nearly blind, you know. How will I cope when my sight goes completely?'

'It won't, will it? It's not got any worse for two years now. They said at the hospital, you never go totally blind with dry macular degeneration.'

'You do.'

'You don't. I was there, remember.'

Poll stood up, trembling with rage. '*Them as calls their grandmother a liar Is in danger of hell fire,*' she chanted, jabbing me in the chest for good measure.

I made the mistake of laughing, and before I knew it, she'd slapped me hard across the face. I couldn't believe she'd done it. I put up my hand to rub away the sensation of her cold bony fingers on my cheek, and to relieve the stinging. 'My *God.*'

'Now, Poll,' said Maggie, trying to draw her away from me, 'I know it's hard, but there are these stages you need to go through. Reeling, Feeling, Kneeling and Healing. No, not Kneeling, Dealing. That's how you cope with a big loss. It's in a book I've got. So you're at the Reeling stage at the moment, which is natural, 'cause it's been a shock, but then you come out of that and go into Dealing, I think, is it? But don't tek it out on Katherine, she's only doing what the young ones do. I wept buckets when Dawn left and she were only on t' new estate round the back. It's nature, flying the nest.'

'I'll get a new care package sorted before I go,' I said. 'I know I've left it late but Maggie'll help out till it's in place. The Rehab Officer's coming on Monday for a chat, and you know she's a lovely woman.'

'Is it that lame one with the long fair hair?' said Maggie, letting go of Poll's cardigan. 'Oh, she's smashing, in't she? She knows what it's like to be crippled.'

But Poll was still in a fury. 'Oh, oh, my heart,' she cried, sinking onto the sofa. 'You've killed me.'

I stayed where I was, but Maggie bent stiffly to help. She patted Poll's forehead and took her hand, then straightened up, half turning to me. 'It's hard for her. She loves you, you see.'

'No, she doesn't,' I said, 'she just wants to keep me here as an unpaid carer. She's frightened of having to cope on her own.'

'You're the one as is frightened,' Poll moaned from her sickbed. 'All I've ever tried to do is protect you.'

'Shall I telephone for a doctor, do you think?' asked Maggie. 'I can feel her heart pounding away and she's very pale. What do you reckon?'

I started to walk to the door. 'I'm sorry, Maggie, I'm not staying around for the performance. Do what you like, call a whole fleet of ambulances if you want. The Bailey's is on the sideboard. I'm off.'

'That's right, run away,' called Poll, raising her

head briefly.

'That's exactly what I am going to do,' I said.

*　　*　　*

'It's Maggie I feel sorry for,' I told Cissie as we sat by the picture window watching the gardener hoover up leaves from the lawn. 'Too much falls on her shoulders. She'll be cursing me before Christmas is here.'

'No, she won't,' replied Cissie. 'She likes it, fussing over Poll. It meks her feel important. There are some people in life who need to be needed; Maggie's one of them. Soon as her daughter left home, she was on the lookout for someone to mither. She'll enjoy stepping into the breach till social services get themselves into gear. And really, Poll doesn't need that much practical help, does she? There's plenty worse off than her.'

'It's more emotional support she needs at the moment.' I sighed. 'You don't think people'll criticize me for going away and leaving her?'

'They'll be clapping you on the back and cheering, more like. Eeh, love, you've your own life to live as well. Get on, enjoy yourself while you're young. It soon passes.' She looked mournfully down at her own body. 'Then you end up like this. Just look at them ankles.'

Ally stumped across the lawn in front of us and shouted something at the gardener, who laughed and switched his hoover off. They stood chatting happily for a minute, and I saw him glancing down her blouse a few times. As she walked off she wiggled her bottom at him and he put his lips together like he was whistling. Where did she get that kind of confidence from?

'Can I ask you something?'

Cissie stopped scrutinizing her legs and turned her face to me. 'What, love?'

'Tell me honestly, what was my dad really like?'

She made a noncommittal noise and stared into the middle distance.

'No, tell me. I know you didn't like him; I know about his affair. But what was he like as a person?'

'The trouble with you,' said Cissie, 'is that you see people as either all good or all bad. Nowt in between. When, in reality, everyone's mixed up nice and nasty. That's the way humans are. Some are nastier than others, of course.'

'Like my dad?'

'No, love; no. Being absolutely truthful, I never took to him especially, but he weren't a bad lad. Well, he were, but not really *evil*. Spoilt, of course. That were his mother. But not a cruel boy. You can't blame him for loving life. I'm sure he never meant to hurt anyone's feelings when he took up with that other woman, he probably just didn't think it through.'

I pictured Mum and Jude, side by side, smiling hopefully. 'So who did he love, in the end?'

'Himself, chiefly,' said Cissie. 'Poll had always taught him the sun shone out of his own backside. How was he to know any better?'

Afterwards, I wondered if I'd ever tell her about finding Mum. One day.

Over my head there were white railway tracks in the blue, guiding me off into infinity.

'Oh, fuck off,' I shouted into the air. 'There's no such thing as sky messages. There never was.'

308

*   *   *

My dad used to say, when I was little, Softly softly catchee monkey. I didn't get it at the time. But I know now it means go slowly. I'll have her, if it takes years. What else have I got to do with my life?

Chapter Twenty-Five

The postcard had been sent to the library, but it was Miss Dragon who handed it to me, not Mum.

> *Kat*
> *So so so so <u>sorry</u>. I HAVE to talk to you. Midday Friday?*

The front showed a portrait of Charlotte Brontë and there was no signature, but I knew who it was from and where he'd be.

Miss Dragon raised her eyebrows as I put the card in my coat pocket. 'I don't mean to interfere, Kat,' she said. 'But if you don't want to see him again, I can field him for you. Pass on a message.'

I glanced round the library to make sure no one was listening in. No sign of Mum, anyway.

'You didn't like him, did you?'

'Since you ask, no. Much too charming. I thought he was lovely, for about ten minutes. Have you two fallen out?'

'You could say that.' I replayed his face coming towards mine through the half-light, and it was like a kick in the chest. Mrs Dragon watched me with concern. 'Listen, have you told anyone else who he said he was? I mean, *anyone*?'

'Absolutely not.'

I could have kissed her for her old-fashioned rectitude, her bobbly check skirt, her brogues.

'Thanks. I'll really miss you when I go.'

'Of course you won't, you'll be far too busy having an interesting time. But thank you.'

'And there's no need to worry about Callum. I'll face him. It's something that has to be done.'

She gave me a long, fond look. 'If you say so. But I'll disembowel him if he does anything untoward; tell him that from me.'

*   *   *

He was sitting outside on the library bench when I saw him again. Too chicken to go in, I thought. His hair had grown slightly but the glasses were back, and he had an army greatcoat round his shoulders.

'Where do you want to go?' he said, standing as I approached. 'I don't want to stay round here. Too many people.'

For what? 'Let's go to the cemetery, then,' I said, my mouth dry with nerves and anger. 'Oh, and I've got this for you.' I held out the little paper bag to him.

'Not the pendant? Please don't get rid of that.'

'No. This photo. You might as well have the original. What would I want a picture of my dad's mistress for?'

He looked mortified as he recognized again the pregnant woman leaning on the Metro, but he didn't say a word. I wondered whether I should have ripped the photo up in his face; too late now, though. The bag went in his pocket and we set off down the village.

I'd intended not to talk till we got there, but I couldn't stop myself. 'I feel like I'll never be able to trust anything you ever tell me again,' I said bitterly as we walked past the school road. 'I don't understand why you had to deceive me like that. I thought we were friends, that you liked me. So why couldn't you have told me the truth from the start? Or keep up the deception, one or the other. In fact, why did you have to go rooting around at all?'

He hung his head. 'It's important for boys to know about their dads. I've always wanted to find out about him; Mum would never give.'

No bloody wonder, I nearly said.

'So I got fed up with it and took matters into my own hands. I posted on a Web site that tries to match up people who've lost each other, adoptees mainly. Not that Friends Reunited, this one's called Lookup. The day after my posting appeared, three people emailed and told me there was only one person called Pollyanna Millar registered in England; two of the emails included your address and phone number.'

'Why? Why would complete strangers send you that sort of information? I don't believe you.'

He shrugged. 'Try it for yourself. They're Internet fiends with nothing better to do, maybe. One of them said she was a private detective, and for a small fee she'd gather information on you, or facilitate a meeting. I didn't reply to any of them. But what would you have done, this phone number sitting in front of you, begging you to ring it? I came and had a look at the house before I met you, you know.'

'Freak.'

311

'I wanted to take my time. Get it right. Ironically.'

We'd drawn level with the Methodists' when a voice called out: 'Ooh, hello again.' It was old Janey Marshall, carrying bunches of flowers into the Methodist church. 'You two still doing your, what is it, research?' She gave a huge, ugly wink.

'We've finished all that,' said Callum. 'Thanks for asking. Now we're just going off for a shag. See you around.'

Janey's face froze.

'Let's hope the old cow has a stroke or something,' he said loudly, quickening his pace. 'Can't you walk a hundred yards in this God-forsaken place without someone poking their nose into your business?'

I was stunned. 'What the hell was that in aid of? Jesus, Callum. I have to live here, you know.'

'I thought you were going to Oxford. Or didn't you get in?'

'Yes I bloody did, actually. I'm going on Sunday. Poll says it's fine and she'll look after herself.'

'Well, then. Bye bye, Bank Top.'

'It's still my home. God, the terms only last eight weeks. I'll be back in no time.'

'Eight weeks and the Methodists'll have forgotten all about it,' said Callum, thrusting his hands into his pockets. 'It'll all get lost in the excitement of knitting toilet-roll covers for the Christmas Fair. Stop getting so agitated. There's more to life than Bank bloody Top, Kat.'

I was so furious I had to stop myself speaking for a minute, in case I said something I regretted. I wanted to ask him so much stuff, get it straight in my mind, before I told him to disappear forever. I

312

didn't want to start the row too early.

We made it to the wrought-iron gates before I really turned on him.

'Go on, then, explain; why the story about being my cousin? Why didn't you tell the truth from the start?'

'Because you'd have hated me. If I'd burst in on the scene and announced your dad had kept a mistress that you knew nothing about, you'd have been livid.'

'I'd have been shocked. But I'd have come round. I had a right to know.'

Callum shook his head and carried on up the gravel path. 'Well, you know now. I'm *sorry*, OK? It was my chance to find out something about my dad. If you'd flown into a rage and said you'd never wanted to see me again because of who I was, I'd have learned nothing. I'd have blown my one opportunity. I had a right as well.'

'You should have asked your mother.'

'I did, last week. We've been talking about it. I told her about coming here and meeting you, and she was pretty gutted. She threw a cup at me. But when she'd calmed down, she told me a load of stuff. It's been great, we've got really close.'

'Bully for you.'

'Yeah, all right, all right. Anyway, back then, all she'd tell me was that Dad had died in a car accident and that he was already with someone. And there was a baby.'

'So when you found me, back in July, did you already know about my mum running off?'

He stopped under a yew tree, screwing up his eyes against the sun. 'Yeah. It was in a letter I found, how she went when you were less than a year old. Of course, I didn't know whether she might have come back in the meantime. But I thought, if you did suddenly whip a mother out of the hat, I'd say I'd got confused and that it was Miller I was searching for. Something like that. I've usually got an idea up my sleeve.'

'You shit,' I said. 'I don't even know whether you're telling me the truth now.'

'I am.'

'And what was this letter? Was it your mum's? Who was it from?'

'Your paternal granddad. Vince.'

'Fuck.' I walked away from him a few yards, then came back. 'And *why* was he writing to your mum?'

Callum kicked at the gravel with his shoe. 'Because he was giving us money. He gave some to your mum too. I think he felt responsible; Mum says he was one of those people who likes to go round trying to put things right. After he left your grandma, he traced Mum through the university, and came all the way over to Sheffield to look after her. She let him stay for a while, because she'd been so ill. Then, after about six months, he left us. God knows where he went after that. But he always sent money, every month. We wouldn't have managed otherwise.'

'Where did he get all this money from?' I thought of how Poll had struggled for cash all these years.

'Dunno. It's stopped now, though. We haven't had anything from him since I was about nine, ten, Mum says. He just disappeared. He might even be dead, I suppose.'

I found myself scanning the sky, but all there was in the air was my cold breath. 'You are such a huge

314

fucking liar.'

'I'm telling you the truth now.'

'So that makes it all right?'

I stalked off round the back of the chapel to the war memorial and sat on the icy stone steps. Who could you trust, really? If I'd had a gun, I swear I'd have shot him as he came, now, round the corner; blasted a big hole in that stupid greatcoat of his. I'd have stood over him as he died, and laughed.

'How many more times can I say it?' he called. 'I'm sorry.'

Don't you dare sit next to me, I thought. He must have picked up the vibes, because he leant against the chapel wall a few feet away and stared at his boots.

'Did she ever get married, your mum, like you said?'

'No. I think our dad spoilt her for another man.'

Your mother and mine. 'You don't especially look like him, you know.'

'Neither do you.'

'It was a mean trick to play with the photo, letting me think it was Elizabeth. That was really low.'

Callum spread his hands. 'You said it was the only picture you had. I couldn't take that away from you. I couldn't destroy your illusion like that.'

'God.' I struck the stone column with my fist. 'You've an answer for everything. Why does everyone think I need protecting all the bloody time?'

He said nothing, and the white skin on my hand flushed and welled into tiny beads of blood. Below us, Harrop stretched away into moorland and sky. I can leave all this behind, I was thinking. Two days.

'Listen,' he said, coming closer, his voice gentler, 'there's another reason I came back to see you. As well as to tell you the truth.'

'What?'

'You know, in the club, right, when we, when I—'

'Oh no, don't start that again. You're either a liar or a pervert, one of the two. I don't want anything to do with it.'

'I wasn't lying about the kiss. You need to know. You're lovely, you're like Blanche Ingram.'

'*Blanche Ingram*?' I almost sniggered. 'She was a scheming cow, wasn't she?'

'No, not that way.' There was a sort of smile on his lips that made me angry and warm at the same time. 'Looks-wise. Tall, curvy, strong. You glow.'

'Fuck off.'

'You do. All right, never mind that. I'm not about to leap on you, I've got a new girlfriend, actually. So you're not in any danger. But I hate the way you think you're ugly when you're not. If I wasn't your brother—'

'Which you are.'

'I know. Didn't you feel like you were in tune with me, though? That there was a sort of pull between us?'

'No.' I stood up. 'Have you any more revelations for today, or have we finished?'

'Kat.' He took my fingers in his. 'Jesus, you're like ice. Look, I wanted to say, nothing funny, but you're my sister, I don't want to walk away from that. Now I've found you.'

'People walk away from their families every day,' I said, withdrawing my hands and putting them behind my back.

'Yeah, but it doesn't make them not exist.

316

They're still there. You might as well close your eyes and expect to go invisible.'

'I don't know. I need time to think.'

'Kat.' He went to put his arms round me.

'Get off. I told you, I need time. I need to stop hating you.'

He looked miserable at that. Good, I thought. I bet you assumed you could talk me round with a bit of charm and flattery. Well, you were wrong.

'I've got your number,' I said. 'I'll be busy for the next eight or nine weeks, but I'll give you a call before Christmas.'

'That long?'

'That long. But I will call. Promise.'

He walked me to the gate and tried again to hug me, but I ducked away.

'I turn right here,' I said. 'You're going left, for the station.'

'OK,' he said. 'Fair enough. One last thing, though. If you hate me anyway, I might as well say. My mum reckons your mum was mentally ill. I mean, really bonkers. Sectioned at one point. So, if you ever do find her, if she ever does come out of the woodwork, watch yourself. Go steady. Be careful you don't end up looking after her instead of after your grandma.'

I watched his tall grey figure walk away till it was out of sight.

*   *   *

This time I was going to get it right.

317

Chapter Twenty-Six

So in the end, my policy of cowardice and inaction paid off. Oxford has turned out to be brilliant, because everyone here's a bit weird so I don't stand out. They all call me Kat, at any rate.

This is where I'm up to now: six weeks into term and I'm technically in college but spending most of my time round at the flat Mum rents in Summertown. She moved in two weeks ago, after she'd worked out her notice at the library. When she finds a job, she'll put her Bolton house on the market and buy a place here. Then I can move in. That's what we've said, anyway.

She's easy enough to live with. We have our own kitchen cupboards, and I've accepted the fact she doesn't eat just like she's accepted the fact that sometimes, after a meal, I lock the bathroom door and play the radio loudly. But even that's not happening as often as it used to. Food's not the same in her house, somehow.

One day I saw her standing in silhouette by the window and she was so slim it took my breath away. 'Why don't I look more like you?' I couldn't help saying. She laughed. 'That's a fallacy, children always looking like their parents. Children aren't clones, they look like themselves because they're new individuals. You wouldn't want to be me, I promise you.'

I'm still finding out about her. Once, as she was unpacking, she showed me a ring box containing a dried-up old conker, like a little brown brain. 'Your dad gave me that,' she said. Last of the big

318

spenders, I thought, but I didn't say so. It obviously meant a lot.

Another time I was looking through her box of Everyman novels and I found a folder full of hole-punched sheets and dividers to mark off the years. I flicked through the pages and they were just lists of books. I wondered why she'd kept them, then I began to recognize some of the titles. Turning to the most recent, I could see they were the ones I'd taken out from Bank Top Library. She'd catalogued every single book I'd ever borrowed.

Other surprises we keep hidden. She's never mentioned Callum, except once to say she was sorry I'd fallen out with my boyfriend. I didn't reply and the conversation went no further. One thing about my mum, she certainly gives you your space.

Although I don't call her Mum. I call her Ann. If anyone asks, I say she's my friend. I don't encourage a lot of questions because I'm frightened of tying myself in knots. I certainly haven't told anyone she's my mother, because I'm not sure she really is. Oh, I don't doubt she gave birth to me, but it's not the same thing.

So far I've had postcards from Becks (*I went to a club last night!!!*), from Donna (*Saw this and thought of you*—picture of Clever Cat from Letterland—*keep rolling the tubes*), and from Maggie (*We are all free from colds here but dickie has put a nail through his foot hope you are wearing your winter coat*). Nothing from Poll, but she does have difficulty writing. I'm not too worried, I'll see her at Christmas and we'll make up. I've not heard anything from Callum either. Perhaps I'll ring him when I get back, perhaps I won't. Perhaps I'll invite him on a Trisha show, 'I Temporarily Fell for my

319

Lying Love-rat Brother'. Christmas is also when we're planning to tell Miss Dragon; Dinah, I'm going to have to start calling her.

Maybe we could all get round the table and pull crackers together.

There are parts of my dad's story, and therefore mine, that only I know; parts that only Poll knows, parts that only Vince would know, parts that only Ann and Jude know. Only all of us together would stand a chance of seeing the whole picture, and maybe not even then. I know that every time I leave the flat, Ann turns my photograph of Dad to the wall, but there's no way I'm going to take it down for her.

One thing I've learned in my short life is that no bugger's who you think they are. That's OK, though; you just have to keep on your toes.

CHRISTMAS POSTSCRIPT

I had vaguely meant to go and see Poll back before the end of term, but there hadn't been time. They work you really hard at Oxford. I like that.

Ann had a job interview so I travelled on my own. I managed the changes and everything, and no one stole my luggage or pulled the communication cord or showed me their penis. I got off at Bank Top and hauled my bags up the Brow to Poll's.

Oddly, there was no one in and, by the looks of the post on the doormat, there'd been no one for a day or two, at least. And yet I'd written to say when I was coming home. Where was everyone? I used my key and went through to the living room. There were two free papers and a slip from the window cleaner on the table, but everywhere else looked unnaturally tidy. Most of the ornaments and pictures were gone. The kitchen had been cleared out, though not cleaned, and when I went upstairs to use the toilet, all the soaps and bottle had disappeared off the window-sill. My room was more or less as I'd left it, but Poll's bed was stripped and her quilted dressing gown absent from behind the door. The place *smelt* empty.

I didn't know what to do. Was Poll in hospital again? Had she died? But no, Maggie or someone would have phoned and told me, surely.

I hunted for a note or a letter to tell me what was going on; nothing. I phoned Maggie and Dogman, but there was no reply from either. Finally I called a taxi and went to see Cissie at the home.

Mr Poole was in reception, wearing a Santa hat on his head. It was jingle all the way. 'I'll fill your stocking,' I heard him say to Ally as I signed in.

'Honest,' she rolled her eyes at me, and her face was the colour of a cricket ball, 'they're like a class of infants. There's still three weeks to go, you know. Come here if you want that tinsel sticking on your Zimmer.'

I found Cissie in her room. She was looking distracted.

'Thank God you've come,' she said when she saw me. 'I've had a message from the Railway.'

'How do you mean?' I was thinking I'd left something on the train, maybe.

'The Railway Arms. Maggie gave them my number to get in touch with you because she thought you'd come here. She was supposed to meet you off the train, but she's fell on some black ice and they had to carry her into the pub. They think she might have broken her cheekbone. She's been tekken to the Royal Bolton, anyroad. They're like glass at the best of times, them cobbles down to the station. They want tarmacking.'

'Oh God, poor Maggie.'

'I know, it's a shame. She's a kind woman. Too kind. She were bothered about you, they said.'

I sat down on the bed. 'Yeah, what's going on? Is Poll all right? The house is deserted.'

Cissie pursed her lips. 'All right? I should say she's all right. She's flitted, that's all.'

'*Moved house*, after all this time?'

'And how.'

'She didn't think to tell me. Typical. God, that's my home.'

'Not any more, it in't. That's why Maggie were meeting you, to bring you up to speed. Poll decided, a couple of months back, she wanted a new bungalow. She came to see me last week. I thought there must be summat up. Brought a box of Roses and delivers this bombshell.' She reached for the chocolates and shook the carton. 'Oh. I was going to say have one, but they've all gone.'

'Never mind. So where is she?'

'Well, you know Coslett's farm? Right at t' other end of the village, on t' way to Ambley? There, in a bungalow for the disabled.'

I was following the route in my head. 'Next to the white farmhouse?'

'That's right. John Coslett built it for his mother, and then she died, and then a chap from Harrop had it awhile. And it's come on the market again.'

'So Poll's sold our house?' It was unbelievable.

'No. Not yet.'

'So how's she funded it? Is it a social services thing? You're going to have to talk me through this, Cissie, 'cause I don't get it at all.'

'No, well, you wouldn't. It was a shock to me. I'll tell you what she said. She reckoned, if she was going to have to live on her own, she wanted somewhere easier to cope with. Hand rails, no steps, a special bath, big windows. It's very deluxe, she showed me the details; a beautiful garden. That I've no problem with. "But," I asked her, "who's paid for it?" And she said, "Me, I have." So I said, "How have you done that? Have you come up on t' lottery?" And she said—'

'What?'

'She's been collecting money from Vince for years. Or should I say, Dickie has, on her behalf.

323

He had property, Vince. I don't know how many houses he owned, but he'd been buying to rent since his grandad and then his mum left him their houses. He'd used the rent to buy others, and so it went on. Nowt flash, just little terraces, but it all added up. I knew he'd owned a couple, way back, but I thought they'd had to be sold to pay off a debt. Turns out that was completely wrong.

'Now, when he went, Poll couldn't get at these houses because they were in his name. But six years ago he wrote to her out of the blue and said she could have the rent.'

'Bloody *hell*. Does she know where he is, then?'

'No, he didn't say. Just sent this parcel of keys and deeds. So Poll med Dickie her rent man and handyman, he's been going round collecting the money and doing general maintenance. She pays him a wage, you know. Cash in hand.'

'And where is all this money?' I thought of our threadbare sofa and the flaking fridge. 'Christ, Cissie; how much is there?'

'She refused to say. I told her she'd get done for not declaring it, but she said it's all legal. She says, get this, that she's got an accountant.'

'No way.'

'It's what she said. I don't know whether to believe her or not. This bungalow's real enough, though. You'll be amazed when you see it, if it's owt like the photos.'

'Oh, Cissie.' We sat in silence for a minute, then I said, 'Why would Vince have given her all that money, though?'

'He probably felt guilty, I should think. Perhaps he heard she were going blind. Or maybe he'd bought some more houses since and thought he didn't need them all. Or he could have hooked up with a rich widow, or gone on the streets, or topped hisself. We'll never know. But he were never very interested in wealth, weren't Vince. I think property was more of a hobby.'

'Some hobby. And where's Dickie now? Has he moved in with her?'

'He's in an annexe, apparently.' She raised her eyebrows. 'I don't know how they carry on aside from that. I don't ask. So there you are. Oh, she's going to employ a carer, she says, in the New Year. Someone she can boss about properly. I pity that person, I do.'

'Who wants a mince pie?' called Ally from the other side of the door. 'Come on, boys and girls, get them while they're hot.'

Neither Cissie nor I had any appetite, but we had three each.

'Will you be seeing Poll now? I've her new number written on that pad by the bed.'

'I'm so angry, Cissie, I don't know what I'm going to do.'

She picked an escaped raisin off her skirt and ate it. 'It's going to be a rum sort of Christmas for you,' she said.

*   *   *

Christmas Eve found me in Oxford with Ann. We went to Midnight Mass together and walked home under sparkling frost. Where the pavement narrowed, I had to step in the road.

'Steady,' I said, my voice loud in the quiet street. I felt drunk.

She looked at me and laughed. 'We are all of us

in the gutter, but some of us are looking at the stars.'

'Oscar Wilde?'

'The Pretenders. But I think they stole it from him.' We craned our necks back to see the constellations. 'Do you know their names?'

'Most of them. I had a Ladybird book on it. Do you?'

'Yes,' she said, pointing, 'Big W, the Saucepan, Mini Saucepan, the Bow-tie.' Her breath came out in little spurts of cloud. I wanted to catch hold of her hand and run all the way back to town, keep the magic going.

'Doesn't a night sky make you feel small?'

'No,' she said. 'Shall I show you why?' And she came up close and put her arms round me. 'Watch the stars.'

She turned me round slowly, as if we were dancing, and the sky moved.

'What are you doing?'

'We're the axis of the universe,' she said. 'You have to believe that.'

*   *   *

I didn't want it to be Christmas Day.

But it wasn't as bad as I'd thought. We listened to Radio Four and unwrapped our presents to each other; a velvet tunic and a professional hair-shaping set for me; an antique brooch in the shape of a basket for her. Then I was busy getting the dinner on, and Dinah Dragon arrived saying how quiet the motorways were, and Ann put the BBC2 opera on, and we were all grinning with nerves because our relationships had shifted round and

326

nobody was quite sure how to behave any more. But then I took Dinah next door and showed her the guest room, where Ann was going to make me a study, and she asked me whether I was truly happy with the way things had turned out, and I said, I thought I was as near to it as made no difference. Then she said, was I missing Poll.

'Yes,' I admitted.

'Give her a ring,' she said.

I looked doubtful.

'Go on, because whatever she says to you, you won't settle till you do.'

'Won't Ann mind?'

Dinah said, 'I'm going to take her out for a walk now. We'll be gone about half an hour.'

I'd so wanted to go and see Poll, even if it was just to give her a good slapping, but I hadn't had the courage. After the interview with Cissie, I'd gone back to Ann and stayed there. I hadn't seen Poll now for nearly three months.

The phone rang and rang, till Maggie eventually picked up. 'Hello?'

'It's Kat. What are you doing at Poll's? I thought you'd be at Dawn's.'

'I've only popped round to give her her present, I'm off in a minute. Oh, love, it's good to hear from you. Poll's been missing you. Are you all right? Did your tutors let you stay in Oxford, in the end? You're not on your own, are you? Are there a few of you?'

In the background I could hear the music to *The Snowman*, and Dogman's voice shouting, 'What's this bloody rubbish? Bloody snowmen? Who's on t' phone?'

'Dawn,' Maggie told him promptly.

'Yeah, everything's fine; can I speak to Poll?' I said, my heart pounding.

'She's just on t' lavvy. She'll only be a minute.'

'Has she been to Cissie's?'

'We went this morning. She's looking very well, ankles a bit thick. Sends her love.'

'Look—' I was losing my nerve. 'Tell Poll happy Christmas from me, OK? And I'll see her in the New Year. We'll talk then.'

'She says—' Maggie lowered her voice—'it's all coming to you when she dies, you know. Every penny.'

'Not to a dog's home, or Dickie, then?' I could hear the bitterness in my own voice.

'She says not. She says it won't be long now, she's tired of this world.'

I could make out Poll yelling something about Bailey's. It sounded serious. 'What's going on, Maggie?'

'Oh, she's got a new puppy, that's all. Tilly. Dickie give it her this morning, she were ovver t' moon. It's another Westie, but it's not like Winston. This one's a little demon, I think Dickie got it from a home. It's knocked her glass and her drink's gone on t' floor.'

'I towd you not to get cream carpets,' Dogman was saying. 'Every mark shows. Come here, I'll have a go at it.'

'Let me put her on,' said Maggie. 'I know she'd love to chat.'

'Not now,' I said quickly, and put the phone down.

Explanations, apologies, recriminations; it could all wait till after Christmas.

Later, I watched Ann chase a lone turkey

drumstick round and round her plate, while Dinah told us stories about her father's time in the army and I tried not to panic about feeling full; there was no way I was going to make myself sick on Christmas Day. I imagined a stranger walking in and seeing us sitting round the table with our tissue hats. Hearty Dinah, with her ruddy cheeks and faint moustache; quiet Ann, with her skeletal arms; me. We must look a pretty strange party. But this was the family I'd chosen, for now.

My life as it stands is a web of deceit. Not just my own, either: I've taken on other people's too. But then, whose isn't? What family isn't held together by a cartilage of lies? In these fractured times, these days of spin, you have to make the family you can.

Bring on the New Year; I'll be ready.

CHIVERS LARGE PRINT –direct–

If you have enjoyed this Large Print book and would like to build up your own collection of Large Print books, please contact

Chivers Large Print Direct

Chivers Large Print Direct offers you a full service:

- Prompt mail order service

- Easy-to-read type

- The very best authors

- Special low prices

For further details either call
Customer Services on (01225) 336552
or write to us at Chivers Large Print Direct,
FREEPOST, Bath BA1 3ZZ

Telephone Orders:
FREEPHONE 08081 72 74 75